WHAT THE REVIEWERS SAID:

'Bestselling author Koontz exploits and occasionally skewers many novel and film conventions – including telepathic mind control games and the obligatory surprise blizzard during the climatic battle – to great effect while building tension in this gripping parable about the real cost of getting away from it all'

Publishers Weekly

'A master of the thriller genre'

Washington Post

'Koontz's art is in making the reader believe the impossible . . . sit back and enjoy it'

Sunday Telegraph

By Dean Koontz and available from Headline

BY THE LIGHT OF THE MOON
ONE DOOR AWAY FROM HEAVEN
FROM THE CORNER OF HIS EYE
FALSE MEMORY
SEIZE THE NIGHT
FEAR NOTHING
SOLE SURVIVOR
INTENSITY
DARK RIVERS OF THE HEART
MR MURDER
DRAGON TEARS
HIDEAWAY
COLD FIRE
THE BAD PLACE
MIDNIGHT
LIGHTNING
WATCHERS
TICKTOCK
STRANGE HIGHWAYS
DEMON SEED
ICEBOUND
WINTER MOON
THE FUNHOUSE
THE FACE OF FEAR
THE MASK
SHADOWFIRES
THE EYES OF DARKNESS
THE SERVANTS OF TWILIGHT
THE DOOR TO DECEMBER
THE KEY TO MIDNIGHT
THE HOUSE OF THUNDER
PHANTOMS
WHISPERS
SHATTERED
CHASE
TWILIGHT EYES
THE VOICE OF THE NIGHT
STRANGERS
DARKFALL
THE VISION
NIGHT CHILLS

DEAN KOONTZ

WINTER MOON

headline

First published in Great Britain in 1994 by
HEADLINE BOOK PUBLISHING

First published in paperback in Great Britain in 1994 by
HEADLINE BOOK PUBLISHING

This edition was published in 2016 by
HEADLINE PUBLISHING GROUP

3

Cataloguing in Publication Data is available from the British Library

ISBN 978 1 4722 4030 9

Typeset in Fournier MT by Palimpsest Book Production Ltd, Falkirk, Stirlingshire

Printed and bound by CPI Group (UK) Ltd, Croydon CR0 4YY

Headline's policy is to use papers that are natural, renewable and recyclable
products and made from wood grown in well-managed forests and other
controlled sources. The logging and manufacturing processes are expected to
conform to the environmental regulations of the country of origin.

HEADLINE PUBLISHING GROUP
An Hachette UK Company
Carmelite House
50 Victoria Embankment
London EC4Y 0DZ

www.headline.co.uk
www.hachette.co.uk

To Gerda,
who knows a thousand reasons why,
with much love.

PART ONE
The City of the Dying Day

Beaches, surfers, California girls.
Wind scented with fabulous dreams.
Bougainvillea, groves of oranges.
Stars are born, everything gleams.

A weather change. Shadows fall.
New scent upon the wind – decay.
Cocaine, Uzis, drive-by shootings.
Death is a banker. Everyone pays.

—*The Book of Counted Sorrows*

1

DEATH WAS driving an emerald-green Lexus. It pulled off the street, passed the four self-service pumps, and stopped in one of the two full-service lanes.

Standing in front of the station, Jack McGarvey noticed the car but not the driver. Even under a bruised and swollen sky that hid the sun, the Lexus gleamed like a jewel, a sleek and lustrous machine. The windows were darkly tinted, so he couldn't have seen the driver clearly even if he had tried.

As a thirty-two-year-old cop with a wife, a child, and a big mortgage, Jack had no prospects of buying an expensive luxury car, but he didn't envy the owner of the Lexus. He often remembered his dad's admonition that envy was mental theft. If you coveted another man's possessions, Dad said, then you should be willing to take on his responsibilities, heartaches, and troubles along with his money.

He stared at the car for a moment, admiring it as he might a priceless painting at the Getty Museum or a first edition of a James M. Cain novel in a pristine dust jacket, with no strong desire to possess it, taking pleasure merely from the fact of its existence.

In a society that often seemed to be spinning toward anarchy, where ugliness and decay made new inroads every day, his spirits were lifted by any proof that the hands of men and women were capable of producing things of beauty and quality. The Lexus, of course, was an import, designed and manufactured on foreign shores; however, it was the entire human species that seemed damned, not just his countrymen, and evidence of standards and dedication was heartening regardless of where he found it.

An attendant in a gray uniform hurried out of the office and approached the gleaming car, and Jack gave his full attention once more to Hassam Arkadian.

'My station is an island of cleanliness in a filthy sea, an eye of sanity in a storm of madness,' Arkadian said, speaking earnestly, unaware of sounding melodramatic.

He was slender, about forty, with dark hair and a neatly trimmed mustache. The creases in the legs of his gray cotton work pants were knife-sharp, and his matching work shirt and jacket were immaculate.

'I had the aluminum siding and the brick treated with a new sealant,' he said, indicating the facade of the service station with a sweep of his arm. 'Paint won't stick to it. Not even metallic paint. Wasn't cheap. But now when these gang kids or crazy-stupid taggers come around at night and spray their trash all over the walls, we scrub it off, scrub it right off the next morning.'

With his meticulous grooming, singular intensity, and quick slender hands, Arkadian might have been a surgeon about to begin his work day in an operating theater. He was, instead, the owner-operator of the service station.

'Do you know,' he said incredulously, 'there are professors who have written books on the value of graffiti? The *value* of graffiti? The *value*?'

'They call it street art,' said Luther Bryson, Jack's partner.

Arkadian gazed up disbelievingly at the towering black cop. 'You think what these punks do is *art*?'

'Hey, no, not me,' Luther said.

At six-three and two-hundred-ten pounds, he was three inches taller than Jack and forty pounds heavier, with maybe eight inches and seventy pounds on Arkadian. Though he was a good partner and a good man, his granite face seemed incapable of the flexibility required for a smile. His deeply set eyes were unwaveringly forthright. *My Malcolm X glare*, he called it. With or without his uniform, Luther Bryson could intimidate anyone from the Pope to a purse snatcher.

He wasn't using the glare now, wasn't trying to intimidate Arkadian, was in complete agreement with him. 'Not me. I'm just saying, that's what the candy-ass crowd calls it. Street art.'

The service-station owner said, 'These are *professors*. Educated men and women. Doctors of art and literature. They have the benefit of an education my parents couldn't afford to give me, but they're *stupid*. There's no other word for it. Stupid, stupid, stupid.' His expressive face revealed frustration and anger that Jack encountered with increasing frequency in the City of Angels. 'What *fools* do universities produce these days?'

Arkadian had labored to make his operation special. Bracketing the property were wedge-shaped brick planters in which grew queen palms, azaleas laden with clusters of red flowers, and impatiens in pinks and purples. There was no grime, no litter. The portico covering the pumps was supported by brick columns, and the whole station had a quaint colonial appearance.

In any age, the station would have seemed misplaced in Los Angeles. Freshly painted and clean, it was doubly out of place in the grunge that had been spreading like a malignancy through the city during the nineties.

'Come on, come look, look,' Arkadian said, and headed toward the south end of the building.

'Poor guy's gonna blow out an artery in the brain over this,' Luther said.

'Somebody should tell him it's not fashionable to give a damn these days,' Jack said.

A low and menacing rumble of thunder rolled through the distended sky.

5

Looking at the dark clouds, Luther said, 'Weatherman predicted it wouldn't rain today.'

'Maybe it wasn't thunder. Maybe somebody finally blew up city hall.'

'You think? Well, if the place was full of politicians,' Luther said, 'we should take the rest of the day off, find a bar, do some celebrating.'

'Come on, officers,' Arkadian called to them. He had reached the south corner of the building, near where they had parked their patrol car. 'Look at this, I want you to see this, I want you to see my bathrooms.'

'His bathrooms?' Luther said.

Jack laughed. 'Hell, you got anything better to do?'

'A lot safer than chasing bad guys,' Luther said, following Arkadian.

Jack glanced at the Lexus again. Nice machine. Zero to sixty in how many seconds? Eight? Seven? Must handle like a dream.

The driver had gotten out of the car and was standing beside it. Jack noticed little about the guy, only that he was wearing a loose-fitting, double-breasted Armani suit.

The Lexus, on the other hand, had wire wheels and chrome guards around the wheel wells. Reflections of storm clouds moved slowly across its windshield and made mysterious smoky patterns in the depths of its jewel-green finish.

Sighing, Jack followed Luther past the two open bays of the repair garage. The first stall was empty, but a gray BMW was on the hydraulic lift in the second space. A young Asian man in mechanic's coveralls was at work on the car. Tools and supplies were neatly racked along the walls, floor to ceiling, and the two bays looked cleaner than the average kitchen in a four-star restaurant.

At the corner of the building stood a pair of soft-drink vending machines. They purred and clinked as if formulating and bottling the beverages within their own guts.

Around the corner were the men's and women's restrooms, where

6

Arkadian had opened both doors. 'Take a look, go ahead, I want you to see my bathrooms.'

Both small rooms had white ceramic-tile floors and walls, white commodes, white swing-top waste cans, white sinks, gleaming chrome fixtures, and large mirrors above the sinks.

'Spotless,' Arkadian said, talking fast, running his sentences together in his quiet anger. 'No streaks on the mirrors, no stains in the sinks, we check them after every customer uses them, disinfect them every day, you could *eat* off those floors and it would be as safe as eating off the plates from your own mother's kitchen.'

Looking at Jack over Arkadian's head, Luther smiled and said, 'I think I'll have a steak and baked potato. What about you?'

'Just a salad,' Jack said. 'I'm trying to lose a few pounds.'

Even if he had been listening to them, Mr Arkadian couldn't have been joked out of his bleak mood. He jangled a ring of keys.

'I keep them locked, give the keys only to customers. City inspector stops around, he tells me a new rule says these are public facilities, so you've got to let them open for the public, whether they buy anything at your place or not.'

He jangled the keys again, harder, more angrily, then harder still. Neither Jack nor Luther tried to comment above the strident ring and rattle.

'Let them fine me. I'll pay the fine. When these are unlocked, the drunks and junkie bums who live in alleys and parks, they use my bathrooms, urinate on the floor, vomit in the sinks. You wouldn't *believe* the mess they make, disgusting, things I'd be embarrassed to talk about.'

Arkadian was actually blushing at the thought of what he could have told them. He waved the jangling keys in the air in front of each open door, and he reminded Jack of nothing so much as a voodoo priest casting a spell – in this case, to ward off the riffraff who would despoil his restrooms. His face was as mottled and turbulent as the stormy sky.

'Let me tell you something. Hassam Arkadian works sixty and seventy hours a week, Hassam Arkadian employs eight people full time, and Hassam Arkadian pays half of what he earns in taxes, but Hassam Arkadian is *not* going to spend his life cleaning up vomit because a bunch of stupid bureaucrats have more compassion for some lazy-drunken-psycho-junkie bums than they have for people who are trying their damnedest to lead decent lives.'

He finished his speech in a rush, breathless. Stopped jangling the keys. Sighed. He closed the doors and locked them.

Jack felt useless. He could see that Luther was uncomfortable too. Sometimes a cop couldn't do much more for a victim than nod in sympathy and shake his head in sorry amazement at the depths into which the city was sinking. That was one of the worst things about the job.

Mr Arkadian went around the corner to the front of the station again. He wasn't walking as fast as before. His shoulders were slumped and for the first time he looked more dejected than angry, as if he had decided, perhaps on a subconscious level, to give up the fight.

Jack hoped that wasn't the case. In his daily life, Hassam was struggling to realize a dream of a better future, a better world. He was one of a dwindling number who still had enough guts to resist entropy. Civilization's soldiers, warring on the side of hope, were already too few to make a satisfactory army.

Adjusting their gunbelts, Jack and Luther followed Arkadian past the soft-drink dispensers.

The man in the Armani suit was standing at the second vending machine, studying the selections. He was about Jack's age, tall, blond, clean-shaven, with a golden-bronze complexion that could have been gotten locally at that time of year only from a tanning bed. As they walked by him, he pulled a handful of change from one pocket of his baggy trousers and picked through the coins.

Out at the pumps, the attendant was washing the windshield of

8

the Lexus, though it had looked freshly washed when the car first pulled in from the street.

Arkadian stopped at the plate-glass window that occupied half the front wall of the station office. 'Street art,' he said softly, sadly, as Jack and Luther joined him. 'Only a fool would call it anything but vandalism. Barbarians are loose.'

Lately, some vandals had traded spray cans for stencils and acid paste. They etched their symbols and slogans on the glass of parked cars and the windows of businesses that were unprotected by security shutters at night.

Arkadian's front window was permanently marred by half a dozen different personal marks by members of the same gang, some of them repeated two and three times. In four-inch-high letters, they had also etched the words THE BLOODBATH IS COMING.

These antisocial acts often reminded Jack of an event in Nazi Germany about which he'd once read: before the war had even begun, when psychopathic thugs had roamed the streets during one long night – *Kristallnacht* – defacing walls with hateful words, smashing windows of homes and stores owned by Jews until the streets glittered as if paved with crystal. Sometimes it seemed to him that the barbarians to which Arkadian referred were the new fascists, from both ends of the political spectrum this time, hating not just Jews but anyone with a stake in social order and civility. Their vandalism was a slow-motion *Kristallnacht*, conducted over years instead of hours.

'It's worse on the next window,' Arkadian said, leading them around the corner to the north side of the station.

That wall of the office featured another large sheet of glass on which, in addition to gang symbols, etched block letters also proclaimed ARMENIAN SHITHEAD.

Even the sight of the racial slur couldn't rekindle Hassam Arkadian's anger. He stared sad-eyed at the offensive words and said, 'I've always tried to treat people well. I'm not perfect, not

9

without sin. Who is? But I've done my best to be a good man, fair, honest – and now this.'

'Won't make you feel any better,' Luther said, 'but if it was up to me, the law would let us take the creeps who do this and stencil that second word right above their eyes. Shithead. Etch it into their skin with acid just like they did to your glass. Make 'em walk around like that for a couple of years and see how their attitude improves before maybe we give them some plastic surgery.'

'You think you can find who did it?' Arkadian asked, though he surely knew the answer.

Luther shook his head, and Jack said, 'Not a chance. We'll file a report, of course, but there's no manpower to work on small crime like this. Best thing you can do is install roll-down metal shutters the same day you replace the windows, so they're covered at night.'

'Otherwise, you'll be putting in new glass every week,' Luther said, 'and pretty soon your insurance company will drop you.'

'They already dropped my vandalism coverage after one claim,' Hassam Arkadian said. 'About the only thing they'll cover me for now is earthquake, flood, and fire. Not even fire if it happens in a riot.'

They stood in silence, staring at the window, brooding about their powerlessness.

A cool March wind sprang up. In the nearby planter, the queen palms rustled, and soft creaking noises arose from where the stems of the big fronds joined the trunks.

'Well,' Jack said at last, 'it could be worse, Mr Arkadian. I mean, at least you're in a pretty good part of the city here on the Westside.'

'Yeah, and doesn't it break your heart,' Arkadian said, 'this is a *good* neighborhood?'

Jack didn't even want to think about that.

Luther started to speak but was interrupted by a loud crash and a shout of anger from the front of the station. As the three of them hurried around the corner, a violent gust of wind made the plate-glass windows thrum.

Fifty feet away, the man in the Armani suit kicked the vending machine again. A foaming can of Pepsi lay behind him, contents spreading across the blacktop.

'Poison,' he shouted at the machine, 'poison, damn it, damn you, damn you, poison!'

Arkadian rushed toward the customer. 'Sir, please, I'm sorry, if the machine gave you the wrong selection—'

'Hey, wait right there,' Luther said, speaking as much to the station owner as to the infuriated stranger.

In front of the office door, Jack caught up with Arkadian, put a hand on his shoulder, stopped him, and said, 'Better let us handle this.'

'Damn poison,' the customer said furiously, and he made a fist as if he wanted to punch the vending machine.

'It's just the machine,' Arkadian told Jack and Luther. 'They keep *saying* it's fixed, but it keeps giving you Pepsi when you push Orange Crush.'

As bad as things were in the City of Angels these days, Jack found it difficult to believe that Arkadian was accustomed to seeing people fly off the handle every time an unwanted can of Pepsi dropped into the dispensing tray.

The customer turned away from the machine and from them, as if he might walk off and leave his Lexus. He seemed to be shaking with anger, but it was mostly the blustery wind shivering the loosely fitted suit.

'What's wrong here?' Luther asked, heading toward the guy as thunder tolled across the lowering sky and the palms in the south planter thrashed against a backdrop of black clouds.

Jack started to follow Luther before he saw the suit jacket billow out behind the blond, flapping like bat wings. Except the coat had been buttoned a moment ago. Double-breasted, buttoned twice.

11

The angry man faced away from them still, shoulders hunched, head lowered. Because of the loose and billowing fabric of his suit, he seemed less than human, like a hunchbacked troll. The guy began to turn, and Jack would not have been surprised to see the deformed muzzle of a beast, but it was the same tan and clean-shaven face as before.

Why had the son of a bitch unbuttoned the coat unless there was something under it that he needed, and what might an irrational and angry man need that he kept under his jacket, his loose-fitting suit jacket, his roomy goddamned jacket?

Jack called a warning to Luther.

But Luther sensed trouble too. His right hand moved toward the gun holstered on his hip.

The perp had the advantage because he was the initiator. No one knew violence was at hand until he unleashed it, so he swung all the way around to face them, holding a weapon in both hands, before Luther or Jack had even touched their revolvers.

Automatic gunfire hammered the day. Bullets pounded Luther's chest, knocked the big man off his feet, hurled him backward, and Hassam Arkadian spun from the impact of one-two-three hits, went down hard, screaming in agony.

Jack threw himself against the glass door to the office. He almost made it to cover before taking a hit to the left leg. He felt as if he'd been clubbed across the thigh with a tire iron, but it was a bullet not a blow.

He dropped face down on the office floor. The door swung shut behind him, gunfire shattered it, and gummy chunks of tempered glass cascaded across his back.

Hot pain boiled sweat from him.

A radio was playing. Golden oldies. Dionne Warwick. Singing about the world needing love, sweet love.

Outside, Arkadian was still screaming, but there wasn't a sound from Luther Bryson.

Luther was dead. Jack couldn't think about that. Dead. Didn't dare think about it. Dead. *Wouldn't* think about it.

The chatter of more gunfire.

Someone else screamed. Probably the attendant at the Lexus. It wasn't a lasting scream. Brief, quickly choked off.

Outside, Arkadian wasn't screaming any more, either. He was sobbing and calling for Jesus.

Hard, chill wind made the plate-glass windows vibrate. It hooted through the shattered door.

The gunman would be coming.

2

JACK WAS stunned at the quantity of his own blood on the vinyl-tile floor around him. Nausea squirmed through him, and greasy sweat streamed down his face. He couldn't take his eyes off the spreading stain that darkened his pants.

He had never been shot before. The pain was terrible but not as bad as he would have expected. Worse than the pain was the sense of violation and vulnerability, a terrible frantic awareness of the true fragility of the human body.

He might not be able to hold on to consciousness for long. A hungry darkness was already eating away at the edges of his vision.

He probably couldn't put much weight on his left leg, and he didn't have time to pull himself up on his right alone, not while in such an exposed position. Shedding broken glass as a bright-scaled snake might shed an old skin, unavoidably leaving a trail of blood, he crawled fast on his belly alongside an L-shaped work counter behind which Arkadian kept the cash register.

The gunman would be coming.

From the sound the weapon made and the brief glimpse he'd gotten of it, Jack figured it was a submachine gun – maybe a Micro Uzi. The Micro was less than ten inches long with the wire stock folded forward but a lot heavier than a pistol, weighing about two kilos if it had a single magazine, heavier if it featured two magazines welded at right angles to give it a forty-round capacity. It would

14

be like carrying a standard-size bag of sugar in a sling, sure to cause chronic neck pain but not too big to fit an oversize shoulder holster under an Armani suit – and worth the trouble if a man had snake-mean enemies. Could be an FN P90, too, or maybe a British Bushman 2, but probably not a Czech Skorpion because a Skorpion fired only .32 ACP ammo. Judging by how hard Luther had gone down, this seemed to be a gun with more punch than a Skorpion, which the 9mm Micro Uzi provided. Forty rounds in the Uzi to start, and the son of a bitch had fired twelve, sixteen at most, so at least twenty-four rounds were left, and maybe a pocketful of spare cartridges.

Thunder boomed, the air felt heavy with pent-up rain, wind shrieked through the ruined door, and the gun rattled again. Outside, Hassam Arkadian's cries to Jesus abruptly ended.

Jack desperately pulled himself around the end of the counter, thinking the unthinkable. Luther Bryson dead. Arkadian dead. The attendant dead. Most likely the young Asian mechanic too. All of them wasted. The world had been turned upside down in less than a minute.

Now it was one-on-one, survival of the fittest, and Jack wasn't afraid of that game. Though Darwinian selection tended to favor the guy with the biggest gun and best supply of ammunition, cleverness could outweigh caliber. He had been saved by his wits before and might be again.

Surviving could be easier when he had his back to the wall, the odds were stacked high against him, and he had no one to worry about but himself. With only his own sorry ass on the line, he was more focused, free to risk inaction or recklessness, free to be a coward or a kamikaze fool, whatever the occasion demanded.

Then he dragged himself entirely into the sheltered space behind the counter and discovered he didn't, after all, enjoy the freedom of a sole survivor. A woman was huddled there: petite, long dark hair, attractive. Gray shirt, work pants, white socks, black shoes with thick rubber soles. She was in her mid thirties, maybe five or six years younger than Hassam Arkadian. Could be his wife. No, not a wife any more. Widow. She was sitting on the floor, knees drawn up against her chest, arms wrapped tightly around her legs, trying to make herself as small as possible, straining for invisibility.

Her presence changed everything for Jack, put him on the line, and reduced his own chances of survival. He couldn't choose to hide, couldn't even opt for recklessness any longer. He had to think hard and clearly, determine the best course of action, and do the right thing. He was responsible for her. He had sworn an oath to serve and protect the public, and he was old-fashioned enough to take oaths seriously.

The woman's eyes were wide with terror and shimmering with unspilled tears. Even in the midst of fear for her own life, she seemed to comprehend the meaning of Arkadian's sudden lapse into silence.

Jack drew his revolver.

Serve and protect.

He was shivering uncontrollably. His left leg was hot, but the rest of him was freezing, as if all his body heat was draining out through the wound.

Outside, a sustained rattle of automatic-weapon fire ended in an explosion that rocked the service station, tipped over a candy-vending machine in the office, and blew in both big windows on which the gang symbols had been etched. The huddled woman covered her face with her hands, Jack squeezed his eyes shut, and glass spilled over the counter into the space where they had taken shelter.

When he opened his eyes, endless phalanxes of shadows and light charged across the office. The wind coming through the shattered door was no longer chilly but hot, and the phantasms swarming over the walls were reflections of fire. The maniac with the Uzi had shot up one or more of the gasoline pumps.

Cautiously Jack pulled himself up against the counter, putting no weight on his left leg. Though his misery still seemed inadequate to the wound, he figured it would get worse suddenly and soon.

16

He didn't want to precipitate it by any action of his own for fear that a sufficiently fierce flash of pain would make him pass out.

Under considerable pressure, jets of burning gasoline were squirting from one of the riddled pumps, splashing like molten lava on to the blacktop. The pavement sloped toward the busy street and scintillant rivers of fire spread in that direction.

The explosion had ignited the roof of the portico that sheltered the pumps. Flames licked rapidly toward the main building.

The Lexus was on fire. The lunatic bastard had destroyed his own car, which in some strange way made him seem more completely out of control and dangerous than anything else he'd done.

Amidst the inferno, which became more panoramic by the second as the gasoline streamed across the blacktop, the killer was nowhere to be seen. Maybe he'd regained at least some of his senses and fled on foot.

More likely, he was in the two-bay garage, coming at them by that route rather than making a bold approach through the shattered front entrance. Less than fifteen feet from Jack, a painted metal door connected the garage to the office. It was closed.

Leaning against the counter, he gripped his revolver in both hands and aimed at the door, arms extended rigidly in front of him, ready to blow the perp to hell at the first opportunity. His hands were shaking. So cold. He strained to hold the gun steady, which helped, but he couldn't entirely repress the tremors.

The darkness at the edges of his vision had retreated. Now it began to encroach again. He blinked furiously, trying to wash away the frightening peripheral blindness as he might have tried to expel a speck of dust, but to no avail.

The air smelled of gasoline and hot tar. Shifting wind blew smoke into the room, not much, just enough to make him want to cough. He clenched his teeth, making only a low choking sound in his throat, because the killer might be on the far side of the door, hesitating and listening.

Still directing the revolver squarely at the entrance from the garage, he glanced outside into whirlwinds of tempestuous fire and churning shrouds of black smoke, afraid he was wrong. The gunman might erupt, after all, from that conflagration, like a demon out of perdition.

The metal door again. Painted the palest blue. Like deep clear water seen through a layer of crystalline ice.

The color made him cold. Everything made him cold – the hollow iron-hard *thunk-thunk* of his laboring heart, the whisper-soft weeping of the woman huddled on the floor behind him, the glittering debris of broken glass. Even the roar and crackle of the fire chilled him.

Outside, seething flames had traveled the length of the portico and reached the front of the service station. The roof must be ablaze by now.

The pale-blue door.

Open it, you crazy sonofabitch. Come on, come on, come on.

Another explosion.

He had to turn his head completely away from the door to the garage and look directly at the front of the station to see what had happened because he had lost nearly all of his peripheral vision.

The fuel tank of the Lexus. The vehicle was engulfed, reduced to just the black skeleton of a car enwrapped by greedy tongues of fire that stripped it of its lustrous emerald paint, fine leather uphol-stery, and other plush appointments.

The blue door remained closed.

The revolver seemed to weigh a hundred pounds. His arms ached. He couldn't hold the weapon steady. Could barely hold it at all.

He wanted to lie down and close his eyes. Sleep a little. Dream a little dream, green pastures, wild flowers, a blue sky, the city long forgotten.

When he looked down at his leg, he discovered he was standing in a pool of blood. An artery must have been nicked, maybe torn, and he was going fast, dizzy just from looking down, nausea swelling anew, a trembling in his gut.

18

Fire on the roof. He could hear it overhead, distinctly different from the crackle and roar of the blaze in front of the station, shingles popping, rafters creaking as construction joints were tortured by the fierce, dry heat. They might have only seconds before the ceiling exploded into flames or caved in on them.

He didn't understand how he could be getting colder by the moment when fire was all around them. The sweat streaming down his face was like ice water.

Even if the roof didn't cave in for a couple of minutes, he might be dead or too weak to pull the trigger when at last the killer rushed them. He couldn't wait any longer.

He had to give up the two-hand grip on the gun. He needed his left hand to brace himself against the Formica top of the counter as he circled the end of it, keeping all weight off his left leg.

But when he reached the end of the counter, he was too dizzy to hop the ten or twelve feet to the blue door. He had to use the toe of his left foot as a balance point, applying the minimum pressure required to stay erect as he hitched across the office.

Surprisingly, the pain was bearable. Then he realized it was tolerable only because his leg was going numb. A cool tingle coursed through the limb from hip to ankle. Even the wound itself was no longer hot, not even warm.

The door. His left hand on the knob looked so far away, as if he were peering at it through the wrong end of a pair of binoculars.

Revolver in the right hand. Hanging down at his side. Like a massive dumbbell. The effort required to raise the weapon caused his stomach to eel over on itself repeatedly.

The killer might be waiting on the other side, watching the knob, so Jack pushed the door open and went through it fast, the revolver thrust out in front of him. He stumbled, almost fell, and stepped past the door, swinging the gun right and left, heart pounding so hard it jolted his weakening arms, but there was no target. He could see all the way across the garage because the BMW was up on the service rack. The only person in sight was the Asian mechanic, as dead as the concrete on which he was sprawled.

Jack turned to the blue door. It was black on this side, which seemed ominous, glossy black, and it had shut behind him.

He took a step toward it, meaning to pull it open. He fell against it instead.

Harried by the changeable wind, a tide of bitter tarry smoke washed into the double-bay garage.

Coughing, Jack wrenched open the door. The office was filled with smoke, an antechamber to Hell.

He shouted for the woman to come to him, and he was dismayed to hear that his shout was barely more than a thin wheeze.

She was already on the move, however, and before he could try to shout again, she appeared out of the roiling smoke, with one hand clamped over her nose and mouth.

At first, when she leaned against him, Jack thought she was seeking support, strength he didn't have to give, but he realized she was urging *him* to rely on *her*. He was the one who had taken the oath, who had sworn to serve and defend. He felt dismally inadequate because he couldn't scoop her up in his arms and carry her out of there as a hero might have done in a movie.

He leaned on the woman as little as he dared and turned left with her in the direction of the open bay door, which was obscured by the smoke. He dragged his left leg. No longer any feeling in it whatsoever, no pain, not even a tingle. Dead weight. Eyes squeezed shut against the stinging smoke, bursts of color coruscating across the backs of his eyelids. Holding his breath, resisting a powerful urge to vomit. Somebody screaming, a shrill and terrible scream, on and on. No, not a scream. Sirens. Rapidly drawing closer. Then he and the woman were in the open, which he detected by a change in the wind, and he gasped for breath, which came cold and clean into his lungs.

When he opened his eyes, the world was blurred by tears that the abrasive smoke had rubbed from him, and he blinked frantically until his sight cleared somewhat. Because of blood loss or shock, he was reduced to tunnel vision. It was like looking at the world through twin gun barrels, because the surrounding darkness was as smooth as the curve of a steel bore.

To his left, everything was enveloped in flames. The Lexus. Portico. Service station. Arkadian's body was on fire. Luther's was not afire yet, but hot embers were falling on it, flaming bits of shingles and wood, and at any moment his uniform would ignite. Burning gasoline still arced from the riddled pumps and streamed toward the street. The blacktop along the perimeter of the blaze was melting, boiling. Churning masses of thick black smoke rose high above the city, blending into the pendulous black and gray storm clouds.

Someone cursed.

Jack jerked his head to the right, away from the terrible but hypnotically fascinating inferno, and focused his narrowed field of vision on the soft-drink machines at the corner of the station. The killer was standing there, as if oblivious of the destruction he had wrought, feeding coins into the first of the two vending machines.

Two more discarded cans of Pepsi lay on the asphalt behind him. The Micro Uzi was in his left hand, at his side, muzzle pointing at the pavement. He slammed the flat of his fist against one of the buttons on the selection board.

Feebly shoving the woman away, Jack whispered, '*Get down!*'

He turned clumsily toward the killer, swaying, barely able to remain on his feet.

The can of soda clattered into the delivery tray. The gunman leaned forward, squinting, then cursed again.

Shuddering violently, Jack struggled to raise his revolver. It seemed to be shackled to the ground on a short length of chain, requiring him to lift the entire world in order to bring the weapon high enough to aim.

21

Aware of him, responding with an arrogant leisureliness, the psychopath in the expensive suit turned and advanced a couple of steps, bringing up his own weapon.

Jack squeezed off a shot. He was so weak, the recoil knocked him backward and off his feet.

The killer loosed a burst of six or eight rounds.

Jack was already falling out of the line of fire. As bullets cut the air over his head, he fired another shot, and then a third as he crumpled on to the blacktop.

Incredibly, the third round slammed the killer in the chest and pitched him backward into the vending machine. He bounced off the machine and dropped on to his knees. He was badly hurt, perhaps mortally wounded, his white silk shirt turning red as swiftly as a trick scarf transformed by a magician's deft hands, but he wasn't dead yet, and he still had the Micro Uzi.

The sirens were extremely loud. Help was nearly at hand, but it was probably going to come too late.

A blast of thunder breached a dam in the sky, and torrents of icy rain suddenly fell by the megaton.

With an effort that nearly caused him to black out, Jack sat up and clasped his revolver in both hands. He squeezed off a shot that was wide of the mark. The recoil induced a muscle spasm in his arms. All the strength went out of his hands, and he lost his grip on the revolver, which clattered on to the blacktop between his spread legs.

The killer loosed two-three-four shots, and Jack took two hits in the chest. He was knocked flat. The back of his skull bounced painfully off the pavement.

He tried to sit up again. He could only raise his head, and not far, just far enough to see the killer had gone down after squeezing off that last barrage, facedown on the blacktop. The round in the chest had taken him out, though not fast enough.

Jack's head lolled to his left. Even as his tunnel vision constricted further, he saw a black-and-white swing off the street, into the station at high speed, fishtailing to a stop as the driver stood on the brakes.

Jack's vision closed down altogether. He was totally blind.

He felt as helpless as a baby, and he began to cry.

He heard doors opening, officers shouting.

It was over.

Luther was dead. Almost one year since Tommy Fernandez had been shot down beside him. Tommy then Luther. Two good partners, good friends, in one year. But it was over.

Voices. Sirens. A crash that might have been the portico collapsing over the service-station pumps.

Sounds were increasingly muffled, as if someone was steadily packing his ears full of cotton. His hearing was fading in much the same way that his vision had gone.

Other senses too. He repeatedly pursed his dry mouth, trying unsuccessfully to work up some saliva and get a taste of something, even the acrid fumes of gasoline and burning tar. He couldn't smell anything, either, although a moment ago the air had been ripe with foul odors.

Couldn't feel the pavement under him. Or the blustery wind. No pain any more. Not even a tingle. Just cold. Deep, penetrating cold.

Utter deafness overcame him.

Holding desperately to the spark of life in a body that had become an insensate receptacle for his mind, he wondered if he would ever see Heather and Toby again. When he tried to summon their faces from memory, he could not recall what they looked like, his wife and son, two people he loved more than life itself, couldn't remember their eyes or the color of their hair, which scared him, *terrified* him. He knew he was shaking with grief, as if *they* had died, but he couldn't feel the shakes, knew he was crying but couldn't feel the tears, strained harder to bring their precious faces to mind, Toby and Heather, Heather and Toby, but his imagination was as blind

23

as his eyes. His interior world wasn't a bottomless pit of darkness but a blank wintry whiteness, like a vision of driving snow, a blizzard, frigid, glacial, arctic, unrelenting.

3

LIGHTNING FLASHED, followed by a crash of thunder so powerful it rattled the kitchen windows. The storm began not with a sprinkle or drizzle but with a sudden downpour, as if clouds were hollow structures that could shatter like egg shells and spill their entire contents at once.

Heather was standing at the counter beside the refrigerator, scooping orange sherbet out of a carton into a bowl, and she turned to look at the window above the sink. Rain was falling so hard it almost appeared to be snow, a white deluge. The branches of the ficus benjaminas in the backyard drooped under the weight of that vertical river, their longest trailers touching the ground.

She was relieved she wouldn't be on the freeways later in the day, commuting home from work. Due to a lack of regular experience, Californians weren't good at driving in rain; they either slowed to a crawl and took such extreme precautions that they halted traffic, or they proceeded in their usual gonzo fashion and careened into one another with a recklessness approaching enthusiasm. Later, a lot of people would find their usual hour-long evening commute stretching into a two-and-a-half-hour ordeal.

There was, after all, a bright side to being unemployed. She just hadn't been looking hard enough for it. No doubt, if she put her mind to it, she'd think of a long list of other benefits. Like not having to buy any new clothes for work. Look how much she had

25

saved right there. Didn't have to worry about the stability of the bank in which they had their savings account, either, because at the rate they were going, they wouldn't *have* a savings account in a few months, not on just Jack's salary since the city's latest financial crisis had required him to take a pay cut. Taxes had gone up again, too, both state and federal, so she was saving all the money that the government would have taken and squandered in her name if she'd been on someone's payroll. Gosh, when you *really* thought about it, being laid off after ten years at IBM wasn't a tragedy, not even a crisis, but a virtual *festival* of life-enhancing change.

'Give it a rest, Heather,' she warned herself, closing up the carton of sherbet and returning it to the freezer.

Jack, ever the grinning optimist, said nothing could be gained by dwelling on bad news, and he was right, of course. His upbeat nature, genial personality, and resilient heart had made it possible for him to endure a nightmarish childhood and adolescence that would have broken many people.

More recently his philosophy had served him well as he'd struggled through the worst year of his career with the Department. After almost a decade together on the streets, he and Tommy Fernandez had been as close as brothers. Tommy had been dead more than eleven months now, but at least one night a week Jack woke from vivid dreams in which his partner and friend was dying again. He always slipped from bed and went to the kitchen for a post-midnight beer or to the living room just to sit alone in the darkness awhile, unaware that Heather had been awakened by the soft cries that escaped him in his sleep. On other nights, months ago, she had learned that she could neither do nor say anything to help him; he needed to be by himself. After he left the room, she often reached out beneath the covers to put her hand on the sheets, which were still warm with his body heat and damp with the perspiration wrung out of him by anguish.

In spite of everything, Jack remained a walking advertisement for the power of positive thinking. Heather was determined to match his cheerful disposition and his capacity for hope.

At the sink, she rinsed the residue of sherbet off the scoop.

Her own mother, Sally, was a world-class whiner who viewed every piece of bad news as a personal catastrophe, even if the event that disturbed her had occurred at the farthest end of the earth and had involved only total strangers. Political unrest in the Philippines could set Sally off on a despairing monologue about the higher prices she believed she would be forced to pay for sugar and for everything containing sugar if the Philippine cane crop was destroyed in a bloody civil war. A hangnail was as troublesome to her as a broken arm to an ordinary person, a headache invariably signaled an impending stroke, and a minor ulcer in the mouth was a sure sign of terminal cancer. The woman *thrived* on bad news and gloom.

Eleven years ago, when Heather was twenty, she'd been delighted to cease being a Beckerman and to become a McGarvey – unlike some friends, in that era of burgeoning feminism, who had continued to use their maiden names after marriage or resorted to hyphenated surnames. She wasn't the first child in history who became determined to be nothing whatsoever like her parents, but she liked to think she was extraordinarily diligent about ridding herself of parental traits.

As she got a spoon out of a drawer, picked up the bowl full of sherbet, and went into the living room, Heather realized another upside to being unemployed was that she didn't have to miss work to care for Toby when he was home sick from school or hire a sitter to look after him. She could be right there where he needed her and suffer none of the guilt of a working mom.

Of course, their health insurance had covered only eighty percent of the cost of the visit to the doctor's office on Monday morning, and the twenty-percent co-payment had caught her attention as never before. It had seemed huge. But that was Beckerman thinking, not McGarvey thinking.

27

Toby was in his pajamas in an armchair in the living room, in front of the television, legs stretched out on a footstool, covered in blankets. He was watching cartoons on a cable channel that programmed exclusively for kids.

Heather knew to the penny what the cable subscription cost. Back in October, when she'd still had a job, she'd have had to guess at the amount and might not have come within five dollars of it.

On the TV, a tiny mouse was chasing a cat, which had apparently been hypnotized into believing that the mouse was six feet tall with fangs and blood-red eyes.

'Gourmet orange sherbet,' she said, handing Toby the bowl and spoon, 'finest on the planet, brewed it up myself, hours upon hours of drudgery, had to kill and skin two dozen sherbets to make it.'

'Thanks, Mom,' he said, grinning at her, then grinning even more broadly at the sherbet before raising his eyes to the TV screen and locking on to the cartoon again.

Sunday through Tuesday, he had stayed in bed without making a fuss, too miserable even to agitate for television time. He had slept so much that she'd begun to worry, but evidently sleep had been what he needed. Last night, for the first time since Sunday, he'd been able to keep more than clear liquids on his stomach; he'd asked for sherbet and hadn't gotten sick on it. This morning he'd risked two slices of unbuttered white toast, and now sherbet again. His fever had broken; the flu seemed to be running its course.

Heather settled into another armchair. On the end table beside her, a coffee-pot-shaped thermos and a heavy white ceramic mug with red and purple flowers stood on a plastic tray. She uncapped the thermos and refilled the mug with a premium coffee flavored with almond and chocolate, relishing the fragrant steam, trying not to calculate the cost per cup of this indulgence.

After curling her legs on the chair, pulling an Afghan over her lap, and sipping the brew, she picked up a paperback edition of a Dick Francis novel. She opened to the page she had marked with a slip of paper, and she tried to return to a world of English manners, morals, and mysteries.

She felt guilty, though she was not neglecting anything to spend time with a book. No housework needed doing. When they'd both held jobs, she and Jack had shared chores at home. They still shared them. When she'd been laid off, she'd insisted on taking over his domestic duties, but he'd refused. He probably thought that letting her fill her time with housework would lead her to the depressing conviction that she would never find another job. He'd always been as sensitive about other people's feelings as he was optimistic about his own prospects. As a result, the house was clean, the laundry was done, and her only chore was to watch over Toby, which wasn't a chore at all because he was such a good kid. Her guilt was the irrational if inescapable result of being, by nature and by choice, a working woman who, in this deep recession, was not permitted to work.

She had submitted applications to twenty-six companies. Now all she could do was wait. And read Dick Francis.

The melodramatic music and comic voices on the television didn't distract her. Indeed, the fragrant coffee, the comfort of the chair, and the cold sound of winter rain drumming on the roof combined to take her mind off her worries and let her slip into the novel.

Heather had been reading fifteen minutes when Toby said, 'Mom?'

'Hmmmm?' she said, without looking up from her book.

'Why do cats always want to kill mice?'

Marking her place in the book with her thumb, she glanced at the television, where a different cat and mouse were involved in another slapstick chase, the former pursuing the latter this time.

'Why can't they be friends with mice,' the boy asked, 'instead of wanting to kill them all the time?'

'It's just a cat's nature,' she said.

'But why?'

'It's the way God made cats.'

'Doesn't God like mice?'

'Well, He must, because He made mice too.'

'Then why make cats to kill them?'

'If mice didn't have natural enemies like cats and owls and coyotes, they'd overrun the world.'

'Why would they overrun the world?'

'Because they give birth to litters, not single babies.'

'So?'

'So, if they didn't have natural enemies to control their numbers, there'd be a trillion-billion mice eating up all the food in the world with nothing left for cats *or* us.'

'If God didn't want mice to overrun the world, why didn't He just make them so they have single babies at a time?'

Adults always lost the Why Game, because eventually the train of questions led to a dead-end track with no answer.

Heather said, 'You got me there, kiddo.'

'I think it's mean to make mice have a lot of babies and then make cats to kill them.'

'You'll have to discuss that with God, I'm afraid.'

'You mean when I go to bed tonight and say my prayers?'

'Best time,' she said, freshening the coffee in her mug with the supply in the thermos.

Toby said, 'I always ask Him questions, then I always fall asleep before He answers me. Why does He let me fall asleep before I can get the answer?'

'That's the way God works. He only talks to you in your sleep. If you listen, then you wake up with the answer.'

She was proud of that one. She seemed to be holding her own.

Frowning, Toby said, 'But usually I still don't know the answer when I wake up. Why don't I know it if He told me?'

Heather took a few sips of coffee to gain time. Then she said, 'Well, see, God doesn't want to just *give* you all the answers. The reason we're here on this world is to find the answers ourselves, to learn and gain understanding by our own efforts.'

Good. Very good. She felt modestly exhilarated, as if she'd held on longer than she'd any right to expect in a tennis match with a world-class player.

Toby said, 'Mice aren't the only things get chased and killed. For every animal, there's another animal wants to tear it to pieces.' He glanced at the TV. 'See, there, like dogs want to murder cats.'

The cat that had been chasing the mouse was now, in turn, being pursued by a fierce-looking bulldog in a spiked collar.

Looking at his mother again, Toby said, 'Why does every animal have another animal that wants to kill it? Would cats overrun the world without their natural enemies?'

The Why Game train had come to another dead-end in the track. Oh, yes, she could have discussed the concept of original sin, told him how the world had been a serene realm of peace and plenty until Eve and Adam had fallen from grace and let death into the world. But all of that seemed to be heavy stuff for an eight-year-old. Besides, she wasn't sure she believed any of it, though it was the explanation for evil, violence, and death with which she herself had grown up.

Fortunately, Toby spared her from the admission that she had no answer. 'If I was God, I woulda made just one mom and dad and kid of each kind of thing. You know? Like one mother golden retriever and one father golden retriever and one puppy.'

He had long wanted a golden retriever, but they'd been delaying because their five-room house seemed too small for such a large dog.

'Nothing would ever die or grow old,' Toby said, continuing to describe the world he would have made, 'so the puppy would always be a puppy, and there could never be more of any one thing to overrun the world, and then nothing would have to kill anything else.'

That, of course, was the paradise that supposedly once had been.

'I wouldn't make *any* bees or spiders or cockroaches or snakes,' he said, wrinkling his face in disgust. 'That *never* made any sense. God musta been in a really weird mood that day.'

31

Heather laughed. She loved this kid to pieces.

'Well, He musta been,' Toby insisted, turning his attention to the television again.

He looked so like Jack. He had Jack's beautiful gray-blue eyes and open guileless face. Jack's nose. But he had her blond hair, and he was slightly small for his age, so it was possible he also had inherited more of his body type from her than from his father. Jack was tall and solidly built; Heather was five-four, slender. Toby was obviously the son of both and sometimes, like now, his existence seemed miraculous. He was the living symbol of her love for Jack and of Jack's love for her, and if death was the price to be paid for the miracle of procreation, then perhaps the bargain made in Eden wasn't as lopsided as it sometimes seemed.

On TV, Sylvester the cat was trying to kill Tweetie the canary, but unlike real life, the tiny bird was getting the best of the sputtering feline.

The telephone rang.

Heather put her book on the arm of the chair, flung the afghan aside, and got up. Toby had eaten all the sherbet, and she plucked the empty bowl from his lap on her way to the kitchen.

The phone was on the wall beside the refrigerator. She put the bowl on the counter and picked up the receiver. 'Hello?'

'Heather?'

'Speaking.'

'It's Lyle Crawford.'

Crawford was the captain of Jack's division, the man to whom he answered.

Maybe it was the fact that Crawford had never called her before, maybe it was something in the tone of his voice, or maybe it was just the instincts of a cop's wife, but she knew at once that something was terribly wrong. Her heart began to race, and for a moment she couldn't breathe. Then suddenly she was breathing shallowly, rapidly, and expelling the same word with each exhalation: 'No, no, no, no.'

32

Crawford was saying something, but Heather couldn't make herself listen to him, as if whatever had happened to Jack would not *really* have happened as long as she refused to hear the ugly facts put into words.

Someone was knocking at the back door.

She turned, looked. Through the window in the door, she saw a man in uniform, dripping rain, Louie Silverman, another cop from Jack's division, a good friend for eight years, nine years, maybe longer, Louie with the rubbery face and unruly red hair. Because he was a friend, he had come around to the back door instead of knocking at the front, not so formal that way, not so damn cold and horribly formal, just a friend at the back door, oh God, just a friend at the back door with some news.

Louie said her name. Muffled by the glass. So forlorn, the way he said her name.

'Wait, wait,' she told Lyle Crawford, and she took the receiver away from her ear, held it against her breast.

She closed her eyes, too, so she wouldn't have to look at poor Louie's face pressed to the window in the door. So gray, his face, so drawn and gray. He loved Jack too. Poor Louie.

She chewed on her lower lip and squeezed her eyes tightly shut and held the phone in both hands against her chest, searching for the strength she was going to need, praying for the strength.

She heard a key in the back door. Louie knew where they hid the spare on the porch.

The door opened. He came inside with the sound of rain swelling behind him. 'Heather,' he said.

The sound of the rain. The rain. The cold merciless sound of the rain.

33

4

THE MONTANA morning was high and blue, pierced by mountains with peaks as white as angels' robes, graced by forests green and by the smooth contours of lower meadows still asleep under winter's mantle. The air was pure and so clear it seemed possible to look all the way to China if not for the obstructing terrain.

Eduardo Fernandez stood on the front porch of the ranch house, staring across the down-sloping, snow-covered fields to the woods a hundred yards to the east. Sugar pines and yellow pines crowded close to one another and pinned inky shadows to the ground, as if the night never quite escaped their needled grasp even with the rising of a bright sun in a cloudless sky.

The silence was deep. Eduardo lived alone, and his nearest neighbor was two miles away. The wind was still abed, and nothing moved across that vast panorama except for two birds of prey – hawks, perhaps – circling soundlessly high overhead.

Shortly after one o'clock in the morning, when the night usually would have been equally steeped in silence, Eduardo had been awakened by a strange sound. The longer he had listened, the stranger it had seemed. As he had gotten out of bed to seek the source, he had been surprised to find he was afraid. After seven decades of taking what life threw at him, having attained spiritual peace and an acceptance of the inevitability of death, he'd not been frightened of anything in a long time. He was unnerved, therefore, when last night he had felt his heart thudding furiously and his gut clenching with dread merely because of a queer sound.

Unlike many seventy-year-old men, Eduardo rarely had difficulty attaining plumbless sleep for a full eight hours. His days were filled with physical activity, his evenings with the solace of good books; a lifetime of measured habits and moderation left him vigorous in old age, without troubling regrets, content. Loneliness was the only curse of his life, since Margarite had died three years ago, and on those infrequent occasions when he woke in the middle of the night, it was a dream of his lost wife that harried him from sleep.

The sound had been less loud than all-pervasive. A low throbbing that swelled like a series of waves rushing toward a beach. Beneath the throbbing, an undertone that was almost subliminal, quaverous, an eerie electronic oscillation. He'd not only heard it but *felt* it, vibrating in his teeth, his bones. The glass in the windows hummed with it. When he placed a hand flat against the wall, he swore that he could feel the waves of sound cresting through the house itself, like the slow beating of a heart beneath the plaster.

Accompanying that pulse had been a sense of pressure, as if he had been listening to someone or something rhythmically straining against confinement, struggling to break out of a prison or through a barrier.

But who?

Or what?

Eventually, after scrambling out of bed, pulling on pants and shoes, he had gone out on to the front porch, where he had seen the light in the woods. No, he had to be more honest with himself. It hadn't been merely a light in the woods, nothing as simple as that.

He wasn't superstitious. Even as a young man, he had prided himself on his levelheadedness, common sense, and unsentimental grasp of the realities of life. The writers whose books lined his study were those with a crisp, simple style and with no patience for fantasy, men with a cold clear vision, who saw the world for what

35

it was and not for what it might be: men like Hemingway, Raymond Carver, Ford Madox Ford.

The phenomenon in the lower woods was nothing that his favorite writers — every last one of them a realist — could have incorporated into their stories. The light had not been from an object within the forest, against which the pines had been silhouetted; rather, it had come from the pines themselves, mottled amber radiance that appeared to originate within the bark, within the boughs, as if the tree roots had siphoned water from a subterranean pool contaminated by a greater percentage of radium than the paint with which watch dials had once been coated to allow time to be told in the dark.

A cluster of ten to twenty pines had been involved. Like a glowing shrine in the otherwise night-black fastness of timber.

Unquestionably, the mysterious source of the light was also the source of the sound. When the former had begun to fade, so had the latter. Quieter and dimmer, quieter and dimmer. The March night had become silent and dark again in the same instant, marked only by the sound of his own breathing and illuminated by nothing stranger than the silver crescent of a quarter-moon and the pearly phosphorescence of the snow-shrouded fields.

The event had lasted about seven minutes.

It had seemed much longer.

Back inside the house, he had stood at the windows, waiting to see what would happen next. Eventually, when that seemed to have been the sum of it, he returned to bed.

He had not been able to get back to sleep. He had lain awake . . . wondering.

Every morning he sat down to breakfast at six-thirty, with his big shortwave radio tuned to a station in Chicago that provided international news twenty-four hours a day. The peculiar experience during the previous night hadn't been a sufficient interruption of the rhythms of his life to make him alter his schedule. This morning he'd eaten the entire contents of a large can of grapefruit sections, followed by two eggs over easy, home fries, a quarter-pound of bacon, and four slices of buttered toast. He hadn't lost his hearty appetite with age, and a lifelong dedication to the foods that were hardest on the heart had only left him with the constitution of a man more than twenty years his junior.

Finished eating, he always liked to linger over several cups of black coffee, listening to the endless troubles of the world. The news unfailingly confirmed the wisdom of living in a far place with no neighbors in view.

This morning, though he had lingered longer than usual with his coffee, and though the radio had been on, he hadn't been able to remember a word of the news when he pushed back his chair and got up from breakfast. The entire time he had been studying the woods through the window beside the table, trying to decide if he should go down to the foot of the meadow and search for evidence of the enigmatic visitation.

Now, standing on the front porch in knee-high boots, jeans, sweater, and sheepskin-lined jacket, wearing a cap with fur-lined ear-flaps tied under his chin, he still hadn't decided what he was going to do.

Incredibly, fear was still with him. Bizarre as they might have been, the tides of pulsating sound and the luminosity in the trees had not harmed him. Whatever threat he perceived was entirely subjective, no doubt more imaginary than real.

Finally he became sufficiently angry with himself to break the chains of dread. He descended the porch steps and strode across the front yard.

The transition from yard to meadow was hidden under a cloak of snow six to eight inches deep in some places and knee-high in others, depending on where the wind had scoured it away or piled it. After thirty years on the ranch, he was so familiar with the contours of the land and the ways of the wind that he unthinkingly chose the route that offered the least resistance.

White plumes of breath steamed from him. The bitter air brought a pleasant flush to his cheeks. He calmed himself by concentrating on – and enjoying – the familiar effects of a winter day.

He stood for a while at the end of the meadow, studying the very trees that, last night, had glowed a smoky amber against the black backdrop of the deeper woods, as if they had been imbued with a divine presence, like God in the bush that burned without being consumed. This morning they looked no more special than a million other sugar and ponderosa pines, the former somewhat greener than the latter.

The specimens at the edge of the forest were younger than those rising behind them, only about thirty to thirty-five feet tall, as young as twenty years. They had grown from seeds fallen to the earth when he had already been on the ranch a decade, and he felt as if he knew them more intimately than he had known most people in his life.

The woods had always seemed like a cathedral to him. The trunks of the great evergreens were reminiscent of the granite columns of a nave, soaring high to support a vaulted ceiling of green boughs. The pine-scented silence was ideal for meditation. Walking the meandering deer trails, he often had a sense that he was in a sacred place, that he was not just a man of flesh and bone but an heir to eternity.

He had always felt safe in the woods.

Until now.

Stepping out of the meadow and into the random-patterned mosaic of shadows and sunlight beneath the interlaced pine branches, Eduardo found nothing out of the ordinary. Neither the trunks nor the boughs showed signs of heat damage, no charring, not even a singed curl of bark or blackened cluster of needles. The thin layer of snow under the trees had not melted anywhere, and the only tracks in it were those of deer, raccoon, and smaller animals.

He broke off a piece of bark from a sugar pine and crumbled it between the thumb and forefinger of his gloved right hand. Nothing unusual about it.

He moved deeper into the woods, past the place where the trees had stood in radiant splendor in the night. Some of the older pines were over two hundred feet tall. The shadows grew more numerous and blacker than ash-buds in the front of March, while the sun found fewer places to intrude.

His heart would not be still. It thudded hard and fast.

He could find nothing in the woods but what had always been there, yet his heart would not be still.

His mouth was dry. The full curve of his spine was clad in a chill that had nothing to do with the wintry air.

Annoyed with himself, Eduardo turned back toward the meadow, following the tracks he had left in the patches of snow and the thick carpet of dead pine needles. The crunch of his footsteps disturbed a slumbering owl from its secret perch in some high bower.

He felt a wrongness in the woods. He couldn't put a finer point on it than that. Which sharpened his annoyance. A wrongness. What the hell did that mean? A wrongness.

The hooting owl.

Spiny black pinecones on white snow.

Pale beams of sunlight lancing through the gaps in the gray-green branches.

All of it ordinary. Peaceful. Yet *wrong*.

As he returned to the perimeter of the forest, with snow-covered fields visible between the trunks of the trees ahead, he was suddenly certain that he was not going to reach open ground, that something was rushing at him from behind, some creature as indefinable as the *wrongness* that he sensed around him. He began to move faster. Fear swelled step by step. The hooting of the owl seemed to sour into a cry as alien as the shriek of a nemesis in a nightmare. He stumbled on an exposed root, his heart trip-hammered, and he spun around with a cry of terror to confront whatever demon was in pursuit of him.

He was, of course, alone.

Shadows and sunlight.

The hoot of an owl. A soft and lonely sound. As ever.

Cursing himself, he headed for the meadow again. Reached it. The trees were behind him. He was safe.

Then, dear sweet Jesus, the fear again, worse than ever, the absolute dead certainty that it was coming – what? – that it was for sure gaining on him, that it would drag him down, that it was bent upon committing an act infinitely worse than murder, that it had an inhuman purpose and unknown uses for him so strange they were beyond both his understanding and conception. This time he was in the grip of a terror so black and profound, so mindless, that he could not summon the courage to turn and confront the empty day behind him – if, indeed, it proved to be empty this time. He raced toward the house, which appeared far more distant than a hundred yards, a citadel beyond his reach. He kicked through shallow snow, blundered into deeper drifts, ran and churned and staggered and flailed uphill, making wordless sounds of blind panic – 'Uh, uh, uhhhhh, uh, uh' – all intellect repressed by instinct, until he found himself at the porch steps, up which he scrambled, at the top of which he turned, at last, to scream – '*No!*' – at the clear, crisp, blue Montana day.

The pristine mantle of snow across the broad field was marred only by his own trail to and from the woods.

He went inside.

He bolted the door.

In the big kitchen he stood for a long time in front of the brick fireplace, still dressed for the outdoors, basking in the heat that poured across the hearth – yet unable to get warm.

Old. He was an old man. Seventy. An old man who had lived alone too long, who sorely missed his wife. If senility had crept up on him, who was around to notice? An old, lonely man with cabin fever, imagining things.

40

'Bullshit,' he said after a while.

He was lonely, all right, but he wasn't senile.

After stripping out of his hat, coat, gloves, and boots, he got the hunting rifles and shotguns out of the locked cabinet in the study. He loaded all of them.

5

MAE HONG, who lived across the street, came over to take care of Toby. Her husband was a cop, too, though not in the same division as Jack. Because the Hongs had no children of their own yet, Mae was free to stay as late as necessary, in the event Heather needed to put in a long vigil at the hospital.

While Louie Silverman and Mae remained in the kitchen, Heather lowered the sound on the television and told Toby what had happened. She sat on the footstool and, after tossing the blankets aside, he perched on the edge of the chair. She held his small hands in hers.

She didn't share the grimmest details with him, in part because she didn't know all of them herself but also because an eight-year-old could handle only so much. On the other hand, she couldn't gloss over the situation, either, because they were a police family. They lived with the repressed expectation of just such a disaster as had struck that morning, and even a child had the need and the right to know when his father had been seriously wounded.

'Can I go to the hospital with you?' Toby asked, holding more tightly to her hands than he probably realized.

'It's best for you to stay here right now, honey.'

'I'm not sick any more.'

'Yes, you are.'

'I feel good.'

'You don't want to give your germs to your dad.'

'He'll be all right, won't he?'

She could give him only one answer even if she couldn't be certain it would prove to be correct. 'Yes, baby, he's going to be all right.'

His gaze was direct. He wanted the truth. Right at that moment he seemed to be far older than eight. Maybe cops' kids grew up faster than others, faster than they should.

'You're sure?' he said.

'Yes. I'm sure.'

'W-where was he shot?'

'In the leg.'

Not a lie. It was one of the places he was shot. In the leg and two hits in the torso, Crawford had said. Two hits in the torso. Jesus. What did that mean? Take out a lung? Gutshot? The heart? At least he hadn't sustained head wounds. Tommy Fernandez had been shot in the head, no chance.

She felt a sob of anguish rising in her, and she strained to force it down, didn't dare give voice to it, not in front of Toby.

'That's not so bad, in the leg,' Toby said, but his lower lip was trembling. 'What about the bad guy?'

'He's dead.'

'Daddy got him?'

'Yes, he got him.'

'Good,' Toby said solemnly.

'Daddy did what was right, and now we have to do what's right, too, we have to be strong. Okay?'

'Yeah.'

He was so small. It wasn't fair to put such a weight on a boy so small.

She said, 'Daddy needs to know we're okay, that we're strong, so he doesn't have to worry about us and can concentrate on getting well.'

'Sure.'

43

'That's my boy.' She squeezed his hands. 'I'm real proud of you, do you know that?'

Suddenly shy, he looked at the floor. 'Well . . . I'm . . . I'm proud of Daddy.'

'You should be, Toby. Your dad's a hero.'

He nodded but couldn't speak. His face was screwed up as he strained to avoid tears.

'You be good for Mae.'

'Yeah.'

'I'll be back as soon as I can.'

'When?'

'As soon as I can.'

He sprang off the chair, into her arms, so fast and with such force he almost knocked her off the stool. She hugged him fiercely. He was shuddering as if with fever chills, though that stage of his illness had passed almost two days ago. Heather squeezed her eyes shut, bit down on her tongue almost hard enough to draw blood, being strong, being strong even if, damn it, no one should ever *have* to be so strong.

'Gotta go,' she said softly.

Toby pulled back from her.

She smiled at him, smoothed his tousled hair.

He settled into the armchair and propped his legs on the stool again. She tucked the blankets around him, then turned the sound up on the television once more.

Elmer Fudd trying to terminate Bugs Bunny. Cwazy wabbit. Boom-boom, bang-bang, whapitta-whapitta-whap, thud, clunk, hoo-ha, around and around in perpetual pursuit.

In the kitchen, Heather hugged Mae Hong and whispered, 'Don't let him watch any regular channels, where he might see a news brief.'

Mae nodded. 'If he gets tired of cartoons, we'll play games.'

'Those bastards on the TV news, they always have to show you the blood, get the ratings. I don't want him seeing his father's blood on the ground.'

*

The storm washed all the color out of the day. The sky was as charry as burnt-out ruins and, from a distance of even half a block, the palm trees looked black. Wind-driven rain, gray as iron nails, hammered every surface, and gutters overflowed with filthy water.

Louie Silverman was in uniform, driving a squad car, so he used the emergency beacons and siren to clear the surface streets ahead of them, staying off the freeways.

Sitting in the shotgun seat beside Louie, hands clasped between her thighs, shoulders hunched, shivering, Heather said, 'Okay, it's just us now, Toby can't overhear, so tell me straight.'

'It's bad. Left leg, lower right abdomen, upper right side of the chest. The perp was armed with a Micro Uzi, nine-millimeter ammunition, so they weren't light rounds. Jack was unconscious when we hit the scene, paramedics couldn't bring him around.'

'And Luther's dead.'

'Yeah.'

'Luther always seemed . . .'

'Like a rock.'

'Yeah. Always going to be there. Like a mountain.'

They rode in silence for a block.

Then she asked, 'How many others?'

'Three. One of the station owners, mechanic, pump jockey. But because of Jack, the other owner, Mrs Arkadian, she's alive.'

They were still a mile or so from the hospital when a Pontiac ahead of them refused to pull over to let the black-and-white pass. It had oversize tires, a jacked-up front end, and air scoops front and back. Louie waited for a break in oncoming traffic, then crossed the solid yellow line to get around the car. Passing the Pontiac,

Heather saw four angry-looking young men in it, hair slicked back and tied behind, affecting a modern version of the gangster look, faces hard with hostility and defiance.

'Jack's going to make it, Heather.'

The wet black streets glimmered with serpentine patterns of frost-cold light, reflections of the headlights of oncoming traffic.

'He's tough,' Louie said.

'We all are,' she said.

*

Jack was still in surgery at Westside General Hospital when Heather arrived at a quarter past ten. The woman at the information desk supplied the surgeon's name – Dr Emil Procnow – and suggested waiting in the visitors' lounge outside the Intensive Care Unit rather than in the main lobby.

Theories of the psychological effects of color were at work in the lounge. The walls were lemon yellow, and the padded vinyl seats and backrests of the gray tubular-steel chairs were bright orange – as if any intensity of worry, fear, or grief could be dramatically relieved by a sufficiently cheerful decor.

Heather wasn't alone in that circus-hued room. Besides Louie, three cops were present – two in uniform, one in street clothes – all of whom she knew. They hugged her, said Jack was going to make it, offered to get her coffee, and in general tried to keep her spirits up. They were the first of a stream of friends and fellow officers from the Department who would participate in the vigil because Jack was well liked but also because, in an increasingly violent society where respect for the law wasn't cool in some circles, cops found it more necessary than ever to take care of their own.

In spite of the well-meaning and welcome company, the wait was excruciating. Heather seemed no less alone than if she had been by herself.

46

Bathed in an abundance of harsh fluorescent light, the yellow walls and the shiny orange chairs seemed to grow brighter minute by minute. Rather than diluting her anxiety, the decor made her twitchy, and periodically she had to close her eyes.

By 11:15, she had been in the hospital for an hour, and Jack had been in surgery an hour and a half. Those in the support group – which now numbered six – were unanimous in their judgment that so much time under the knife was a good sign. If Jack had been mortally wounded, they said, he would have been in the operating room only a short while, and bad news would have come quickly.

Heather wasn't so sure about that. She wouldn't allow her hopes to rise because that would just leave her farther to fall if the news was bad after all.

Torrents of hard-driven rain clattered against the windows and streamed down the glass. Through the distorting lens of water, the city outside appeared to be utterly without straight lines and sharp edges, a surreal metropolis of molten forms.

Strangers arrived, some red-eyed from crying, all quietly tense, waiting for news about other patients, their friends and relatives. Some of them were damp from the storm, and they brought with them the odors of wet wool and cotton.

She paced. She looked out the window. She drank bitter coffee from a vending machine. She sat with a month-old copy of *Newsweek*, trying to read a story about the hottest new actress in Hollywood, but every time she reached the end of a paragraph, she couldn't recall a word of it.

By 12:15, when Jack had been under the knife for two and a half hours, everyone in the support group continued to pretend no news was good news and that Jack's prognosis improved with every minute the doctors spent on him. Some, including Louie, found it more difficult to meet Heather's eyes, however, and they were speaking softly, as if in a funeral parlor instead of a hospital. The grayness of the storm outside had seeped into their faces and voices.

Staring at *Newsweek* without seeing it, she began to wonder what she'd do if Jack didn't make it. Such thoughts seemed traitorous, and at first she suppressed them, as if the very act of imagining life without Jack would contribute to his death.

He couldn't die. She needed him, and Toby needed him.

The thought of conveying the news of Jack's death to Toby made her nauseous. A thin cold sweat broke out along the nape of her neck. She felt as if she might throw up, ridding herself of the bad coffee.

At last a man in surgical greens entered the lounge. 'Mrs McGarvey?'

As heads turned toward her, Heather put the magazine on the end table beside her chair and got to her feet.

'I'm Doctor Procnow,' he said as he approached her. The surgeon who had been working on Jack. He was in his forties, slender, with curly black hair and dark yet limpid eyes which were – or which she imagined were – compassionate and wise. 'Your husband's in the post-op recovery room. We'll be moving him into ICU shortly.'

Jack was *alive*.

'Is he going to be all right?'

'He's got a good chance,' Procnow said.

The support group reacted with enthusiasm, but Heather was more cautious, not quick to embrace optimism. Nevertheless, relief made her legs weak. She thought she might crumple to the floor.

As if reading her mind, Procnow guided her to a chair. He pulled another chair up at a right angle to hers and sat facing her.

'Two of the wounds were especially serious,' he said. 'One in the leg and one in the abdomen, lower right side. He lost a lot of blood and was in deep shock by the time paramedics got to him.'

'But he'll be all right?' she asked again, sensing that Procnow had news he was reluctant to deliver.

'Like I said, he's got a good chance. I really mean that. But he's not out of the woods yet.'

Emil Procnow's deep concern was visible in his kind face and eyes, and Heather couldn't tolerate being the object of such profound sympathy because it meant that surviving surgery might have been the least of the challenges facing Jack. She lowered her eyes, unable to meet the surgeon's gaze.

'I had to remove his right kidney,' Procnow said, 'but otherwise there was remarkably little internal damage. Some minor blood-vessel problems, a nicked colon. But we've cleaned that up, done repairs, put in temporary abdominal drains, and we'll keep him on antibiotics to prevent infection. No trouble there.'

'A person can live . . . can live on one kidney, right?'

'Yes, certainly. He won't notice any difference in his quality of life from that.'

What *will* make a difference in the quality of his life, what other wound, what damage? she wanted to ask, but she didn't have the courage.

The surgeon had long, supple fingers. His hands looked lean but strong, like those of a concert pianist. She told herself that Jack could have received neither better care nor more tender mercy than those skilled hands had provided.

'Two things concern us now,' Procnow continued. 'Severe shock combined with a heavy loss of blood can sometimes have . . . cerebral consequences.'

Oh, God, please. Not this.

He said, 'It depends on how long there was a decrease in the supply of blood to the brain and how severe the decrease was, how deoxygenated the tissues became.'

She closed her eyes.

'His EEG looks good, and if I were to base a prognosis on that, I'd say there's been no brain damage. We have every reason to be optimistic. But we won't know until he regains consciousness.'

'When?'

'No way of telling. We'll have to wait and see.'

Maybe never.

She opened her eyes, fighting back tears but not with complete success. She took her purse off the end table and opened it.

As she blew her nose and blotted her eyes, the surgeon said, 'There's one more thing. When you visit him in the ICU, you'll see he's been immobilized with a restraining jacket and bed straps.'

At last Heather met his eyes again.

He said, 'A bullet or fragment struck the spinal cord. There's bruising of the spine, but we don't see a fracture.'

'Bruising. Is that serious?'

'It depends on whether any nerve structures were crushed.'

'Paralysis?'

'Until he's conscious and we can run some simple tests, we can't know. If there *is* paralysis, we'll take another look for a fracture. The important thing is, the cord hasn't been severed, nothing as bad as that. If there's paralysis and we find a fracture, we'll get him into a body cast, apply traction to the legs to get the pressure off the sacrum. We can treat a fracture. It isn't catastrophic. There's an excellent chance we can get him on his feet again.'

'But no guarantees,' she said softly.

He hesitated. Then he said, 'There never are.'

6

THE CUBICLE, one of eight, had large windows that looked into the staff area of the ICU. The drapes had been pulled aside so the nurses could keep a direct watch on the patient even from their station in the center of the wheel-shaped chamber. Jack was attached to a cardiac monitor that transmitted continuous data to a terminal at the central desk, an intravenous drip that provided him with glucose and antibiotics, and a bifurcated oxygen tube that clipped gently to the septum between his nostrils.

Heather was prepared to be shocked by Jack's condition – but he looked even worse than she expected. He was unconscious, so his face was slack, of course, but the lack of animation was not the only reason for his frightening appearance. His skin was bone-white, with dark-blue circles around his sunken eyes. His lips were so gray that she thought of ashes, and a biblical phrase passed through her mind with unsettling resonance, as if it had actually been spoken aloud – *ashes to ashes, dust to dust*. He seemed ten or fifteen pounds lighter than when he had left home this morning, as if his struggle for survival had taken place over a week, not just a few hours.

A lump in her throat made it difficult to swallow as she stood at the side of the bed, and she was unable to speak. Though he was unconscious, she didn't want to talk to him until she was sure she could control her speech. She'd read somewhere that even patients in comas might be able to hear people around them; on some deep

51

level, they might understand what was said and benefit from encouragement. She didn't want Jack to hear a tremor of fear or doubt in her voice – or anything else that might upset him or exacerbate what fear and depression already gripped him.

The cubicle was unnervingly quiet. The heart-monitor sound had been turned off, leaving only a visual display. The oxygen-rich air escaping through the nasal inserts hissed so faintly she could hear it only when she leaned close to him, and the sound of his shallow breathing was as soft as that of a sleeping child. Rain drummed on the world outside, ticked and tapped against the single window, but that quickly became a gray noise, just another form of silence.

She wanted to hold his hand worse than she'd ever wanted anything. But his hands were hidden in the long sleeves of the restraining jacket. The IV line, which was probably inserted in a vein on the back of his hand, disappeared under the cuff.

Hesitantly she touched his cheek. He looked cold but felt feverish.

Eventually she said, 'I'm here, babe.'

He gave no sign he had heard her. His eyes didn't move under their lids. His gray lips remained slightly parted.

'Doctor Procnow says everything's looking good,' she told him. 'You're going to come out of this just fine. Together we can handle this, no sweat. Hell, two years ago, when my folks came to stay with us for a week? Now *that* was a disaster and an ordeal, my mother whining nonstop for seven days, my dad drunk and moody. This is just a bee-sting by comparison, don't you think?'

No response.

'I'm here,' she said. 'I'll stay here. I'm not going anywhere. You and me, okay?'

On the screen of the cardiac monitor, a moving line of bright-green light displayed the jagged and critical patterns of atrial and ventricular activity, which proceeded without a single disruptive blip, weak but steady. If Jack had heard what she'd said, his heart did not respond to her words.

52

A straight-backed chair stood in one corner. She moved it next to the bed. She watched him through the gaps in the railing.

Visitors in the ICU were limited to ten minutes every two hours, so as not to exhaust patients and interfere with the nurses.

However, the head nurse of the unit, Maria Alicante, was the daughter of a policeman. She gave Heather a dispensation from the rules. 'You stay with him as long as you want,' Maria said. 'Thank God, nothing like this ever happened to my dad. We always expected it would, but it never did. Of course, he retired a few years ago, just as everything started getting even crazier out there.'

Every hour or so, Heather left the ICU to spend a few minutes with the members of the support group in the lounge. The faces kept changing, but there were never fewer than three and sometimes as many as six or seven, male and female officers in uniform, plain-clothes detectives.

Other cops' wives stopped by too. Each of them hugged her. At one moment or another, each of them was on the verge of tears. They were sincerely sympathetic, shared the anguish. But Heather knew that every last one of them was glad it had been Jack and not *her* husband who'd taken the call at Arkadian's service station.

Heather didn't blame them for that. She'd have sold her soul to have Jack change places with any of their husbands – and would have visited them in an equally sincere spirit of sorrow and sympathy.

The Department was a closely knit community, especially in this age of social dissolution, but every community was formed of smaller units, of families with shared experiences, mutual needs, similar values and hopes. Regardless of how tightly woven the fabric of the community, each family first protected and cherished its own. Without the intense and all-excluding love of wife for husband, husband for wife, parents for children, and children for parents, there would be no compassion for people in the larger community beyond the home.

In the ICU cubicle with Jack, she relived their life together in memory, from their first date, to the night Toby had been born, to breakfast this morning. More than twelve years. But it seemed so short a span. Sometimes she put her head against the bed railing and spoke to him, recalling a special moment, reminding him of how much laughter they had shared, how much joy.

Shortly before five o'clock, she was jolted from her memories by the sudden awareness that something had changed.

Alarmed, she got up and leaned over the bed to see if Jack was still breathing. Then she realized he must be all right because the cardiac monitor showed no change in the rhythms of his heart.

What *had* changed was the sound of the rain. It was gone. The storm had ended.

She stared at the opaque window. The city beyond, which she couldn't see, would be glimmering in the aftermath of the day-long downpour. She had always been enchanted by Los Angeles after a rain – sparkling drops of water dripping off the points of palm fronds as if the trees were exuding jewels, streets washed clean, the air so clear that the distant mountains reappeared from out of the usual haze of smog, everything fresh.

If the window had been clear and the city had been there for her to see, she wondered if it would seem enchanting this time. She didn't think so. This city would never gleam for her again, even if rain scrubbed it for forty days and forty nights.

In that moment she knew their future – Jack's, Toby's, and her own – lay in some far place. This wasn't home any more. When Jack recovered, they would sell the house and go . . . somewhere, anywhere, to new lives, a fresh start. There was a sadness in that decision, but it gave her hope as well.

When she turned away from the window, she discovered that Jack's eyes were open and that he was watching her.

Her heart stuttered.

She remembered Procnow's bleak words. Massive blood loss. Deep shock. Cerebral consequence. Brain damage.

She was afraid to speak for fear his response would be slurred, tortured, and meaningless.

He licked his gray, chapped lips.

His breathing was wheezy.

Leaning against the side of the bed, bending over him, summoning all her courage, she said, 'Honey?'

Confusion and fear played across his face as he turned his head slightly left, then slightly right, surveying the room.

'Jack? Are you with me, baby?'

He focused on the cardiac monitor, seemed transfixed by the moving green line, which was spiking higher and far more often than at any time since Heather had first entered the cubicle.

Her own heart was pounding so hard that it shook her. His failure to respond was terrifying.

'Jack, are you okay, can you hear me?'

Slowly he turned his head to face her again. He licked his lips, grimaced. His voice was weak, whispery. 'Sorry about this.'

Startled, she said, 'Sorry?'

'Warned you. Night I proposed. I've always been . . . a little bit of a fuck-up.'

The laugh that escaped her was perilously close to a sob. She leaned so hard against the bed railing that it pressed painfully into her midriff, but she managed to kiss his cheek, his pale and feverish cheek, and then the corner of his gray lips. 'Yeah, but you're *my* fuck-up,' she said.

'Thirsty,' he said.

'Sure, okay, I'll get a nurse, see what you're allowed to have.'

Maria Alicante hurried through the door, alerted to Jack's change of condition by telemetry data on the cardiac monitor at the central desk.

'He's awake, alert, he says he's thirsty,' Heather reported, running her words together in quiet jubilation.

'A man has a right to be a little thirsty after a hard day, doesn't he?' Maria said to Jack, rounding the bed to the nightstand on which stood an insulated carafe of ice-water.

'Beer,' Jack said.

Tapping the IV bag, Maria said, 'What do you think we've been dripping into your veins all day?'

'Not Heineken.'

'Oh, you like Heineken, huh? Well, we have to control medical costs, you know. Can't use that imported stuff.' She poured a third of a glass of water from the carafe. 'From us you get Budweiser intravenously, take it or leave it.'

'Take it.'

Opening a nightstand drawer and plucking out a flexible plastic straw, Maria said to Heather, 'Doctor Procnow's back in the hospital, making his evening rounds, and Doctor Delaney just got here too. As soon as I saw the change on Jack's EEG, I had them paged.'

Walter Delaney was their family doctor. Though Procnow was nice and obviously competent, Heather felt better just knowing there was about to be a familiar face on the medical team dealing with Jack.

'Jack,' Maria said, 'I can't put the bed up because you have to keep lying flat. And I don't want you to try to raise your head by yourself, all right? Let me lift your head for you.'

Maria put one hand behind his neck and raised his head a few inches off the thin pillow. With her other hand, she held the glass. Heather reached across the railing and put the straw to Jack's lips.

'Small sips,' Maria warned him. 'You don't want to choke.'

After six or seven sips, with a pause to breathe between each, he'd had enough.

Heather was delighted out of all proportion to her husband's modest accomplishment. However, his ability to swallow a thin liquid without choking probably meant there was no paralysis of his throat muscles, not even minimal. She realized how profoundly their lives had changed when such a mundane act as drinking water without choking was a triumph, but that grim awareness did not diminish her delight.

As long as Jack was alive, there was a road back to the life they had known. A long road. One step at a time. Small, small steps. But there was a road, and nothing else mattered right now.

*

While Emil Procnow and Walter Delaney examined Jack, Heather used the phone at the nurses' station to call home. She talked to Mae Hong first, then Toby, and told them that Jack was going to be all right. She knew she was putting a rose tint on reality, but a little positive thinking was good for all of them.

'Can I see him?' Toby asked.

'In a few days, honey.'

'I'm much better. Got better all day. I'm not sick any more.'

'I'll be the judge of that. Anyway, your dad needs a few days to get his strength back.'

'I'll bring peanut-butter-and-chocolate ice cream. That's his favorite. They won't have that in a hospital, will they?'

'No, nothing like that.'

'Tell Dad I'm gonna bring him some.'

'All right,' she said.

'I want to buy it myself. I have money, from my allowance.'

'You're a good boy, Toby. You know that?'

His voice became soft and shy. 'When are you coming home?'

'I don't know, honey. I'll be here a while. Probably after you're in bed.'

'Will you bring me something from Dad's room?'

'What do you mean?'

'Something from his room. Anything. Just something was in his room, so I can have it and know there's a room where he is.'

The chasm of insecurity and fear revealed by the boy's request

57

was almost more than Heather could bear without losing the emotional control she had thus far maintained with such iron-willed success. Her chest tightened, and she had to swallow hard before she dared to speak. 'Sure, okay, I'll bring you something.'

'If I'm asleep, wake me.'

'Okay.'

'Promise?'

'I promise, peanut. Now I gotta go. You be good for Mae.'

'We're playing Five Hundred Rummy.'

'You're not betting, are you?'

'Just pretzel sticks.'

'Good. I wouldn't want to see you bankrupt a good friend like Mae,' Heather said, and the boy's giggle was sweet music.

*

To be sure she didn't interfere with the nurses, Heather leaned against the wall beside the door that led out of the ICU. She could see Jack's cubicle from there. His door was closed, privacy curtains drawn at the big observation windows.

The air in the ICU smelled of various antiseptics. She ought to have been used to those astringent and metallic odors by now. Instead, they became increasingly noxious and left a bitter taste as well.

When at last the doctors stepped out of Jack's cubicle and walked toward her, they were smiling, but she had the disquieting feeling they had bad news. Their smiles ended at the corners of their mouths; in their eyes was something worse than sorrow – perhaps pity.

Dr Walter Delaney was in his fifties and would have been perfect as the wise father in a television sitcom in the early sixties. Brown hair going to gray at the temples. A handsome if soft-featured face. He radiated quiet authority yet was as relaxed and mellow as Ozzie Nelson or Robert Young.

'You okay, Heather?' Delaney asked.

She nodded. 'I'm holding up.'

'How's Toby?'

'Kids are resilient. He'll be all right as long as he can see his dad in a couple of days.'

Delaney sighed and wiped one hand down his face. 'Jesus, I hate this world we've made.' Heather had never before seen him angry. 'When I was a kid, people didn't shoot each other on the street every day. We had respect for police, we knew they stood between us and the barbarians. When did it all change?'

Neither Heather nor Procnow had an answer to that.

Delaney said, 'Seems like I just turned around, and I'm living in a sewer, a madhouse. The world's crawling with people who don't respect anyone or anything, but we're supposed to respect *them*, have compassion for the killers because they've been so poorly treated by life.' He sighed again and shook his head. 'Sorry. This is the day I donate time to the children's hospital, and we have two little kids in there who were caught in the middle of gang shootings, one of them three years old, the other six. Babies, for God's sake. Now Jack.'

'I don't know if you've heard the latest news,' Emil Procnow said, 'but the man who shot up the service station this morning was carrying cocaine and PCP in his pockets. If he was using both drugs simultaneously . . . well, that's psycho soup for sure.'

'Like nuking your own brain, for God's sake,' Delaney said disgustedly.

Heather knew they were genuinely frustrated and angry, but she also suspected they were delaying the bad news. To the surgeon, she said, 'He came through without brain damage. You were worried about that, but he came through.'

'He's not aphasic,' Procnow said. 'He can speak, read, spell, do basic math in his head. Mental faculties appear intact.'

'Which means there's not likely to be any brain-related physical incapacity, either,' Walter Delaney said, 'but it'll be at least a day or two before we can be sure of that.'

Emil Procnow ran one slender hand through his curly black hair. 'He's coming through this really well, Mrs McGarvey. He really is.'

'But?' she said.

The physicians glanced at each other.

'Right now,' Delaney said, 'there's paralysis in both legs.'

'From the waist down,' Procnow said.

'Upper body?' she asked.

'That's fine,' Delaney assured her. 'Full function.'

'In the morning,' Procnow said, 'we'll look again for a spinal fracture. If we find it, then we make up a plaster bed, line it with felt, immobilize Jack from below the neck all the way past the filum terminale, below the buttocks, and put his legs in traction.'

'But he'll walk again?'

'Almost certainly.'

She looked from Procnow to Delaney to Procnow again, waiting for the rest of it, and then she said, 'That's all?'

The doctors exchanged a glance again.

Delaney said, 'Heather, I'm not sure you understand what lies ahead for Jack and for you.'

'Tell me.'

'He'll be in a body cast between three and four months. By the time the cast comes off, he'll have severe muscle atrophy from the waist down. He won't have the strength to walk. In fact, his body will have forgotten *how* to walk, so he'll undergo weeks of physical therapy in a rehab hospital. It's going to be more frustrating and painful than anything most of us will ever have to face.'

'That's it?' she asked.

Procnow said, 'That's more than enough.'

'But it could have been so much worse,' she reminded them.

*

Alone with Jack again, she put down the side railing on the bed and smoothed his damp hair back from his forehead.

'You look beautiful,' he said, his voice still weak and soft.

'Liar.'

'Beautiful.'

'I look like shit.'

He smiled. 'Just before I blacked out, I wondered if I'd ever see you again.'

'Can't get rid of me that easy.'

'Have to actually die, huh?'

'Even that wouldn't work. I'd find you wherever you went.'

'I love you, Heather.'

'I love you,' she said, 'more than life.'

Heat rose in her eyes, but she was determined not to cry in front of him. Positive thinking. Keep the spirits up.

His eyelids fluttered, and he said, 'I'm so tired.'

'Can't imagine why.'

He smiled again. 'Hard day at work.'

'Yeah? I thought you cops didn't do anything all day except sit around in doughnut shops, chowing down, and collect protection money from drug dealers.'

'Sometimes we beat up innocent citizens.'

'Well, yeah, that can be tiring.'

His eyes had closed.

She kept smoothing his hair. His hands were still concealed by the sleeves of the restraining jacket, and she wanted desperately to keep touching him.

Suddenly his eyes popped open, and he said, 'Luther's dead?'

She hesitated. 'Yes.'

'I thought so but . . . I hoped . . .'

'You saved the woman, Mrs Arkadian.'

'That's something.'

His eyelids fluttered again, drooped heavily, and she said, 'You better rest, babe.'

'You seen Alma?'

That was Alma Bryson, Luther's wife.

'Not yet, babe. I've been sort of tied up here, you know.'

'Go see her,' he whispered.

'I will.'

'Now. I'm okay. She's the one . . . needs you.'

'All right.'

'So tired,' he said, and slipped into sleep again.

*

The support group in the ICU lounge numbered three when Heather left Jack for the evening – two uniformed officers whose names she didn't know and Gina Tendero, the wife of another officer. They were elated when she reported that Jack had come around, and she knew they would put the word on the department grapevine. Unlike the doctors, they understood when she refused to focus gloomily on the paralysis and the treatment required to overcome it.

'I need someone to take me home,' Heather said, 'so I can get my car. I want to go see Alma Bryson.'

'I'll take you there and then home,' Gina said. 'I want to see Alma myself.'

Gina Tendero was the most colorful spouse in the division and perhaps in the entire Los Angeles Police Department. She was twenty-three years old but looked fourteen. Tonight she was wearing five-inch heels, tight black leather pants, red sweater, black leather jacket, an enormous silver medallion with a brightly colored enamel portrait of Elvis in the center, and large multiple-hoop earrings so complex they might have been variations of those puzzles that were supposed to relax harried businessmen if they concentrated totally on disassembling them. Her fingernails were painted neon purple, a shade reflected slightly more subtly in her eye shadow. Her jet-black hair was a mass of curls that spilled over her shoulders; it looked as much like a wig as any Dolly Parton had ever worn, but it was all her own.

Though she was only five-three without shoes and weighed maybe a hundred and five pounds dripping wet, Gina always seemed bigger than anyone around her. As she walked along the hospital corridors with Heather, her footsteps were louder than those of a man twice her size, and nurses turned to frown disapprovingly at the *tock-tock-tock* of her high heels on the tile floors.

'You okay, Heth?' Gina asked as they headed for the four-story parking garage attached to the hospital.

'Yeah.'

'I mean really.'

'I'll make it.'

At the end of a corridor they went through a green metal door into the parking garage. It was bare gray concrete, chilly, with low ceilings. A third of the fluorescent lights were broken in spite of the wire cages that protected them, and the shadows among the cars offered countless places of concealment.

Gina fished a small aerosol can from her purse, holding it with her index finger on the trigger, and Heather said, 'What's that?'

'Red-pepper mace. You don't carry?'

'No.'

'Where you think you're living, girl – Disneyland?'

As they walked up a concrete ramp with cars parked on both sides, Heather said, 'Maybe I should buy some.'

'Can't. The bastard politicians made it illegal. Wouldn't want to give some poor misguided rapist a skin rash, would you? Ask Jack or one of the guys, they can still get it for you.'

Gina was driving an inexpensive blue Ford compact, but it had an alarm system, which she disengaged from a distance with a

63

remote-control device on her key ring. The headlights flashed, the alarm beeped once, and the doors unlocked.

Looking around at the shadows, they got in and immediately locked up again.

After starting the car, Gina hesitated before putting it in gear. 'You know, Heth, you want to cry on my shoulder, my clothes are all drip-dry.'

'I'm all right. I really am.'

'Sure you're not into denial?'

'He's alive, Gina. I can handle anything else.'

'Forty years, Jack in a wheelchair?'

'Doesn't matter if it comes to that, as long as I have him to talk to, hold him at night.'

Gina stared hard at her for long seconds. Then: 'You mean it. You know what it's gonna be like, but you still mean it. Good. I always figured you for one, but it's good to know I was right.'

'One what?'

Popping the handbrake and shifting the Ford into reverse, Gina said, 'One tough damned bitch.'

Heather laughed. 'I guess that's a compliment.'

'Fuckin' A, it's a compliment.'

When Gina paid the parking fee at the exit booth and pulled out of the garage, a glorious gold-and-orange sunset gilded the patchy clouds to the west. However, as they crossed the metropolis through lengthening shadows and a twilight that gradually filled with blood-red light, the familiar streets and buildings were as alien as any on a distant planet. She had lived her entire adult life in Los Angeles, but Heather McGarvey felt like a stranger in a strange land.

*

The Brysons' two-story Spanish house was in the Valley, on the edge of Burbank, lucky number 777 on a street lined with sycamores.

The leafless limbs of the big trees made spiky arachnid patterns against the muddy yellow-black night sky, which was filled with too much ambient light from the urban sprawl ever to be perfectly inky. Cars were clustered in the driveway and street in front of 777, including one black-and-white.

The house was filled with relatives and friends of the Brysons. A few of the former and most of the latter were cops in uniforms or civilian clothes. Blacks, Hispanics, Whites, and Asians had come together in companionship and mutual support in a way they seldom seemed capable of associating in the larger community any more.

Heather felt at home the moment she crossed the threshold, so much safer than she had felt in the world outside. As she made her way through the living room and dining room, seeking Alma, she paused to speak briefly with old friends – and discovered that word of Jack's improved condition was already on the grapevine.

More acutely than ever, she was aware of how completely she had come to think of herself as part of the police family rather than as an Angeleno or a Californian. It hadn't always been that way. But it was difficult to maintain a spiritual allegiance to a city swimming in drugs and pornography, shattered by gang violence, steeped in Hollywood-style cynicism, and controlled by politicians as venal and demagogic as they were incompetent. Destructive social forces were fracturing the city – and country – into clans, and even as she took comfort in her police family, she recognized the danger of descending into an us-against-them view of life.

Alma was in the kitchen with her sister, Faye, and two other women, all of whom were busy at culinary tasks. Chopping vegetables, peeling fruit, grating cheese. Alma was rolling out pie dough on a marble slab, working at it vigorously. The kitchen was filled with the delicious aromas of cakes baking.

When Heather touched Alma's shoulder, the woman looked up from the pie dough, and her eyes were as blank as those of a mannequin. Then she blinked and wiped her flour-coated hands on her apron. 'Heather, you didn't have to come, you should've stayed with Jack.'

They embraced, and Heather said, 'I wish there was something I could do, Alma.'

'So do I, girl. So do I.'

As they leaned back from each other, Heather said, 'What's all this cooking?'

'We're going to have the funeral tomorrow afternoon. No delay. Get the hard part over with. A lot of family and friends will be by tomorrow after the services. Got to feed them.'

'Others will do this for you.'

'I'd rather help,' Alma said. 'What else am I going to do? Sit and think? I sure don't want to think. If I don't stay busy, keep my mind occupied, then I'm just going to go stark raving crazy. You know what I mean?'

Heather nodded. 'Yes. I know.'

'The word is,' Alma said, 'Jack's going to be in the hospital then rehab for maybe months, and you and Toby are going to be alone. Are you ready for that?'

'We'll see him every day. We're in this together.'

'That's not what I mean.'

'Well, I know it's going to be lonely but—'

'That's not what I mean, either. Come on, I want to show you something.'

Heather followed Alma into the master bedroom, and Alma closed the door. 'Luther always worried about me being alone if anything happened to him, so he made sure I knew how to take care of myself.'

Sitting on the vanity bench, Heather watched with amazement as Alma retrieved a variety of weapons from concealment.

She got a pistol-grip shotgun from under the bed. 'This is the best home-defense weapon you can get. Twelve gauge. Powerful enough to knock down some creep high on PCP, thinks he's Superman. You don't have to be able to aim perfectly, just point it and pull the trigger, and the spread will get him.' She placed the shotgun on the beige chenille bedspread.

From the back of a closet Alma fetched a heavy, wicked-looking rifle with a vented barrel, a scope, and a large magazine. 'Heckler and Koch HK91 assault rifle,' she said. 'You can't buy these in California so easy any more.' She put it on the bed beside the shotgun.

She opened a nightstand drawer and plucked out a formidable handgun. 'Browning 9mm semiautomatic. There's one like it in the other nightstand.'

Heather said, 'My God, you've got an arsenal here.'

'Just different guns for different uses.'

Alma Bryson was five feet eight but by no means an Amazon. She was attractive, willowy, with delicate features, a swanlike neck, and wrists almost as thin and fragile as those of a ten-year-old girl. Her slender, graceful hands appeared incapable of controlling some of the heavy weaponry she possessed, but she was evidently proficient with all of it.

Getting up from the vanity bench, Heather said, 'I can see having a handgun for protection, maybe even that shotgun. But an assault rifle?'

Looking at the Heckler & Koch, Alma said, 'Accurate enough at a hundred yards to put a three-shot group in a half-inch circle. Fires a 7.62 NATO cartridge so powerful it'll penetrate a tree, a brick wall, even a car, and still take out the guy who's hiding on the other side. Very reliable. You can fire hundreds of rounds, until it's almost too hot to touch, and it still won't jam. I think you should have one, Heather. You should be ready.'

Heather felt as if she had followed the white rabbit down a burrow into a strange, dark world. 'Ready for what?'

Alma's gentle face hardened, and her voice was tight with anger. 'Luther saw it coming years ago. Said politicians were tearing down a thousand years of civilization brick by brick but weren't building anything to replace it.'

'True enough, but—'

'Said cops would be expected to hold it all together when it started to collapse, but by then cops would've been blamed for so much and been painted as the villains so often, no one would respect them enough to *let* them hold it together.'

Rage was Alma Bryson's refuge from grief. She was able to hold off tears only with fury.

Although Heather worried that her friend's method of coping wasn't healthy, she could think of nothing to offer in its place. Sympathy was inadequate. Alma and Luther had been married sixteen years and had been devoted to each other. Because they'd been unable to have children, they were especially close. Heather could only imagine the depth of Alma's pain. It was a hard world. Real love, true and deep, wasn't easy to find even once. Nearly impossible to find twice. Alma must feel the best times of her life were past, though she was only thirty-eight. She needed more than kind words, more than just a shoulder to cry on. She needed someone or something at which to be furious – politicians, the system.

Perhaps her anger wasn't unhealthy, after all. Maybe if a lot more people had gotten angry enough decades ago, the country wouldn't have reached such perilous straits.

'You have guns?' Alma asked.

'One.'

'What is it?'

'A pistol.'

'You know how to use it?'

'Yes.'

'You need more than just a pistol.'

'I feel uncomfortable with guns, Alma.'

'It's on the TV now, going to be all over the papers tomorrow – what happened at Arkadian's station. People are going to know you and Toby are alone, people who don't like cops or cops' wives.

68

Some jackass reporter will probably even print your address. You've got to be ready for anything these days, anything.'

Alma's paranoia, which came as such a surprise and which seemed so out of character, chilled Heather. Even as she shivered at the icy glint in her friend's eyes, however, a part of her wondered if Alma's assessment of the situation was more rational than it sounded. That she could seriously consider such a paranoid view was enough to make her shiver again, harder than before.

'You've got to prepare for the worst,' Alma Bryson said, picking up the shotgun, turning it over in her hands. 'It's not just your life on the line. You've got Toby to think about too.'

She stood there, a slender and pretty black woman, an aficionado of jazz and opera, a lover of museums, educated and refined, as warm and loving a person as anyone Heather had ever known, capable of a smile that would charm wild beasts and a musical laugh that angels might have envied, holding a shotgun that looked absurdly large and evil in the hands of someone so lovely and delicate, embracing rage because the only alternative to rage was suicidal despair. Alma was like a figure on a poster urging revolution, not a real person but a wildly romanticized symbol. Heather had the disquieting feeling that she was not looking at merely one troubled woman struggling to elude the grasp of bitter grief and disabling hopelessness but at the grim future of their entire troubled society, a harbinger of an all-obliterating storm.

'Tearing it down brick by brick,' Alma said solemnly, 'but building nothing to replace it.'

7

For twenty-nine uneventful nights, the Montana stillness was disturbed only by periodic fits of winter wind, the hoot of a hunting owl, and the distant forlorn howling of timber wolves. Gradually Eduardo Fernandez regained his usual confidence and ceased to regard each oncoming dusk with quiet dread.

He might have recovered his equilibrium quickly if he'd had more work to occupy him. Inclement weather prevented him from performing routine maintenance around the ranch; with electric heat and plenty of cordwood for the fireplaces, he had little to do during the winter months except hunker down and wait for spring.

It had never been a working ranch since he had managed it. Thirty-four years ago, he and Margarite had been hired by Stanley Quartermass, a wealthy film producer, who had fallen in love with Montana and wanted a second home there. No animals or crops were raised for profit; the ranch was strictly a secluded hideaway.

Quartermass loved horses, so he built a comfortable, heated stable with ten stalls a hundred yards south of the house. He spent about two months per year at the ranch, in one- and two-week visits, and it was Eduardo's duty, in the producer's absence, to ensure the horses received first-rate care and plenty of exercise. Tending to the animals and keeping the property in good repair had constituted the largest part of his job, and Margarite had been the housekeeper.

Until eight years ago, Eduardo and Margarite had lived in the

70

cozy, two-bedroom, single-story caretaker's house. That fieldstone structure stood eighty or ninety yards behind – and due west of – the main house, cloistered among pines at the edge of the higher woods. Tommy, their only child, had been raised there until city life had exerted its fatal attraction when he was eighteen.

When Stanley Quartermass died in a private-plane crash, Eduardo and Margarite had been surprised to learn the ranch had been left to them, along with sufficient funds to allow immediate retirement. The producer had taken care of his four ex-wives while he was alive and had fathered no children from any of his marriages, so he used the greater part of his estate to provide generously for key employees.

They had sold the horses, closed up the caretaker's house, and moved into the Victorian-style main house with its gables, decorative shutters, scalloped eaves, and wide porches. It felt strange to be a person of property, but the security was welcome even – or perhaps especially – when it came late in life.

Now Eduardo was a widowed retiree with plenty of security but with too little work to occupy him. And with too many strange thoughts preying on his mind. Luminous trees . . .

On three occasions during March, he drove his Jeep Cherokee into Eagle's Roost, the nearest town. He ate at Jasper's Diner because he liked their Salisbury steak, home fries, and pepper slaw. He bought magazines and a few paperback books at the High Plains Pharmacy, and he shopped for groceries at the only supermarket. His ranch was just sixteen miles from Eagle's Roost, so he could have gone daily if he'd wished, but three times a month was usually enough. The town was small, three to four thousand souls; however, even in its isolation, it was too much a part of the modern world to appeal to a man as accustomed to rural peace as he was.

Each time he'd gone shopping, he'd considered stopping at the county sheriff's substation to report the peculiar noise and strange lights in the woods. But he was sure the deputy would figure him for an old fool and do nothing but file the report in a folder labeled CRACKPOTS.

In the third week of March, spring officially arrived – and the following day a storm put down eight inches of new snow. Winter was not quick to relinquish its grasp there on the eastern slopes of the Rockies.

He took daily walks, as had been his habit all his life, but he stayed on the long driveway, which he plowed himself after each snowfall, or he crossed the open fields south of the house and stables. He avoided the lower woods, which lay east and downhill from the house, but he also stayed away from those to the north and even the higher forests to the west.

His cowardice irritated him, not least of all because he was unable to understand it. He'd always been an advocate of reason and logic, always said there was too little of either in the world. He was scornful of people who operated more from emotion than from intellect. But reason failed him now, and logic could not overcome the instinctual awareness of danger that caused him to avoid the trees and the perpetual twilight under their boughs.

By the end of March, he began to think that the phenomenon had been a singular occurrence without notable consequences. A rare but natural event. Perhaps an electromagnetic disturbance of some kind. No more threat to him than a summer thunderstorm.

On 1 April, he unloaded the two rifles and two shotguns. After cleaning them, he returned the guns to the cabinet in the study.

However, still slightly uneasy, he kept the .22 target pistol on his nightstand. It didn't pack a tremendous punch but, loaded with hollow-point cartridges, it could do some damage.

*

In the dark hours of the morning, 4 April, Eduardo was awakened by the low throbbing which swelled and faded, swelled and faded.

72

As in early March, that pulsating sound was accompanied by an eerie electronic oscillation.

He sat straight up in bed, blinking at the window. During the three years since Margarite had died, he'd not slept in the master bedroom at the front of the house, which they had shared. Instead, he bunked down in one of two back bedrooms. Consequently, the window faced west, a hundred and eighty degrees around the compass from the eastern woods where he had seen the strange light. The night sky was deep and black beyond the window.

The Stiffel lamp on the nightstand had a pull-chain instead of a thumb switch. Just before he turned it on, he had the feeling that something was in the room with him, something he would be better off not seeing. He hesitated, fingers tightly pinching the metal beads of the pull. Intently he searched the darkness, his heart pounding, as if he had wakened *into* a nightmare replete with a monster. When at last he tugged the chain, however, the light revealed that he was alone.

He picked up his wristwatch from the nightstand and checked the time. Nineteen minutes past one o'clock.

He threw off the covers and got out of bed. He was in his long underwear. His blue jeans and a flannel shirt were close at hand, folded over the back of an armchair, beside which stood a pair of boots. He was already wearing socks because his feet often got cold during the night if he slept without them.

The sound was louder than it had been a month before, and it pulsed through the house with noticeably greater effect than before. In March, Eduardo had experienced a sense of pressure along with the rhythmic pounding – which, like the sound, crested repeatedly in a series of waves. Now the pressure had increased dramatically. He didn't merely sense it but felt it, indescribably different from the pressure of turbulent air, more like the invisible tides of a cold sea washing across his body.

By the time he hurriedly dressed and snatched the loaded .22

73

pistol from the nightstand, the pull-chain was swinging wildly and clinking against the burnished brass body of the lamp. The window panes vibrated. The paintings rattled against the walls, askew on their wires.

He rushed downstairs into the foyer, where there was no need to switch on a light. In the front door, the beveled edges of the leaded panes in the oval window sparkled with reflections of the mysterious glow outside. It was far brighter than it had been the previous month. The bevels broke down the amber radiance into all the colors of the spectrum, projecting bright prismatic patterns of blue and green and yellow and red across the ceiling and walls, so it seemed as if he was in a church with stained-glass murals.

In the dark living room to his left, where no light penetrated from outside because the drapes were drawn, a collection of crystal paperweights and other bibelots rattled and clinked against the end tables on which they stood and against one another. Porcelain vibrated on the glass shelves of a display cabinet.

To his right, in the book-lined study, the marble-and-brass desk set bounced on the blotter, a pencil drawer popped open and banged shut in time with the pressure waves, and the executive chair behind the desk wobbled around enough to make its wheels creak.

As Eduardo opened the front door, most of the spots and spears of colored light flew away, vanished as if into another dimension, and the rest fled to the right-hand wall of the foyer, where they melted together in a vibrant mosaic.

The woods were luminous precisely where they had been luminous last month. The amber glow emanated from the same group of closely packed trees and from the ground beneath, as if the evergreen needles and cones and bark and dirt and stones and snow were the incandescent elements of a lamp, shining brightly without being consumed. This time the light was more dazzling than before, just as the throbbing was louder and the waves of pressure more forceful.

He found himself at the head of the steps but did not remember exiting the house or crossing the porch. He looked back and saw that he had closed the front door behind him.

Punishing waves of bass sound throbbed through the night at the rate of perhaps thirty a minute, but his heart was beating six times faster. He wanted to turn and run back into the house.

He looked down at the pistol in his hand. He wished the shotgun had been loaded and beside his bed.

When he raised his head and turned his eyes away from the gun, he was startled to see that the woods had moved closer to him. The glowing trees loomed.

Then he realized that he, not the woods, had moved. He glanced back again and saw the house thirty to forty feet behind him. He had descended the steps without being aware of it. His tracks marred the snow.

'No,' he said shakily.

The swelling sound was like a surf with an undertow that pulled him relentlessly from the safety of the shore. The ululant electronic wail seemed like a siren's song, penetrating him, speaking to him on a level so deep that he seemed to understand the message without hearing the words, a music in his blood, luring him toward the cold fire in the woods.

His thoughts grew fuzzy.

He peered up at the star-punctured sky, trying to clear his head. A delicate filigree of clouds shone against the black vault, rendered luminous by the silver light of the quarter moon.

He closed his eyes. Found the strength to resist the pull of each ebbing wave of sound.

But when he opened his eyes, he discovered his resistance was imaginary. He was even closer to the trees than before, only thirty feet from the perimeter of the forest, so close he had to squint against the blinding brightness emanating from the branches, the trunks, and the ground under the pines.

The moody amber light was now threaded with red, like blood in an egg yolk.

Eduardo was scared, miles past fear into sheer terror, fighting a looseness in his bowels and a weakness in his bladder, shaking so violently that he would not have been surprised to hear his bones rattling together – yet his heart was no longer racing. It had slowed drastically and now matched the steady thirty-beats-per-minute of the pulsating sound that seemed to issue from every radiant surface.

He couldn't possibly stay on his feet when his heartbeat was so slow, the blood supply to his brain so diminished. He ought to be either in severe shock or unconscious. His perceptions must be untrustworthy. Perhaps the throbbing had escalated to match the pace of his hammering heart.

Curiously, he was no longer aware of the frigid air. Yet no heat accompanied the enigmatic light. He was neither hot nor cold.

He couldn't feel the earth under his feet. No sense of gravity, weight, or weariness of muscle. Might as well have been floating.

The odors of the winter were no longer perceptible. Gone was the faint, crisp, ozone-like scent of snow. Gone, the fresh smell of the pine forest that rose just in front of him. Gone, the faint sour stink of his own icy sweat.

No taste on his tongue. That was the weirdest of all. He had never before realized there was always an endless and subtly changing series of tastes in his mouth even when he wasn't eating anything. Now a blandness. Neither sweet nor sour. Neither salty nor bitter. Not even a blandness. Beyond blandness. Nothing. *Nada*. He worked his mouth, felt saliva flooding it, but still no taste.

All of his powers of sensory perception seemed to be focused solely on the ghost light shining from within the trees and on the punishing, insistent sound. He no longer felt the throbbing bass washing in cold waves across his body; rather, the sound was coming from *within* him now, and it surged out of him in the same way that it issued from the trees.

Suddenly he was standing at the edge of the woods, on ground as effulgent as molten lava. *Inside* the phenomenon. Gazing down, he saw his feet seemed to be planted on a sheet of glass beneath which a sea of fire churned, a sea as deep as the stars were distant. The extent of that abyss made him cry out in panic, although not even the thinnest whisper escaped him.

Fearfully and reluctantly, yet wonderingly, Eduardo looked at his legs and body, and saw that the amber light also radiated from *him* and was riddled with bursts of red. He appeared to be a man from another world, filled with alien energy, or a holy Indian spirit that had walked out of the high mountains in search of the ancient nations once in dominion over the vast Montana wilderness but long lost: Blackfeet, Crow, Sioux, Assiniboin, Cheyenne.

He raised his left hand to examine it more closely. His skin was transparent, his flesh translucent. At first he could see the bones of his hand and fingers, well-articulated gray-red forms within the molten amber substance of which he seemed to be made. Even as he watched, his bones became transparent, too, and he was entirely a man of glass, no substance to him at all any more; he had become a window through which could be seen an unearthly fire, just as the ground under him was a window, just as the stones and trees were windows.

The crashing waves of sound and the electronic squeal arose from within the currents of fire, ever more insistent. As on that night in March, he had an almost clairvoyant perception of something straining against confinement, struggling to break out of a prison or through a barrier.

Something trying to force open a door.

He was standing in the intended doorway.

On the threshold.

He was seized by the bizarre conviction that if the door opened while he was standing in the way, he would shatter into disassociated atoms as if he'd never existed. He would *become* the door. An

77

unknown caller would enter through him, out of the fire and *through* him.

Jesus, help me, he prayed, though he wasn't a religious man.

He tried to move.

Paralyzed.

Within his raised hand, within his entire body, within the trees and stones and earth, the fire grew less amber, more red, hotter, entirely red, scarlet, seething. Abruptly it was marbled with blue-white veins to rival the consuming brightness at the very heart of a star. The malevolent pulsations swelled, exploded, swelled, exploded, like the pounding of colossal pistons, booming, booming, pistons in the perpetual engines that drove the universe itself, harder, harder, pressure escalating, his glass body vibrating, fragile as crystal, pressure, expanding, demanding, hammering, fire and thunder, fire and thunder, fireandthunder—

Blackness.

Silence.

Cold.

When he woke, he was lying at the perimeter of the forest, in the light of a quarter moon. Above him, the trees stood sentinel, dark and still.

He was in possession of all his senses again. He smelled the ozone crispness of snow, dense masses of pines, his own sweat – and urine. He had lost control of his bladder. The taste in his mouth was unpleasant but familiar: blood. In his terror or when he'd fallen, he must have bitten his tongue.

Evidently, the door in the night had not opened.

8

THAT SAME night, Eduardo removed the weapons from the cabinet in the study and reloaded them. He distributed them throughout the house, so one firearm or another would always be within reach.

The following morning, 4 April, he drove into Eagle's Roost, but he didn't go to the sheriff's substation. He still had no evidence to back up his story.

He went, instead, to Custer's Appliances. Custer's was housed in a yellow-brick building dating from about 1920, and the glittering high-tech merchandise in its display windows was as anachronistic as tennis shoes on a Neanderthal. Eduardo purchased a video-cassette recorder, a video camera, and half a dozen blank tapes.

The salesman was a long-haired young man who looked like Mozart in boots, jeans, a decoratively stitched cowboy shirt, and a string tie with a turquoise clasp. He kept up a continuous chatter about the multitude of features the equipment offered, using so much jargon that he seemed to be speaking a foreign language.

Eduardo just wanted to record and play back. Nothing more. He didn't care if he could watch one show while taping another, or whether the damned gadgets could cook his dinner, make his bed, and give him a pedicure.

The ranch already had a television capable of receiving a lot of channels because, shortly before his death, Mr Quartermass had installed a satellite dish behind the stables. Eduardo seldom watched a program, maybe three or four times a year, but he knew the TV worked.

From the appliance store he went to the library. He checked out a stack of novels by Robert A. Heinlein and Arthur C. Clarke, plus collections of stories by H. P. Lovecraft, Algernon Blackwood, and M. R. James.

He felt no less of a fool than if he had selected lurid volumes of flapdoodle purporting to be non fiction accounts of the Abominable Snowman, the Loch Ness Monster, the Lost Continent of Atlantis, the Bermuda Triangle, and the true story of Elvis Presley's faked death and sex-change operation. He fully expected the librarian to sneer at him or at least favor him with a pitying and patronizing smile, but she processed the books as if she found nothing frivolous about his taste in fiction.

After stopping at the supermarket, as well, he returned to the ranch and unpacked his purchases.

He needed two full days and more beers than he would ordinarily have allowed himself in order to get the hang of the video system. The damned equipment had more buttons and switches and readouts than the cockpit of an airliner, and at times it seemed the manufacturers had complicated their products for no good reason, out of a sheer love of complication. The instruction books read as if they'd been written by someone for whom English was a second language – which was very likely the case, as both the recorder and the camcorder were made by the Japanese.

'Either I'm getting feeble-minded,' he groused aloud in one fit of frustration, 'or the world's going to hell in a handbasket.'

Maybe both.

*

Warmer weather arrived sooner than usual. April was often a winter month at that latitude and altitude, but this year the daytime temperatures rose into the forties. The season-long accumulation of snow melted, and gurgling freshets filled every gully and declivity.

The nights remained peaceful.

Eduardo read most of the books he'd borrowed from the library. Blackwood and especially James wrote in a style far too mannered for his taste, heavy on atmosphere and light on substance. They were purveyors of ghost stories, and he had trouble suspending disbelief long enough to become involved in their tales.

If Hell existed, he supposed the unknown entity trying to open a door in the fabric of the night might have been a damned soul or a demon forcing its way out of that fiery realm. But that was the sticking point: he didn't believe Hell existed, at least not as the carnival-gaudy kingdom of evil portrayed in cheap films and books.

To his surprise, he found Heinlein and Clarke to be entertaining and thought-provoking. He preferred the crustiness of the former to the sometimes naive humanism of the latter, but they both had value.

He wasn't sure what he hoped to discover in their books that would help him to deal with the phenomenon in the woods. Had he harbored, in the back of his mind, the absurd expectation that one of these writers had produced a story about an old man who lived in an isolated place and who made contact with something not of this earth? If such was the case, then he was so far around the bend that he would meet himself coming the other way at any moment.

Nevertheless, it was more likely that the presence he sensed beyond the phantom fire and pulsating sound was extraterrestrial rather than Hellborn. The universe contained an infinite number of stars. An infinite number of planets, circling those stars, might have provided the right conditions for life to have arisen. That was scientific fact, not fantasy.

He might also have imagined the whole business. Hardening of the arteries that supplied blood to the brain. An Alzheimer-induced hallucination. He found it easier to believe in that explanation than in demons *or* aliens.

He had bought the video camera more to assuage self-doubt than to gather evidence for the authorities. If the phenomenon could be captured on tape, he wasn't dotty, after all, and was competent to continue to live alone. Until he was killed by whatever finally opened that doorway in the night.

*

On 15 April, he drove into Eagle's Roost to buy fresh milk and produce – and a Sony Discman with quality headphones.

Custer's Appliance also had a selection of audiotapes and compact discs. Eduardo asked the Mozart look-alike for the loudest music to which teenagers were listening these days.

'Gift for your grandkid?' the clerk asked.

It was easier to agree than to explain. 'That's right.'

'Heavy metal.'

Eduardo had no idea what the man was talking about.

'Here's a new group that's getting really hot,' the clerk said, selecting a disc from the display bins. 'Call themselves Wormheart.'

Back at the ranch, after putting away the groceries, Eduardo sat at the kitchen table to listen to the disc. He installed batteries in the Discman, inserted the disc, put on the headphones, and pressed the PLAY button. The blast of sound nearly burst his eardrums, and he hastily lowered the volume.

He listened for a minute or so, half convinced he'd been sold a faulty disc. But the clarity of the sound argued that he was hearing exactly what Wormheart had intended to record. He listened for another minute or two, waiting for the cacophony to become music, before realizing it apparently *was* music by the modern definition.

He felt old.

He remembered, as a young man, necking with Margarite to the music of Benny Goodman, Frank Sinatra, Mel Torme, Tommy Dorsey. Did young people still neck? Did they know what the word meant? Did they cuddle? Did they pet? Or did they just get naked and tear at each other straightaway?

It sure didn't sound like music you'd play as background to love-making. What it sounded like, to him anyway, was music you'd play as background to violent homicide, maybe to drown out the victim's screams.

He felt ancient.

Aside from not being able to hear *music* in the music, he didn't understand why any group would call itself Wormheart. Groups should have names like The Four Freshmen, The Andrews Sisters, The Mills Brothers. He could even handle The Four Tops or James Brown and the Famous Flames. *Loved* James Brown. But Wormheart? It brought disgusting images to mind.

Well, he wasn't hip and didn't try to be. They probably didn't even use the word 'hip' any more. In fact, he was sure they didn't. He hadn't a clue as to what word meant 'hip' these days.

Older than the sands of Egypt.

He listened to the music for another minute, then switched it off and removed the headphones.

Wormheart was exactly what he needed.

*

By the last day of April, the winter shroud had melted except for deeper drifts that enjoyed the protection of shadows during a large part of the day, although even they were dwindling steadily. The ground was damp but not muddy any longer. Dead brown grass, crushed and matted from the weight of the vanished snow, covered hills and fields; within a week, however, a carpet of tender green shoots would brighten every corner of the now-dreary land.

Eduardo's daily walk took him past the east end of the stables and across open fields to the south. At eleven in the morning, the day was sunny, the temperature near fifty, with a receding armada of high white clouds to the north. He wore khakis and a flannel shirt, and was so warmed by exertion that he rolled up his sleeves. On the return trip he visited the three graves that lay west of the stables.

Until recently, the State of Montana had been liberal about allowing the establishment of family cemeteries on private property. Soon after acquiring the ranch, Stanley Quartermass had decided he wanted to spend eternity there, and he had obtained a permit for as many as twelve burial plots.

The graveyard was on a small knoll near the higher woods. That hallowed ground was defined only by a foot-high fieldstone wall and by a pair of four-foot-high columns at the entrance. Quartermass had not wanted to obstruct the panoramic view of the valley and mountains – as if he thought his spirit would sit upon his grave and enjoy the scenery like a ghost in that old, light-hearted movie *Topper*.

Only three granite headstones occupied a space designed to accommodate twelve. Quartermass. Tommy. Margarite.

Specified by the producer's will, the inscription on the first monument read, 'Here lies Stanley Quartermass/ dead before his time/ because he had to work/ with so damned many/ actors and writers,' followed by the dates of his birth and death. He had been sixty-six when his plane crashed. However, if he'd been five hundred years old, he still would have felt that his span had been too short, for he had been a man who embraced life with great energy and passion.

Tommy's and Margarite's stones bore no humorous epitaphs – just 'beloved son' and 'beloved wife'. Eduardo missed them.

The hardest blow had been the death of his son, who had been killed in the line of duty only a little more than a year ago at the age of thirty-two. At least Eduardo and Margarite had enjoyed a long life together. It was a terrible thing for a man to outlive his own child.

He wished they were with him again. That was a wish frequently made, and the fact that it could never be fulfilled usually reduced him to a melancholy mood which he found difficult to shake. At best, longing to see his wife and son again, he drifted into nostalgic mists, reliving favorite days of years gone by.

This time, however, the familiar wish had no sooner flickered through his mind than he was inexplicably overcome by dread. A chill wind seemed to whistle through his spine as if it were hollow end to end.

Turning, he wouldn't have been surprised to find someone looming behind him. He was alone.

The sky was entirely blue, the last of the clouds having slipped across the northern horizon, and the air was warmer than it had been at any time since last autumn. Nonetheless, the chill persisted. He rolled down his sleeves, buttoned the cuffs.

When he looked at the headstones again, Eduardo's imagination was suddenly crowded with unwanted images of Tommy and Margarite not as they had been in life but as they might be in their coffins: decaying, worm-riddled, eye sockets empty, lips shriveled back from yellow-toothed grins. Trembling uncontrollably, he was gripped by an absolute conviction that the earth in front of the granite markers was going to shift and cave inward, that the corrupted hands of their corpses were going to appear in the crumbling soil, digging fiercely, and then their faces, eyeless faces, as they pulled themselves out of the ground.

He backed away from the graves a few steps but refused to flee. He was too old to believe in the living dead or in ghosts.

The dead-brown grass and spring-thawed earth did not move. After a while he stopped *expecting* them to move.

When he was in full control of himself again, he walked between the low stone columns and out of the graveyard. All the way to the house, he wanted to spin around and look back. He didn't do it.

He entered the house through the back door and locked it behind him. Ordinarily he never locked doors.

85

Though it was time for lunch, he had no appetite. Instead, he opened a bottle of Corona.

He was a three-beers-a-day man. That was his usual limit, not a minimum requirement. There were days when he didn't drink at all. Though not lately. Recently, in spite of his limit, he had been downing more than three a day. Some days – a lot more.

Later that afternoon, sitting in a living-room armchair, trying to read Thomas Wolfe and sipping a third bottle of Corona, he became convinced, against his will, that the experience in the graveyard had been a vivid premonition. A warning. But a warning of what?

*

As April passed with no recurrence of the phenomenon in the lower woods, Eduardo had become more – not less – tense. Each of the previous events had transpired when the moon was in the same phase, a quarter full. That celestial condition seemed increasingly pertinent as the April moon waxed and waned without another disturbance. The lunar cycle might have nothing whatsoever to do with these peculiar events – yet still be a calendar by which to anticipate them.

Beginning the night of 1 May, which boasted a sliver of the new moon, he slept fully clothed. The .22 was in a soft leather holster on the nightstand. Beside it was the Discman with headphones, Wormheart album inserted. A loaded Remington 12-gauge shotgun lay under the bed, within easy reach. The video camera was equipped with fresh batteries and a blank cassette. He was prepared to move fast.

He slept only fitfully, but the night passed without incident.

He didn't actually expect trouble until the early morning hours of 4 May.

Of course, the strange spectacle might never be repeated. In fact, he hoped he wouldn't have to witness it again. In his heart, however, he knew what his mind could not entirely admit: that events of significance had been set in motion, that they were gathering momentum, and that he could no more avoid playing a role in them than a condemned man, in shackles, could avoid the noose or guillotine.

As it turned out, he didn't have to wait quite as long as he had expected. Because he'd had little sleep the night before, he went to bed early on 2 May – and was awakened past midnight, in the first hour of 3 May, by those ominous and rhythmic pulsations.

The sound was no louder than it had been before, but the wave of pressure that accompanied each beat was half again as powerful as anything he had previously experienced. The house shook all the way into its foundations, the rocking chair in the corner arced back and forth as if a hyperactive ghost was working off a superhuman rage, and one of the paintings flew off the wall and crashed to the floor.

By the time he turned on the lamp, threw back the covers, and got out of bed, Eduardo felt himself being lulled into a trancelike state similar to the one that had gripped him a month ago. If he fully succumbed, he might blink and discover he'd left the house without being aware of having taken a single step from the bed.

He snatched up the Discman, slipped the headphones over his ears, and hit the PLAY button. The music of Wormheart assaulted him.

He suspected that the unearthly throbbing sound operated on a frequency with a natural hypnotic influence. If so, the trancelike effect might be countered by blocking the mesmeric sound with sufficient chaotic noise.

He raised the volume of Wormheart until he could hear neither the bass throbbing nor the underlying electronic oscillation. He was sure his ear drums were in danger of bursting; however, with the heavy-metal band in full shriek, he was able to shrug off the trance before he was entirely enthralled.

He could still feel the waves of pressure surging over him and see the effects on objects around him. As he had suspected, however, only the sound itself elicited a lemming-like response; by blocking it, he was safe.

After clipping the Discman to his belt, so he wouldn't have to hold it, he strapped on the hip holster with the .22 pistol. He retrieved the shotgun from under the bed, slung it over his shoulder by its field strap, grabbed the camcorder, and rushed downstairs, outside.

The night was chilly.

The quarter moon gleamed like a silver scimitar.

The light emanating from the cluster of trees and the ground at the edge of the lower woods was already blood-red, no amber in it whatsoever.

Standing on the front porch, Eduardo taped the eerie luminosity from a distance. He panned back and forth to get it in perspective to the landscape.

Then he plunged down the porch steps, hurried across the brown lawn, and raced into the field. He was afraid that the phenomenon was going to be of shorter duration than it had been a month before, just as that second occurrence had been noticeably shorter but more intense than the first.

He stopped twice in the meadow to tape for a few seconds from different distances. By the time he halted warily within ten yards of the uncanny radiance, he wondered if the camcorder was getting anything or was overwhelmed by the sheer quantity of light.

The heatless fire was fiercely bright, shining through from some other place or time or dimension.

Pressure waves battered Eduardo. No longer like a crashing storm surf. Hard, punishing. Rocking him so forcefully he had to concentrate on keeping his balance.

Again he was aware of something struggling to be free of constraint, break loose of confinement, and burst full-born into the world.

The apocalyptic roar of Wormheart was the ideal accompaniment to the moment, brutal as a sledgehammer yet thrilling, atonal yet

88

compelling, anthems to animal need, shattering the frustrations of human limitations, liberating. It was the darkly gleeful music of doomsday.

The throbbing and the electronic whine must have grown to match the brilliance of the light and the power of the escalating pressure waves. He began to hear them again and was aware of being seduced.

He cranked up the volume on Wormheart.

The sugar and Ponderosa pines, previously as still as trees on a painted stage backdrop, suddenly began to thrash, though no wind had risen. The air was filled with whirling needles.

The pressure waves grew so fierce that he was pushed backward, stumbled, fell on his ass. He stopped recording, dropped the video camera on the ground beside him.

The Discman, clipped to his belt, began to vibrate against his left hip. A wail of Wormheart guitars escalated into a shrill electronic shriek that replaced the music and was as painful as jamming nails into his ears might have been.

Screaming in agony, he stripped off the headphones. Against his hip, the vibrating Discman was smoking. He tore it loose, threw it to the ground, scorching his fingers on the hot metal case.

The metronomic throbbing surrounded him, as if he were adrift inside the beating heart of a leviathan.

Resisting the urge to walk into the light and become part of it forever, Eduardo struggled to his feet. Shrugged the shotgun off his shoulder.

Blinding light forcing him to squint, serial shockwaves knocking the breath out of him, evergreen boughs churning, a trembling in the earth, the electronic oscillation like the high-pitched squeal of a surgeon's bone saw, and the whole night throbbing, the sky and the earth throbbing as something pushed repeatedly and relentlessly at the fabric of reality, throbbing, throbbing—

Whoooosh.

The new sound was like – but enormously louder than – the

gasp of a vacuum-packed can of coffee or peanuts being opened, air rushing to fill a void. Immediately after that single brief *whoooosh* a pall of silence fell across the night and the unearthly light vanished in an instant.

Eduardo Fernandez stood in stunned disbelief under the crescent moon, staring at a perfect sphere of pure blackness that towered over him, like a gargantuan ball on a cosmic billiards table. It was so flawlessly black, it stood out against the ordinary darkness of the May night as prominently as the flare of a nuclear explosion would stand out against the backdrop of even the sunniest summer day. Huge. Thirty feet in diameter. It filled the space once occupied by the radiant pine trees and earth.

A ship.

For a moment he thought that he was gazing up at a ship with a windowless hull as smooth as pooled oil. He waited in paralytic terror for a seam of light to appear, a portal to crack open, a ramp to extrude.

In spite of the fear that clouded his thinking, Eduardo quickly realized he was not looking at a solid object. The moonglow wasn't reflected on its surface. Light just fell into it as it would fall into a well. Or tunnel. Except that it revealed no curving walls within. Instinctively, without needing to touch that smooth inky surface, he knew the sphere had no weight, no mass at all; he had no primitive sense whatsoever that it was looming over him, as he should have had if it had been solid.

The object *wasn't* an object, not a sphere but a circle. Not three dimensional but two.

A doorway.

Open.

The dark beyond the threshold was unrelieved by gleam, glint, or faintest glimmer. Such perfect blackness was neither natural nor within human experience, and staring at it made Eduardo's eyes ache with the strain of seeking dimension and detail where none existed.

He wanted to run.

He approached the doorway instead.

His heart thudded, and his blood pressure no doubt pushed him toward a stroke. He clutched the shotgun with what he knew was pathetic faith in its efficacy, shoving it out in front of him as a primitive tribesman might brandish a talismanic staff carved with runes, inset with wild-animal teeth, lacquered with sacrificial blood and crowned with a shock of a witch doctor's hair.

However, his fear of the door – and of the unknown realms and entities beyond it – was not as debilitating as the fear of senility and the self-doubt with which he had been living lately. While the chance existed to gather proof of this experience, he intended to explore as far and as long as his nerves would hold out. He hoped never to wake another morning with the suspicion that his brain was addled and his perceptions no longer trustworthy.

Moving cautiously across the dead and flattened meadow grass, feet sinking slightly into the spring-softened soil, he remained alert for any change within the circle of exceptional darkness: a lesser blackness, shadows within the gloom, a spark, a hint of movement, anything that might signal the approach of . . . a traveller. He stopped three feet from the brink of that eye-baffling tenebrity, leaning forward slightly, as wonder-struck as a man in a fairy tale gazing into a magical mirror, the biggest damned magical mirror the Brothers Grimm ever imagined, one which offered no reflections – enchanted or otherwise – but which gave him a hair-raising glimpse of eternity.

Holding the shotgun in one hand, he reached down and picked up a stone as large as a lemon. He tossed it gently at the portal. He more than half expected the stone to bounce off the blackness with a hard metallic *tonk*, for it was still easier to believe he was looking at an object rather than peering into infinity. But it crossed the vertical plane of the doorway and vanished without a sound.

He edged closer.

Experimentally, he pushed the barrel of the Remington shotgun across the threshold. It didn't fade into the gloom. Instead, the blackness so totally claimed the forward part of the weapon that it appeared as if someone had run a high-speed saw through the barrel and the forearm slide handle, neatly truncating them.

He pulled back on the Remington, and the forward part of the gun reappeared. It seemed to be intact.

He touched the steel barrel and the checkered wood grip on the slide. Everything felt as it should feel.

Taking a deep breath, not sure whether he was brave or insane, he raised one trembling hand, as if signaling 'hello' to someone, and eased it forward, feeling for the transition point between this world and . . . whatever lay beyond the doorway. A tingle against his palm and the pads of his fingers. A coolness. It felt almost as if his hand rested on a pool of water but too lightly to break the surface tension.

He hesitated.

'You're seventy years old,' he grumbled. 'What've you got to lose?'

Swallowing hard, he pushed his hand through the portal, and it disappeared in the same manner as the shotgun. He encountered no resistance, and his wrist terminated in a neat stump.

'Jesus,' he said softly.

He made a fist, opened and closed it, but he couldn't tell if his hand responded on the other side of the barrier. All feeling ended at the point at which that hellish blackness cut across his wrist.

When he withdrew his hand from the doorway, it was as unchanged as the shotgun had been. He opened his fist, closed it, opened it. Everything worked as it should, and he had full feeling again.

Eduardo looked around at the deep and peaceful May night. The forest flanking the impossible circle of darkness. Meadow sloping upward, palely frosted by the glow of the quarter moon. The house at the higher end of the meadow. Some windows dark and others filled with light. Mountain peaks in the west, caps of snow phosphorescent against the post-midnight sky.

The scene was too detailed to be a place in a dream or part of the hallucination-riddled world of senile dementia. He was not a demented old fool, after all. Old, yes. A fool, probably. But not demented.

He returned his attention to the doorway again – and suddenly wondered what it looked like from the side. He imagined a long tube of perfectly non-reflective ebony leading straight off into the night more or less like an oil pipeline stretching across Alaskan tundra, boring through mountains in some cases and suspended in thin air when it crossed less lofty territories, until it reached the curve of the earth, where it continued straight and true, unbending, off into space, a tunnel to the stars.

When he walked to one end of the thirty-foot-wide blot and looked at the side of it, he discovered something utterly different from – but quite as strange as – the pipeline image in his mind. The forest lay behind the enormous portal, unchanged as far as he could tell: the moon shone down, the trees rose as if responding to the caress of that silvery light, and an owl hooted far away. The doorway disappeared when viewed from the side. Its width, if it had any width at all, was as thin as a thread or as a well-stropped razor blade.

He walked all the way around to the back of it.

Viewed from a point a hundred and eighty degrees from his first position, the doorway was the same thirty-foot circle of featureless mystery. From that reverse perspective, it seemed to have swallowed not part of the forest but the meadow and the house at the top of the rise. It was like a great paper-thin black coin balanced on edge.

He moved to take another look at the side of it. From that angle, he couldn't make out even the finest filament of supernatural blackness against the lesser darkness of the night. He felt for the edge with one hand, but he encountered only empty air.

From the side, the doorway simply didn't exist – which was a concept that made him dizzy.

He faced the invisible edge of the damned thing, then leaned to his left, looking around at what he thought of as the 'front' of the doorway. He shoved his left hand into it as deeply as before.

He was surprised at his boldness and knew he was being too quick to assume that the phenomenon was, after all, harmless. Curiosity, that old killer of cats – and not a few human beings – had him in its grip.

Without withdrawing his left hand, he leaned to the right and looked at the 'back' of the doorway. His fingers had not poked through the far side.

He pushed his hand deeper into the front of the portal, but it still did not appear out of the back. The doorway was as thin as a razor blade, yet he had about fourteen to sixteen inches of hand and forearm thrust into it.

Where had his hand gone?

Shivering, he withdrew his hand from the enigma and returned to the meadow, once more facing the 'front' of the portal.

He wondered what would happen to him if he stepped through the doorway, both feet, all the way, with no tether to the world he knew. What would he discover beyond? Would he be able to get back if he didn't like what he found?

He didn't have enough curiosity to take such a fateful step. He stood at the brink, wondering – and gradually began to feel that something was coming. Before he could decide what to do, that pure essence of darkness seemed to pour out of the doorway, an ocean of night that sucked him down into a dry but drowning sea.

*

When he regained consciousness, Eduardo was face down in the dead and matted grass, head turned to his left, gazing up the long meadow toward the house.

Dawn had not yet come, but time had passed. The moon had

set, and the night was dull and bleak without its silvery enhancement.

He was initially confused, but his mind cleared. He remembered the doorway.

He rolled on to his back, sat up, looked toward the woods. The razor-thin coin of blackness was gone. The forest stood where it had always stood, unchanged.

He crawled to where the doorway had been, stupidly wondering if it had fallen over and was now flat on the ground, transformed from a doorway into a bottomless well. But it was just gone.

Shaky and weak, wincing at a headache as intense as a hot wire through his brain, he got laboriously to his feet. He swayed like a drunkard sobering from a week-long binge.

He staggered to where he remembered putting down the video camera.

It wasn't there.

He searched in circles, steadily widening the pattern from the point where the camcorder should have been, until he was certain that he was venturing into areas where he had not gone earlier. He couldn't find the camera.

The shotgun was missing, as well. And the discarded Discman with its headphones.

Reluctantly he returned to the house. He made a pot of strong coffee. Almost as bitter and black as espresso. With the first cup, he washed down two aspirin.

He usually made a weak brew and limited himself to two or three cups. Too much caffeine could cause prostate problems. This morning he didn't care if his prostate swelled as big as a basketball. He *needed* coffee.

He took off the holster, with the pistol still in it, and put it on the kitchen table. He pulled out a chair and sat within easy reach of the weapon.

He repeatedly examined his left hand, which he had thrust through the doorway, as if he thought it might abruptly turn to dust. And why not? Was that any more fantastic than anything else that had happened?

At first light, he strapped on the holster and returned to the meadow at the perimeter of the lower woods, where he conducted another search for the camera, the shotgun, and the Discman.

Gone.

He could do without the shotgun. It wasn't his only defense.

The Discman had served its purpose. He didn't need it any more. Besides, he remembered how smoke had seeped from its innards and how hot the casing had been when he'd unclipped it from his belt. It was probably ruined.

However, he badly wanted the camcorder because, without it, he had no proof of what he'd seen. Maybe that was why it had been taken.

In the house again he made a fresh pot of coffee. What the hell did *he* need a prostate for, anyway?

From the desk in the study, he fetched a legal-size tablet of ruled yellow paper and a couple of ballpoint pens.

He sat at the kitchen table, working on the second pot of coffee and filling up tablet pages with his neat, strong handwriting. On the first page, he began with:

My name is Eduardo Fernandez and I have witnessed a series of strange and unsettling events. I am not much of a diarist. Often I've resolved to start a diary with the new year, but I have always lost interest before the end of January. However, I am sufficiently worried to put down here everything that I've seen and may yet see in the days to come, so there will be a record in the event that something happens to me.

He strove to recount his peculiar story in simple terms, with a minimum of adjectives and no sensationalism. He even avoided speculating about the nature of the phenomenon or the power behind the creation of the doorway. In fact, he hesitated to call it a doorway, but he finally used that term because he knew, on a deep level beyond language and logic, that a doorway was precisely what it had been. If he died – face it, if he was killed – before he could obtain proof of these bizarre goings-on, he hoped that whoever read his account would be impressed by its cool, calm style and would not disregard it as the ravings of a demented old man.

He became so involved in his writing that he worked through the lunch hour and well into the afternoon before pausing to prepare a bite to eat. Because he'd skipped breakfast, too, he had quite an appetite. He sliced a cold chicken breast left over from dinner the previous night, and he built a couple of tall sandwiches with cheese, tomato, lettuce, and mustard. Sandwiches and beer were the perfect meal because that was something he could eat while still writing in the yellow legal tablet.

By twilight, he had brought the story up to date. He finished with: *I don't expect to see the doorway again because I suspect it has already served its purpose. Something has come through it. I wish I knew what that something was. Or perhaps I don't.*

9

A SOUND woke Heather. A soft thunk, then a brief scraping, the source unidentifiable. She sat straight up in bed, instantly alert.

The night was silent again.

She looked at the clock. Ten minutes past two in the morning.

A few months ago, she would have attributed her apprehension to some fright in an unremembered dream, and she would have rolled over and gone back to sleep. Not any more.

She had fallen asleep atop the covers. Now she didn't have to disentangle herself from the blankets before getting out of bed.

For weeks, she had been sleeping in sweatsuits instead of her usual T-shirt and panties. Even in pajamas, she would have felt too vulnerable. Sweats were comfortable enough in bed, and she was dressed for trouble if something happened in the middle of the night.

Like now.

In spite of the continued silence, she picked up the gun from the nightstand. It was a Korth .38 revolver, made in Germany by Waffenfabrik Korth and perhaps the finest handgun in the world, with tolerances unmatched by any other maker.

The revolver was one of the weapons she had purchased since the day Jack had been shot, with the consultation of Alma Bryson. She'd spent hours with it on the police firing range. When she picked it up, it felt like a natural extension of her hand.

The size of her arsenal now exceeded Alma's, which sometimes amazed her. More amazing still: she worried that she was not well enough armed for every eventuality.

New laws were soon going into effect, making it more difficult to purchase firearms. She was going to have to weigh the wisdom of spending more of their limited income on defenses they might never need against the possibility that even her worst-case scenarios would prove to be too optimistic.

Once, she would have regarded her current state of mind as a clear-cut case of paranoia. Times had changed. What once had been paranoia was now sober realism.

She didn't like to think about that. It depressed her.

When the night remained suspiciously quiet, she crossed the bedroom to the hall door. She didn't need to turn on any lights. During the past few months, she had spent so many nights restlessly walking through the house that she could now move from room to room in the darkness as swiftly and silently as a cat.

On the wall just inside the bedroom, there was a panel for the alarm system that she'd had installed a week after the events at Arkadian's service station. In luminous green letters, the lighted digital monitor strip informed her that all was SECURE.

It was a perimeter alarm, involving magnetic contacts at every exterior door and window, so she could be confident the noise that awakened her hadn't been made by an intruder already in the premises. Otherwise, a siren would have sounded, and a microchip recording of an authoritarian male voice would have announced: *You have violated a protected dwelling. Police have been called. Leave at once.*

Barefoot, she stepped into the dark second-floor hallway and moved along to Toby's room. Every evening she made sure both his and her doors were open, so she would hear him if he called to her.

For a few seconds she stood by her son's bed, listening to his soft snoring. The boy-shape beneath the covers was barely visible in the weak ambient light that passed from the city night through the narrow slats of the Levolor blinds. He was dead to the world and couldn't have been the source of the sound that had interrupted her dreams.

Heather returned to the hall. She crept to the stairs and went down to the first floor.

In the cramped den and then in the living room, she eased from window to window, checking outside for anything suspicious. The quiet street looked so peaceful that it might have been located in a small Midwestern town instead of Los Angeles. No one was up to foul play on the front lawn. No one skulking along the north side of the house, either.

Heather began to think the suspicious sound had been part of a nightmare, after all.

She seldom slept well any more, but usually she remembered her dreams. They were more often than not about Arkadian's service station, though she'd only driven by the place once on the day after the shootout. The dreams were operatic spectacles of bullets and blood and fire, in which Jack was sometimes burned alive, in which she and Toby were often present during the gunplay, one or both of them shot down with Jack, one or both of them afire, and sometimes the well-groomed blond man in the Armani suit knelt beside her where she lay riddled with bullets, put his mouth to her wounds, and drank her blood. The killer was frequently blind, with hollow eye sockets full of roiling flames. His smile revealed teeth as sharp as the fangs of a viper, and once he said to her, *I'm taking Toby down to Hell with me — put the little bastard on a leash and use him as a guide dog.*

Considering that her remembered nightmares were so bad, how gruesome must be the ones that she blocked from memory?

By the time she had circled the living room, returned to the archway, and crossed the hall to the dining room, she decided that her imagination had gotten the better of her. There was no immediate danger. She no longer held the Korth in front of her but held

100

it at her side with the muzzle aimed at the floor and her finger on the trigger guard rather than on the trigger itself.

The sight of someone outside moving past a dining-room window brought her to full alert again. The drapes were open, but the sheers under them were drawn all the way shut. Backlit by a street lamp, the prowler cast a shadow that pierced the glass and rippled across the soft folds of the translucent chiffon. It passed quickly, like the shadow of a night bird, but she suffered no doubt that it had been made by a man.

She hurried into the kitchen. The tile floor was cold under her bare feet.

Another alarm-system control panel was on the wall beside the connecting door to the garage. She punched in the deactivating code.

With Jack in the hospital for an unthinkably long convalescence, herself out of work, and their financial future uncertain, Heather had been hesitant to spend precious savings on a burglar alarm. She had always assumed security systems were for mansions in Bel Air and Beverly Hills, not for middle-class families like theirs. Then she'd learned that six other homes, out of the sixteen on their block, already relied on such high-tech protection.

Now the glowing green letters on the readout strip changed from SECURE to the less comforting READY TO ARM.

She could have set off the alarm, summoning the police. But if she did that, the creeps outside would run. By the time a patrol car arrived, there would be no one to arrest. She was pretty sure she knew what they were – though not who – and what mischief they were up to. She wanted to surprise them and hold them at gunpoint until help arrived.

As she quietly disengaged the dead-bolt lock, opened the door – NOT READY TO ARM, the system warned – and stepped into the garage, she knew she was out of control. Fear should have had her in its thrall. She was afraid, yes, but fear was not what made her heart beat hard and fast. Anger was the engine that drove her.

She was infuriated by repeated victimization and determined to make her tormentors pay regardless of the risks.

The concrete floor of the garage was even colder than the kitchen tiles.

She rounded the back end of the nearer car. Stopping between the fenders of the two vehicles, she waited, listened.

The only light came through a series of six-inch-square windows high in the double-wide garage doors. The sickly yellow glow of the street lamps. The deep shadows seemed contemptuous of it, refusing to withdraw.

There. Whispering outside. Soft footfalls on the service walkway along the south side of the house. Then the telltale hiss for which she'd been waiting.

Bastards.

Heather walked quickly between the cars to the man-size door in the back wall of the garage. The lock had a thumb-turn on the inside. She twisted it slowly, easing the dead-bolt out of the striker plate without the *clack* that it made if opened unthinkingly. She turned the knob, carefully pulled the door inward, and stepped on to the sidewalk behind the house.

The May night was mild. The full moon, well on its westward course, was mostly hidden by an overcast.

She was being irresponsible. She wasn't protecting Toby. If anything, she was putting him in greater jeopardy. Over the top. Out of control. She knew it. Couldn't help it. She'd had enough. Couldn't take any more. Couldn't stop.

To her right lay the covered rear porch, the patio in front of it. The backyard was lit only patchily by what moonlight penetrated the ragged veil of clouds. Tall eucalyptuses, smaller benjaminas, and low shrubs were dappled with lunar silver.

She was on the west side of the house. She moved to her left along the walkway, toward the south.

At the corner she halted, listening. Because there was no wind, she could clearly hear the vicious hissing, a sound that only stoked her anger.

Murmurs of conversation. Couldn't catch the words.

Stealthy footsteps hurrying toward the back of the house. A low, suppressed laugh, almost a giggle. Having such a good time at their game.

Judging the moment of his appearance by the sound of his swiftly approaching footsteps, intending to scare the living hell out of him, Heather moved forward. With perfect timing, she met him at the turn in the sidewalk.

She was surprised to see he was taller than she was. She had expected them to be ten years old, eleven, twelve at the oldest.

The prowler let out a faint, '*Ah!*' of alarm.

Putting the fear of God into them was going to be a harder proposition than if they'd been younger. And no retreating now. They'd drag her down. And then . . .

She kept moving, collided with him, rammed him backward across the eight-foot-wide set-back and into the ivy-covered concrete-block wall that marked the southern property line. The can of spray-paint flew out of his hand, clattered against the sidewalk.

The impact knocked the wind out of him. His mouth sagged open, and he gasped for breath.

Footsteps. The second one. Running toward her.

Pressed against the first boy, face to face, even in the darkness, she saw that he was sixteen or seventeen, maybe older. Plenty old enough to know better.

She rammed her right knee up between his spread legs and turned away from him as he fell, wheezing and retching, into the flower bed along the wall.

The second boy was coming at her fast. He didn't see the gun, and she didn't have time to stop him with a threat.

She stepped toward him instead of away, spun on her left foot, and kicked him in the crotch with her right. Because she'd moved into him, it was a deep kick; she caught him with her ankle and the upper part of the bridge of her foot instead of with her toes.

He crashed past her, slammed into the sidewalk, and rolled against the first boy, afflicted by an identical fit of retching.

A third one was coming at her along the sidewalk from the front of the house, but he skidded to a halt fifteen feet away and started to back up.

'Stop right there,' she said, 'I've got a gun.' Though she raised the Korth, holding it in a two-hand grip, she did not raise her voice, and her calm control made the order more menacing than if she had shouted it in anger.

He stopped, but maybe he couldn't see the revolver in the dark. His body language said he was still contemplating making a break for it.

'So help me God,' she said, still at a conversational level, 'I'll blow your brains out.' She was surprised by the cold hatred in her voice. She wouldn't really have shot him. She was sure of that. Yet the sound of her own voice frightened her . . . and made her wonder.

His shoulders sagged. His entire posture changed. He believed her threat.

A dark exhilaration filled her. Nearly three months of intense tae kwon do and women's defense classes, provided free to members of police families three times a week at the division gym, had paid off. Her right foot hurt like blazes, probably almost as badly as the second boy's crotch hurt him. She might have broken a bone in it, would certainly be hobbling around for a week even if there wasn't a fracture, but she felt so good about nailing the three vandals that she was happy to suffer for her triumph.

'Come here,' she said. 'Now, come on, come on.'

The third kid raised his hands over his head. He was holding a spray can in each of them.

'Get down on the ground with your buddies,' she demanded, and he did as he was told.

The moon sailed out from behind the clouds, which was like slowly bringing up the stage lights to quarter power on a darkened set. She could see well enough to be sure they were all older teenagers, sixteen to eighteen.

She could also see they didn't fit any popular stereotypes of taggers. They weren't black or Hispanic. They were white boys. And they didn't look poor, either. One of them wore a well-cut leather jacket, and another wore a cable-knit cotton sweater with what appeared to be a complicated and beautifully knitted pattern.

The night quiet was broken only by the miserable gagging and groaning of the two she'd disabled. The confrontation had unfolded so swiftly in the eight-foot-wide space between the house and the property wall, and in such relative silence, that they hadn't even awakened any neighbors.

Keeping the gun on them, Heather said, 'You been here before?'

Two of them couldn't yet have answered her if they'd wanted to, but the third was also unresponsive.

'I asked if you'd been here before,' she said sharply, 'done this kind of crap here before.'

'Bitch,' the third kid said.

She realized it was possible to lose control of the situation even when she was the only one with a gun, especially if the crotch-bashed pair recovered more easily than she expected. She resorted to a lie that might convince them she was more than just a cop's wife with a few smart moves: 'Listen, you little snots, I can kill all of you, go in the house and get a couple of knives, plant them in your hands before the first black-and-white gets here. Maybe they'll drag me into court and maybe they won't. But what jury's going to put the wife of a hero cop and the mother of a little eight-year-old boy in prison?'

'You wouldn't do that,' the third kid said, although he spoke only after a hesitation. A thread of uncertainty fluttered in his voice.

She continued to surprise herself by speaking with an intensity and bitterness she didn't have to fake. 'Wouldn't I, huh? Wouldn't

I? My Jack, two partners shot down beside him in one year, and him lying in the hospital since the first of March, going to be in there weeks yet, months yet, God knows what pain he might have the rest of his life, whether he'll ever walk entirely right, and here I am out of work since October, savings almost gone, can't sleep for worrying, being harassed by crud like you. You think I wouldn't like to see somebody else hurting for a change, think I wouldn't actually get a *kick* out of hurting you, hurting you real bad? Wouldn't I? Huh? Huh? Wouldn't I, you little snot?'

Jesus. She was shaking. She hadn't been aware that anything this dark was in her. She felt her gorge rising in the back of her throat and had to fight hard to keep it down.

From all appearances, she had scared the three taggers even more than she had scared herself. Their eyes were wide with fright in the moonlight.

'We . . . been here . . . before,' gasped the kid whom she'd kicked.

'How often?'

'T-Twice.'

The house had been hit twice before, once in late March, once in the middle of April.

Glowering down at them, she said, 'Where you from?'

'Here,' said the kid she hadn't hurt.

'Not from this neighborhood, you aren't.'

'L.A.,' he said.

'It's a big city,' she pressed.

'The Hills.'

'Beverly Hills?'

'Yeah.'

'All three of you?'

'Yeah.'

'Don't screw around with me.'

'It's true, that's where we're from, why wouldn't it be true?'

The unhurt boy put his hands to his temples as if he'd just been overcome with remorse, though it was far more likely to be a sudden headache. Moonlight glinted off his wristwatch and the beveled edges of the shiny metal band.

'What's that watch?' she demanded.

'Huh?'

'What make is it?'

'Rolex,' he said.

That was what she'd thought it was, although she couldn't help but express astonishment: 'Rolex?'

'I'm not lying. I got it for Christmas.'

'Jesus.'

He started to take it off. 'Here, you can have it.'

'Leave it on,' she said scornfully.

'No, really.'

'Who gave it to you?'

'My folks. It's the gold one.' He had taken it off. He held it out, offering it to her. 'No diamonds, but all gold, the watch and the band.'

'What is that,' she asked incredulously, 'fifteen thousand bucks, twenty thousand?'

'Something like that,' one of the hurt boys said. 'It's not the most expensive model.'

'You can have it,' the owner of the watch repeated.

Heather said, 'How old are you?'

'Seventeen.'

'You're still in high school?'

'Senior. Here, take the watch.'

'You're still in high school, you get a fifteen-thousand-dollar watch for Christmas?'

'It's yours.'

Crouching in front of the huddled trio, refusing to acknowledge the pain in her right foot, she leveled the Korth at the face of the boy with the watch. All three drew back in terror.

She said, 'I might blow your head off, you spoiled little creep, I sure might, but I wouldn't steal your watch even if it was worth a million. *Put it on.*'

The gold links of the Rolex band rattled as he nervously slipped it on to his wrist again and fumbled with the clasp.

She wanted to know why, with all the privileges and advantages their families could give them, three boys from Beverly Hills would sneak around at night defacing the hard-earned property of a cop who had nearly been killed trying to preserve the very social stability that made it possible for them to have enough food to eat, let alone Rolex watches. Where did their meanness come from, their twisted values, their nihilism? Couldn't blame it on deprivation. Then who or what *was* to blame?

'Show me your wallets,' she said harshly.

They fumbled wallets out of hip pockets, held them out to her. They kept glancing back and forth from her to the Korth. The muzzle of the .38 must have looked like a cannon to them.

She said, 'Take out whatever cash you're carrying.'

Maybe the trouble with them was just that they'd been raised in a time when the media assaulted them, first, with endless predictions of nuclear war and then, after the fall of the Soviet Union, with ceaseless warnings of a fast-approaching worldwide environmental catastrophe. Maybe the unremitting but stylishly produced gloom and doom that got high Nielson ratings for electronic news had convinced them that they had no future. And black kids had it even worse because they were also being told they couldn't make it, the system was against them, unfair, no justice, no use even trying.

Or maybe none of that had anything to do with it.

She didn't know. She wasn't sure she even cared. Nothing she could say or do would turn them around.

Each boy was holding cash in one hand, a wallet in the other, waiting expectantly.

She almost didn't ask the next question, then decided she'd better: 'Any of you have credit cards?'

Incredibly, two of them did. High-school students with credit cards. The boy she had driven backward into the wall had American Express and Visa cards. The boy with the Rolex had a Mastercard.

Staring at them, meeting their troubled eyes in the moonlight, she took solace from the certainty that most kids weren't like these three. Most were struggling to deal with an immoral world in a moral fashion, and they would finish growing up to be good people. Maybe even these brats would be all right eventually, one or two of them anyway. But what was the percentage who'd lost their moral compass these days, not merely among teenagers but in any age group? Ten percent? Surely more. So much street crime and white-collar crime, so much lying and cheating, greed and envy. Twenty per cent? And what percentage could a democracy tolerate before it collapsed?

'Throw your wallets on the sidewalk,' she said, indicating a spot beside her.

They did as instructed.

'Put the cash and credit cards in your pockets.'

Looking perplexed, they did that too.

'I don't want your money. I'm no petty criminal like you.'

Holding the revolver in her right hand, she gathered up the wallets with her left. She stood and backed away from them, refusing to favor her right foot, until she came up against the garage wall.

She didn't ask them any of the questions that had been running through her mind. Their answers – if they had any answers – would be glib. She was sick of glibness. The modern world creaked along on a lubricant of facile lies, oily evasions, slick self-justifications.

'All I want is your identification,' Heather said, raising the fist in which she clenched the wallets. 'This'll tell me who you are, where I can find you. You ever give us any more grief, you so much as drive by and spit on the front lawn, I'll come after all of you, take my time, catch you at just the right moment.' She cocked the hammer on the Korth, and their gazes all dropped from her eyes to the gun. 'Bigger gun than this, higher calibre ammunition, something with a hollow point, shoot you in the leg and it shatters the bone so bad they have to amputate. Shoot you in both legs, you're in a wheelchair the rest of your life. Maybe one of you gets it in the balls, so you can't bring any more like you into the world.'

The moon slid behind clouds.

The night was deep.

From the backyard came the coarse singing of toads.

The three boys stared at her, not sure that she meant for them to go. They had expected to be turned over to the police.

That, of course, was out of the question. She had hurt two of them. Each of the injured still had a hand cupped tenderly over his crotch, and both were grimacing with pain. Furthermore, she had threatened them with a gun *outside* her home. The argument against her would be that they had represented no real threat because they hadn't crossed her threshold. Although they had spray-painted her house with hateful and obscene graffiti on three separate occasions, though they had done financial and emotional damage to her and her child, she knew that being the wife of a heroic cop was no guarantee against prosecution on a variety of charges that inevitably would result in her imprisonment instead of theirs.

'Get out of here,' she said.

They rose to their feet but then hesitated as if afraid she would shoot them in the back.

'Go,' she said. '*Now*.'

At last they hurried past her, along the side of the house, and she followed at a distance to be sure they actually cleared out. They kept glancing back at her.

On the front lawn, standing in the dew-damp grass, she got a good look at what they had done to at least two and possibly three sides of the house. The red, yellow, and sour-apple-green paint seemed to glow in the light of the street lamps. They had scrawled their personal tagger symbols everywhere, and they had favored the F word with and without a variety of suffixes, as noun and verb and adjective. But the central message was as it had been the previous two times they'd struck: KILLER COP.

The three boys – two of them limping – reached their car, which was parked nearly a block to the north. A black Infiniti. They took off with a squeal of spinning tires, leaving clouds of blue smoke in their wake.

KILLER COP.

WIDOWMAKER.

ORPHANMAKER.

Heather was more deeply disturbed by the irrationality of the graffiti than by the confrontation with the three taggers. Jack had not been to blame. He'd been doing his duty. How was he supposed to have taken a machine gun from a homicidal maniac *without* resorting to lethal force? She was overcome with a feeling that civilization was sinking in a sea of mindless hatred.

ANSON OLIVER LIVES!

Anson Oliver was the maniac with the Micro Uzi, a promising young film director with three features released in the past four years. Not surprisingly, he made angry movies about angry people. Since the shootout, Heather had seen all three films. Oliver had made excellent use of the camera and had had a powerful narrative style. Some of his scenes were dazzling. He might even have been a genius and, in time, might have been honored with Oscars and other awards. But there was a disquieting moral arrogance in his work, a smugness and bullying, that now appeared to have been an early sign of much deeper problems exacerbated by too many drugs.

ASSASSIN.

She wished that Toby didn't have to see his father labeled a murderer. Well, he'd seen it before. Twice before, all over his own house. He had heard it at school, as well, and had been in two fights because of it. He was a little guy, but he had guts. Though he'd lost both of the fights, he would no doubt disregard her advice to turn the other cheek and would wade into more battles.

In the morning, after she drove him to school, she would paint over the graffiti. As before, some of the neighbors would probably help. Multiple coats were required over the affected areas because their house was a pale yellow-beige.

Even so, it was a temporary repair because the spray paint had a chemical composition that ate through the house paint. Over a few weeks, each defacement gradually reappeared like spirit writing on a medium's tablet at a seance, messages from souls in Hell.

In spite of the mess on her house, her anger faded. She didn't have the energy to sustain it. These last few months had worn her down. She was tired, so very tired.

Limping, she re-entered the house by the back garage door and locked up after herself. She also locked the connecting door between the garage and the kitchen, and punched in the activating code to arm the alarm system again.

SECURE.

Not really. Not ever.

She went upstairs to check on Toby. He was still sound asleep.

Standing in the doorway of her son's room, listening to him snore, she understood why Anson Oliver's mother and father had been unable to accept that their son had been capable of mass murder. He had been their baby, their little boy, their fine young man, the embodiment of the best of their own qualities, a source of pride and hope, heart of their heart. She sympathized with them, pitied them, prayed that she would never have to experience a pain like theirs – but wished they would shut up and go away.

Oliver's parents had conducted an effective media campaign to portray their son as a kind, talented man incapable of what he was said to have done. They claimed the Uzi found at the scene had not belonged to him. No record existed to prove he had purchased or registered such a weapon. But the fully automatic Micro Uzi was an illegal gun these days, and Oliver no doubt paid cash for it on the black market. No mystery about the lack of a receipt or registration.

Heather left Toby's room and returned to her own. She sat on the edge of the bed and switched on the lamp.

She put down the revolver and occupied herself with the contents of the three wallets. From their driver's licenses, she learned that one of the boys was sixteen years old and two were seventeen. They did, indeed, live in Beverly Hills.

In one wallet, among snapshots of a cute high-school-age blonde and a grinning Irish setter, Heather found a two-inch-diameter decal at which she stared in disbelief for a moment before she fished it out of the plastic window. It was the kind of thing often sold on novelty racks in stationery stores, pharmacies, record shops and book stores; kids decorated school notebooks and countless other items with them. A paper backing could be peeled off to reveal an adhesive surface. This one was glossy black with embossed silver-foil letters: ANSON OLIVER LIVES.

Someone was already merchandising his death. Sick. Sick and strange. What unnerved Heather most was that, apparently, a market existed for Anson Oliver as legendary figure, perhaps even as martyr.

Maybe she should have seen it coming. Oliver's parents weren't the only people assiduously polishing his image since the shootout.

The director's fiancée, pregnant with his child, claimed he didn't use drugs any more. He'd been arrested twice for driving under the influence of narcotics; however, those slips from the pedestal were said to have been a thing of the past. The fiancée was an actress, not merely beautiful but with a fey and vulnerable quality that ensured plenty of TV-news time; her large, lovely eyes always seemed on the verge of filling with tears.

Various film-community associates of the director had taken out full-page ads in the *Hollywood Reporter* and *Daily Variety*, mourning the loss of such a creative talent, making the observation that his controversial films had angered a lot of people in positions of power, and suggesting that he had lived and died for his art.

The implications of all this were that the Uzi had been planted on him, as had the cocaine and PCP. Because everyone up and down the street from Arkadian's station had dived for cover at the sound of all that gunfire, no one had witnessed Anson Oliver with a gun in his hands except the people who died – and Jack. Mrs Arkadian had never seen the gunman while she'd been hiding in the office; when she'd come out of the service station with Jack, she'd been virtually blind because smoke and soot had mucked up her contact lenses.

Within two days of the shootout, Heather had been forced to change their phone number for a new unlisted one because fans of Anson Oliver were calling at all hours. Many had made accusations of sinister conspiracies in which Jack figured as the triggerman.

It was nuts.

The guy was just a filmmaker, for God's sake, not President of the United States. Politicians, corporate chiefs, military leaders, and police officials didn't quiver in terror and plot murder out of fear that some crusading Hollywood film director was going to take a swipe at them in a movie. Hell, if they were *that* sensitive, there would hardly be any directors left.

And did these people actually believe that Jack had shot his own partner and three other men at the service station, then pumped three rounds into himself, all of this in broad daylight where it well *might* have been witnesses, risking death, subjecting himself to enormous pain and suffering and an arduous rehabilitation merely to make his story about Anson Oliver's death look more credible?

The answer, of course, was yes. They *did* believe such nonsense.

She found proof in another plastic window in the same wallet. Another decal, also a two-inch-diameter circle. Black background, red letters, three names stacked above one another: OSWALD, CHAPMAN, MCGARVEY?

114

She was filled with revulsion. To compare a troubled film director who'd made three flawed movies to John Kennedy (Oswald's victim) or even to John Lennon (Mark David Chapman's victim) was disgusting. But to liken Jack to a pair of infamous murderers was an abomination.

OSWALD, CHAPMAN, MCGARVEY?

Her first thought was to call an attorney in the morning, find out who was producing this trash, and sue them for every penny they had. As she stared at the hateful decal, however, she had a sinking feeling that the purveyor of this crap had protected himself by the use of that question mark.

OSWALD, CHAPMAN, MCGARVEY?

Speculation wasn't the same thing as accusation. The question mark made it speculation and probably provided protection against a successful prosecution for slander or libel.

Suddenly she had enough energy to sustain her anger, after all. She gathered up the wallets and threw them into the bottom drawer of the nightstand, along with the decals. She slammed the drawer shut – then hoped she hadn't wakened Toby.

It was an age when a great many people would rather embrace a patently absurd conspiracy theory than bother to research the facts and accept a simple, observable truth. They seemed to have confused real life with fiction, eagerly seeking Byzantine schemes and cabals of maniacal villains straight out of Ludlum novels. But the reality was nearly always far less dramatic and immeasurably less flamboyant. It was probably a coping mechanism, a means by which they tried to bring order to – and make sense of – a high-tech world in which the pace of social and technological change dizzied and frightened them.

Coping mechanism or not, it was sick.

And speaking of sick, she had *hurt* two of those boys. Never mind that they deserved it. She had never hurt anyone in her life before. Now that the heat of the moment was past, she felt . . . not

remorse, exactly, because they *had* earned what she'd done to them
. . . but a sadness that it had been necessary. She felt soiled. Her
exhilaration had fallen with her adrenalin levels.

She examined her right foot. It was beginning to swell, but the
pain was tolerable.

'Good God, woman,' she admonished herself, 'who did you think
you were – one of the Ninja Turtles?'

She got two Excedrin from the bathroom medicine cabinet, washed
them down with tepid water.

In the bedroom again, she switched off the bedside lamp.

She wasn't afraid of the darkness.

What she feared was the damage people were capable of doing
to one another either in darkness or at high noon.

10

THE TENTH of June was not a day to be cooped up inside. The sky was delft blue, the temperature hovered around eighty degrees, and the meadows were still a dazzling green because the heat of summer had not yet seared the grass.

Eduardo spent most of the balmy afternoon in a bentwood hickory rocking chair on the front porch. A new video camera, loaded with tape and fully charged batteries, lay on the porch floor beside the rocker. Next to the camera was a shotgun. He got up a couple of times to fetch a fresh bottle of beer or to use the bathroom. And once he went for a half-hour walk around the nearer fields, carrying the camera. For the most part, however, he remained in the chair – waiting.

It was in the woods.

Eduardo knew in his bones that something had come through the black doorway in the first hour of 3 May, over five weeks ago. *Knew* it, felt it. He had no idea what it was or where it had begun its journey, but he knew it had travelled from some strange world into that Montana night.

Thereafter, it must have found a hiding place into which it had crawled. No other analysis of the situation made sense. Hiding. If it had wanted its presence to be known, it would have revealed itself to him that night or later. The woods, vast and dense, offered an infinite number of places to go to ground.

Although the doorway had been enormous, that didn't mean the traveller – or the vessel carrying it, if a vessel existed – was also large. Eduardo had once been to New York City and driven through the Holland Tunnel, which had been a lot bigger than any car that used it. Whatever had come out of that death-black portal might be no larger than a man, perhaps even smaller, and able to hide almost anywhere among those timbered vales and ridges.

The doorway indicated nothing about the traveller, in fact, except that it was undoubtedly intelligent. Sophisticated science and engineering lay behind the creation of that gate.

He had read enough Heinlein and Clarke – and selected others in their vein – to have exercised his imagination, and he had realized that the intruder might have a variety of origins. More likely than not, it was extraterrestrial. However, it might also be something from another dimension or from a parallel world. It might even be a human being, opening a passage into this age from the far future.

The numerous possibilities were dizzying, and he no longer felt like a fool when he speculated about them. He also had ceased being embarrassed about borrowing fantastical literature from the library – though the cover art was often trashy even when well drawn – and his appetite for it had become voracious.

Indeed, he found that he no longer had the patience to read the realist writers who had been his lifelong favorites. Their work simply wasn't as realistic as it had seemed before. Hell, it wasn't realistic at all to him any longer. Now, when he was just a few pages into a book or story by one of them, Eduardo got the distinct feeling that their point of view consisted of an extremely narrow slice of reality, as if they looked at life through the slit of a welder's hood. They wrote well, certainly, but they were writing about only the tiniest sliver of the human experience in a big world and an infinite universe.

He now preferred writers who could look beyond this horizon, who knew that humanity would one day reach childhood's end, who believed intellect could triumph over superstition and ignorance, and who dared to dream.

He was also thinking about buying a second Discman and giving Wormheart another try.

He finished a beer, put the bottle on the porch beside the rocker, and wished he could believe the thing that had come through the doorway *was* just a person from the distant future, or at least something benign. But it had gone into hiding for more than five weeks, and its secretiveness did not seem to indicate benevolent intentions. He was trying not to be xenophobic. But instinct told him that he'd had a brush with something not merely different from humanity but inherently hostile to it.

Although his attention was focused, more often than not, on the lower woods to the east, at the edge of which the doorway had opened, Eduardo wasn't comfortable venturing near the northern and western woods, either, because the evergreen wilderness on three sides of the ranch house was contiguous, broken only by the fields to the south. Whatever had entered the lower woods could easily make its way under the cover of the trees into any arm of the forest.

He supposed it was possible that the traveller had not chosen to hide anywhere nearby but had circled into the pines on the western foothills and from there into the mountains. It might long ago have retreated into some high redoubt, secluded ravine, or cavern in the remote reaches of the Rocky Mountains, many miles from Quartermass Ranch.

But he didn't think that was the case.

Sometimes, when he was walking near the forest, studying the shadows under the trees, looking for anything out of the ordinary, he was aware of . . . a presence. Simple as that. Inexplicable as that. A presence. On those occasions, though he neither saw nor heard anything unusual, he was aware that he was no longer alone.

So he waited.

Sooner or later something new would happen.

On those days when he grew impatient, he reminded himself of two things. First, he was well accustomed to waiting; since Margarite had died three years ago, he hadn't been doing anything but waiting for the time to come when he could join her again. Second, when at last something *did* happen, when the traveller finally chose to reveal itself in some fashion, Eduardo more likely than not would wish that it had remained concealed and secretive.

Now he picked up the empty beer bottle, rose from the rocking chair, intending to get another brew – and saw the raccoon. It was standing in the yard, about eight or ten feet from the porch, staring at him. He hadn't noticed it before because he'd been focused on the distant trees – the once-luminous trees – at the foot of the meadow.

The woods and fields were heavily populated with wildlife. The frequent appearance of squirrels, rabbits, foxes, possums, deer, big-horn sheep, and other animals was one of the charms of such a deeply rural life.

Raccoons, perhaps the most adventurous and interesting of all the creatures in the neighborhood, were highly intelligent and rated higher still on any scale of cuteness. However, their intelligence and aggressive scavenging made them a nuisance, and the dexterity of their almost handlike paws facilitated their mischief. In the days when horses had been kept in the stables, before Stanley Quartermass died, raccoons – although primarily carnivores – had been endlessly inventive in the raids they launched on apples and other equestrian supplies. Now, as then, trash cans had to be fitted with raccoon-proof lids, though these masked bandits still made an occasional assault on the containers, as if they'd been in their dens, brooding about the situation for weeks, and had devised a new technique they wanted to try out.

The specimen in the front yard was an adult, sleek and fat, with a shiny coat that was somewhat thinner than the thick fur of winter.

It sat on its hindquarters, forepaws against its chest, head held high, watching Eduardo. Though raccoons were communal and usually roamed in pairs or groups, no others were visible either in the front yard or along the edge of the meadow.

They were also nocturnal. They were rarely seen in the open in broad daylight.

With no horses in the stables and the trash cans well secured, Eduardo had long ago stopped chasing raccoons away – unless they got on to the roof at night. Engaged in raucous play or mouse chasing across the top of the house, they could make sleeping impossible.

He moved to the head of the porch steps, taking advantage of this uncommon opportunity to study one of the critters in bright sunlight at such close range.

The raccoon moved its head to follow him.

Nature had cursed the rascals with exceptionally beautiful fur, doing them the tragic disservice of making them valuable to the human species, which was ceaselessly engaged in a narcissistic search for materials with which to bedeck and ornament itself. This one had a particularly bushy tail, ringed with black, glossy and glorious.

'What're you doing out and about on a sunny afternoon?' Eduardo asked.

The animal's anthracite-black eyes regarded him with almost palpable curiosity.

'Must be having an identity crisis, think you're a squirrel or something.'

With a flurry of paws, the raccoon busily combed its facial fur for maybe half a minute, then froze again and regarded Eduardo intently.

Wild animals – even species as aggressive as raccoons – seldom made such direct eye contact as this fellow. They usually tracked people furtively, with peripheral vision or quick glances. Some said this reluctance to meet a direct gaze for more than a few seconds was an acknowledgment of human superiority, the animal's way of humbling itself as a commoner might do before a king, while others said it indicated that animals – innocent creatures of God – saw in men's eyes the stain of sin and were ashamed for humanity. Eduardo had his own theory: animals recognized that people were the most vicious and unrelenting beasts of all, violent and unpredictable, and avoided direct eye contact out of fear and prudence.

Except for this raccoon. It seemed to have no fear whatsoever, to feel no humility in the presence of a human being.

'At least not this particular sorry old human being, huh?'

The raccoon just watched him.

Finally the coon was less compelling than his thirst, and Eduardo went inside to get another beer. The hinge springs sang when he pulled open the screen door – which he'd hung for the season only two weeks ago – and again when he eased it shut behind him.

He expected the strange sound to startle the coon and send it scurrying away, but when he looked back through the screen, he saw the critter had come a couple of feet closer to the porch steps and more directly in line with the door, keeping him in sight.

'Funny little bugger,' he said.

He walked to the kitchen at the end of the hall and, first thing, looked at the clock above the double ovens because he wasn't wearing a watch. Twenty past three.

He had a pleasing buzz on, and he was in the mood to sustain it all the way to bedtime. However, he didn't want to get downright sloppy. He decided to have dinner an hour early, at six instead of seven, get some food on his stomach. He might take a book to bed and turn in early as well.

This waiting for something to happen was getting on his nerves.

He took another Corona from the refrigerator. It had a twist-off cap, but he had a touch of arthritis in his hands. The bottle opener was on the cutting board by the sink.

As he popped the cap off the bottle, he happened to glance out the window above the sink – and saw the raccoon in the backyard. It was twelve or fourteen feet from the rear porch. Sitting on its hindquarters, forepaws against its chest, head held high. Because the yard rose toward the western woods, the coon was in a position to look over the porch railing, directly at the kitchen window.

It was watching him.

Eduardo went to the back door, unlocked and opened it.

The raccoon moved from its previous position to another from which it could continue to study him.

He pushed open the screen door, which made the same screaky sound as the one at the front of the house. He went on to the porch, hesitated, then descended the three back steps to the yard.

The animal's dark eyes glittered.

When Eduardo closed half the distance between them, the raccoon dropped to all fours, turned, and scampered twenty feet farther up the slope. There it stopped, turned to face him again, sat erect on its hindquarters, and regarded him as before.

Until then he had thought it was the same raccoon that had been watching him from the front yard. Suddenly he wondered if, in fact, it was a different beast altogether.

He walked quickly around the north side of the house, cutting a wide enough berth to keep the raccoon at the back in sight. He came to a point, well to the north of the house, from which he could see the front and back yards – and two ring-tailed sentinels.

They were both staring at him.

He proceeded toward the raccoon in front of the house.

When he drew close, the coon put its tail to him and ran across the front yard. At what it evidently regarded as a safe distance, it stopped and sat watching him with its back against the higher, unmown grass of the meadow.

'I'll be damned,' he said.

He returned to the front porch and sat in the rocker.

The waiting was over. After more than five weeks, things were beginning to happen.

Eventually he realized he'd left his open beer by the kitchen sink. He went inside to retrieve it because, now more than ever, he needed it.

He had left the back door standing open, though the screen door had closed behind him when he'd gone outside. He locked up, got his beer, stood at the window watching the backyard raccoon for a moment, and then returned to the front porch.

The first raccoon had crept forward from the edge of the meadow and was again only ten feet from the porch.

Eduardo picked up the video camera and recorded the critter for a couple of minutes. It wasn't anything amazing enough to convince skeptics that a doorway from beyond had opened in the early morning hours of 3 May; however, it was peculiar for a nocturnal animal to pose so long in broad daylight, making such obviously direct eye contact with the operator of the camcorder, and it might prove to be the first small fragment in a mosaic of evidence.

After he finished with the camera, he sat in the rocker, sipping beer and watching the raccoon as it watched him, waiting to see what would happen next. Occasionally the ring-tailed sentinel smoothed its whiskers, combed its face fur, scratched behind its ears, or performed some other small act of grooming. Otherwise, there were no new developments.

At five-thirty he went inside to make dinner, taking his empty beer bottle, camcorder, and shotgun with him. He closed and locked the front door.

Through the oval, beveled-glass window, he saw the coon still on duty.

*

At the kitchen table, Eduardo enjoyed an early dinner of rigatoni and spicy sausage with thick slabs of heavily buttered Italian bread. He kept the yellow legal-size tablet beside his plate and, while he ate, wrote about the intriguing events of the afternoon.

He had almost brought the account up to date when a peculiar clicking noise distracted him. He glanced at the electric stove, then at each of the two windows to see if something was tapping on the glass.

When he turned in his chair, he saw that a raccoon was in the kitchen behind him. Sitting on its hindquarters. Staring at him.

He shoved his chair back from the table and got quickly to his feet.

Evidently the animal had entered the room from the hallway. How it had gotten inside the house in the first place, however, was a mystery.

The clicking he'd heard had been its claws on the pegged-oak floor. They rattled against the wood again, though it didn't move.

Eduardo realized it was wracked by severe shivers. At first he thought it was frightened of being in the house, feeling threatened and cornered.

He backed away a couple of steps, giving it space.

The raccoon made a thin mewling sound that was neither a threat nor an expression of fear, but the unmistakable voice of misery. It was in pain, injured or ill.

His first reaction was, *Rabies*.

The .22 pistol lay on the table, as he always kept a weapon close at hand these days. He picked it up, though he did not want to have to kill the raccoon in the house.

He saw now that the creature's eyes were protruding unnaturally and that the fur under them was wet and matted with tears. The small paws clawed at the air, and the black-ringed tail swished back and forth furiously across the oak floor. Gagging, the coon dropped off its haunches, flopped on its side. It twitched convulsively, sides heaving as it struggled to breathe. Abruptly blood bubbled from its nostrils and trickled from its ears. After one final spasm that rattled its claws against the floor again, it lay still, silent.

Dead.

'Dear Jesus,' Eduardo said, and put one trembling hand to his brow to blot away the sudden dew of perspiration that had sprung up along his hairline.

The dead raccoon didn't seem as large as either of the sentinels he'd seen outside, and he didn't think that it looked smaller merely because death had diminished it. He was pretty sure it was a third individual, perhaps younger than the other two; or maybe they were males, and this was a female.

He remembered leaving the kitchen door open when he'd walked around the house to see if the front and back sentries were the same animal. The screen door had been closed. But it was light, just a narrow pine frame and screen. The raccoon might have been able to pry it open wide enough to insinuate its snout, its head, then its body, sneaking into the house before he'd returned to close the inner door.

Where had it hidden in the house when he'd been passing the late afternoon in the rocking chair? What had it been up to while he was cooking dinner?

He went to the window at the sink. Because he had eaten early and because the summer sunset was late, twilight had not yet arrived, so he could clearly see the masked observer. It was in the backyard, sitting on its hindquarters, dutifully watching the house.

Stepping carefully around the pitiful creature on the floor, Eduardo went down the hall, unlocked the front door, and stepped outside to see if the other sentry was still in place. It was not in the front yard, where he'd left it, but on the porch, a few feet from the door. It was lying on its side, blood pooled in the one ear that he could see, blood at its nostrils, eyes wide and glazed.

Eduardo raised his attention from the coon to the lower woods at the bottom of the meadow. The declining sun, balanced on the peaks of the mountains in the west, threw slanting orange beams between the trunks of those trees but was incapable of dispelling the stubborn shadows.

By the time he returned to the kitchen and looked out the window

126

again, the backyard coon was running frantically in circles. When he went out on to the porch, he could hear it squealing in pain. Within seconds it fell, tumbled. It lay with its sides heaving for a moment, and then it was motionless.

He looked uphill, past the dead raccoon on the grass, to the woods that flanked the fieldstone house where he had lived when he'd been the caretaker. The darkness among those trees was deeper than in the lower forest because the westering sun illuminated only their highest boughs as it slid slowly behind the Rockies.

Something was in the woods.

Eduardo didn't think the raccoons' strange behavior resulted from rabies or, in fact, from an illness of any kind. Something was . . . controlling them. Maybe the means by which that control was exerted had proved so physically taxing to the animals that it had resulted in their sudden, spasmodic deaths.

Or maybe the entity in the woods had purposefully killed them to exhibit the extent of its control, to impress Eduardo with its power, and to suggest that it might be able to waste him as easily as it had destroyed the raccoons.

He felt he was being watched – and not just through the eyes of other raccoons.

The bare peaks of the highest mountains loomed like a tidal wave of granite. The orange sun slowly submerged into that sea of stone.

A steadily inkier darkness rose under the evergreen boughs, but Eduardo didn't think that even the blackest condition in nature could match the darkness in the heart of the watcher in the woods – if, in fact, it had a heart at all.

*

Although he was convinced that disease had not played a role in the behavior and death of the raccoons, Eduardo could not be certain of his diagnosis, so he took precautions when handling the bodies.

He tied a bandanna over his nose and mouth, and wore a pair of rubber gloves. He didn't handle the carcasses directly but lifted each with a short-handled shovel and slipped it into its own large plastic trash bag. He twisted the top of each bag, tied a knot in it, and put it in the cargo area of the Cherokee station wagon in the garage. After hosing off the small smears of blood on the front porch, he used several cotton cloths to scrub the kitchen floor with pure Lysol. Finally he threw the cleaning rags into a bucket, stripped off the gloves and dropped them on top of the rags, and set the bucket on the back porch to be dealt with later.

He also put a loaded 12-gauge shotgun and the .22 pistol in the Cherokee. He took the video camera with him, because he didn't know when he might need it. Besides, the tape currently in the camera contained the footage of the raccoons, and he didn't want that to disappear as had the tape he'd taken of the luminous woods and the black doorway. For the same reason, he took the yellow tablet that was half filled with his handwritten account of these recent events.

By the time he was ready to drive into Eagle's Roost, the long twilight had surrendered to night. He didn't relish returning to a dark house, though he had never been skittish about that before. He turned on lights in the kitchen and the downstairs hall. After further thought, he switched on lamps in the living room and study.

He locked up, backed the Cherokee out of the garage – and thought too much of the house remained dark. He went back inside to turn on a couple of upstairs lights. By the time he returned to the Cherokee and headed down the half-mile driveway toward the county road to the south, every window on both floors of the house glowed.

The Montana vastness appeared to be emptier than ever before. Mile after mile, up into the black hills on one hand and across the timeless plains on the other, the few tiny clusters of lights that he saw were always in the distance. They seemed adrift on a sea, as if they were the lights of ships moving inexorably away toward one horizon or another.

Though the moon had not yet risen, he didn't think its glimmer would have made the night seem any less enormous or more welcoming. The sense of isolation that troubled him had more to do with his interior landscape than with the Montana countryside.

He was a widower, childless, and most likely in the last decade of his life, separated from so many of his fellow men and women by age, fate, and inclination. He had never needed anyone but Margarite and Tommy. After losing them, he had been resigned to living out his years in an almost monkish existence – and had been confident that he could do so without succumbing to boredom or despair. Until recently he'd gotten along well enough. Now, however, he wished that he had reached out to make friends, at least one, and had not so single-mindedly obeyed his hermit heart.

Mile by lonely mile, he waited for the distinctive rustle of plastic in the cargo space behind the back seat.

He was certain the raccoons were dead. He didn't understand why he should expect them to revive and tear their way out of the bags, but he did.

Worse, he knew that if he heard them ripping at the plastic, sharp little claws busily slicing, they would not be the raccoons he had shoveled into the bags, not exactly, maybe not much like them at all, but *changed*.

'Foolish old coot,' he said, trying to shame himself out of such morbid and peculiar contemplations.

Eight miles after leaving his driveway, he finally encountered other traffic on the county route. Thereafter, the closer he drew to Eagle's Roost, the busier the two-lane blacktop became, though no one would ever have mistaken it for the approach road to New York City – or even Missoula.

He had to drive through town to the far side, where Dr Lester Yeats maintained his professional offices and his home on the same five-acre property where Eagle's Roost again met rural fields. Yeats was a veterinarian who, for years, had cared for Stanley Quartermass's horses – a white-haired, white-bearded, jolly man who would have made a good Santa Claus if he'd been heavy instead of whip-thin.

The house was a rambling gray clapboard structure with blue shutters and a slate roof. Because there were also lights on in the one-story barnlike building that housed Yeats's offices and in the adjacent stables where four-legged patients were kept, he drove a few hundred feet past the house to the end of the graveled lane.

As Eduardo was getting out of the Cherokee, the front door of the office barn opened, and a man came out in a wash of fluorescent light, leaving the door ajar behind him. He was tall, in his early thirties, rugged-looking, with thick brown hair. He had a broad and easy smile. 'Howdy, what can I do for you?'

'Lookin' for Lester Yeats,' Eduardo said.

'Doctor Yeats?' The smile faded. 'You an old friend or something?'

'Business,' Eduardo said. 'Got some animals I'd like him to take a look at.'

Clearly puzzled, the stranger said, 'Well, sir, I'm afraid Les Yeats isn't doing business any more.'

'Oh? He retire?'

'Died,' the young man said.

'He did? Doctor Yeats?'

'More than six years ago.'

That startled Eduardo. 'Sorry to hear it.' He hadn't quite realized so much time had passed since he'd last seen Yeats.

A warm breeze sprang up, stirring the larches that were grouped at various points around the buildings.

The stranger said, 'My name's Travis Potter. I bought the house and practice from Mrs Yeats. She moved to a smaller place in town.'

They shook hands, and instead of identifying himself, Eduardo said, 'Doctor Yeats took care of our horses out at the ranch.'

'What ranch would that be?'

'Quartermass Ranch.'

'Ah,' Travis Potter said, 'then you must be the . . . Mr Fernandez, is it?'

'Oh, sorry, yeah, Ed Fernandez,' he replied, and had the uneasy feeling that the vet had been about to say *the one they talk about* or something of the sort, as if he was a local eccentric.

He supposed that might, in fact, be the case. Inheriting his spread from his rich employer, living alone, a recluse with seldom a word for anyone even when he ventured into town on errands, he might have become a minor enigma about whom townspeople were curious. The thought of it made him cringe.

'How many years since you've had horses?' Potter asked.

'Eight. Since Mr Quartermass died.'

He realized how odd it was – not having spoken with Yeats in eight years, then showing up six years after he died, as if only a week had gone by.

They stood in silence a moment. The June night around them was filled with cricket songs.

'Well,' Potter said, 'where are these animals?'

'Animals?'

'You said you had some animals for Doctor Yeats to look at.'

'Oh. Yeah.'

'He was a good vet, but I assure you I'm his equal.'

'I'm sure you are, Doctor Potter. But these are dead animals.'

'Dead animals?'

'Raccoons.'

'Dead raccoons?'

'Three of them.'

'Three dead raccoons?'

Eduardo realized that, if he *did* have a reputation as a local eccentric, he was only adding to it now. He was so out of practice at conversation that he couldn't get to the point.

He took a deep breath and said what was necessary without going

131

into the story of the doorway and other oddities: 'They were acting funny, out in broad daylight, running in circles. Then one by one they dropped over.' He succinctly described their death throes, the blood in their nostrils and ears. 'What I wondered was – could they be rabid?'

'You're up against those foothills,' Potter said. 'There's always a little rabies working its way through the wild populations. That's natural. But we haven't seen evidence of it around here for a while. Blood in the ears? Not a rabies symptom. Were they foaming at the mouth?'

'Not that I saw.'

'Running in a straight line?'

'Circles.'

A pickup truck drove by on the highway, country music so loud on its radio that the tune carried all the way to the back of Potter's property. Loud or not, it was a mournful song.

'Where are they?' Potter asked.

'Got them bagged in plastic in the Cherokee here.'

'You get bitten?'

'No,' Eduardo said.

'Scratched?'

'No.'

'Any contact with them whatsoever?'

Eduardo explained about the precautions he'd taken: the shovel, bandanna, rubber gloves.

Cocking his head, looking puzzled, Travis Potter said, 'You telling me everything?'

'Well, I think so,' he lied. 'I mean, their behavior was pretty strange, but I've told you everything important, no other symptoms I noticed.'

Potter's gaze was forthright and penetrating, and for a moment Eduardo considered opening up and revealing the whole bizarre story.

Instead, he said, 'If it isn't rabies, does it sound like maybe it could be plague?'

132

Potter frowned. 'Doubtful. Bleeding from the ears? That's an uncommon symptom. You get any flea bites being around them?'

'I'm not itchy.'

The warm breeze pumped itself into a gust of wind, rattling the larches and startling a night bird out of the branches. It flew low over their heads with a shriek that startled them.

Potter said, 'Well, why don't you leave these raccoons with me, and I'll have a look.'

They removed the three green plastic bags from the Cherokee and carried them inside. The waiting room was deserted; Potter had evidently been doing paper work in his office. They went through a door and down a short hallway to the white-tiled surgery, where they put the bags on the floor beside a stainless-steel examination table.

The room felt cool and looked cold. Harsh white light fell on the enamel, steel, and glass surfaces. Everything gleamed like snow and ice.

'What'll you do with them?' Eduardo asked.

'I don't have the means to test for rabies here. I'll take tissue samples, send them up to the state lab, and we'll have the results in a few days.'

'That's all?'

'What do you mean?'

Poking one of the bags with the toe of his boot, Eduardo said, 'You going to dissect one of them?'

'I'll store them in one of my cold lockers and wait for the state lab's report. If they're negative for rabies then, yeah, I'll perform an autopsy on one of them.'

'Let me know what you find?'

Potter gave him that penetrating stare again. 'You *sure* you weren't bitten or scratched? Because if you were, and if there's any reason at all to suspect rabies, you should get to a doctor now and start the vaccine right away, tonight—'

'I'm no fool,' Eduardo said. 'I'd tell you if there was any chance I'd been infected.'

Potter continued to stare at him.

Looking around the surgery, Eduardo said, 'You really modernized the place from the way it was.'

'Come on,' the veterinarian said, turning to the door, 'I have something I want to give you.'

Eduardo followed him into the hall and through another door into Potter's private office. The vet rummaged in the drawers of a white, enameled-metal storage cabinet and handed him a couple of pamphlets – one on rabies, one on bubonic plague.

'Read up on the symptoms for both,' Potter said. 'You notice anything similar in yourself, even *similar*, get to your doctor.'

'Don't like doctors much.'

'That's not the point. You *have* a doctor?'

'Never need one.'

'Then you call me, and I'll get a doctor to you, one way or the other. Understand?'

'All right.'

'You'll do it?'

'Sure will.'

Potter said, 'You have a telephone out there?'

'Of course. Who doesn't have a phone these days?'

The question seemed to confirm that he had an image as a hermit and an eccentric. Which maybe he deserved. Because now that he thought about it, he hadn't used the phone to receive or place a call in at least five or six months. He doubted if it'd rung more than three times in the past year, and one of those was a wrong number.

Potter went to his desk, picked up a pen, pulled a notepad in front of him, and wrote the number down as Eduardo recited it. He tore off another sheet of notepaper and gave it to Eduardo because it was imprinted with his office address and his own phone numbers.

Eduardo folded the paper into his wallet. 'What do I owe you?'

'Nothing,' Potter said. 'These weren't your pet raccoons, so why should you pay? Rabies is a community problem.'

Potter accompanied him out to the Cherokee.

The larches rustled in the warm breeze, crickets chirruped, and a frog croaked like a dead man trying to talk.

As he opened the driver's door, Eduardo turned to the vet and said, 'When you do that autopsy . . .'

'Yes?'

'Will you look just for signs of known diseases?'

'Disease pathologies, trauma.'

'That's all?'

'What else would I look for?'

Eduardo hesitated, shrugged, and said, 'Anything . . . strange.'

That stare again. 'Well, sir,' Potter said, 'I will now.'

*

All the way home through that dark and forlorn land, Eduardo wondered if he had done the right thing. As far as he could see, there were only two alternatives to the course of action he'd taken, and both were problematic.

He could have disposed of the raccoons on the ranch and waited to see what would happen next. But he might have been destroying important evidence that something not of this earth was hiding in the Montana woods.

Or he could have explained to Travis Potter about the luminous trees, throbbing sounds, waves of pressure, and black doorway. He could have told him about the raccoons keeping him under surveillance – and the sense he'd had that they were serving as surrogate eyes for the unknown watcher in the woods. If he *was* generally regarded as the old hermit of Quartermass Ranch, however, he wouldn't be taken seriously.

Worse, once the veterinarian had spread the story, some busybody

135

public official might get it in his head that poor old Ed Fernandez was senile or even flat-out deranged, a danger to himself and others. With all the compassion in the world, sorrowful-eyed and soft-voiced, shaking their heads sadly and telling themselves they were doing it for his own good, they might commit him against his will for medical examinations and a psychiatric review.

He was loath to be carted away to a hospital, poked and prodded and spoken to as if he had reverted to infancy. He wouldn't react well. He knew himself. He would respond to them with stubbornness and contempt, irritating the do-gooders to such an extent they might induce a court to take charge of his affairs and order him transferred to a nursing home or other facility for the rest of his days.

He had lived a long time and had seen how many lives were ruined by people operating with the best intentions and a smug assurance of their own superiority and wisdom. The destruction of one more old man wouldn't be noticed, and he had no wife or children, no friend or relative, to stand with him against the killing kindness of the state.

Giving the dead animals to Potter to be tested and autopsied was, therefore, as far as Eduardo had dared to go. He only worried that, considering the inhuman nature of the entity that controlled the coons, he might have put Travis Potter at risk in some way he couldn't foresee.

Eduardo *had* hinted at a strangeness, however, and Potter had seemed to have his share of common sense. The vet knew the risks associated with disease. He would take every precaution against contamination, which would probably also be effective against whatever unguessable and unearthly peril the carcasses might pose in addition to microbiotic infection.

Beyond the Cherokee, the home lights of unmet families shone far out on the sea of night. For the first time in his life, Eduardo wished that he knew them, their names and faces, their histories and hopes.

136

He wondered if some child might be sitting on a distant porch or at a window, staring across the rising plains at the headlights of the Cherokee progressing westward through the June darkness. A young boy or girl, full of plans and dreams, might wonder who was in the vehicle behind those lights, where he was bound, and what his life was like.

The thought of such a child out there in the night gave Eduardo the strangest sense of community, an utterly unexpected feeling that he *was* part of a family whether he wanted to be or not, the family of humanity, more often than not a frustrating and contentious clan, flawed and often deeply confused, but also periodically noble and admirable, with a common destiny that every member shared.

For him, that was an unusually optimistic and philosophically generous view of his fellow men and women, uncomfortably close to sentimentality. But he was warmed as well as astonished by it.

He was convinced that whatever had come through the doorway was inimical to humankind, and his brush with it had reminded him that all of nature was, in fact, hostile. It was a cold and uncaring universe, either because God made it that way as a test to determine good souls from bad, or simply because that's the way it was. No man could survive in civilized comfort without the struggles and hard-won successes of all the people who had gone before him and who shared his time on earth with him. If a new evil had entered the world, one to dwarf the evil of which some men and women were capable, humanity would need a sense of community more desperately than ever before in its long and troubled journey.

*

The house came into view when he was a third of the way along the half-mile driveway, and he continued uphill, approaching to within sixty or eighty yards of it before realizing that something was wrong. He braked to a full stop.

137

Prior to leaving for Eagle's Roost, he had turned on lights in every room. He clearly remembered all of the glowing windows as he had driven away. He had been embarrassed by his childlike reluctance to return to a dark house.

Well, it was dark now. As black as the inside of the devil's bowels.

Before he quite realized what he was doing, Eduardo pressed the master lock switch, simultaneously securing all the doors on the station wagon.

He sat for a while, just staring at the house. The front door was closed, and all the windows he could see were unbroken. Nothing appeared out of order.

Except that every light in every room had been turned off. By whom? By what?

He supposed a power failure could have been responsible – but he didn't believe it. Sometimes, a Montana thunderstorm could be a real stemwinder; in the winter, blizzard winds and accumulated ice could play havoc with electrical service. But there had been no bad weather tonight and only the mildest breeze. He hadn't noticed any downed power lines on the way home.

The house waited.

Couldn't sit in the car all night. Couldn't live in it, for God's sake.

He drove slowly along the last stretch of driveway and stopped in front of the garage. He picked up the remote control and pressed the single button.

The automatic garage door rolled up. Inside the three-vehicle space, the overhead convenience lamp, which was on a three-minute timer, shed enough light to reveal that nothing was amiss in the garage.

So much for the power-failure theory.

Instead of pulling forward ten feet and into the garage, he stayed where he was. He put the Cherokee in park but didn't switch off the engine. He left the headlights on too.

He picked up the shotgun from where it was angled muzzle-down in the knee space in front of the passenger seat, and he got out of the station wagon. He left the driver's door wide open.

Door open, lights on, engine running.

He didn't like to think that he would cut and run at the first sign of trouble. But if it was run or die, he was sure as hell going to be faster than anything that might be chasing him.

Although the pump-action 12-gauge shotgun contained only five rounds – one already in the breach and four in the magazine tube – he was unconcerned that he hadn't brought any spare shells. If he was unlucky enough to encounter something that couldn't be brought down with five shots at close range, he wouldn't live long enough to reload anyway.

He went to the front of the house, climbed the porch steps, and tried the front door. It was locked.

His house key was on a bead chain, separate from the car keys. He fished it out of his jeans and unlocked the door.

Standing outside, holding the shotgun in his right hand, he reached cross-body with his left, inside the half-open door, fumbling for the light switch. He expected something to rush at him from out of the coal-dark downstairs hallway – or to put its hand over his as he patted the wall in search of the switch plate.

He flipped the switch, and light filled the hall, spilled over him on to the front porch. He crossed the threshold and took a couple of steps inside, leaving the door open behind him.

The house was quiet.

Dark rooms on both sides of the hallway. Study to his left. Living room to his right.

He hated to turn his back on either room, but finally he moved to the right, through the archway, the shotgun held in front of him. When he turned on the overhead light, the expansive living room proved to be deserted. No intruder. Nothing out of the ordinary.

Then he noticed a dark clump lying on the white fringe at the edge of the Chinese carpet. At first glance he thought it was feces, that an animal had gotten in the house and done its business right there. But when he stood over it and looked closer, he saw it was only a caked wad of damp earth. A couple of blades of grass bristled from it.

Back in the hallway he noticed, for the first time, smaller crumbs of dirt littering the polished oak floor.

He ventured cautiously into the study, where there was no ceiling fixture. The influx of light from the hallway dispelled enough shadows to allow him to find and click on the desk lamp.

Crumbs and smears of dirt, now dry, soiled the blotter on the desk. More of it on the red-leather seat of the chair.

'What the hell?' he wondered softly.

Warily he rolled aside the mirrored doors on the study closet, but no one was hiding in there.

In the hall he checked the foyer closet too. Nobody.

The front door was still standing open. He couldn't decide what to do about it. He liked it open because it offered an unobstructed exit if he wanted to get out fast. On the other hand, if he searched the house top to bottom and found no one in it, he would have to come back, lock the door, and search every room again to guard against the possibility that someone had slipped in behind his back. Reluctantly he closed it and engaged the deadbolt.

The beige wall-to-wall carpet that was used through the upstairs also extended down the inlaid-oak staircase, with its heavy handrail. In the center of a few of the lower treads were crumbled chunks of dry earth, not much, just enough to catch his eye.

He peered up at the second floor.

No. First, the downstairs.

He found nothing in the powder bath, in the closet under the stairs, in the large dining room, in the laundry room, or in the service bath. But there was dirt again in the kitchen, more than elsewhere.

His unfinished dinner of rigatoni, sausage, and butter bread was on the table, for he'd been interrupted in mid-meal by the intrusion of the raccoon – and by its death spasms. Smudges of now dry mud marked the rim of his dinner plate. The table around the plate was littered with pea-size lumps of dry earth, a spade-shaped brown leaf curled into a miniature scroll, and a dead beetle the size of a penny.

The beetle was on its back, six stiff legs in the air. When he flicked it over with one finger, he saw that its shell was iridescent blue-green.

Two flattened wads of dirt, like dollar pancakes, were stuck to the seat of the chair. On the oak floor around the chair was more detritus.

Another concentration of soil lay in front of the refrigerator. Altogether, it amounted to a couple of tablespoons worth, but there were also a few blades of grass, another dead leaf, and an earthworm. The worm was still alive but curled up on itself, suffering from a lack of moisture.

A crawling sensation along the nape of his neck and a sudden conviction that he was being watched made him clutch the shotgun with both hands and spin toward one window, then the other. No pale, ghastly face was pressed to either pane of glass, as he had imagined.

Only the night.

The chrome handle on the refrigerator was dulled by filth, and he did not touch it. He opened the door by gripping the edge. The food and beverages inside seemed untouched, everything just as he'd left it.

The doors of both double ovens were hanging open. He closed them without touching the handles, which were also smeared in places with unidentifiable crud.

Caught on a sharp edge of the oven door was a torn scrap of fabric, half an inch wide and less than an inch long. It was pale blue with a fragmentary curve of darker blue that might have been a portion of a repeating pattern against the lighter background.

Eduardo stared at the fragment of cloth for a personal eternity.

Time seemed to stop, and the universe hung as still as the pendulum of a broken grandfather clock – until icy spicules of profound fear formed in his blood and made him shudder so violently that his teeth actually chattered. *The graveyard* . . . He whipped around again, toward one window, the other, but nothing was there.

Only the night. The night. The blind, featureless, uncaring face of the night.

He searched the upstairs. Telltale chunks, crumbs, and smears of earth – once moist, now dry – could be found in most rooms. Another leaf. Two more dead beetles as dry as ancient papyrus. A pebble the size of a cherry pit, smooth and gray.

He realized that some of the switch plates and light switches were soiled. Thereafter, he flicked the lights on with his sleeve-covered arm or the shotgun barrel.

When he had examined every chamber, probed to the back of every closet, inspected behind and under every piece of furniture where a hollow space might conceivably offer concealment even to something as large as a seven- or eight-year-old child, and when he was satisfied that nothing was hiding on the second floor, he returned to the end of the upstairs hall and pulled on the dangling release cord that lowered the attic trapdoor. He pulled down the folding ladder fixed to the back of the trap.

The attic lights could be turned on from the hall, so he didn't have to ascend into darkness. He searched every shadowed niche in the deep and dusty eaves, where snowflake moths hung in webs like laces of ice and feeding spiders loomed as cold and black as winter shadows.

Downstairs in the kitchen again, he slid aside the brass bolt on the cellar door. It worked only from the kitchen. Nothing could have gone down there and re-locked from the far side.

On the other hand, the front and back doors of the house had been bolted when he'd driven into town. No one could have gotten inside – or locked up again upon leaving – without a key, and *he*

142

had the only keys in existence. Yet the damned bolts were engaged when he'd come home; his search had revealed no broken or unlatched window, but an intruder definitely had come and gone.

He went into the cellar and searched the two large, windowless rooms. They were cool, slightly musty, and deserted.

For the moment, the house was secure.

He was the only resident.

He went outside, locking the front entrance after him, and drove the Cherokee into the garage. He put down the door with the remote control before getting out of the wagon.

For the next several hours, he scrubbed and vacuumed the mess in the house with an urgency and unflagging energy that approached a state of frenzy. He used liquid soap, strong ammonia water, and Lysol spray, determined that every soiled surface should be not merely clean but disinfected, as close to sterile as possible outside of a hospital surgery or laboratory. He broke into a sustained sweat that soaked his shirt and pasted his hair to his scalp. The muscles in his neck, shoulders, and arms began to ache from the repetitive scouring motions. The mild arthritis in his hands flared up; his knuckles swelled and reddened from gripping the scrub brushes and rags with almost manic ferocity, but his response was to grip them tighter still, until the pain dizzied him and brought tears to his eyes.

Eduardo knew he was striving not merely to sanitize the house but to cleanse himself of certain terrible ideas that he could not tolerate, would not explore, absolutely *would not*. He made himself into a cleaning machine, an insensate robot, focusing so intently and narrowly on the menial task at hand that he was purged of all unwanted thoughts, breathing deeply of the ammonia fumes as if they could disinfect his mind, seeking to exhaust himself so thoroughly that he would be able to sleep and, perhaps, even forget.

As he cleaned, he disposed of all used paper towels, rags, brushes, and sponges in a large plastic bag. When he was finished, he knotted the top of the bag and deposited it outside in a trash can. Ordinarily, he would have rinsed and saved sponges and brushes for re-use, but not this time.

Instead of removing the disposable paper bag from the vacuum sweeper, he put the entire machine out with the trash. He didn't want to think about the origin of the microscopic particles now trapped in its brushes and stuck to the inside of its plastic suction hose, most of them so tiny that he could never be sure they were expunged unless he disassembled the sweeper to scrub every inch and reachable crevice with bleach, and maybe not even then.

From the refrigerator, he removed all the foods and beverages that might have been touched by . . . the intruder. Anything in plastic wrap or aluminum foil had to go, even if it didn't appear to have been tampered with: Swiss cheese, cheddar, leftover ham, half a Bermuda onion. Resealable containers had to be tossed: a one-pound tub of soft butter with a snap-on plastic lid; jars of dill and sweet pickles, olives, maraschino cherries, mayonnaise, mustard, and more; bottles with screw-top caps – salad dressing, soy sauce, ketchup. An open box of raisins, an open carton of milk. The thought of anything touching his lips which had first been touched by the intruder made him gag and shudder. By the time he finished with the refrigerator, it held little more than unopened cans of soft drinks and bottles of beer.

But, after all, he was dealing with contamination. Couldn't be too careful. No measure was too extreme.

Not merely bacterial contamination, either. If only it was that simple. God, if only. Spiritual contamination. A darkness capable of spreading through the heart, seeping deep into the soul.

Don't even think about it. Don't. *Don't.*

Too tired to think. Too old to think. Too scared.

From the garage he fetched a blue Styrofoam cooler into which he emptied the entire contents of the bin under the automatic ice-maker in the freezer. He wedged eight bottles of beer into the ice and stuck a bottle opener in his hip pocket.

Leaving all the lights on, he carried the cooler and the shotgun upstairs to the back bedroom where he had been sleeping for the past three years. He put the beer and the gun beside the bed.

The bedroom door had only a flimsy privacy latch in the knob, which he engaged by pushing a brass button. All that was needed to break through from the hallway was one good kick, so he tilted a straight-backed chair under the knob and jammed it tightly in place.

Don't think about what might come through the door.

Shut the mind down. Focus on the arthritis, muscle pain, sore neck, let it blot out thought.

He took a shower, washing himself as assiduously as he had scoured the soiled portions of the house. He finished only when he had used the entire supply of hot water.

He dressed but not for bed. Socks, chinos, a T-shirt. He stood his boots beside the bed, next to the shotgun.

Although the nightstand clock and his watch agreed that it was 2:50 in the morning, Eduardo was not sleepy. He sat on the bed, propped against a pile of pillows and the headboard.

Using the remote control, he switched on the television and checked out the seemingly endless array of channels provided by the satellite dish behind the stables. He found an action movie, cops and drug dealers, lots of running and jumping and shooting, fist fights and car chases and explosions. He turned the volume all the way off because he wanted to be able to hear whatever sounds might arise elsewhere in the house.

He drank the first beer fast, staring at the television. He was not trying to follow the plot of the movie, just letting his mind fill with the abstract whirl of motion and the bright ripple-flare of changing colors. Scrubbing at the dark stains of those terrible thoughts. Those stubborn stains.

Something ticked against the west-facing window.

He looked at the draperies, which he had drawn tightly shut.

Another tick. Like a pebble thrown against the glass.

His heart began to pound.

He forced himself to look at the TV again. Motion. Color. He finished the beer. Opened a second.

Tick. And again, almost at once. *Tick.*

Perhaps it was just a moth or a scarab beetle trying to reach the light that the closed drapes couldn't entirely contain.

He could get up, go to the window, discover it was just a flying beetle that was banging against the glass, relieve his mind.

Don't even think about it.

He took a long swallow of the second beer.

Tick.

Something standing on the dark lawn below, looking up at the window. Something that knew exactly where he was, wanted to make contact.

But not a raccoon this time.

Don't, don't, don't.

No cute furry face with a little black mask this time. No beautiful coat and black-ringed tail.

Motion, color, beer. Scrub out the diseased thought, purge the contamination.

Tick.

Because, if he didn't rid himself of the monstrous thought that soiled his mind, he would sooner or later lose his grip on sanity. Sooner.

Tick.

If he went to the window and parted the draperies and looked down at the thing on the lawn, even insanity would be no refuge. Once he had seen, once he *knew*, then there would be only a single way out. Shotgun barrel in his mouth, one toe hooked in the trigger.

Tick.

He turned up the volume control on the television. Loud. Louder. He finished the second beer. Turned the volume up even louder, until the raucous soundtrack of the violent movie seemed to shake the room. Popped the cap off a third beer. Purging his thoughts. Maybe in the morning he would have forgotten the sick, demented considerations that plagued him so persistently tonight, forgotten them or washed them away in tides of alcohol. Or perhaps he would die in his sleep. He almost didn't care which. He poured down a long swallow of the third beer, seeking one form of oblivion or another.

11

THROUGH MARCH, April, and May, as Jack lay cupped in felt-lined plaster with his legs often in traction, he suffered pain, cramps, spastic muscle twitches, uncontrollable nerve tics, and itchy skin where it could not be scratched inside a cast. He endured those discomforts and others with few complaints, and he thanked God that he would live to hold his wife again and see his son grow up.

His health worries were even more numerous than his discomforts. The risk of bedsores was ever-present, though the body cast had been formed with great care and though most of the nurses were concerned, solicitous, and skilled. Once a pressure sore became ulcerated, it was not easily healed, and gangrene could set in quickly. Because he was periodically catheterized, his chances of contracting an infection of the urethra were increased, which could lead to a more serious case of cystitis. Any patient immobilized for long periods was in jeopardy of developing blood clots that could break loose and spin through the body, lodge in the heart or brain, killing him or causing substantial brain damage; though Jack was medicated to reduce the danger of that complication, it was the one that most deeply concerned him.

He worried, as well, about Heather and Toby. They were alone, which troubled him in spite of the fact that Heather, under Alma Bryson's guidance, seemed to be prepared to handle everything from a lone burglar to a foreign invasion. Actually, the thought of all those weapons in the house – and what the need for them said about Heather's state of mind – disturbed him nearly as much as the thought of someone breaking into the place.

Money worried him more than cerebral embolisms. He was on disability and had no idea when he might be able to work again full time. Heather was still unemployed, the economy showed no signs of emerging from the recession, and their savings were virtually exhausted. Friends in the department had opened a trust account for his family at a branch of Wells Fargo Bank, and contributions from policemen and the public at large now totaled more than twenty-five thousand dollars. But medical and rehabilitation expenses were never entirely covered by insurance, and he suspected that even the trust fund would not return them to the modest level of financial security they had enjoyed before the shootout at Arkadian's service station. By September or October, making the mortgage payment might be impossible.

However, he was able to keep all of those worries to himself, partly because he knew that other people had worries of their own and that some of them might be more serious than his, but also because he was an optimist, a believer in the healing power of laughter and positive thinking. Though some of his friends thought his response to adversity was cockeyed, he couldn't help it. As far as he could recall, he had been born that way. Where a pessimist looked at a glass of wine and saw it as half empty, Jack not only saw it as half full but also figured there was the better part of a bottle still to be drunk. He was in a body cast and temporarily disabled, but he felt he was blessed to have escaped permanent disability and death. He was in pain, sure, but there were people in the same hospital in more pain than he was. Until the glass was empty and the bottle as well, he would always anticipate the next sip of wine rather than regret that so little was left.

On his first visit to the hospital back in March, Toby had been frightened to see his father so immobilized, and his eyes had filled with tears even as he bit his lip and kept his chin up and struggled to be brave. Jack had done his best to minimize the seriousness of his condition, insisted he looked in worse shape than he was, and strove with growing desperation to lift his son's spirits. Finally he got the boy to laugh by claiming he wasn't really hurt at all, was in the hospital as a participant in a secret new police program, and would emerge in a few months as a member of their new Teenage Mutant Ninja Turtle Task Force.

'Yeah,' he said, 'it's true. See, that's what all this plaster is, a shell, a turtle shell that's being applied to my back. When it's dry and coated with Kevlar, bullets will just bounce off.'

Smiling in spite of himself, wiping at his eyes with one hand, Toby said, 'Get real, Dad.'

'It's true.'

'You don't know tae kwon do.'

'I'll be taking lessons, soon as the shell's dry.'

'A Ninja has to know how to use swords, too, swords and all kinda stuff.'

'More lessons, that's all.'

'Big problem.'

'What's that?'

'You're not a real turtle.'

'Well, of course, I'm not a real turtle. Don't be silly. The department isn't allowed to hire anything but human beings. People don't much like it when they're given traffic tickets by members of another species. So we have to make do with an *imitation* Teenage Mutant Ninja Turtle Task Force. So what? Is Spider-Man really a spider? Is Batman really a bat?'

'You got a point there.'

'You're damned right I do.'

'But.'

'But what?'

Grinning, the boy said, 'You're no teenager.'

150

'I can pass for one.'

'No way. You're an old guy.'

'Is that so?'

'A real old guy.'

'You're in big trouble when I get out of this bed, mister.'

'Yeah, but until your shell's dry, I'm safe.'

The next time Toby came to the hospital – Heather visited every day, but Toby was limited to once or twice a week – Jack was wearing a colorful headband. Heather had gotten him a red-and-yellow scarf, which he'd folded and tied around his head. The ends of the knot hung rakishly over his right ear.

'Rest of the uniform is still being designed,' he told Toby.

A few weeks later, one day in mid-April, Heather pulled the privacy curtain around Jack's bed and gave him a sponge bath and damp-sponge shampoo to save the nurses a little work. She said, 'I'm not sure I like other women bathing you. I'm getting jealous.'

He said, 'I swear I can explain where I was last night.'

'There's not a nurse in the hospital hasn't gone out of her way to tell me that you're their favorite patient.'

'Well, honey, that's meaningless. *Anybody* can be their favorite patient. It's easy. All you've got to do is avoid puking on them and don't make fun of their little hats.'

'That easy, huh?' she said, sponging his left arm.

'Well, you also have to eat everything on your dinner tray, never hassle them to give you massive injections of heroin without a doctor's prescription, and never ever fake cardiac arrest just to get attention.'

'They say you're so sweet, brave, and funny.'

'Aw, shucks,' he said with exaggerated shyness, but he was genuinely embarrassed.

'A couple of them told me how lucky I am, married to you.'

'You punch them?'

'Managed to control myself.'

'Good. They'd only take it out on me.'

'I *am* lucky,' she said.

'And some of these nurses are strong, they probably pack a pretty hard punch.'

'I love you, Jack,' she said, leaning over the bed and kissing him full on the mouth.

The kiss took his breath away. Her hair fell across his face; it smelled of a lemony shampoo.

'Heather,' he said softly, putting one hand against her cheek, 'Heather, Heather,' repeating the name as if it was sacred, which it was, not only a name but a prayer that sustained him, the name and face that made his nights less dark, that made his pain-filled days pass more quickly.

'I'm so lucky,' she repeated.

'Me too. Finding you.'

'You'll be home with me again.'

'Soon,' he said, though he knew he would be weeks in that bed and weeks more in a rehabilitation hospital.

'No more lonely nights,' she said.

'No more.'

'Always together.'

'Always.' His throat was tight, and he was afraid he was going to cry. He was not ashamed to cry, but he didn't think either of them dared indulge in tears yet. They needed all their strength and resolve for the struggles that still lay ahead. He swallowed hard and whispered, 'When I get home . . .?'

'Yes?'

'And we can go to bed together again?'

Face to face with him, she whispered too: 'Yes?'

'Will you do something special for me?'

'Of course, silly.'

'Would you dress up like a nurse? That really turns me on.'

She blinked in surprise for a moment, burst out laughing, and shoved a cold sponge in his face. 'Beast.'

'Well, then how about a nun?'

'Pervert.'

'A Girl Scout?'

'But a sweet, brave, and funny pervert.'

If he hadn't possessed a good sense of humor, he wouldn't have been able to be a cop. Laughter, sometimes dark laughter, was the shield that made it possible to wade, without being stained, through the filth and madness in which most cops had to function these days.

A sense of humor aided his recovery, too, and made it possible not to be consumed by pain and worry, although there was one thing about which he had difficulty laughing – his helplessness. He was embarrassed about being assisted with his basic bodily functions and subjected to regular enemas to counteract the effects of extreme inactivity. Week after week, the lack of privacy in those matters became more rather than less humiliating.

It was even worse to be trapped in bed, in the rigid grip of the cast, unable to run or walk or even crawl if a sudden catastrophe struck. Periodically he became convinced that the hospital was going to be swept by fire or damaged in an earthquake. Although he knew the staff was well trained in emergency procedures and that he would not be abandoned to the ravages of flames or the mortal weight of collapsing walls, he was occasionally seized by an irrational panic, often in the dead of night, a blind terror that squeezed him tighter and tighter, hour after hour, and that succumbed only gradually to reason or exhaustion.

By the middle of May, he had acquired a deep appreciation and limitless admiration for quadriplegics who did not let life get the best of them. At least he had the use of his hands and arms, and he could exercise by rhythmically squeezing rubber balls and doing curls with light hand weights. He could scratch his nose if it itched, feed himself to some extent, blow his nose. He was in awe of people who suffered permanent below-the-neck paralysis but held fast to their joy in life and faced the future with hope, because he knew he didn't possess their courage or character, no matter whether he was voted favorite patient of the week, month, or century.

If he'd been deprived of his legs *and* hands for three months, he would have been weighed down by despair. And if he hadn't known that he would get out of the bed and be learning to walk again by the time spring became summer, the prospect of long-term helplessness would have broken his sanity.

Beyond the window of his third-floor room, he could see little more than the crown of a tall palm tree. Over the weeks he spent countless hours watching its fronds shiver in mild breezes, toss violently in storm winds, bright green against sunny skies, dull green against somber clouds. Sometimes birds wheeled across that framed section of the heavens, and Jack thrilled to each brief glimpse of their flight.

He swore that, once back on his feet, he would never be helpless again. He was aware of the hubris of such an oath; his ability to fulfill it depended on the whims of fate. Man proposes, God disposes. But on this subject he could not laugh at himself. He would never be helpless again. Never. It was a challenge to God: leave me alone or kill me, but don't put me in this vise again.

*

Jack's division captain, Lyle Crawford, visited him for the third time in the hospital on the evening of 3 June.

Crawford was a nondescript man, of average height and average weight, with close-cropped brown hair, brown eyes and brown skin all of virtually the same shade. He was wearing Hush Puppies, chocolate-brown slacks, tan shirt, and a chocolate-brown jacket, as if his fondest desire was to be *so* nondescript that he would blend into any background and perhaps even attain invisibility. He also wore a brown cap which he took off and held in both hands as he stood by the bed. He was soft-spoken and quick to smile, but he also had more commendations for bravery than any two other cops in the entire department, and he was the best natural-born leader of men that Jack had ever encountered.

'How you doing?' Crawford asked.

'My serve has improved, but my backhand's still lousy,' Jack said.

'Don't choke the racket.'

'You think that's my problem?'

'That and not being able to stand up.'

Jack laughed. 'How're things in the division, Captain?'

'The fun never stops. Two guys walk into a jewelry store on Westwood Boulevard this morning, right after opening, silencers on their guns, shoot the owner and two employees, kill 'em deader than old King Tut before anyone can set off an alarm. No one outside hears a thing. Cases full of jewelry, big safe's open in the back room, full of estate pieces, millions worth. Looks like a cake-walk from there on. Then the two perps start to argue about what to take first and whether they have time to take everything. One of them makes a comment about the other one's old lady, and the next thing you know, they shoot each other.'

'Jesus.'

'So a little time passes, and a customer walks in on this. Four dead people plus a half-conscious perp sprawled on the floor wounded so bad he can't even crawl out of the place and try to get away. The customer stands there, shocked by the blood, which is splattered all to hell over. He's just paralyzed by the sight of this mess. The wounded perp waits for the customer to do something, and when the guy just stands there, gaping, frozen, the perp says, "For the love of God, mister, call an ambulance!"'

'"For the love of God",' Jack said.

'"For the love of God". When the paramedics show up, first thing he asks them for is a Bible.'

Jack rolled his head back and forth on the pillow in disbelief. 'Nice to know not all the scum out there are godless scum, isn't it?'

'Warms my heart,' Crawford said.

At the moment Jack was the only patient in the room. His most recent roommate, a fifty-year-old estate-planning specialist, in residence for three days, had died yesterday of complications from routine gall-bladder surgery.

Crawford sat on the edge of the vacant bed. 'I got some good news for you.'

'I can use it.'

'Internal Affairs submitted its final report on the shootings, and you're cleared across the board. Better yet, both the Chief and the Commission are going to accept it as definitive.'

'Why don't I feel like dancing?'

'We both know the whole demand for a special investigation was bullshit. But we also both know . . . once they open that door they don't always close it again without slamming it on some poor innocent bastard's fingers. So we'll count our blessings.'

'They clear Luther too?'

'Yes, of course.'

'All right.'

Crawford said, 'I put your name in for a commendation – Luther, too, posthumously. Both are going to be approved.'

'Thank you, Captain.'

'Deserved.'

'I don't give a damn about the dickheads on the Commission, and the Chief can take a hike to Hell, too, for all I care. But it means something to me because it was you put in our names.'

Lowering his gaze to his brown cap, which he turned around and around in his brown hands, Crawford said, 'I appreciate that.'

They were both silent a while.

Jack was remembering Luther. He figured Crawford was too.

Finally Crawford looked up from his cap and said, 'Now for the bad news.'

'Always has to be some.'

'Not actively bad, just irritating. You hear about the Anson Oliver movie?'

'Which one? There were three.'

'So you haven't heard. His parents and his pregnant fiancée made a deal with Warner Brothers.'

'Deal?'

'Sold the rights to Anson Oliver's life story for one million dollars?'

Jack was speechless.

Crawford said, 'The way they tell it, they made the deal for two reasons. First, they want to provide for Oliver's unborn son, make sure the kid's future is secure.'

'What about my kid's future?' Jack asked angrily.

Crawford cocked his head. 'You really pissed?'

'Yes!'

'Hell, Jack, since when did our kids ever matter to people like them?'

'Since never.'

'Exactly. You and me and our kids, we're here to applaud them when they do something artistic or high-minded – and clean up after them when they make a mess.'

'It isn't fair,' Jack said. He laughed at his own words, as if any experienced cop could still expect life to be fair, virtue to be rewarded, and villainy to be punished. 'Ah, hell.'

'You can't hate them for that. It's just the way they are, the way they think. They'll never change. Might as well hate lightning, hate ice being cold and fire being hot.'

Jack sighed, still angry but only smouldering. 'You said they had two reasons for making the deal. What's number two?'

'To make a movie that will be "a monument to the genius of

Anson Oliver,"' Crawford said. 'That's how the father put it. "A monument to the genius of Anson Oliver."'

'For the love of God.'

Crawford laughed softly. 'Yeah, for the love of God. And the fiancée, mother of the heir-to-be, she says this movie's going to put Anson Oliver's controversial career and his death in historical perspective.'

'*What* historical perspective? He made movies, he wasn't the leader of the Western world, he just made movies.'

Crawford shrugged. 'Well, by the time they're done building him up, I suspect he'll have been an anti-drug crusader, a tireless advocate for the homeless—'

Jack picked it up: 'A devout Christian who once considered dedicating his life to missionary work—'

'—until Mother Teresa told him to make movies instead—'

'—and because of his effective efforts on behalf of justice, he was killed by a conspiracy involving the CIA, the FBI—'

'—the British royal family, the International Brotherhood of Boilermakers and Pipe Fitters—'

'—the late Joseph Stalin—'

'—Kermit the Frog—'

'—and a cabal of pill-popping rabbis in New Jersey,' Jack finished.

They laughed because the situation was too ridiculous to respond with anything *but* laughter – and because, if they didn't laugh at it, they were admitting the power of these people to hurt them.

'They better not put me in this damn movie of theirs,' Jack said after his laughter had devolved into a fit of coughing. 'I'll sue their asses.'

'They'll change your name, make you an Asian cop named Wong, ten years older and six inches shorter, married to a redhead named Bertha, and you won't be able to sue for spit.'

'People are still gonna know it was me in real life.'

'Real life? What's that? This is Lala Land.'

'Jesus, how can they make a *hero* out of this guy?'

Crawford said, 'They made heroes out of Bonnie and Clyde.'

'Anti-heroes.'

'Okay, then, Butch Cassidy and the Sundance Kid.'

'Still.'

'They made heroes out of Jimmy Hoffa and Bugsy Siegel. Anson Oliver's a snap.'

That night, long after Lyle Crawford had gone, when Jack tried to ignore his thousand discomforts and get some sleep, he couldn't stop thinking about the movie, the million dollars, the harassment Toby had taken at school, the vile graffiti with which their house had been covered, the inadequacy of their savings, his disability checks, Luther in the grave, Alma alone with her arsenal, and Anson Oliver portrayed on-screen by some young actor with chiseled features and melancholy eyes, radiating an aura of saintly compassion and noble purpose exceeded only by his sex appeal.

Jack was overwhelmed by a sense of helplessness far worse than anything he had felt before. The cause of it was only partly the claustrophobic confinement of the body cast and the bed. It arose, as well, from the fact that he was tied to this City of Angels by a house that had declined in value and was currently hard to sell in a recessionary market, from the fact that he was a good cop in an age when the heroes were gangsters, and from the fact that he was unable to imagine either earning a living or finding meaning in life as anything *but* a cop. He was as trapped as a rat in a giant laboratory maze. Unlike the rat, he didn't even have the illusion of freedom.

*

On 6 June the body cast came off. The spinal fracture was entirely healed. He had full feeling in both legs. Undoubtedly he would learn to walk again.

Initially, however, he couldn't stand without the assistance of either two nurses or one nurse and a wheeled walker. His thighs had withered. Though his calf muscles had received some passive exercise, they were atrophied to a degree. For the first time in his life, he was soft and flabby in the middle, which was the only place he'd gained weight.

A single trip around the room, assisted by nurses and a walker, broke him out in a sweat and made his stomach muscles flutter as if he had attempted to bench-press five hundred pounds. Nevertheless, it was a day of celebration. Life went on. He felt reborn.

He paused by the window that framed the crown of the tall palm tree and, as if by the grace of an aware and benign universe, a trio of sea gulls appeared in the sky, having strayed inland from the Santa Monica shoreline. They hovered on rising thermals for half a minute or so, like three white kites. Suddenly the birds wheeled across the blue in an aerial ballet of freedom and disappeared to the west. Jack watched them until they were gone, his vision blurring, and he turned away from the window without once lowering his gaze to the city beyond and below him.

Heather and Toby visited that evening and brought Baskin & Robbins peanut-butter-and-chocolate ice cream. In spite of the flab around his waist, Jack ate his share.

That night he dreamed of sea gulls. Three. With gloriously wide wingspans. As white and luminous as angels. They flew steadily westward, soaring and diving, spiraling and looping spiritedly, but always westward, and he ran through fields below, trying to keep pace with them. He was a boy again, spreading his arms as if they were wings, zooming up hills, down grassy slopes, wild flowers lashing his legs, easily imagining himself taking to the air at any moment, free of the bonds of gravity, high in the company of the gulls. Then the fields ended when he was gazing up at the gulls, and he found himself pumping his legs in thin air, over the edge of a bluff, with pointed and bladed rocks a few hundred feet below, powerful waves exploding among them, white spray cast high into the air, and he was falling, falling. He knew, then, that it was only a dream, but he couldn't wake up when he tried. Falling and falling, always closer to death but never quite there, falling and falling toward the jagged black maw of the rocks, toward the cold deep gullet of the hungry sea, falling, falling . . .

*

After four days of increasingly arduous therapy at Westside General, Jack was transferred to Phoenix Rehabilitation Hospital on 11 June. Although the spinal fracture had healed, he had sustained some nerve damage. Nevertheless, his prognosis was excellent.

His room might have been in a motel. Carpet instead of a vinyl-tile floor, green-and-white-striped wallpaper, nicely framed prints of bucolic landscapes, garishly patterned but cheerful drapes at the window. The two hospital beds, however, belied the Holiday Inn image.

The physical therapy room, where he was taken in a wheelchair for the first time at six-thirty in the morning, 12 June, was well-equipped with exercise machines. It smelled more like a hospital than like a gym, which wasn't bad. And, perhaps because he had at least an idea of what lay ahead of him, he thought the place looked less like a gym than like a torture chamber.

His physical therapist, Moshe Bloom, was in his late twenties, six feet four, with a body so pumped and well carved that he looked as if he was in training to go one-on-one with an army tank. He had curly black hair, brown eyes flecked with gold, and a dark complexion enhanced by the California sun to a lustrous bronze shade. In white sneakers, white cotton slacks, white T-shirt, and skullcap, he was like a radiant apparition, floating a fraction of an inch above the floor, come to deliver a message from God, which turned out to be, 'No pain, no gain.'

'Doesn't sound like advice the way you say it,' Jack told him.

'Oh?'

'Sounds like a threat.'

'You'll cry like a baby after the first several sessions.'

'If that's what you want, I can cry like a baby right now, and we can both go home.'

'You'll fear the pain to start with.'

'I've had some therapy at Westside General.'

'That was just a game of patty-cake. Nothing like the hell I'm going to put you through.'

'You're so comforting.'

Bloom shrugged his immense shoulders. 'You've got to have no illusions about any easy rehabilitation.'

'I'm the original illusionless man.'

'Good. You'll fear the pain at first, dread it, cower from it, beg to be sent home half crippled rather than finish the program—'

'Gee, I can hardly wait to start.'

'—but I'll teach you to hate the pain instead of fear it—'

'Maybe I should just go to some UCLA extension classes, learn Spanish instead.'

'—and then I'll teach you to *love* the pain because it's a sure sign that you're making progress.'

'You need a refresher course in how to inspire your patients.'

'You've got to inspire yourself, McGarvey. My main job is to challenge you.'

'Call me Jack.'

The therapist shook his head. 'No. To start, I'll call you McGarvey, you call me Bloom. This relationship is always adversarial at first. You'll *need* to hate me, to have a focus for your anger. When that time comes, it'll be easier to hate me if we aren't using first names.'

'I hate you already.'

Bloom smiled. 'You'll do all right, McGarvey.'

12

AFTER THE night of 10 June, Eduardo lived in denial. For the first time in his life, he was unwilling to face reality, although he knew it had never been more important to do so. It would have been healthier for him to visit the one place on the ranch where he would find – or fail to find – evidence to support his darkest suspicions about the nature of the intruder who had come into the house when he had been at Travis Potter's office in Eagle's Roost. Instead, it was the one place that he assiduously avoided. He didn't even look toward that knoll.

He drank too much and didn't care. For seventy years he had lived by the motto 'moderation in all things', and that prescription for life had led him only to this point of humbling loneliness and horror. He wished the beer – which he occasionally spiked with good bourbon – would have a greater numbing effect on him. He seemed to have an uncanny tolerance for alcohol. And even when he had poured down enough to turn his legs and spine to rubber, his mind remained far too clear to suit him.

He escaped into books, reading exclusively in the genre for which he'd recently developed an appreciation. Heinlein, Clarke, Bradbury, Sturgeon, Benford, Clement, Wyndham, Christopher, Niven, Zelazny. Whereas he had first found, to his surprise, that fiction of the fantastic could be challenging and meaningful, he now found it also could be narcotizing, a better drug than any volume of beer and less taxing on the bladder. The effect – either enlightenment and wonder or intellectual and emotional anesthesia – was strictly at the discretion of the reader. Spaceships, time machines, teleportation cubicles, alien worlds, colonized moons, extraterrestrials, mutants, intelligent plants, robots, androids, clones, computers alive with artificial intelligence, telepathy, starship war fleets engaged in battles in far reaches of the galaxy, the collapse of the universe, time running backward, the end of all things! He lost himself in a fog of the fantastic, in a tomorrow that would never be, to avoid thinking about the unthinkable.

The traveler from the doorway became quiescent, holed up in the woods, and days passed without new developments. Eduardo didn't understand why it would have come across billions of miles of space or thousands of years of time, only to proceed with the conquest of the earth at a turtle's pace.

Of course, the very essence of something truly and deeply *alien* was that its motivations and actions would be mysterious and perhaps even incomprehensible to a human being. The conquest of earth might be of no interest whatsoever to the thing that had come through the doorway, and its concept of time might be so radically different from Eduardo's that days were like minutes to it.

In science-fiction novels, there were essentially three kinds of aliens. The good ones generally wanted to help humanity reach its full potential as an intelligent species and thereafter co-exist in fellowship and share adventures for eternity. The bad ones wanted to enslave human beings, feed on them, plant eggs in them, hunt them for sport, or eradicate them because of a tragic misunderstanding or out of sheer viciousness. The third – and least-encountered – type of extraterrestrial was neither good nor bad, but so utterly alien that its purpose and destiny was as enigmatic to human beings as was the mind of God; this third type usually did the human race a great good service or a terrible evil merely by passing through on its way to the galactic rim, like a bus running across a column of busy ants on a highway, and was never even aware of the encounter, let alone that it had impacted the lives of *intelligent* beings.

Eduardo hadn't a clue as to the larger intentions of the watcher in the woods, but he knew instinctively that, on a personal level, it didn't wish him well. It wasn't seeking eternal fellowship and shared adventures. It wasn't blissfully unaware of him, either, so it was not one of the third type. It was strange and malevolent, and sooner or later it would kill him.

In the novels, good aliens outnumbered bad. Science fiction was basically a literature of hope.

As the warm June days passed, hope was in far shorter supply on Quartermass Ranch than in the pages of those books.

On the afternoon of 17 June, while Eduardo was sitting in a living-room armchair, drinking beer and reading Walter M. Miller, the telephone rang. He put down the book but not the beer, and went into the kitchen to take the call.

Travis Potter said, 'Mr Fernandez, you don't have to worry.'

'Don't I?'

'I got a fax from the state lab, results of the tests on the tissue samples from those raccoons, and they aren't infected.'

'They sure are dead,' Eduardo said.

'But not from rabies. Not from plague, either. Nothing that appears to be infectious, or communicable by bite or fleas.'

'You do an autopsy?'

'Yes, sir, I did.'

'So was it boredom that killed them, or what?'

Potter hesitated. 'The only thing I could find was severe brain inflammation and swelling.'

'Thought you said there was no infection?'

'There isn't. No lesions, no abscesses or pus, just inflammation and extreme swelling. Extreme.'

'Maybe the state lab ought to test that brain tissue.'

'Brain tissue was part of what I sent them in the first place.'

'I see.'

'I've never encountered anything like it,' Potter told him.

Eduardo said nothing.

'Very odd,' Potter said. 'Have there been more of them?'

'More dead raccoons? No. Just the three.'

'I'm going to run some toxicological studies, see if maybe we're dealing with a poison here.'

'I haven't put out any poisons.'

'Could be an industrial toxin.'

'It could? There's no damned industry around here.'

'Well . . . a natural toxin then.'

Eduardo said, 'When you dissected them . . .'

'Yes?'

'. . . opened the skull, saw the brain inflamed and swollen . . .'

'So much pressure, even after death, blood and spinal fluid *squirted* out the instant the bone saw cut through the cranium.'

'Vivid image.'

'Sorry. But that's why their eyes were bulging.'

'Did you just take samples of the brain tissue or . . .'

'Yes?'

'. . . did you actually dissect the brain?'

'I performed complete cerebrotomies on two of them.'

'Opened their brains all the way up?'

'Yes.'

'And you didn't find anything?'

'Just what I told you.'

'Nothing . . . unusual?'

The puzzlement in Potter's silence was almost audible. Then: 'What would you have expected me to find, Mr Fernandez?'

Eduardo did not respond.

'Mr Fernandez?'

'What about their spines?' Eduardo asked. 'Did you examine their spines, the whole length of their spines?'

166

'Yes, I did.'

'You find anything . . . attached?'

'Attached?' Potter said.

'Yes.'

'What do you mean, "attached"?'

'Might have . . . might have looked like a tumor.'

'*Looked* like a tumor?'

'Say a tumor . . . something like that?'

'No. Nothing like that. Nothing at all.'

Eduardo took the telephone handset away from his head long enough to swallow some beer.

When he put the phone to his ear again, he heard Travis Potter saying, '—know something you haven't told me?'

'Not that I'm aware of,' Eduardo lied.

The veterinarian was silent this time. Maybe he was sucking on a beer of his own. Then: 'If you come across any more animals like this, will you call me?'

'Yes.'

'Not just raccoons.'

'All right.'

'Any animals at all.'

'Sure.'

'Don't move them,' Potter said.

'I won't.'

'I want to see them in situ, just where they fell.'

'Whatever you say.'

'Well . . .'

'Goodbye, Doctor.'

Eduardo hung up and went to the sink. He stared out the window at the forest at the top of the sloped backyard, west of the house.

He wondered how long he would have to wait. He was sick to death of waiting.

'Come on,' he said softly to the hidden watcher in the woods.

He was ready. Ready for Hell or Heaven or eternal nothingness, whatever came. He wasn't afraid of dying.

What frightened him was the *how* of dying. What he might have to endure. What might be done to him in the final minutes or hours of his life. What he might *see*.

*

On the morning of 21 June, as he was eating breakfast and listening to the world news on the radio, he looked up and saw a squirrel at the window in the north wall of the kitchen. It was perched on the window stool, gazing through the glass at him. Very still. Intense. As the raccoons had been.

He watched it for a while, then concentrated on his breakfast again. Each time he looked up, it was on duty.

After he washed the dishes, he went to the window, crouched, and came face to face with the squirrel. Only the pane of glass was between them. The animal seemed unfazed by this close inspection.

He snapped one fingernail against the glass directly in front of its face.

The squirrel didn't flinch.

He rose, twisted the thumb-turn latch, and started to lift the lower half of the double-hung window.

The squirrel leaped down from the stool and fled to the side yard, where it turned and regarded him intently once more.

He closed and locked the window and went out to sit on the front porch. Two squirrels were already out there on the grass, waiting for him. When Eduardo sat in the hickory rocking chair, one of the small beasts remained in the grass, but the other climbed to the top porch step and kept a watch on him from that angle.

That night, abed in his barricaded room again, seeking sleep, he heard squirrels scampering on the roof. Small claws scratching at the shingles.

When he finally slept, he dreamed of rodents.

The following day, 22 June, the squirrels remained with him. At windows. In the yard. On the porches. When he went for a walk, they trailed him at a distance.

The twenty-third was the same but, on the morning of the twenty-fourth, he found a dead squirrel on the back porch. Clots of blood in its ears. Dried blood in its nostrils. Eyes protruding from the sockets. He found two more squirrels in the yard and a fourth on the front porch steps, all in the same condition.

They had survived control longer than the raccoons.

Apparently the traveler was learning.

Eduardo considered calling Dr Potter. Instead, he gathered up the four bodies and carried them to the center of the eastern meadow. He dropped them in the grass, where scavengers could find and deal with them.

He thought, also, of the imagined child in the faraway ranch that might have been watching the Cherokee's headlights on the way back from the vet's two weeks ago. He told himself that he owed it to that child – or to other children who really existed – to tell Potter the whole story. He should try to involve the authorities in the matter, as well, even though getting anyone to believe him would be a frustrating and humiliating ordeal.

Maybe it was the beer he still drank from morning until bedtime, but he could no longer summon the sense of community that he had felt that night. He'd spent his whole life avoiding people. He couldn't suddenly find it within himself to embrace them.

Besides, everything changed for him when he'd come home and found the evidence of the intruder: the crumbling clumps of soil, the dead beetles, the earthworm, the scrap of blue cloth caught in the frame of the oven door. He was waiting in dread for the next move in *that* part of the game, yet refusing to speculate about it, instantly blocking every forbidden thought that started to rise in his tortured mind. When that fearful confrontation occurred, at last, he could not possibly share it with strangers. The horror was too personal, for him alone to witness and endure.

He still maintained the diary of these events, and in that yellow tablet he wrote about the squirrels. He hadn't the will or the energy to record his experiences in as much detail as he had done at first. He wrote as succinctly as possible without leaving out any pertinent information. After a lifetime of finding journal-keeping too burdensome, he was now unable to stop keeping this one.

He was seeking to understand the traveler by writing about it. The traveler . . . and himself.

*

On the last day of June, he decided to drive into Eagle's Roost to buy groceries and other supplies. Considering that he now lived deep in the shadow of the unknown and the fantastic, every mundane act – cooking a meal, making his bed every morning, shopping – seemed to be a pointless waste of time and energy, an absurd attempt to paint a facade of normality over an existence that was now twisted and strange. But life went on.

As Eduardo backed the Cherokee out of the garage, into the driveway, a large crow sprang off the front-porch railing and flew across the hood of the wagon with a great flapping of wings. He jammed on the brakes and stalled the engine. The bird soared high into a mottled-gray sky.

Later, in town, when Eduardo walked out of the supermarket, pushing a cart filled with supplies, a crow was perched on the hood ornament of the station wagon. He assumed it was the same creature that had startled him less than two hours before.

It remained on the hood, watching him through the windshield, as he went around to the back of the Cherokee and opened the cargo hatch. As he loaded the bags into the space behind the rear seat, the crow never looked away from him. It continued to watch

170

him as he pushed the empty cart back to the front of the store, returned, and got in behind the steering wheel. The bird took flight only when he started the engine.

Across sixteen miles of Montana countryside, the crow tracked him from on high. He could keep it in view either by leaning forward over the wheel to peer through the upper part of the windshield or simply by looking out his side window, depending on the position from which the creature chose to monitor him. Sometimes it flew parallel to the Cherokee, keeping pace, and sometimes it rocketed ahead so far that it became only a speck, nearly vanished into the clouds, only to double back and take up a parallel course once more. It was with him all the way home.

While Eduardo ate dinner, the bird perched on the exterior stool of the window in the north wall of the kitchen, where he had first seen one of the sentinel squirrels. When he got up from his meal to raise the bottom half of the window, the crow scrammed, as the squirrel had.

He left the window open while he finished dinner. A refreshing breeze skimmed in off the twilight meadows. Before Eduardo had eaten his last bite, the crow returned.

The bird remained in the open window while Eduardo washed the dishes, dried them, and put them away. It followed his every move with its bright black eyes.

He got another beer from the refrigerator and returned to the table. He settled in a different chair from the one in which he'd sat before, closer to the crow. Only an arm's length separated them.

'What do you want?' he asked, surprised that he didn't feel at all foolish talking to a damned bird.

Of course, he *wasn't* talking to the bird. He was addressing whatever controlled the bird. The traveller.

'Do you just want to watch me?' he asked.

The bird stared.

'Would you like to communicate?'

The bird lifted one wing, tucked its head underneath, and pecked at its feathers as if plucking out lice.

After another swallow of beer, Eduardo said, 'Or would you like to control me the way you do these animals?'

The crow shifted back and forth from foot to foot, shook itself, cocked its head to peer at him with one eye.

'You can act like a damned bird all you want, but I know that's not what you are, not *all* you are.'

The crow grew still again.

Beyond the window, twilight had given way to night.

'*Can* you control me? Maybe you're limited to simpler creatures, less complex neurological systems.'

Black eyes glittering. Sharp orange beak parted slightly.

'Or maybe you're learning the ecology here, the flora and fauna, figuring out how it works in this place, honing your skills. Hmmm? Maybe you're working your way up to me. Is that it?'

Watching.

'I know there's nothing of you in the bird, nothing physical. Just like you weren't in the raccoons. An autopsy established that much. Thought you might have to insert something into an animal to control it, something electronic, I don't know, maybe even something biological. Thought maybe there were a lot of you out in the woods, a hive, a nest, and maybe one of you actually had to enter an animal to control it. Half expected Potter would find some strange slug living in the raccoon's brain, some damned centipede thing hooked to its spine. A seed, an unearthly-looking spider, *something*. But you don't work that way, huh?'

He took a swallow of Corona.

'Ahhhh. Tastes good.'

He held the beer out to the crow.

It stared at him over the top of the bottle.

'Teetotaler, huh? I keep learning things about you. We're an inquisitive bunch, we human beings. We learn fast and we're good at applying what we learn, good at meeting challenges. Does that worry you any?'

The crow raised its tail feather and crapped.

'Was that a comment,' Eduardo wondered, 'or just part of doing a good bird imitation?'

The sharp beak opened and closed, opened and closed, but no sound issued from the bird.

'Somehow you control these animals from a distance. Telepathy, something like that? From quite a distance, in the case of this bird. Sixteen miles into Eagle's Roost. Well, maybe fourteen miles as the crow flies.'

If the traveler knew that Eduardo had made a lame pun, it gave no indication through the bird.

'Pretty clever, whether it's telepathy or something else. But it sure as hell takes a toll of the subject, doesn't it? You're getting better, though, learning the limitations of the local slave population.'

The crow pecked for more lice.

'Have you made any attempts to control me? Because, if you have, I don't think I was aware of it. Didn't feel any probing at my mind, didn't see alien images behind my eyes, none of the stuff you read about in novels.'

Peck, peck, peck.

Eduardo chugged the rest of the Corona. He wiped his mouth on his sleeve.

Having nailed the lice, the bird watched him serenely, as though it would sit there all night and listen to him ramble, if that was what he wanted.

'I think you're going slow, feeling your way, experimenting. This world seems normal enough to those of us born here, but maybe to you it's one of the weirdest places you've ever seen. Could be you're not too sure of yourself here.'

He had not begun the conversation with any expectation that the crow would answer him. He wasn't in a damned Disney movie. Yet

173

its continued silence was beginning to frustrate and annoy him, probably because the day had sailed by on a tide of beer and he was full of drunkard's anger.

'Come on. Let's stop farting around. Let's do it.'

The crow just stared.

'Come here yourself, pay me a visit, the *real* you, not in a bird or squirrel or raccoon. Come as yourself. No costumes. Let's do it. Let's get it over with.'

The bird flapped its wings once, half unfurling them, but that was all.

'You're worse than Poe's raven. You don't even say a single word, you just sit there. What good are you?'

Staring, staring.

And the raven never flitting, still is sitting, still is sitting . . .

Though Poe had never been one of his favorites, only a writer he had read while discovering what he really admired, he began quoting aloud to the feathered sentry, infusing the words with the vehemence of the troubled narrator that the poet had created: '"And his eyes have all the seeming of a demon's that is dreaming, and the lamplight o'er him streaming throws his shadow on the floor—"'

Abruptly he realized, too late, that the bird and the poem and his own treacherous mind had brought him to a confrontation with the horrific thought that he'd repressed ever since cleaning up the soil and other leavings on 10 June. At the heart of Poe's 'The Raven' was a lost maiden, young Lenore, lost to death, and a narrator with a morbid belief that Lenore had come back from—

Eduardo slammed down a mental door on the rest of that thought. With a snarl of rage, he threw the empty beer bottle. It hit the crow. Bird and bottle tumbled into the night.

He leaped off his chair and to the window.

The bird fluttered on the lawn, then sprang into the air with a furious flapping of wings, up into the dark sky.

Eduardo closed the window so hard he nearly shattered the glass, locked it, and clasped both hands to his head, as if he would tear out the fearful thought if it would not be repressed again.

He got very drunk that night. The sleep he finally found was as good an approximation of death as any he had known.

If the bird came to his bedroom window while he slept, or walked the edges of the roof above him, he did not hear it.

*

He didn't wake until ten minutes past noon on 1 July. For the rest of that day, coping with his hangover and trying to cure it preoccupied him and kept his mind off the morbid verses of a long-dead poet.

The crow was with him 1, 2 and 3 July, from morning through night, without surcease, but he tried to ignore it. No more staring matches as with the other sentries. No more one-sided conversations. Eduardo did not sit on the porches. When he was inside, he did not look toward the windows. His narrow life became more constricted than ever.

At three o'clock on the afternoon of the fourth, suffering a bout of claustrophobia from being too long within four walls, he planned a cautious itinerary and, taking the shotgun, went for a walk. He did not look at the sky above him, only toward distant horizons. Twice, however, he saw a swift shadow flash over the ground ahead of him, and he knew that he did not walk alone.

He was returning to the house, only twenty yards from the front porch, when the crow plummeted out of the sky. Its wings flapped uselessly, as if it had forgotten how to fly, and it met the earth with only slightly more grace than a stone dropped from a similar height. It flopped and shrieked on the grass but was dead by the time he reached it.

Without looking closely at the crow, he picked it up by the tip of one wing. He carried it into the meadow to throw it where he had tossed the four squirrels on 24 June.

He expected to find a macabre pile of remains, well plucked and dismembered by carrion eaters, but the squirrels were gone. He would not have been surprised if one or even two of the carcasses had been dragged off to be devoured elsewhere. But most carrion eaters would strip the squirrels where they were found, leaving at least several bones, the inedible feet, scraps of fur-covered hide, a well-gnawed and pecked-at skull.

The lack of any remains whatsoever could only mean the squirrels had been removed by the traveler. Or by its sorcerously controlled surrogates.

Perhaps, having tested them to destruction, the traveler wanted to examine them to determine why they failed – which it had not been able to do with the raccoons because Eduardo had intervened and taken them to the veterinarian. Or it might feel that they were, like the raccoons, evidence of its presence. It might prefer to leave as few loose ends as possible until its position on this world was more firmly established.

He stood in the meadow, staring at the place where the dead squirrels had been. Thinking.

He raised his left hand, from which dangled the broken crow, and stared at the now-sightless eyes. As shiny as polished ebony and bulging from the sockets.

'Come on,' he whispered.

Finally, he took the crow into the house. He had a use for it. A plan.

*

The wire-mesh colander was held together by sturdy stainless-steel rings at top and bottom, and stood on three short steel legs. It was

176

the size of a two- or three-quart bowl. He used it to drain pasta when he cooked large quantities to make salads or to ensure there would be plenty of leftovers. Two steel-loop handles were fixed to the top ring, by which to shake it when it was filled with steaming pasta that needed encouragement to fully drain.

Turning the colander over and over in his hands, Eduardo thought through his plan one more time – then began to put it into action.

Standing at a kitchen counter, he folded the wings of the dead crow. He tucked the whole bird into the colander.

With needle and thread, he fixed the crow to the wire mesh in three places. That would prevent the limp body from slipping out when he tilted the colander.

As he put the needle and thread aside, the bird rolled its head loosely and shuddered.

Eduardo recoiled from it and took a step back from the counter in surprise.

The crow issued a feeble, quavery cry.

He knew it had been dead. Stone dead. For one thing, its neck had been broken. Its swollen eyes had been virtually hanging out of the sockets. Apparently it had died in mid-flight of a massive brain seizure like those that had killed the raccoons and squirrels. Dropping from a great height, it had hit the ground with sickening force, sustaining yet more physical damage. Stone dead.

Now, stitched to the wire mesh of the colander, the reanimated bird was unable to lift its head off its breast, not because it was hampered by the threads with which he'd secured it but because its neck was *still* broken. Smashed legs flopped uselessly. Crippled wings tried to flutter and were hampered more by the damage to them than by the entangling threads.

Overcoming his fear and revulsion, Eduardo pressed one hand against the crow's breast. He couldn't feel a heartbeat.

The heart of any small bird pounded extremely fast, much faster than the heart of any mammal, a racing little engine, *putta-putta-putta-putta-putta*. It was always easy to detect because the whole body reverberated with the rapid beats.

The crow's heart was definitely not beating. As far as he was able to tell, the bird wasn't breathing, either. And its neck was broken.

He had hoped that he was witnessing the traveller's ability to bring a dead creature back to life, a miracle of sorts. But the truth was darker than that.

The crow was dead.

Yet it moved.

Trembling with disgust, Eduardo lifted his hand from the small squirming corpse.

The traveler could re-establish control of a carcass without resuscitating the animal. To some extent, it had power over the inanimate as well as the animate.

Eduardo desperately wanted to avoid thinking about that.

But he couldn't turn his mind off. Couldn't avoid that dreaded line of inquiry any longer.

If he had not taken the raccoons away at once to the vet, would they eventually have shuddered and pulled themselves to their feet again, cold but moving, dead but animated?

In the colander, the crow's head wobbled loosely on its broken neck, and its beak opened and closed with a faint clicking.

Perhaps nothing had carried the four dead squirrels out of the meadow, after all. Maybe those carcasses, stiff with rigor mortis, had responded to the insistent call of the puppetmaster on their own, cold muscles flexing and contracting awkwardly, rigid joints cracking and snapping as demands were put upon them. Even as their bodies had entered the early stages of decomposition, perhaps they twitched and lifted their heads, crawled and hitched and dragged themselves out of the meadow, into the woods, to the lair of the thing that commanded them.

178

Don't think about it. Stop. Think about something else, for Christ's sake. Anything else. Not this, not this.

If he released the crow from the colander and took it outside, would it flop and flutter along the ground on its broken wings, all the way up the sloped backyard, making a nightmarish pilgrimage into the shadows of the higher woods?

Did he dare follow it into that heart of darkness?

No. No, if there was to be an ultimate confrontation, it had to happen here on his own territory, not in whatever strange nest the traveller had made for itself.

Eduardo was stricken by the blood-freezing suspicion that the traveler was alien to such an extreme degree that it didn't share humanity's perception of life and death, didn't draw the line between the two in the same place at all. Perhaps its kind never died. Or they died in a true biological sense yet were reborn in a different form out of their own rotting remains – and expected the same to be true of creatures on this world. In fact, the nature of their species – especially its relationship with death – might be unimaginably more bizarre, perverse, and repellent than anything his imagination could conceive.

In an infinite universe, the potential number of intelligent life-forms was also infinite – as he had discovered from the books he'd been reading lately. Theoretically, anything that could be imagined must exist in an infinite realm. When referring to extraterrestrial lifeforms, alien meant *alien*, maximum strange, one weirdness wrapped in another, beyond easy understanding and possibly beyond all hope of comprehension.

He had brooded about this issue before, but only now did he fully grasp that he had about as much chance of understanding this traveler, *really* understanding it, as a mouse had of understanding the intricacies of the human experience, the workings of the human mind.

The dead crow shuddered, twitched its broken legs. From its

179

twisted throat came a wet cawing sound that was a grotesque parody of the cry of a living crow.

A spiritual darkness filled Eduardo, because he could no longer deny, to any extent whatsoever, the identity of the intruder who had left a vile trail through the house on the night of 10 June. He had known all along what he was repressing. Even as he had drunk himself into oblivion, he had known. Even as he had pretended not to know, he had known. And he knew now. He knew. Dear sweet Jesus, he knew.

Eduardo had not been afraid to die.

He'd almost welcomed death.

Now he was again afraid to die. Beyond fright. Physically ill with terror. Trembling, sweating.

Though the traveler had shown no signs of being able to control the body of a *living* human being, what would happen when he was dead?

He picked up the shotgun from the table, snatched the keys to the Cherokee off the pegboard, went to the connecting door between the kitchen and garage. He had to leave at once, no time to waste, get out and far away. To hell with learning more about the traveler. To hell with forcing a confrontation. He should just get in the Cherokee, jam the accelerator to the floorboards, run down anything that got in his way, and put a lot of distance between himself and whatever had come out of the black doorway into the Montana night.

He jerked the door open but halted on the threshold between the kitchen and the garage. He had nowhere to go. No family left. No friends. He was too old to begin another life.

And no matter where he went, the traveller would still be *here*, learning its way in this world, performing its perverse experiments, befouling what was sacred, committing unspeakable outrages against everything that Eduardo had ever cherished.

He could not run from this. He had never run from anything in his life; however, it was not pride that stopped him before he had taken one full step into the garage. The only thing preventing him from leaving was his sense of what was right and wrong, the basic values that had gotten him through a long life. If he turned his back on those values and ran like a gutless wonder, he wouldn't be able to look at himself in a mirror any more. He was old and alone, which was bad enough. To be old, alone, and eaten by self-loathing would be intolerable. He wanted so desperately to run from this, but that option was not open to him.

He stepped back from the threshold, closed the door to the garage, and returned the shotgun to the table.

He knew a bleakness of the soul that perhaps no one outside of Hell had ever known before him.

The dead crow thrashed, trying to tear loose of the colander. Eduardo had used heavy thread and tied secure knots, and the bird's muscles and bones were too badly damaged for it to exert enough force to break free.

His plan seemed foolish now. An act of meaningless bravado – and insanity. He proceeded with it, anyway, preferring to act rather than wait meekly for the end.

On the back porch, he held the colander against the outside of the kitchen door. The imprisoned crow scratched and thumped. With a pencil, Eduardo marked the wood where the openings in the handles met it.

He hammered two standard nails into those marks and hung the colander on them.

The crow, still struggling weakly, was visible through the wire mesh, trapped against the door. But the colander could be too easily lifted off the nails.

Using two U-shaped nails on each side, he fixed both handles securely to the solid oak door. The hammering carried up the long slope of the yard and echoed back to him from the pine walls of the western forest.

To remove the colander and get at the crow, the traveller or its surrogate would have to pry loose the U-shaped nails to free at least one of the handles. The only alternative was to cut the mesh with heavy shears and pull out the feathered prize.

Either way, the dead bird could not be snatched up quickly or silently. Eduardo would have plenty of warning that something was after the contents of the colander – especially as he intended to spend the entire night in the kitchen if necessary.

He could not be sure the traveler would covet the dead crow. Perhaps he was wrong, and it had no interest in the failed surrogate. However, the bird had lasted longer than the squirrels, which had lasted longer than the raccoons, and the puppetmaster might find it instructive to examine the carcass to help it discover why.

It wouldn't be working through a squirrel this time. Or even a clever raccoon. Greater strength and dexterity were required for the task as Eduardo had arranged it. He prayed that the traveler itself would rise to the challenge and put in its first appearance. *Come on.* However, if it sent the other thing, the unspeakable thing, the lost Lenore, that terror could be faced.

Amazing, what a human being could endure. Amazing, the strength of a man even in the shadow of oppressive terror, even in the grip of horror, even filled with bleakest despair.

The crow was motionless once more. Silent. Stone dead.

Eduardo turned to look at the high woods.

Come on. Come on, you bastard. Show me your face, show me your stinking ugly face. Come on, crawl out where I can see you. Don't be so gutless, you fucking freak.

Eduardo went inside. He shut the door but didn't lock it.

After closing the blinds at the windows, so nothing could look in at him without his knowledge, he sat at the kitchen table to bring his diary up to date. Filling three more pages with his neat script, he concluded what he supposed might be his final entry.

In case something happened to him, he wanted the yellow tablet

182

to be found – but not too easily. He inserted it in a large Ziploc plastic bag, sealed it against moisture, and put it in the freezer half of the refrigerator, among packages of frozen foods.

Twilight had arrived. The time of truth was fast approaching. He had not expected the entity in the woods to put in an appearance in daylight. He sensed it was a creature of nocturnal habits and preferences, spawned in darkness.

He got a beer from the refrigerator. What the hell. It was his first in several hours.

Although he wanted to be sober for the confrontation to come, he didn't want to be *entirely* clear-headed. Some things could be faced and dealt with better by a man whose sensibilities had been mildly numbed.

Nightfall had barely settled all the way into the west and he had not finished that first beer when he heard movement on the back porch. A soft thud and a scrape and a thud again. Definitely not the crow stirring. Heavier noises than that. It was a clumsy sound made by something awkwardly but determinedly climbing the three wooden steps from the lawn.

Eduardo got to his feet and picked up the shotgun. His palms were slick with sweat, but he could still handle the weapon.

Another thud and a gritty scraping.

His heart was beating bird-fast, faster than the crow's had ever beaten when it had been alive.

The visitor – whatever its world of origin, whatever its name, whether dead or alive – reached the top of the steps and moved across the porch toward the door. No thudding any longer. All dragging and shuffling, sliding and scraping.

Because of the type of reading he had been doing these past few months, in but an instant Eduardo conjured image after image of different unearthly creatures that might produce such a sound instead of ordinary footsteps, each more malevolent in appearance than the one before it, until his mind swam with monsters. One monster

183

among them was not unearthly, belonged more to Poe than to Heinlein or Sturgeon or Bradbury, gothic rather than futuristic, not only from Earth but from the *earth*.

It drew nearer the door, nearer still, and finally it was *at* the door. The unlocked door.

Silence.

Eduardo had only to take three steps, grab the doorknob, pull inward, and he would stand face to face with the visitor. He could not move. He was as rooted to the floor as any tree was rooted to the hills that rose behind the house. Though he had devised the plan that had precipitated the confrontation, though he had not run when he'd had the chance, though he had convinced himself that his sanity depended on facing this ultimate terror forthrightly and putting it behind him, he was paralyzed and suddenly not so sure that running would have been wrong.

The thing was silent. It was *there* but silent. Inches from the far side of the door.

Doing what? Waiting for Eduardo to move first? Or studying the crow in the colander? The porch was dark, and only a little kitchen light was emitted by the covered windows, so could it really see the crow?

Yes. Oh, yes, it could see in the dark, bet on that, it could see in the dark better than any damned cat could see, because it was *of* the dark.

He could hear the kitchen clock ticking. Though it had been there all along, he hadn't heard it in years, because it had become part of the background, white noise, but he heard it now, louder than it had ever been, like one stick striking slow measured beats on a felt-softened snare drum at a state funeral.

Come on, come on, let's do it. This time he was not urging the traveler to come out of hiding. He was goading himself. *Come on, you bastard, you coward, you stupid old ignorant fool, come on, come on, come on.*

He moved to the door and stood slightly to one side of it, so he could open it past himself.

To grasp the knob, he would have to let go of the shotgun with one hand, but he couldn't do that. No way.

His heart was knocking painfully against his ribs. He could feel the pulse in his temples, pounding, pounding.

He smelled the thing through the closed door. A nauseating odor, sour and putrescent, beyond anything in his long lifetime of experience.

The doorknob in front of him, the knob that he could not bring himself to grasp, round and polished, yellow and gleaming, began to turn. Scintillant light, a reflection of the kitchen fluorescents, trickled along the smooth curve of the knob as it slowly revolved. So slowly. The free-moving latchbolt eased out of its notch in the striker plate with the faintest rasp of brass on brass.

Pulse pounding in his temples, booming. Heart swollen in his chest, so swollen and leaping that it crowded his lungs and made breathing difficult, painful.

And now the knob slipped back the other way, and the door remained unopened. The latchbolt eased into its catch once more. The moment of revelation was delayed, perhaps slipping away forever as the visitor withdrew . . .

With an anguished cry that surprised him, Eduardo seized the knob and yanked the door open in one convulsively violent movement, bringing himself face to face with his worst fear. The lost maiden, three years in the grave and now released: a wiry and tangled mass of gray hair matted with filth, eyeless sockets, flesh hideously corrupted and dark in spite of the preserving influence of embalming fluid, glimpses of clean bone in the desiccated and reeking tissues, lips withered back from teeth to reveal a wide but humorless grin. The lost maiden stood in her ragged and worm-eaten burial dress, the blue-on-blue fabric grossly stained with the fluids of decomposition, risen and returned to him, reaching for him with one hand. The sight of her filled him not merely with terror and revulsion but with despair, oh God, he was sinking in a sea of cold black despair that Margarite should have come to this, reduced to the unspeakable fate of all living things—

It's not Margarite, not this thing, unclean thing, Margarite's in a better place, Heaven, sits with God, must be a God, Margarite deserves a God, not just this, not an ending like this, sits with God, sits with God, long gone from this body and sits with God.

—and after the first instant of confrontation, he thought he was going to be all right, thought he was going to be able to hold on to his sanity and bring up the shotgun and blast the hateful thing backward off the porch, pump round after round into it until it no longer bore the vaguest resemblance to his Margarite, until it was nothing but a pile of bone fragments and organic ruins with no power to plunge him into despondency.

Then he saw that he hadn't been visited only by this heinous surrogate but by the traveller itself, two confrontations in one. The alien was entwined with the corpse, hanging upon its back but also intruding within the cavities of it, riding on and in the dead woman. Its own body appeared to be soft and poorly designed for gravity as heavy as that it had encountered here, so perhaps it needed support to permit locomotion in these conditions. Black, it was, black and slick, irregularly stippled with red, and seemed to be comprised only of a mass of entwined and writhing appendages that one moment appeared as fluid and smooth as snakes but the next moment seemed as spiky and jointed as the legs of a crab. Not muscular like the coils of snakes or armored like crabs but oozing and jellid. He saw no head or orifice, no familiar feature that could help him tell the top of it from the bottom, but he had only a few seconds to absorb what he was seeing, merely the briefest glimpse. The sight of those shiny black tentacles slithering in and out of the cadaver's rib cage brought him to the realization that less flesh remained on the three-year-old corpse than he had at first believed, and that the bulk of the apparition before him was the rider on the bones. Its tangled appendages bulged where her heart and lungs had once been, twined like vines around clavicles and scapulae, around humerus and radius and ulna, around femur and tibia, even filled the empty skull and churned frenziedly just behind the rims of the hollow sockets. This was more than he could tolerate and more than his books had prepared him for, beyond *alien*, an obscenity he couldn't bear. He heard himself screaming, heard it but was unable to stop, could not lift the gun because all of his strength was in the scream.

Although it seemed like an eternity, only five seconds elapsed from the moment he yanked open the door until his heart was wrenched by fatal spasms. In spite of the thing that loomed on the threshold of the kitchen, in spite of the thoughts and terrors that exploded through his mind in that sliver of time, Eduardo knew the number of seconds was precisely five because a part of him continued to be aware of the ticking of the clock, the funereal cadence, five ticks, five seconds. Then a searing pain blazed through him, the mother of all pain, not from an assault by the traveler but arising from within, accompanied by white light as bright as the eye of a nuclear explosion might be, an all-obliterating whiteness that erased the traveler from his view and all the cares of the world from his consideration. Peace.

13

BECAUSE HE had suffered some nerve damage in addition to the spinal fracture, Jack required a longer course of therapy at Phoenix Rehabilitation Hospital than he had anticipated. As promised, Moshe Bloom taught him to make a friend of pain, to see it as evidence of rebuilding and recovery. By early July, four months from the day he had been shot down, gradually diminishing pain had been a constant companion for so long that it was not just a friend but a brother.

On 17 July, when he was discharged from Phoenix, he was able to walk again, although he still required the assurance of not one but two canes. He seldom actually used both, sometimes neither, but was fearful of falling without them, especially on a staircase. Although slow, he was for the most part steady on his feet; however, influenced by an occasional vagrant nerve impulse, either leg could go entirely limp without warning, causing his knee to buckle. Those unpleasant surprises became less frequent by the week. He hoped to be rid of one cane by August and the other by September.

Moshe Bloom, as solid as sculpted rock but still appearing to drift along as if propelled on a thin cushion of air, accompanied Jack to the front entrance, while Heather brought the car from the parking lot. The therapist was dressed all in white, as usual, but his skullcap was crocheted and colorful. 'Listen, you be sure to keep up those daily exercises.'

'All right.'

'Even after you're able to give up the canes.'

'I will.'

'The tendency is to slack off. Sometimes when the patient gets most of the function back, regains his confidence, he decides he doesn't have to work at it any more. But the healing is still going on even if he doesn't realize it.'

'I hear you.'

Holding open the front door for Jack, Moshe said, 'Next thing you know, he has problems, has to come back here on an out-patient basis to gain back the ground he's lost.'

'Not me,' Jack assured him, caning outside into the gloriously hot summer day.

'Take your medication when you need it.'

'I will.'

'Don't try to tough it out.'

'I won't.'

'Hot baths with Epsom salts when you're sore.'

Jack nodded solemnly. 'And I swear to God, every day I'll eat my chicken soup.'

Laughing, Moshe said, 'I don't mean to mother you.'

'Yes, you do.'

'No, not really.'

'You've been mothering me for weeks.'

'Have I? Yes, all right, I *do* mean to do it.'

Jack hooked one cane over his wrist so he could shake hands. 'Thank you, Moshe.'

The therapist shook hands, then hugged him. 'You've made a hell of a comeback. I'm proud of you.'

'You're damned good at this job, my friend.'

As Heather and Toby pulled up in the car, Moshe grinned. 'Of course I'm good at it. We Jews know all about suffering.'

*

189

For a few days, just being in his own home and sleeping in his own bed was such a delight that Jack needed to make no effort to sustain optimism. Sitting in his favorite armchair, eating meals whenever he wanted rather than when a rigid institutional schedule said he must, helping Heather to cook dinner, reading to Toby before bedtime, watching television after ten o'clock in the evening without having to wear headphones – these things were more satisfying to him than all the luxuries and pleasures to which a Saudi Arabian prince might be entitled.

He remained concerned about family finances, but he had hope on that front too. He expected to be back at work in some capacity by August, at last earning a paycheck again. Before he could return to duty on the streets, however, he would be required to pass a rigorous department physical and a psychological evaluation to determine if he had been traumatized in any way that would affect his performance; consequently, for a number of weeks, he would have to serve at a desk.

As the recession dragged on with few signs of a recovery, as every initiative by the government seemed devised solely to destroy more jobs, Heather stopped waiting for her widely seeded applications to bear fruit. While Jack had been in the rehab hospital, Heather had become an entrepreneur – 'Howard Hughes without the insanity,' she joked – doing business as McGarvey Associates. Ten years with IBM as a software designer gave her credibility. By the time Jack came home, Heather had signed a contract to design custom inventory-control and bookkeeping programs for the owner of a chain of eight taverns; one of the few enterprises thriving in the current economy was selling booze and a companionable atmosphere in which to drink it, and her client had lost the ability to monitor his increasingly busy saloons.

Profit from her first contract wouldn't come close to replacing the salary she had stopped receiving the previous October. However, she seemed confident that good word of mouth would bring her more work if she did a first-rate job for the tavern owner.

Jack was pleased to see her contentedly at work, her computers set up on a pair of large folding tables in the spare bedroom, where the mattress and springs of the bed now stood on end against one wall. She had always been happiest when busy, and his respect for her intelligence and industriousness was such that he wouldn't have been surprised to see the humble office of McGarvey Associates grow, in time, to rival the corporate headquarters of Microsoft.

On his fourth day at home, when he told her as much, she leaned back in her office chair and puffed out her chest as if swelling with pride. 'Yep, that's me. Bill Gates without the nerd reputation.'

Leaning against the doorway, already using only one cane, he said, 'I prefer to think of you as Bill Gates with terrific legs.'

'Sexist.'

'Guilty.'

'Besides, how do you know Bill Gates doesn't have better legs than mine? Have you seen his?'

'Okay, I take back everything. I should have said – as far as I'm concerned, you are every bit as much of a nerd as people think Bill Gates is.'

'Thank you.'

'You're welcome,' he said.

'Are they really terrific?'

'What?'

'My legs.'

'You have legs?'

Although he doubted that good word of mouth was going to boost her business fast enough to pay the bills and meet the mortgage, Jack didn't worry unduly about much of anything – until 24 July, when he had been home for a week and when his mood began to slide. When his characteristic optimism started to go, it didn't just crumble slowly but cracked all the way down the middle and soon thereafter shattered altogether.

He couldn't sleep without dreams, which grew increasingly bloody night by night. He routinely woke in the middle of a panic attack three or four hours after he went to bed, and he was unable to doze off again no matter how desperately tired he was.

A general malaise quickly set in. Food seemed to lose much of its flavor. He stayed indoors because the summer sun became annoyingly bright, and the dry California heat that he had always loved now parched him and made him irritable. Though he had always been a reader and owned an extensive book collection, he could find no writer – even among his old favorites – who appealed to him any more; every story, regardless of how liberally festooned with the praises of the critics, was uninvolving, and he often had to reread a paragraph three or even four times until the meaning penetrated his mental haze.

He advanced from malaise to flat-out depression by the twenty-eighth, only eleven days out of rehabilitation. He found himself thinking about the future more than had ever been his habit – and he could find no possible version of it that appealed to him. Once an exuberant swimmer in an ocean of optimism, he became a huddled and frightened creature in a backwater of despair.

He was reading the daily newspaper too closely, brooding about current events too deeply, and spending far too much time watching television news. Wars, genocide, riots, terrorist attacks, political bombings, gang wars, drive-by shootings, child molestations, serial killers on the loose, carjackings, ecological doomsday scenarios, a young convenience-store clerk shot in the head for the lousy fifty bucks and change in his cash-register drawer, rapes and stabbings and strangulations. He knew modern life was more than this. Good will still existed and good deeds were still done. But the media focused on the grimmest aspects of every issue, and so did Jack. Though he tried to leave the newspaper unopened and the TV off, he was as drawn to their vivid accounts of the latest tragedies and outrages as an alcoholic to the bottle or a compulsive gambler to the excitement of the racetrack.

The despair inspired by the news was a down escalator from which he seemed unable to escape. And it was picking up speed.

When Heather casually mentioned that Toby would be entering third grade in a month, Jack began to worry about the drug dealing and violence surrounding so many Los Angeles schools. He became convinced Toby was going to be killed unless they could find a way, in spite of their financial problems, to pay private-school tuition. The conviction that such a once-safe place as a classroom was now as dangerous as a battlefield led him inevitably and swiftly to the conclusion that *nowhere* was safe for his son. If Toby could be killed in school, why not on his own street, playing in his own front yard? Jack became an overly protective parent, which he had never been before, reluctant to let the boy out of his sight.

By 5 August, with his return to work only two days away and the restoration of a more normal life so near at hand, he should have experienced an upswing in his mood, but the opposite was the case. The thought of reporting to the division for reassignment made his palms sweat, even though he was at least a month away from moving off a desk job and back on to patrol.

He believed he had concealed his fears and depressions from everyone. That night he learned differently.

In bed, after he turned off the lamp, he worked up the courage to say in the darkness what he would have been embarrassed to say in the light: 'I'm not going back on the street.'

'I know,' Heather said from her side of the bed.

'I don't mean not just right away. I mean never.'

'I know, baby,' she said tenderly, and reached out to find and hold his hand.

'Is it that obvious?'

'It's been a bad couple of weeks.'

'I'm sorry.'

'You had to go through it.'

'I thought I'd be on the street until I retired. It's all I ever wanted to do.'

'Things change,' she said.

'I can't risk it now. I've lost my confidence.'

'You'll get it back.'

'Maybe.'

'You will,' she insisted. 'But you still won't go back on the street. You can't. You've done your part, you've pushed your luck as far as any cop could be expected to push it. Let someone else save the world.'

'I feel . . .'

'I know.'

'. . . empty . . .'

'It'll get better. Everything does.'

'. . . like a sorry-ass quitter.'

'You're no quitter.' She slid against his side and put her hand on his chest. 'You're a good man and you're brave, too damn brave, as far as I'm concerned. If you hadn't decided to get off the street, I'd have decided it for you. One way or another, I'd have made you do it, because the odds are, next time, I'll be Alma Bryson and your partner's wife will be coming to sit at *my* side, hold *my* hand. I'll be damned to Hell before I'll let that happen. You've had two partners shot down beside you in one year, and there's been seven cops killed here since January. *Seven.* I'm not going to lose you, Jack.'

He put his arm around her, held her close, profoundly grateful to have found her in a hard world where so much seemed to depend on random chance. For a while he couldn't speak; his voice would have been too thick with emotion.

At last he said, 'So I guess from here on out, I'll park my butt in a chair and be a desk jockey of one kind or another.'

'I'll buy you a whole *case* of hemorrhoid cream.'

'I'll have to get a coffee mug with my name on it.'

'And a supply of note pads that say "From the Desk of Jack McGarvey".'

He said, 'It's going to mean a salary cut. Won't pay as much as being on the street.'

'We'll be all right.'

'Will we? I'm not so sure. It's going to be tight.'

She said, 'You're forgetting McGarvey Associates. Inventive and flexible custom programs. Tailored to your needs. Reasonable rates. Timely delivery. Better legs than Bill Gates.'

And that night, in the darkness of their bedroom, it did seem that finding security and happiness again in the City of Angels might be possible, after all.

During the next ten days, however, they were confronted by a series of reality checks that made it impossible to sustain the old L.A. fantasy. Yet another city budget shortfall was rectified in part by reducing the compensation of street cops by five percent and that of the desk-bound in the department by twelve percent; a job that already paid less than Jack's previous position now paid *markedly* less. A day later, government statistics showed the economy slipping again; and a new client, on the verge of signing a contract with McGarvey Associates, was so unnerved by those numbers that he decided against investing in new computer programs for a few months. Inflation was up. Taxes were *way* up. The debt-strapped utility company was granted a rate increase to prevent bankruptcy, which meant electricity rates were going to climb. Water rates had already risen; natural-gas prices were next. They were clobbered with a car-repair bill of six hundred and forty dollars on the same day that Anson Oliver's first film, which had not enjoyed a wide or successful theatrical run in its initial release, was re-issued by Paramount, re-igniting media interest in the shootout and in Jack. And Richie Tendero, husband to the flamboyant and unshakable Gina Tendero of the black leather clothes and red-pepper mace, was hit by a shotgun blast while answering a domestic-dispute call, resulting in the amputation of his left arm and plastic surgery to the left side of his face.

On 15 August, an eleven-year-old girl was caught in gang cross-fire one block from the elementary school that Toby would soon be attending. She was killed instantly.

*

Sometimes, life seems to have a higher meaning. Events unfold in uncanny sequences. Long-forgotten acquaintances turn up again with news that changes lives. A stranger appears and speaks a few words of wisdom, solving a previously insoluble problem, or something in a recent dream transpires in reality. Suddenly the existence of God seems confirmed.

On the afternoon of 18 August, as Heather stood in the kitchen, waiting for the Mr Coffee machine to brew a fresh pot and sorting through mail that had just arrived, she came across a letter from Paul Youngblood, an attorney-at-law from Eagle's Roost, Montana. The envelope was heavy, as if it contained not merely a letter but a document. According to the postmark, it had been sent on the sixth of the month, which led her to wonder about the gypseian route by which the postal service had chosen to deliver it.

She knew she'd heard of Eagle's Roost. She could not recall when or why.

Because she shared a nearly universal aversion to attorneys and associated all correspondence from law firms with trouble, she put the letter on the bottom of the stack, choosing to deal with it last. After throwing away advertisements, she found that the four other remaining items were bills. When she finally read the letter from Paul Youngblood, it proved to be so utterly different from the bad news she had expected – and so astonishing – that immediately after finishing it, she sat down at the kitchen table and read it again from the top.

Eduardo Fernandez, a client of Youngblood's, had died on 4 or 5 July. He had been the father of the late Thomas Fernandez. That was Tommy – murdered at Jack's side eleven months before the events at Hassam Arkadian's service station. Eduardo Fernandez had named Jack McGarvey of Los Angeles, California, as his sole heir. Serving as executor of Mr Fernandez's estate, Youngblood had tried to notify Jack by phone, only to discover that his number was no longer listed. The estate included an insurance policy that would cover the fifty-five percent federal inheritance tax, leaving Jack the unencumbered six-hundred-acre Quartermass Ranch, the four-bedroom main house with furnishings, the caretaker's house, the ten-horse stable, various tools and equipment, and 'a substantial amount of cash'.

Instead of a legal document, six photographs were included with the single-page letter. With shaky hands, Heather spread them in two rows on the table in front of her. The modified Victorian main house was charming, with just enough decorative millwork to enchant without descending into Gothic oppressiveness. It appeared to be twice as large as the house in which they now lived. The mountain and valley views in every direction were breathtaking.

Heather had never been filled with such mixed emotions as she experienced at that moment.

In their hour of desperation, they had been given salvation, a way out of darkness, escape from despair. She had no idea what a Montana attorney would regard as a 'substantial amount of cash', but she figured the ranch alone, if liquidated, must be worth enough to pay off all their bills and their current mortgage, with money left to bank. She felt light-headed with a wild ebullience she hadn't known since she had been a small child and had still believed in fairy tales, miracles.

On the other hand, their good fortune would have been Tommy Fernandez's good fortune if he had not been murdered. That dark and inescapable fact tainted the gift and dampened her pleasure in it.

For a while she brooded, torn between delight and guilt, and at last decided she was responding too much like a Beckerman and too little like a McGarvey. She would have done anything to bring Tommy Fernandez back to life, even if it meant that this inheritance would never have been hers and Jack's; but the cold truth was that Tommy was dead, in the ground over sixteen months now, and beyond the help of anyone. Fate was too often malicious, too seldom generous. She would be a fool to greet this staggering beneficence with a frown.

Her first thought was to call Jack at work. She went to the wall phone, dialled part of the number, then hung up.

This was once-in-a-lifetime news. She would never have another opportunity to spring something this deliriously wonderful on him, and she must not screw it up. For one thing, she wanted to see his face when he heard about the inheritance.

She took the notepad and pencil from the holder beside the phone and returned to the table, where she read the letter again. She wrote out a list of questions for Paul Youngblood, then returned to the phone and called him in Eagle's Roost, Montana.

When Heather identified herself to the attorney's secretary and then to the man himself, her voice was tremulous because she was half afraid he would tell her there had been a mistake. Maybe someone had contested the will. Or maybe a more recent will had been found which negated the one naming Jack as the sole heir. A thousand maybes.

*

Rush-hour traffic was even worse than usual. Dinner was delayed because Jack got home more than half an hour late, tired and frazzled but putting on a good act as a man in love with his new job and happy with his life.

The instant Toby was finished eating, he asked to be excused to watch a favorite television program, and Heather let him go. She wanted to share the news with Jack first, just the two of them, and tell Toby later.

As usual, Jack helped her clean the table and load the dishwasher. When they were finished, he said, 'Think I'll go for a walk, exercise these legs.'

'You having any pain?'

'Just a little cramping.'

Though he had stopped using a cane, she worried that he wouldn't tell her if he was having strength or balance problems. 'You sure you're okay?'

'Positive.' He kissed her cheek. 'You and Moshe Bloom could never be married. You'd always be fighting over whose job it was to do the mothering.'

'Sit down a minute,' she said, leading him to the table and encouraging him into a chair. 'There's something we have to talk about.'

'If Toby needs more dental work, I'll do it myself.'

'No dental work.'

'You see the size of that last bill?'

'Yes, I saw it.'

'Who needs teeth anyway? Clams don't have teeth, and they get along just fine. Oysters don't have teeth. Worms don't have teeth. Lots of things don't have teeth, and they're perfectly happy.'

'Forget about teeth,' she said, fetching Youngblood's letter and the photographs from the top of the refrigerator.

He took the envelope when she offered it. 'What're you grinning about? What's this?'

'Read it.'

Heather sat across from him, her elbows on the table, her face cupped in her hands, watching him intently, trying to guess where he was in the letter by the expressions that crossed his face. The sight of him absorbing the news gladdened her as nothing had in a long time.

'This is . . . I . . . but why on earth . . .' He looked up from the letter and gaped at her. 'Is this true?'

She giggled. She hadn't giggled in ages. 'Yes. Yes! It's true, every incredible word of it. I called Paul Youngblood. He sounds like a very nice man. He was Eduardo's neighbor as well as his attorney. His nearest neighbor but still two miles away. He confirms everything in the letter, all of it. Ask me how much a "substantial amount of cash" might be.'

Jack blinked at her stupidly, as if the news had been a blunt instrument with which he'd been stunned. 'How much?'

'He can't be sure yet, not until he has the final tax figure, but after everything's said and done . . . it's going to be between three hundred and fifty thousand to four hundred thousand dollars.'

Jack paled. 'That can't be right.'

'That's what he told me.'

'*Plus* the ranch?'

'Plus the ranch.'

'Tommy talked about the place in Montana, said his dad loved it, but he hated it. Dull, Tommy said, nothing ever happening, the ass-end of nowhere. He loved his dad, told funny stories about him, but he never said he was *rich*.' He picked up the letter again, which rattled in his hand. 'Why would Tommy's dad leave everything to me, for God's sake?'

'That was one of the questions I asked Paul Youngblood. He says Tommy used to write to his dad about you, what a great guy you were. Talked about you like a brother. So with Tommy gone, his dad wanted you to have everything.'

'What do the other relatives have to say about that?'

'There aren't any relatives.'

Jack shook his head. 'But I never even met' – he consulted the letter – 'Eduardo. This is crazy. I mean, Jesus, it's wonderful but it's crazy. He gives everything to someone he hasn't even met?'

Unable to remain seated, bursting with excitement, Heather got up and went to the refrigerator. 'Paul Youngblood says the idea appealed to Eduardo, because *he* inherited it eight years ago from his former boss, which was a total surprise to him too.'

'I'll be damned,' he said wonderingly.

She removed a bottle of champagne that she had hidden in the vegetable drawer, where Jack wouldn't see it before he heard the news and knew what they were celebrating. 'According to Youngblood, Eduardo thought that surprising you with it . . . well, he seemed to see it as the only way he'd ever be able to repay his boss's kindness.'

When she returned to the table, Jack frowned at the bottle of champagne. 'I'm like a balloon, I'm floating, bouncing off the ceiling but . . . at the same time . . .'

'Tommy,' she said.

He nodded.

Peeling the foil off the champagne bottle, she said, 'We can't bring him back.'

'No, but . . .'

'He'd want us to be happy about this.'

'Yeah, I know. Tommy was a great guy.'

'So let's be happy.'

He said nothing.

Untwisting the wire cage that restrained the cork, she said, 'We'd be idiots if we weren't.'

'I know.'

'It's a miracle, and just when we need one.'

He stared at the champagne.

She said, 'It's not just our future. It's Toby's too.'

'He can keep his teeth now.'

Laughing, Heather said, 'It's a wonderful thing, Jack.'

At last his smile was broad and without reservation. 'You're damn right it's a wonderful thing – now we won't have to listen to him gumming his food.'

Removing the wire from the cork, she said, 'Even if we don't deserve so much good fortune, Toby does.'

'We all deserve it.' He got up, went to a nearby cabinet, and removed a clean dish towel from a drawer. 'Here, let me.' He took the bottle from Heather, draped the cloth over it. 'Might explode.' He twisted the cork, it popped, but the champagne did not foam out of the neck of the bottle.

She brought a couple of glasses, and he filled them.

'To Eduardo Fernandez,' she said by way of a toast.

'To Tommy.'

They drank, standing beside the table, and then he kissed her lightly. His quick tongue was sweet with champagne. 'My God, Heather, do you know what this means?'

They sat down again as she said, 'When we go out to dinner the next time, it can be someplace that serves the food on real plates instead of in paper containers.'

His eyes were shining, and she was thrilled to see him so happy. 'We can pay the mortgage, all the bills, put money away for Toby to go to college one day, maybe even take a vacation – and that's just from the cash. If we sell the farm—'

'Look at the photographs,' she urged, grabbing them, spreading them on the table in front of him.

'Very nice,' he said.

'Better than very nice. It's gorgeous, Jack. Look at those mountains! And look at this one – look, from this angle, standing in front of the house, you can see *forever*!'

He looked up from the snapshots and met her eyes. 'What am I hearing?'

'We don't have to sell it.'

'Live there?'

'Why not?'

'We're city people.'

'And we hate it.'

'Angelenos all our lives.'

'Isn't what it once was.'

She could see the idea intrigued him, and her own excitement grew as he began to come around to her point of view.

'We've wanted change for a long time,' he said. 'But I was never thinking *this* much change.'

'Look at the photographs.'

'Okay, yeah, it's gorgeous. But what would we do there? It's a lot of money but not enough to last forever. Besides, we're young, we can't vegetate, we need to *do* something.'

'Maybe we can start a business in Eagle's Roost.'

'What sort of business?'

'I don't know. Anything,' she said. 'We can go, see what it's like, and maybe we'll spot an opportunity right off the bat. And if not . . . well, we don't have to live there forever. A year, two years, and if we don't like it, we can sell.'

He finished his champagne, poured refreshers for both of them. 'Toby starts school in two weeks . . .'

'They have schools in Montana,' she said, though she knew that was not what concerned him.

He was no doubt thinking about the eleven-year-old girl who'd been shot to death one block from the elementary school that Toby would be attending.

She nudged him: 'He'll have six hundred acres to play on, Jack. How long has he wanted a dog, a golden retriever, and it just seemed like this place was too small for one?'

Staring at one of the snapshots, Jack said, 'At work today, we were talking about all the names this city has, more than other places. Like New York is The Big Apple, and that's it. But L.A. has lots of names – and none of them fit any more, none of them mean anything. Like The Big Orange. But there aren't any orange groves any more, all gone to tract houses and mini-malls and car lots. You can call it The City of Angels, but not much angelic happens here any more, not the way it once did, too many devils on the streets.'

'The City Where Stars Are Born,' she said.

'And nine hundred and ninety-nine out of a thousand kids who come here to be movie stars, what happens to them? Wind up used, abused, broke, and hooked on drugs.'

'The City Where the Sun Goes Down.'

'Well, it still does set in the west,' he acknowledged, picking up another photo from Montana. 'City Where the Sun Goes Down . . . that makes you think of the thirties and forties, swing music, men tipping their hats to one another and holding doors open for ladies in black cocktail dresses, elegant nightclubs overlooking the ocean, Bogart and Bacall, Gable and Lombard, people sipping martinis and watching golden sunsets. All gone. Mostly gone. These days, call it The City of the Dying Day.'

He fell silent. Shuffling the photographs, studying them.

She waited.

At last he looked up and said, 'Let's do it.'

PART TWO
The Land of the Winter Moon

Under the winter moon's pale light,
across the cold and starry night,
from snowy mountains soaring high
to ocean shores echoes the cry.
From barren sands to verdant fields,
from city streets to lonely wealds,
cries the tortured human heart,
seeking solace, wisdom, a chart
by which to understand its plight
under the winter moon's pale light.
Dawn is unable to fade the night.
Must we live 'ever in the blight
under the winter moon's cold light,
lost in loneliness, hate, and fright,
last night, tonight, tomorrow night
under the winter moon's bleak light?

—The Book of Counted Sorrows

14

IN THE distant age of the dinosaurs, fearful creatures as mighty as the Tyrannosaurus rex had perished in treacherous tar pits upon which the visionary builders of Los Angeles later erected freeways, shopping centers, houses, office buildings, theaters, topless bars, restaurants shaped like hot dogs and derby hats, churches, automated car washes, and so much more. Deep beneath parts of the metropolis, those fossilized monsters lay in eternal sleep.

Through September and October, Jack felt the city was still a pit in which *he* was mired. He believed he was obligated to give Lyle Crawford a thirty-day notice. And at the advice of their Realtor, before listing the house for sale, they painted it inside and out, installed new carpets and made minor repairs. The moment Jack made the decision to leave the city, he'd mentally packed and decamped. Now his heart was in the Montana highlands east of the Rockies, while he was still trying to pull his feet out of the L.A. tar.

Because they no longer needed every dollar of equity in the house, they priced it below market value. In spite of poor economic conditions, it moved quickly. By 28 October, they were in a sixty-day escrow with a buyer who appeared qualified, and they felt reasonably confident about embarking upon a new life and leaving the finalization of the sale to their Realtor.

On 4 November, they set out for their new home in a Ford

Explorer purchased with some of their inheritance. Jack insisted on leaving at six in the morning, determined that his last day in the city would not include the frustrating crawl of rush-hour traffic.

They took only suitcases and a few boxes of personal effects, and shipped little more than books. Additional photographs sent by Paul Youngblood had revealed their new house was already furnished in a style to which they could easily adjust. They might have to replace a few upholstered pieces, but many items were antiques of high quality and considerable beauty.

Departing the city on Interstate 5, they never looked back as they crested the Hollywood Hills and went north past Burbank, San Fernando, Valencia, Castaic, far out of the suburbs, into the Angeles National Forest, across Pyramid Lake, and up through the Tejon Pass between the Sierra Madre and Tehachapi Mountains.

Mile by mile, Jack felt himself rising out of an emotional and mental darkness. He was like a swimmer who had been weighed down with iron shackles and blocks, drowning in oceanic depths, now freed and soaring toward the surface, light, air.

Toby was amazed by the vast farmlands flanking the highway, so Heather quoted figures from a travel book. The San Joaquin Valley was more than a hundred and fifty miles long, defined by the Diablo Range on the west and Sierra foothills to the distant east. Those thousands of square miles were the most fertile in the world, producing eighty percent of the entire country's fresh vegetables and melons, half its fresh fruit and almonds, and much more.

They stopped at a roadside produce stand and bought a one-pound bag of roasted almonds for a quarter of what the cost would have been in a supermarket. Jack stood beside the Explorer, eating a handful of nuts, staring at vistas of productive fields and orchards. The day was blessedly quiet, and the air was clean.

Residing in the city, it was easy to forget there were other ways to live, worlds beyond the teeming streets of the human hive. He was a sleeper waking to a real world more diverse and interesting than the dream he had mistaken for reality.

In pursuit of their new life, they reached Reno that night, Salt Lake City the next, and Eagle's Roost, Montana, at three o'clock in the afternoon on the sixth of November.

*

To Kill a Mockingbird was one of Jack's favorite novels, and Atticus Finch, the courageous lawyer of that book, would have been at home in Paul Youngblood's office on the top floor of the only three-story building in Eagle's Roost. The wooden blinds surely dated from mid-century. The mahogany wainscoting, bookshelves, and cabinets were glass-smooth from decades of hand-polishing. The room had an air of gentility, a learned quietude, and the shelves held volumes of history and philosophy as well as law books.

The attorney actually greeted them with, 'Howdy, neighbors! What a pleasure this is, a genuine pleasure.' He had a firm handshake and a smile like soft sunshine on mountain crags.

Paul Youngblood would never have been recognized as a lawyer in L.A., and he might have been removed discreetly but forcefully if he had ever visited the swanky offices of the powerhouse firms quartered in Century City. He was fifty, tall, lanky, with close-cropped iron-gray hair. His face was creased and ruddy from years spent outdoors, and his big, leathery hands were scarred by physical labor. He wore scuffed boots, tan jeans, a white shirt, and a bolo tie with a silver clasp in the form of a bucking bronco. In L.A., people in similar outfits were dentists or accountants or executives, costumed for an evening at a Country-Western bar, and could not disguise their true nature. But Youngblood looked as if he had been born in Western garb, birthed between a cactus and a campfire, and raised on horseback.

Although he appeared to be rough enough to walk into a biker bar and take on a mob of machine-wranglers, the attorney was soft-spoken and so polite that Jack was aware of how badly his own manners had deteriorated under the constant abrasion of daily life in the city.

Youngblood won Toby's heart by calling him 'Scout' and offering to teach him horseback riding 'come spring, starting with a pony of course . . and assuming that's okay with your folks.' When the lawyer put on a suede jacket and a cowboy hat before leading them out to Quartermass Ranch, Toby regarded him with wide-eyed awe.

They followed Youngblood's white Bronco across sixteen miles of country more beautiful than it had appeared to be in photographs. Two stone columns, surmounted by a weathered wooden arch, marked the entrance to their property. Burned into the arch, rustic lettering spelled QUARTERMASS RANCH. They turned off the county route, under the sign, and headed uphill.

'Wow! This all belongs to us?' Toby asked from the back seat, enraptured by the sprawl of fields and forests. Before either Jack or Heather could answer him, he posed the question that he no doubt had been wanting to ask for weeks: 'Can I have a dog?'

'Just a dog?' Jack asked.

'Huh?'

'With this much land, you could have a pet cow.'

Toby laughed. 'Cows aren't pets.'

'You're wrong,' Jack said, striving for a serious tone. 'They're darned good pets.'

'Cows!' Toby said incredulously.

'No, really. You can teach a cow to fetch, roll over, beg for its dinner, shake hands, all the usual dog stuff – plus they make milk for your breakfast cereal.'

'You're putting me on. Mom, is he serious?'

'The only problem is,' Heather said, 'you might get a cow that likes to chase cars – in which case it can do a lot more damage than a dog.'

'That's silly,' the boy said, and giggled.

210

'Not if you're in the car being chased,' Heather assured him.

'Then it's terrifying,' Jack agreed.

'I'll stick with a dog.'

'Well, if that's what you want,' Jack said.

'You mean it? I can have a dog?'

Heather said, 'I don't see why not.'

Toby whooped with delight.

The private lane led to the main residence, which overlooked a meadow of golden-brown grass. In the last hour of its journey toward the western mountains, the sun back-lit the property, and the house cast a long purple shadow. They parked in that shade behind Paul Youngblood's Bronco.

*

They began their tour in the basement. Although windowless and entirely beneath ground level, it was cold. The first room contained a washer, a dryer, a double sink, and a set of pine cabinets. The corners of the ceiling were enlivened by the architecture of spiders and a few cocooning moths. In the second room stood an electric forced-air furnace, and a water heater.

A Japanese-made electric generator, as large as the washing machine, was also provided. It looked capable of producing enough power to light a small town.

'Why do we need this?' Jack wondered, indicating the generator.

Paul Youngblood said, 'Bad storm can knock out the public power supply for a couple of days in some of these rural areas. Since we don't have natural-gas service, and the price of being supplied by a fuel-oil company in this territory can be high, we have to rely on electricity for heating, cooking, everything. It goes out, we have fireplaces, but that's not ideal. And Stan Quartermass was a man who never wanted to be without the comforts of civilization.'

'But this is a monster,' Jack said, patting the dust-sheathed generator.

'Supplies the main house, caretaker's house, and the stables. Doesn't just provide backup power to run a few lights, either. As long as you've got gasoline, you can go on living with all the amenities, just as if you were still on public power.'

'Might be fun to rough it a couple of days now and then,' Jack suggested.

The attorney frowned and shook his head. 'Not when the real temperature is below zero and the wind-chill factor pushes it down to minus thirty or forty degrees.'

'Ouch,' Heather said. She hugged herself at the very thought of such arctic cold.

'I'd call that more than roughing it,' Youngblood said.

Jack agreed. 'I'd call it "suicide". I'll make sure we have a good gasoline supply.'

*

The thermostat had been set low in the two main floors of the untenanted house. A stubborn chill pooled everywhere, like the icy remnant of a flood tide. It surrendered gradually to the electric heat, which Paul switched on after they ascended from the basement and inspected half the ground floor. In spite of her insulated ski jacket, Heather shivered through the entire tour.

The house had both character and every convenience, and would be even easier to settle into than they'd expected. Eduardo Fernandez's personal effects and clothing had not been disposed of; so they would need to empty closets to make room for their own things. In the three months since the old man's sudden death, the place had been closed and unattended; a thin layer of dust coated every surface. However, Eduardo had led a neat and orderly life; there was no great mess with which to deal.

In the final bedroom on the second floor, at the back of the house, coppery late-afternoon sunlight slanted through west-facing windows, and the air glowed like that in front of an open furnace door. It was light without heat, and still Heather shivered.

Toby said, 'This is great, this is terrific!'

The room was more than twice the size of the one in which the boy had slept in Los Angeles, but Heather knew he was less excited by the dimensions than by the almost whimsical architecture, which would have sparked the imagination of any child. The twelve-foot-high ceiling was composed of four groin vaults, and the shadows that lay across those concave surfaces were complex and intriguing.

'Neat,' Toby said, staring up at the ceiling. 'Like hanging under a parachute.'

In the wall to the left of the hall door was a four-foot-deep, six-foot-long, arched niche into which a custom-built bed had been fitted. Behind the headboard on the left and in the back wall of the niche were recessed bookshelves and deep cabinets for the storage of model spaceships, action figures, games, and the other possessions that a young boy cherished. Curtains were drawn back from both sides of the niche and, when closed, could seal it off like a berth on an old-fashioned railroad sleeping car.

'Can this be my room, can it, please?' Toby asked.

'Looks to me like it was made for you,' Jack said.

'Great!'

Opening one of two other doors in the room, Paul said, 'This walk-in closet is so deep you could almost say it's a room itself.'

The last door revealed the head of an uncarpeted staircase as tightly curved as that in a lighthouse. The wooden treads squeaked as the four of them descended.

Heather instantly disliked the stairs. Perhaps she was somewhat claustrophobic in that cramped and windowless space, following Paul Youngblood and Toby, with Jack close behind. Perhaps the inadequate lighting – two widely spaced, bare bulbs in the ceiling – made her uneasy. A mustiness and vague underlying odor of decay didn't add any charm. Neither did spider webs hung with dead moths and beetles. Whatever the reason, her heart began to pound as if they were climbing rather than descending. She was overcome by the bizarre fear – similar to the nameless dread in a nightmare – that something hostile and infinitely strange was waiting for them below.

The last step brought them into a windowless vestibule, where Paul had to use a key to unlock the first of two lower doors.

'Kitchen,' he said.

Nothing fearful waited beyond, merely the room he had indicated.

'We'll go this way,' he said, turning to the second door, which didn't require a key from the inside.

When the thumb-turn on the deadbolt lock proved stiff from lack of use, the few seconds of delay were almost more than Heather could tolerate. Now she was convinced that something was coming down the steps *behind* them, the murderous phantom of a bad dream. She wanted out of that narrow place immediately, desperately— *out*.

The door creaked open.

They followed Paul through the second exit on to the back porch. They were twelve feet to the left of the house's main rear entrance that led into the kitchen.

Heather took several deep breaths, purging her lungs of the contaminated air from the stairwell. Her fear swiftly abated and her racing heart regained a normal pace. She looked back into the vestibule where the steps curved upward out of sight. Of course no denizen of a nightmare appeared, and her moment of panic seemed more foolish and inexplicable by the second.

Jack, unaware of Heather's inner turmoil, put one hand on Toby's head and said, 'Well, if that's going to be your room, I don't want to catch you sneaking girls up the back steps.'

'Girls?' Toby was astonished. 'Yuck. Why would I want to have anything to do with *girls*?'

'I suspect you'll figure that one out all on your own, given a little time,' the attorney said, amused.

'And too fast,' Jack said. 'Five years from now, we'll have to fill those stairs with concrete, seal them off forever.'

Heather found the will to turn her back on the door as the attorney closed it. She was baffled by the episode and relieved that no one had been aware of her odd reaction.

Los Angeles jitters. She hadn't shed the city. She was in rural Montana, where there probably hadn't been a murder in a decade, where most people left doors unlocked day and night – but psychologically, she remained in the shadow of the Big Orange, living in subconscious anticipation of sudden, senseless violence. Just a delayed case of Los Angeles jitters.

'Better show you the rest of the property,' Paul said. 'We don't have much more than half an hour of daylight left.'

They followed him down the porch steps and up the sloping rear lawn toward a smaller, stone house tucked among the evergreens at the edge of the forest. Heather recognized it from the photographs Paul had sent: the caretaker's residence.

As twilight stealthily approached, the sky far to the east was a deep sapphire. It faded to a lighter blue in the west, where the sun hastened toward the mountains.

The temperature had slipped out of the fifties. Heather walked with her hands jammed in jacket pockets and her shoulders hunched.

She was pleased to see that Jack took the hill with vigor, not limping at all. Occasionally his left leg ached and he favored it, but not today. She found it hard to believe that only eight months ago, their lives seemed to have been changed for the worse, forever. No wonder she was still jumpy. Such a terrible eight months. But everything was fine now. Really fine.

The rear lawn hadn't been maintained after Eduardo's death. The grass had grown six or eight inches before the aridity of late summer and the chill of early autumn had turned it brown and pinched off its growth until spring. It crackled faintly under their feet.

215

'Ed and Margarite moved out of the caretaker's house when they inherited the ranch eight years ago,' Paul said as they drew near the stone bungalow. 'Sold the contents, nailed plywood over the windows. Don't think anyone's been in there since. Unless you plan to have a caretaker yourself, you probably won't have a use for it, either. But you ought to take a look just the same.'

Pine trees crowded three sides of the smaller house. The forest was so primeval that darkness dwelt in much of it even before the sun had set. The bristling green of heavy boughs, enfolded with purple-black shadows, was a lovely sight – but those wooded realms had an air of mystery that Heather found disturbing, even a little menacing.

For the first time she wondered what animals might from time to time venture out of those wilds into the yard. Wolves? Bears? Mountain lions? Was Toby safe here?

Oh, for God's sake, Heather.

She was thinking like a city-dweller, always wary of danger, perceiving threats everywhere. In fact, wild animals avoided people and ran if approached.

What do you expect? she asked herself sarcastically. That you'll be barricaded in the house while gangs of bears hammer on the doors and packs of snarling wolves throw themselves through windows like something out of a bad TV movie about ecological disaster?

Instead of a porch, the caretaker's house had a large flagstone-paved area in front of the entrance. They stood there while Paul found the right key on the ring he carried.

The north-east-south panorama from the perimeter of the high woods was stunning, better even than from the main house. Like a landscape in a Maxfield Parrish painting, the descending fields and forests receded into a distant violet haze under a darkly luminous sapphire sky.

The fading afternoon was windless, and the silence was so deep she might have thought she'd gone deaf – except for the clinking of the attorney's keys. After a life in the city, such quiet was eerie.

The door opened with much cracking and scraping, as if an ancient seal had been broken. Paul stepped across the threshold, into the dark living room, and flicked the light switch.

Heather heard it click several times, but the lights didn't come on.

Stepping outside again, Paul said, 'Figures. Ed must've shut off all the power at the breaker box. I know where it is. You wait here, I'll be right back.'

They stood at the front door, staring at the gloom beyond the threshold, while the attorney disappeared around the corner of the house. His departure made Heather apprehensive, though she wasn't sure why. Perhaps because he had gone alone.

'When I get a dog, can he sleep in my room?' Toby asked.

'Sure,' Jack said, 'but not on the bed.'

'Not on the bed? Then where would he sleep?'

'Dogs usually make do with the floor.'

'That's not fair.'

'You'll never hear a dog complain.'

'But why not on the bed?'

'Fleas.'

'I'll take good care of him. He won't have fleas.'

'Dog hairs in the sheets.'

'That won't be a problem, Dad.'

'What – you're going to shave him, have a bald dog?'

'I'll just brush him every day.'

Listening to her husband and son, Heather watched the corner of the house, increasingly certain that Paul Youngblood was never going to return. Something terrible had happened to him. Something—

He reappeared. 'All the breakers were off. We should be in business now.'

217

What's *wrong* with me? Heather wondered. Got to shake this damn L.A. attitude.

Standing inside the front door, Paul flipped the wall switch repeatedly, without success. The dimly visible ceiling fixture in the empty living room remained dark. The carriage lamp outside, next to the door, didn't come on either.

'Maybe he had the electric service discontinued,' Jack suggested.

The attorney shook his head. 'Don't see how that could be. This is on the same line as the main house and the stable.'

'Bulbs might be dead, sockets corroded after all this time.'

Pushing his cowboy hat back on his head, scratching his brow, frowning, Paul said, 'Not like Ed to let things deteriorate. I'd expect him to do routine maintenance, keep the place in good working order in case the next owner had a need for it. That's just how he was. Good man, Ed. Not much of a socializer, but a good man.'

'Well,' Heather said, 'we can investigate the problem in a couple of days, once we're settled down at the main place.'

Paul retreated from the house, pulled the door shut, and locked it. 'You might want to have an electrician out to check the wiring.'

Instead of returning the way they had come, they angled across the sloping yard toward the stable that stood on more level land to the south of the main house. Toby ran ahead, arms out at his sides, making a *brrrrrrrrrrr* noise with his lips, pretending to be an airplane.

Heather glanced back at the caretaker's bungalow a couple of times, and at the woods on both sides of it. She had a peculiar tingly feeling on the back of her neck.

'Pretty cold for the sixth of November,' Jack said.

The attorney laughed. 'This isn't southern California, I'm afraid. Actually, it's been a mild day. Temperature's probably going to drop well below freezing tonight.'

'You get much snow up here?'

'Does Hell get many sinners?'

'When can we expect the first snow – before Christmas?'

'Way before Christmas, Jack. If we had a big storm tomorrow, nobody'd think it was an early season.'

'That's why we got the Explorer,' Heather said. 'Four-wheel drive. That should get us around all winter, shouldn't it?'

'Mostly, yeah,' Paul said, pulling down the brim of his hat, which he had pushed up earlier to scratch his forehead.

Toby had reached the stable. Short legs pumping, he vanished around the side of it before Heather could call out to him to wait.

Paul said, 'But every winter there's one or two times where you're going to be snowbound a day or three, drifts half over the house sometimes.'

'Snowbound? Half over the house?' Jack said, sounding a little like a kid himself. 'Really?'

'Get one of those blizzards coming down out of the Rockies, it can drop two or three feet of snow in twenty-four hours. Winds like to peel your skin off. County crews can't keep the roads open all at once. You have chains for that Explorer?'

'A couple of sets,' Jack said.

Heather walked faster toward the stable, hoping the men would pick up their pace to accompany her, which they did.

Toby was still out of sight.

'What you should also get,' Paul told them, 'soon as you can, is a good plow for the front of it. Even if county crews get the roads open, you have half a mile of private lane to take care of.'

If the boy was just 'flying' around the stable, with his arms spread like wings, he should have reappeared by now.

'Lex Parker's garage,' Paul continued, 'in town, can fit your truck with the armatures, attach the plow, hydraulic arms to raise and lower it, a real fine rig. Just leave it on all winter, remove it in the spring, and you'll be ready for however much butt-kicking Mother Nature has in store for us.'

No sign of Toby.

Heather's heart was pounding again. The sun was about to set.

219

If Toby . . . if he got lost or . . . or something . . . they would have a harder time finding him at night. She restrained herself from breaking into a run.

'Now, last winter,' Paul continued smoothly, unaware of her trepidation, 'was on the dry side, which probably means we're going to take a shellacking this year.'

As they reached the stable and as Heather was about to cry out for Toby, he reappeared. He was no longer playing airplane. He sprinted to her side through the unmown grass, grinning and excited. 'Mom, this place is neat, really neat. Maybe I can really have a pony, huh?'

'Maybe,' Heather said, swallowing hard before she could get the word out. 'Don't go running off like that, okay?'

'Why not?'

'Just don't.'

'Sure, okay,' Toby said. He was a good boy.

She glanced back toward the caretaker's house and the wilderness beyond. Perched on the jagged peaks of the mountains, the sun seemed to quiver like a raw egg yolk just before dissolving around the tines of a prodding fork. The highest pinnacles of rock were gray and black and pink in the fiery light of day's end. Miles of serried forests shelved down to the fieldstone bungalow.

All was still and peaceful.

The stable was a single-story fieldstone building with a slate roof. The long side walls had no exterior stall doors, only small windows high under the eaves. There was a white barn door on the end, which rolled open easily when Paul tried it, and the electric lights came on with the first flip of a switch.

'As you can see,' the attorney said as he led them inside, 'it was every inch a gentleman's ranch, not a spread that had to show a profit in any way.'

Beyond the concrete threshold, which was flush with the ground, the stable floor was composed of soft, tamped earth as pale as sand. Five empty stalls with half-doors stood to each side of the wide

220

center promenade, more spacious than ordinary barn stalls. On the twelve-inch wooden posts between stalls were cast-bronze sconces that threw amber light toward both the ceiling and floor; they were needed because the high-set windows were too small – each about eight inches high by eighteen long – to admit much sunlight even at high noon.

'Stan Quartermass kept this place heated in winter, cooled in the summer,' Paul Youngblood said. He pointed to vent grilles set in the suspended tongue-and-groove ceiling. 'Seldom smelled like a stable, either, because he vented it continuously, pumped fresh air in. And all the ductwork is heavily insulated, so the sound of the fans is too low to bother horses.'

On the left, beyond the final stall, was a large tackroom where saddles, bridles, and other equipment had been kept. It was empty except for a built-in sink as long and deep as a trough.

To the right, opposite the tackroom, were top-access bins where oats, apples, and other feed had been stored, but they were now all empty as well. On the wall near the bins, several tools were racked business-end up: a pitchfork, two shovels, and a rake.

'Smoke alarm,' Paul said, pointing to a device attached to the header above the big door that was opposite the one by which they had entered. 'Wired into the electrical system. You can't make the mistake of letting batteries go dead. It sounds in the house, so Stan wouldn't have to worry about not hearing it.'

'The guy sure loved his horses,' Jack said.

'Oh, he sure did, and he had more Hollywood money than he knew what to do with. After Stan died, Ed took special pains to be sure the people who bought all the animals would treat them well. Stan was a nice man. Seemed only right.'

'I could have *ten* ponies,' Toby said.

'Wrong,' Heather said. 'Whatever business we decide to get into, it won't be a manure factory.'

'Well, I just mean, there's room,' the boy said.

'A dog, ten ponies,' Jack said. 'You're turning into a real farm boy. What's next? Chickens?'

'A cow,' Toby said. 'I been thinking what you said about cows, and you talked me into it.'

'Wiseass,' Jack said, taking a playful swipe at the boy.

Dodging successfully, laughing, Toby said, 'Like father, like son. Mr Youngblood, did you know my Dad says cows can do any tricks dogs can do – roll over and play dead and all that?'

'Well,' the attorney replied, leading them back through the stable toward the door by which they'd entered, 'I know a steer that can walk on his hind feet.'

'Really?'

'More than that. He can do math as well as you or me.'

The claim was made with such calm conviction that the boy looked up wide-eyed at Youngblood. 'You mean, like you ask him a problem, he can pound out the answer with his hoof?'

'He could do that, sure. Or just tell you the answer.'

'Huh?'

'This steer, he can talk.'

'No way,' Toby said, following Jack and Heather outside.

'Sure. He can talk, dance, drive a car, and he goes to church every Sunday,' Paul said, switching off the stable lights. 'Name's Lester Steer, and he owns the Main Street Diner in town.'

'He's a man!'

'Well, of course he's a man,' Paul said, rolling the big door shut. 'Never said he wasn't.'

The attorney winked at Heather, and she realized how much she had come to like him in such a short time.

'Oh, you're tricky,' Toby told Paul. 'Dad, he's tricky.'

'Not me,' Paul said. 'I only told you the truth, Scout. You tricked yourself.'

'Paul is an attorney, son,' Jack said. 'You've always got to be careful of attorneys or you'll end up with no ponies *or* cows.'

Paul laughed. 'Listen to your dad. He's wise. Very wise.'

Only an orange rind of sun remained in view, and in seconds, the irregular blade of mountain peaks peeled it away. Shadows spread toward one another. The somber twilight, all deep blues and funereal purples, hinted at the unrelenting darkness of night in that largely unpeopled vastness.

Looking directly upslope from the stable, toward a knoll at the terminus of the western woods, Paul said, 'No point showing you the cemetery in this poor light. Not that much to see even at noon.'

'Cemetery?' Jack said, frowning.

'You've got a state-certified private cemetery on your grounds,' the attorney said. 'Twelve plots, though only four have been used.'

Staring toward the knoll, where she could vaguely see part of what might have been a low stone wall and a pair of gate posts in the plum-dark light, Heather said, 'Who's buried there?'

'Stan Quartermass, Ed Fernandez, Margarite, and Tommy.'

'Tommy, my old partner, he's buried up there?' Jack asked.

'Private cemetery,' Heather said. She told herself that the only reason she shivered was because the air was growing colder by the minute. 'That's a little macabre.'

'Not so strange around here,' Paul assured her. 'A lot of these ranches, the same family has been on the land for generations. It's not only their home, it's their hometown, the only place they love. Eagle's Roost is just somewhere to shop. When it comes to being put to eternal rest, they want to be part of the land they've given their lives to.'

'Wow,' Toby said, 'how cool can you get? We live in a *graveyard*.'

'Hardly that,' Paul said. 'My grandfolks and my parents are buried over at our place, and there's really nothing creepy about it. Comforting. Gives you a sense of heritage, continuity. Carolyn and I figure to be put to rest there, too, though I can't say what our kids want to do, now they're off in medical school and law school, making new lives that don't have anything to do with the ranch.'

'Darn it, we just missed Halloween,' Toby said more to himself than to them. He stared toward the cemetery, caught up in a personal fantasy that no doubt involved the challenge of walking through a graveyard on All Hallows Eve.

They stood quietly for a moment.

The dusk was heavy, silent, still.

Uphill, the cemetery seemed to cast off the fading light and pull the night down like a shroud, covering itself with darkness faster than any of the land around it.

Heather glanced at Jack to see if he showed any sign of being troubled by having Tommy Fernandez's remains buried nearby. Tommy had died at his side, after all, eleven months before Luther Bryson had been shot down. With Tommy's grave so close, Jack couldn't help but recall, perhaps too vividly, violent events best consigned forever to the deeper vaults of memory.

As if sensing her concern, Jack smiled. 'Makes me feel better to know Tommy found rest in a place as beautiful as this.'

As they walked back to the house, the attorney invited them to dinner and to stay overnight with him and his wife. 'One, you arrived too late today to get the place cleaned and livable. Two, you don't have any fresh food here, only what might be in the freezer. And three, you don't want to have to cook after putting in a long day on the road. Why not relax this evening, get a start on it first thing in the morning, when you're rested?'

Heather was grateful for the invitation, not merely for the reasons Paul had enumerated but because she remained uneasy about the house and the isolation in which it stood. She had decided that her jumpiness was nothing other than a city person's initial response to more wide open spaces than she'd ever seen or contemplated before. A mild phobic reaction. Temporary agoraphobia. It would pass. She simply needed a day or two – perhaps only a few hours – to acclimate herself to this new landscape and way of life. An evening with Paul Youngblood and his wife might be just the right medicine.

After setting the thermostats throughout the house, even in the basement, to be sure it would be warm in the morning, they locked up, got in the Explorer, and followed Paul's Bronco to the county road. He turned east toward town, and so did they.

The brief twilight had vanished under the falling wall of night. The moon had not yet risen. The darkness on all sides was so deep that it seemed as if it could never be banished again even by the ascension of the sun.

The Youngblood ranch was named after the predominant tree within its boundaries. Spotlights at each end of the overhead entrance sign were directed inward to reveal green letters on a white background: PONDEROSA PINES. Under those two words, in smaller letters: *Paul and Carolyn Youngblood*.

The attorney's spread, a working ranch, was considerably larger than their own. On both sides of the entrance lane, which was even longer than the one at Quartermass Ranch, lay extensive complexes of white-trimmed red stables, riding rings, exercise yards, and fenced pastures. The buildings were illuminated by the pearly glow of low-voltage nightlights. White fences divided the rising meadows: dimly phosphorescent, geometric patterns that dwindled into the darkness, like lines of inscrutable hieroglyphics on tomb walls.

The main house, in front of which they parked, was a large, low ranch-style building of river rock and darkly stained pine. It seemed to be an almost organic extension of the land.

As he walked with them to the house, Paul answered Jack's question about the business of Ponderosa Pines. 'We have two basic enterprises, actually. We raise and race quarter horses, which is a popular sport throughout the West, from New Mexico to the Canadian border. Then we also breed and sell several types of show horses that never go out of style, mostly Arabians. We have one of the finest Arabian bloodlines in the country, specimens so perfect and pretty they can break your heart – or make you pull out your wallet if you're obsessed with the breed.'

'No cows?' Toby said as they reached the foot of the steps that led up to the long, deep veranda at the front of the house.

'Sorry, Scout, no cows,' the attorney said. 'Lots of ranches 'round here have cattle, but not us. Howsomever, we *do* have our share of cowboys.' He pointed to a cluster of lighted bungalows approximately a hundred and twenty yards to the east of the house. 'Eighteen wranglers currently live here on the ranch, with their wives if they're married. A little town of our own, sort of.'

'Cowboys,' Toby said in the awed tone of voice with which he had spoken of the private graveyard and of the prospect of having a pony. Montana was proving to be as exotic to him as any distant planet in the comic books and science fiction movies he liked. 'Real cowboys.'

Carolyn Youngblood greeted them at the door and warmly welcomed them. To be the mother of Paul's children, she must have been his age, fifty, but she looked and acted younger. She wore tight jeans and a decoratively stitched red-and-white Western shirt, revealing the lean, limber figure of an athletic thirty-year-old. Her snowy hair – cut short in an easy-care gamine style – wasn't brittle as white hair often was, but thick and soft and lustrous. Her face was far less lined than Paul's, and her skin was silk-smooth.

Heather decided, if this was what life in the ranch country of Montana could do for a woman, she could overcome any aversion to the unnervingly large open spaces, to the immensity of the night, to the spookiness of the woods, and even to the novel experience of having four corpses interred in a far corner of her backyard.

*

After dinner, when Jack and Paul were alone for a few minutes in the study, each of them with a glass of port, looking at the many framed photographs of prize-winning horses that nearly covered one of the knotty-pine walls, the attorney suddenly changed the

226

subject from equestrian bloodlines and quarter-horse champions to Quartermass Ranch. 'I'm sure you folks are going to be happy there, Jack.'

'I think so too.'

'It's a great place for a boy like Toby to grow up.'

'A dog, a pony – it's like a dream come true for him.'

'Beautiful land.'

'So peaceful compared to L.A. Hell, there *is* no comparison.'

Paul opened his mouth to say something, hesitated, and looked instead at the horse photo with which he'd broken off his colorful account of Ponderosa Pines' racing triumphs. When the attorney did speak, Jack had the feeling that what he said was not what he had been *about* to say before the hesitation.

'And though we aren't spitting-distance neighbors, Jack, I hope we'll be close in other ways, get to know each other well.'

'I'd like that.'

The attorney hesitated again, sipping from his glass of port to cover his indecision.

After tasting his own port, Jack said, 'Something wrong, Paul?'

'No, not wrong . . . just . . . What makes you say that?'

'I was a cop for a long time. I have a sort of sixth sense about people holding back something.'

'Guess you do. You'll probably be a good businessman when you decide what it is you want to get into.'

'So what's up?'

Sighing, Paul sat on a corner of his large desk. 'Didn't even know if I should mention this, 'cause I *don't* want you to be concerned about it, don't think there's really any reason to be.'

'Yes?'

'It was a heart attack killed Ed Fernandez, like I told you. Massive heart attack took him down as sudden and complete as a bullet in the head. Coroner couldn't find anything else, only the heart.'

'Coroner? Are you saying an autopsy was performed?'

'Yeah, sure was,' Paul said, and sipped his port.

Jack was certain that, in Montana as in California, autopsies were not performed every time someone died, especially not when the decedent was a man of Eduardo Fernandez's age and all but certain to have expired of natural causes. The old man would have been cut open only under special circumstances, primarily if visible trauma indicated the possibility of death at the hands of another.

'But you said the coroner couldn't find anything but a damaged heart, no wounds.'

Staring at the glimmering surface of the port in his glass, the attorney said, 'Ed's body was found across the threshold between his kitchen and the back porch, lying on his right side, blocking the door open. He was clutching a shotgun with both hands.'

'Ah. Could be suspicious enough circumstances to justify an autopsy. Or it could be he was just going out to do some hunting.'

'Wasn't hunting season.'

'You telling me a little poaching is unheard of in these parts, especially when a man's hunting out of season on his own land?'

The attorney shook his head. 'Not at all. But Ed wasn't a hunter. Never had been.'

'You sure?'

'Yeah. Stan Quartermass was the hunter, and Ed just inherited the guns. And another odd thing – wasn't just a full magazine in that shotgun. He'd also pumped an extra round into the breach. No hunter with half a brain would traipse around with a shell ready to go. He trips and falls, he might blow off his own head.'

'Doesn't make sense to carry it in the house that way, either.'

'Unless,' Paul said, 'there was some immediate threat.'

'You mean, like an intruder or prowler.'

'Maybe. Though that's rarer than steak tartare in these parts.'

'Any signs of burglary, house ransacked?'

'No. Nothing at all like that.'

'Who found the body?'

228

'Travis Potter, veterinarian from Eagle's Roost. Which brings up another oddity. June tenth, more than three weeks before he died, Ed took some dead raccoons to Travis, asked him to examine them.'

The attorney told Jack as much about the raccoons as Eduardo had told Potter, then explained Potter's findings.

'Brain swelling?' Jack asked uneasily.

'But no sign of infection, no disease,' Paul reassured him. 'Travis asked Ed to keep a lookout for other animals acting peculiar. Then . . . when they talked again on June seventeenth, he had the feeling Ed had seen something more but was holding out on him.'

'Why would he hold out on Potter? Fernandez was the one who got Potter involved in the first place.'

The attorney shrugged. 'Anyway, on the morning of July sixth, Travis was still curious, so he went out to Quartermass Ranch to talk to Ed – and found his body instead. Coroner says Ed had been dead no less than twenty-four hours, probably no more than thirty-six.'

Jack paced along the wall of horse photographs and along another wall of bookshelves, and then back again, slowly turning the glass of port around in his hand. 'So you think – what? Fernandez saw some animal behaving *really* strangely, doing something that spooked him enough to go load up the shotgun?'

'Maybe.'

'Could he have been going outside to shoot this animal because it was acting rabid or crazy in some other way?'

'That's occurred to us, yes. And maybe he was so worked up, so excited – that's what brought on the heart attack.'

At the study window, Jack stared at the lights of the cowboys' bungalows, which were unable to press back the densely clotted night. He finished the port. 'I assume, from what you've said, Fernandez wasn't a particularly excitable man, not an hysteric.'

'The opposite. Ed was about as excitable as a tree stump.'

Turning away from the window, Jack said, 'So then what could he have seen that would've gotten his heart pumping so hard? How bizarre would an animal have had to be acting, how much of a threat would it have to've seemed . . . before Fernandez would've worked himself up to a heart attack?'

'There you put your finger on it,' the attorney said, finishing his own port. 'Just doesn't make sense.'

'Seems like we have a mystery here.'

'Fortunate that you were a detective.'

'Not me. I was a patrol officer.'

'Well, now you've been promoted by circumstances.' Paul got up from the corner of his desk. 'Listen, I'm sure there's nothing to be worried about. We *know* those raccoons weren't diseased. And there's probably a reasonable explanation for what Ed was going to do with that gun. This is peaceful country. Damned if I can see what kind of danger could be out there.'

'I suspect you're right,' Jack agreed.

'I brought it up only because . . . well, it seemed odd. I thought if you *did* see something peculiar, you ought to know not just to dismiss it. Call Travis. Or me.'

Jack put his empty glass on the desk beside Paul's. 'I'll do that. Meanwhile . . . I'd appreciate if you didn't mention this to Heather. We've had a real bad year down there in L.A. This is a new start for us in a lot of ways, and I don't want a shadow on it. We're a little shaky. We need this to work, need to stay positive.'

'That's why I chose this moment to tell you.'

'Thanks, Paul.'

'And don't *you* worry about it.'

'I won't.'

''Cause I'm sure there's nothing to it. Just one of life's many little mysteries. People new to this country sometimes get the heebie-jeebies 'cause of all the open space, the wilderness. I don't mean to get you on edge like that.'

230

'Don't worry,' Jack assured him. 'After you've played bullet billiards with some of the crazies loose in L.A., there's nothing any raccoon can do to spoil your mood.'

15

DURING THEIR first four days at Quartermass Ranch – Tuesday through Friday – Heather, Jack, and Toby cleaned the house from top to bottom. They wiped down walls and woodwork, polished furniture, vacuumed upholstery and carpets, washed all the dishes and utensils, put new shelf paper in the kitchen cabinets, disposed of Eduardo's clothes through a church in town that distributed to the needy, and in general made the place their own.

They didn't intend to register Toby for school until the following week, giving him time to adjust to their new life. He was thrilled to be free while other boys his age were trapped in third-grade classrooms.

On Wednesday the moving company arrived with the small shipment from Los Angeles: the rest of their clothes, their books, Heather's computers and related equipment, Toby's toys and games, and the other items they hadn't been willing to give away or sell. The presence of a greater number of their familiar possessions made the new house seem more like home.

Although the days became chillier and more overcast as the week waned, Heather's mood remained bright and cheerful. She was not troubled by anxiety attacks like the one she'd experienced when Paul Youngblood had first shown them around the property Monday evening; day by day that paranoid episode faded from her thoughts.

She swept away spider webs and desiccated insect prey in the back stairs, washed the spiraling treads with pungent ammonia water, and rid that space of mustiness and the faint odor of decay. No uncanny feelings overcame her, and it was hard to believe that she'd felt a superstitious dread of the stairs when she'd first descended them behind Paul and Toby.

From a few second-floor windows, she could see the graveyard on the knoll. It didn't strike her as macabre any longer, because of what Paul had said about ranchers' attachment to the land that had sustained their families for generations. In the dysfunctional family in which she'd been raised, and in Los Angeles, there had been so little tradition and such a weak sense of belonging anywhere or to anything that these ranchers' love of home seemed touching – even spiritually uplifting – rather than morbid or strange.

Heather cleaned out the refrigerator, too, and they filled it with healthy foods for quick breakfasts and lunches. The freezer compartment was already half filled with packaged dinners, but she delayed doing an inventory because more important tasks awaited her.

Four evenings in a row, too weary from their chores to cook, they drove into Eagle's Roost to eat at the Main Street Diner, owned and operated by the steer that could drive a car and do math and dance. The food was first-rate country cooking.

The sixteen-mile journey was insignificant. In southern California, no trip had ever been measured by distance but by the length of time needed to complete it, and even a quick jaunt to the market, in city traffic, had required half an hour. A sixteen-mile drive from one point in L.A. to another could take an hour, two hours, or eternity, depending on traffic and the violent tendencies of other motorists. Who knew? However, they could routinely drive to Eagle's Roost in twenty or twenty-five minutes, which seemed like *nothing*. The perpetually uncrowded highways were exhilarating.

Friday night, as on every night since they'd arrived in Montana, she fell asleep without difficulty. For the first time, however, her sleep was troubled . . .

In her dream, she was in a cold place blacker than a moonless and overcast night, blacker than a windowless room. She was feeling her way forward, as if she had been stricken blind, curious but at first unafraid. She was actually smiling, because she was convinced that something wonderful awaited her in a warm, well-lighted place beyond the darkness. Treasure. Pleasure. Enlightenment, peace, joy, and transcendence waiting for her if she could find her way. Sweet peace, freedom from fear, freedom forever, enlightenment, joy, pleasure more intense than any she had ever known, waiting, waiting. But she fumbled through the impenetrable darkness, feeling with hands extended in front of her, always moving in the wrong direction, turning this way and that, that way and this.

Curiosity became overpowering desire. She wanted whatever lay beyond the wall of night, wanted it as badly as she had ever wanted anything in her life, more than food or love or wealth or happiness, for it was all those things and more. Find the door, the door and the light beyond, the wonderful door, beautiful light, peace and joy, freedom and pleasure, release from sorrow, transformation, so close, achingly close, reach out, reach. Want became need, compulsion became obsession. She *had* to have whatever awaited her – joy, peace, freedom – so she *ran* into the cloying blackness, heedless of danger, *plunged* forward, frantic to find the way, the path, the truth, the door, joy forever, no more fear of death, no fear of anything, paradise, sought it with increasing desperation, but ran always away from it instead.

Now a voice called to her, strange and wordless, frightening but alluring, trying to show her the way, joy and peace and an end to all sadness. Just accept. Accept. It was reaching out for her, if only she would turn the right way, find it, touch it, embrace it.

She stopped running. Abruptly she realized that she didn't have to seek the gift after all, for she was standing in its presence, in the house of joy, the palace of peace, the kingdom of enlightenment. All that she had to do was let it in, open a door *within* herself and let it in, let it in, open herself to inconceivable joy, paradise, paradise, paradise, surrender to pleasure and happiness. She wanted it, she really did oh-so-eagerly want it, because life was hard when it didn't have to be.

But some stubborn part of her resisted the gift, some hateful and proud part of her complex self. She sensed the frustration of him who wished to give this gift, the Giver in the darkness, felt frustration and maybe anger, so she said, *I'm sorry, I'm so sorry*.

Now the gift – joy, peace, love, pleasure – was thrust upon her with tremendous force, brutal and unrelenting pressure, until she felt she would be crushed by it. The darkness around her acquired weight, as if she lay trapped deep in a fathomless sea, though it was far heavier and thicker than water, surrounding her, smothering, crushing. Must submit, useless to resist, let it in, submission was peace, submission was joy, paradise, paradise. Refusal to submit would mean pain beyond anything she could imagine, despair and agony as only those in Hell knew it, so she must submit, open the door within herself, let it in, accept, be at peace. Hammering on her soul, ramming and pounding, fierce and irresistible hammering, hammering: Let it in, let it in, in, in. LET. IT. *IN*.

Suddenly she found the secret door within herself, pathway to joy, gate to peace eternal. She seized the knob, twisted, heard the latch click, pulled inward, shaking with anticipation. Through the slowly widening crack: a glimpse of the Giver. Glistening and dark. Writhing and quick. Hiss of triumph. Coldness at the threshold. *Slam the door, slam the door, slam the door, slamthedoor—*

Heather exploded from sleep, cast back the covers, rolled out of bed on to her feet in one fluid and frantic movement. Her booming heart kept knocking the breath out of her as she tried to inhale.

A dream. Only a dream. But no dream in her experience had ever been so intense.

Maybe the thing beyond the door had followed her out of sleep into the real world.

Crazy thought. Couldn't shake it.

Wheezing thinly, she fumbled with the nightstand lamp, found the switch. The light revealed no nightmare creatures. Just Jack. Asleep on his stomach, head turned away from her, snoring softly.

She managed to draw a breath, though her heart continued to pound. She was damp with sweat and couldn't stop shivering.

Jesus.

Not wanting to wake Jack, Heather switched off the lamp – and twitched as darkness fell around her.

She sat on the edge of the bed, intending to perch there until her heart stopped racing and the shakes passed, then pull a robe over her pajamas and go downstairs to read until morning. According to the luminous green numbers on the digital alarm clock, it was 3:09 A.M., but she was not going to be able to get back to sleep. No way. She might be unable to sleep even *tomorrow* night.

She remembered the glistening, writhing, half-seen presence on the threshold and the bitter cold that flowed from it. The touch of it was still within her, a lingering chill. Disgusting. She felt contaminated, dirty *inside*, where she could never wash the corruption away. Deciding that she needed a hot shower, she got up from the bed.

Disgust swiftly ripened into nausea.

In the dark bathroom she was wracked by dry heaves that left a bitter taste. After turning on the light only long enough to find the bottle of mouthwash, she rinsed away the bitterness. In the dark again, she repeatedly bathed her face in handfuls of cold water.

She sat on the edge of the tub. She dried her face on a towel. As she waited for calm to return, she tried to figure out why a mere dream could have had such a powerful effect on her, but there was no understanding it.

In a few minutes, when she'd regained her composure, she quietly returned to the bedroom. Jack was still snoring softly.

Her robe was draped over the back of a Queen Anne armchair.

She picked it up, slipped out of the room, and eased the door shut behind her. In the hall she pulled on the robe and belted it.

Although she'd intended to go downstairs, brew a pot of coffee, and read, she turned instead toward Toby's room at the end of the hall. Try as she might, Heather was unable to extinguish completely the fear from the nightmare, and her simmering anxiety began to focus on her son.

Toby's door was ajar, and his room was not entirely dark. Since moving to the ranch, he had chosen to sleep with a nightlight again, although he had given up that security a year ago. Heather and Jack were surprised but not particularly concerned by the boy's loss of confidence. They assumed, once he adjusted to his surroundings, he would again prefer darkness to the red glow of the low-wattage bulb that was plugged into a wall socket near the floor.

Toby was tucked under his covers, only his head exposed on the pillow. His breathing was so shallow that, to hear it, Heather had to bend close to him.

Nothing in the room was other than it ought to have been, but she hesitated to leave. Mild apprehension continued to tug at her.

Finally, as Heather reluctantly retreated to the open hall door, she heard a soft scrape that halted her. She turned to the bed, where Toby had not awakened, had not moved.

Even as she glanced at her son, however, she realized the noise had come from the back stairs. It had been the sly, stealthy scrape of something hard, perhaps a boot heel, dragged across a wooden step – recognizable because of the air space under each stair tread, which lent the sound a distinctive hollow quality.

She was instantly afflicted by the same distress which she'd *not* felt while cleaning the stairs but which had plagued her on Monday when she'd followed Paul Youngblood and Toby down that curving well. The sweaty paranoid conviction that somebody – *something?* – was waiting around the next turn. Or descending behind them. An enemy possessed by a singular rage and capable of extreme violence.

She stared at the closed door at the head of those stairs. It was painted white, but it reflected the red glow of the nightlight and seemed almost to shimmer like a portal of fire.

She waited for another sound.

Toby sighed in his sleep. Just a sigh. Nothing more.

Silence again.

Heather supposed she could have been wrong, could have heard an innocent sound from outside – perhaps a night bird settling on to the roof with a rustle of feathers and a scratching of claws against shingles – and could have mistakenly transposed the noise to the stairwell. She was jumpy because of the nightmare. Her perceptions might not be entirely trustworthy. She certainly *wanted* to believe she had been wrong.

Creak-creak.

No mistaking it this time. The new sound was quieter than the first, but it definitely came from behind the door at the head of the back stairs. She remembered how some of the wooden treads had creaked when she first descended to the ground floor during the tour on Monday and how they groaned and complained when she had been cleaning them on Wednesday.

She wanted to snatch Toby from the bed, take him out of the room, go quickly down the hall to the master bedroom, and wake Jack. However, she had never run from anything in her life. During the crises of the past eight months, she'd developed considerably more inner strength and self-confidence than ever before. Although the skin on the back of her neck tingled as if acrawl with hairy spiders, she actually blushed at the mental image of herself fleeing like the frail-hearted damsel of a bad gothic-romance novel, spooked out of her wits by nothing more menacing than a strange sound.

Instead, she went to the stairwell door. The deadbolt lock was securely engaged.

She put her left ear to the crack between door and jamb. The faintest draft of cold air seeped through from the far side, but no sound came with it.

As she listened, she suspected that the intruder was on the upper landing of the stairwell, inches from her, with only the door between them. She could easily imagine him there, a dark and strange figure, his head against the door just as hers was, his ear pressed to the crack, listening for a sound from *her*.

Nonsense. The scraping and creaking had been nothing more than settling noises. Even old houses continued to settle under the unending press of gravity. That damned dream had really spooked her.

Toby muttered wordlessly in his sleep. She turned her head to look at him. He didn't move, and after a few seconds his murmuring subsided.

Heather backed up one step and considered the door for a moment. She didn't want to endanger Toby, but she was beginning to feel more ridiculous than afraid. Just a door. Just a staircase at the back of the house. Just an ordinary night, a dream, a bad case of jumpy nerves.

She put one hand on the knob, the other on the thumb-turn of the dead-bolt lock. The brass hardware was cool under her fingers.

She remembered the urgent need that had possessed her in the dream: *Let it in, let it in, let it in.*

That had been a dream. This was reality. People who couldn't tell them apart were housed in rooms with padded walls, tended by nurses with fixed smiles and soft voices.

Let it in.

She disengaged the lock, turned the knob, hesitated.

Let it in.

Exasperated with herself, she yanked open the door.

She'd forgotten the stairwell lights would be off. That narrow shaft was windowless; no ambient light leached into it from outside. The red radiance in the bedroom was too weak to cross the threshold.

She stood face to face with perfect darkness, unable to tell if anything loomed on the upper steps or even on the landing immediately before her. Out of the gloom wafted the repulsive odor that she'd eradicated two days ago with hard work and ammonia water, not strong but not as faint as before, either: the vile aroma of rotting meat.

Maybe she had only dreamed that she'd awakened but was still in the grip of the nightmare.

Her heart slammed against her breast bone, her breath caught in her throat, and she groped for the light switch, which was on her side of the door. If it had been on the other side, she might not have had the courage to reach into that coiled blackness to feel for it. She missed it on the first and second tries, dared not look away from the darkness before her, felt blindly where she recalled having seen it, almost shouted at Toby to wake up and run, at last found the switch, *thank God*, clicked it.

Light. The deserted landing. Nothing there. Of course. What else? Empty steps curving down and out of sight.

A stair tread creaked below.

Oh, Jesus.

She stepped on to the landing. She wasn't wearing slippers. The wood was cool and rough under her bare feet.

Another creak, softer than before.

Settling noises. Maybe.

She moved off the landing, keeping her left hand against the concave curve of the outer wall to steady herself. Each step that she descended brought a new step into view ahead of her.

At the first glimpse of anyone, she would turn and run back up the stairs, into Toby's room, throw the door shut, snap the deadbolt in place. The lock couldn't be opened from the stairwell, only from inside the house, so they would be safe.

From below came a furtive click, a faint thud – as of a door being pulled shut as quietly as possible.

240

Suddenly she was less disturbed by the prospect of confrontation than by the possibility that the episode would end inconclusively. Needing to *know*, one way or the other, Heather shook off timidity. She *ran* down the stairs, making more than enough noise to reveal her presence, along the convex curve of the inner wall, around, around, into the vestibule at the bottom.

Deserted.

She tried the door to the kitchen. It was locked and required a key to be opened from this side. She had no key. Presumably, an intruder would not have one, either.

The other door led to the back porch. On this side, the dead-bolt operated with a thumb-turn. It was locked. She disengaged it, pulled open the door, stepped on to the porch.

Deserted. And as far as she could see, no one was sprinting away across the backyard.

Besides, although an intruder would not have needed a key to exit by that door, he would have needed one to lock it behind him, for it operated only with a key from the outside.

Somewhere an owl issued a mournful interrogative. Windless, cold, and humid, the night air seemed not like that of the outdoors but like the dank and ever-so-slightly fetid atmosphere of a cellar.

She was alone. But she didn't *feel* alone. She felt . . . watched.

'For God's sake, Heth,' she said, 'what the hell's the matter with you?'

She retreated into the vestibule and locked the door. She stared at the gleaming brass thumb-turn, wondering if her imagination had seized on a few perfectly natural noises to conjure a threat that had even less substance than a ghost.

The rotten smell lingered.

Yes, well, perhaps the ammonia water had not been able to banish the odor for more than a day or two. A rat or other small animal might be dead and decomposing inside the wall.

As she turned toward the stairs, she stepped in something. She

241

lifted her left foot and studied the floor. A clod of dry earth about as large as a plum had partially crumbled under her bare heel.

Climbing to the second floor, she noticed dry crumbs of earth scattered on a few of the treads, which she'd failed to notice in her swift descent. The dirt hadn't been there when she finished cleaning the stairwell on Wednesday. She wanted to believe it was proof the intruder existed. More likely, Toby had tracked a little mud in from the backyard. He was usually a considerate kid, and he was neat by nature, but he was, after all, only eight years old.

Heather returned to Toby's room, locked the door, and snapped off the stairwell light.

Her son was sound asleep.

Feeling no less foolish than confused, she went down the front stairs, directly to the kitchen. If the repulsive smell was a sign of the intruder's recent presence, and if the slightest trace of that stink hung in the kitchen, it would mean he had a key with which he'd entered from the back stairs. In that case she intended to wake Jack and insist they search the house top to bottom – with loaded guns.

The kitchen smelled fresh and clean. No crumbs of dry soil on the floor, either.

She was almost disappointed. She was loath to think that she'd imagined everything, but the facts justified no other interpretation.

Imagination or not, she couldn't rid herself of the feeling that she was under observation. She closed the blinds over the kitchen windows.

Get a grip, Heather thought. You're fifteen years away from the change of life, lady, no excuse for these weird mood swings.

She had intended to spend the rest of the night reading, but she was too agitated to concentrate on a book. She needed to keep busy.

While she brewed a pot of coffee, she inventoried the contents of the freezer compartment in the side-by-side refrigerator. There were half a dozen frozen dinners, a package of frankfurters, two

242

boxes of Green Giant white corn, one box of green beans, two of carrots, and a package of Oregon blueberries, none of which Eduardo Fernandez had opened and all of which they could use.

On a lower shelf, under a box of Eggo waffles and a pound of bacon, she found a Ziploc bag that appeared to contain a legal-size tablet of yellow paper. The plastic was opaque with frost, but she could vaguely see that lines of handwriting filled the first page.

She popped the pressure seal on the bag – but then hesitated. Storing the tablet in such a peculiar place was tantamount to *hiding* it. Fernandez must have considered the contents to be important and extremely personal, and Heather was reluctant to invade his privacy. Though dead and gone, he was the benefactor who had radically changed their lives; he deserved her respect and discretion.

She read the first few words on the top page – *My name is Eduardo Fernandez* – and thumbed through the tablet, confirming it had been written by Fernandez and was a lengthy document. More than two-thirds of the long yellow pages were filled with neat handwriting.

Stifling her curiosity, Heather put the tablet on top of the refrigerator, intending to give it to Paul Youngblood the next time she saw him. The attorney was the closest thing to a friend that Fernandez had known and, in his professional capacity, was privy to all of the old man's affairs. If the contents of the tablet were important and private, only Paul had any right to read them.

Finished with the inventory of frozen foods, she poured a cup of fresh coffee, sat at the kitchen table, and began to make a list of needed groceries and household supplies. Come morning, they would drive to the supermarket in Eagle's Roost and stock not only the refrigerator but the half-empty shelves of the pantry. She wanted to be well-prepared if they were cut off by deep snow for any length of time during the winter.

She paused in her listmaking to scribble a note, reminding Jack to schedule an appointment next week with Parker's Garage for the installation of a plow on the front of the Explorer.

Initially, as she sipped her coffee and composed her list, she was alert for any peculiar sound. However, the task before her was so mundane that it was calming; after a while, she could not sustain a sense of the uncanny.

*

In his sleep, Toby moaned softly.

He said, 'Go away . . . go . . . go away . . .'

After falling silent for a while, he pushed back the covers and got out of bed. In the ruddy glow of the nightlight, his pale-yellow pajamas appeared to be streaked with blood.

He stood beside the bed, swaying as if keeping time to music that only he could hear.

'No,' he whispered, not with alarm but in a flat voice devoid of emotion. 'No . . . no . . . no . . .'

Lapsing into silence again, he walked to the window and gazed into the night.

At the top of the yard, nestled among the pines at the edge of the forest, the caretaker's house was no longer dark and deserted. Strange light, as purely blue as a gas flame, shot into the night from cracks around the edges of the plywood rectangles that covered the windows, from under the front door, and even from the top of the fireplace chimney.

'Ah,' Toby said.

The light was not of constant intensity but sometimes flickered, sometimes throbbed. Periodically, even the narrowest of the escaping beams were so bright that staring at them was painful, although occasionally they grew so dim they seemed about to be extinguished. Even at its brightest, it was a cold light, giving no impression whatsoever of heat.

Toby watched for a long time.

Eventually the light faded. The caretaker's house became dark once more.

The boy returned to the bed.

The night passed.

16

SATURDAY MORNING began with sunshine. A cold breeze swept out of the northwest, and periodic flocks of dark birds wheeled across the sky from the forested Rockies toward the descending land in the east, as if fleeing a predator.

The radio weatherman on a station in Butte – to which Heather and Jack listened as they showered and dressed – predicted snow by nightfall. This was, he said, one of the earliest storms in years, and the total accumulation might reach ten inches.

Judging by the tone of the report, a ten-inch snowfall was not regarded as a blizzard in those northern climes. There was no talk of anticipated road closures, no references to rural areas that might be snowbound. A second storm was rolling toward them in the wake of the first; though expected to arrive early Monday, it was apparently a weaker front than the one that would hit by evening.

Sitting on the edge of the bed, bending forward to tie the laces of her Nikes, Heather said, 'Hey, we've gotta get a couple of sleds.'

Jack was at his open closet, removing a red-and-brown-checkered flannel shirt from a hanger. 'You sound like a little kid.'

'Well, it *is* my first snow.'

'That's right. I forgot.'

In Los Angeles in the winter, when the smog cleared enough to expose them, white-capped mountains served as a distant backdrop to the city, and that was the closest she had ever gotten to snow.

She wasn't a skier. She'd never been to Arrowhead or Big Bear except in the summer, and she was as excited as a kid about the oncoming storm.

Finishing with her shoe laces, she said, 'We've got to make an appointment with Parker's Garage to get that plow on the Explorer before the *real* winter gets here.'

'Already did,' Jack said. 'Ten o'clock Thursday morning.' As he buttoned his shirt, he moved to the bedroom window to look out at the eastern woods and southern lowlands. 'This view keeps hypno-tizing me. I'm doing something, very busy, then I look up, catch a glimpse of it through a window, from the porch, and I just stand and stare.'

Heather moved behind him, put her arms around him, and looked past him at the striking panorama of woods and fields and wide blue sky. 'Is it going to be good?' she asked after a while.

'It's going to be great. This is where we belong. Don't you feel that way?'

'Yes,' she said with only the briefest hesitation. In daylight, the events of the previous night seemed immeasurably less threatening and more surely the work of an overactive imagination. She had seen nothing, after all, and didn't even know quite what she had *expected* to see. Lingering city jitters complicated by a nightmare. Nothing more. 'This is where we belong.'

He turned, embraced her, and they kissed. She moved her hands in lazy circles on his back, gently massaging his muscles, which his exercise program had toned and rebuilt. He felt so good. Exhausted from traveling and from settling in, they had not made love since the night before they'd left Los Angeles. As soon as they made the house their own in *that* way, it would be theirs in every way, and her peculiar uneasiness would probably disappear.

He slid his strong hands down her sides to her hips. He pulled her against him. Punctuating his whispered words with soft kisses to her throat, cheeks, eyes, and the corners of her mouth, he said,

'How about tonight . . . when the snow's falling . . . after we've had . . . a glass of wine or two . . . by the fire . . . romantic music . . . on the radio . . . when we're feeling relaxed . . .'

'. . . relaxed . . .' she said dreamily.

'. . . then we get together . . .'

'. . . mmmmmmm, together . . .'

'. . . and we have a really wonderful, wonderful . . .'

'. . . wonderful . . .'

'Snowball fight.'

She smacked him playfully on the cheek. 'Beast. I'll have rocks in my snowballs.'

'Or we could make love.'

'Sure you don't want to go outside and make snow angels?'

'Not now that I've taken more time to think about it.'

'Get dressed, smartass. We've got shopping to do.'

*

Heather found Toby in the living room, dressed for the day. He was on the floor in front of the TV, watching a program with the sound off.

'Big snow's coming tonight,' she told him from the archway, expecting his excitement to exceed her own because this also would be his first experience with a white winter.

He didn't respond.

'We're going to buy a couple of sleds when we go to town, be ready for tomorrow.'

He was as still as stone. His attention remained entirely on the screen.

From where she stood, Heather couldn't see what show had so gripped him. 'Toby?' She stepped out of the archway and into the living room. 'Hey, kiddo, what're you watching?'

He acknowledged her at last as she approached him. 'Don't know what it is.' His eyes appeared to be out of focus, as though he wasn't actually seeing her, and he gazed once more at the television.

The screen was filled with a constantly evolving flow of amoebic forms, reminiscent of those Lava lamps that had once been so popular. The lamps had always been in two colors, however, while this display progressed in infinite shades of all the primary colors, now bright, now dark. Ever-changing shapes melted together, curled and flexed, streamed and spurted, drizzled and purled and throbbed in a ceaseless exhibition of amorphic chaos, surging at a frenzied pace for a few seconds, then oozing sluggishly, then faster again.

'What is this?' Heather asked.

Toby shrugged.

Endlessly recomposing itself, the colorful curvilinear abstract was interesting to watch and frequently beautiful. The longer she stared at it, however, the more disturbing it became, although for no reason she could discern. Nothing in its patterns was inherently ominous or menacing. Indeed, the fluid and dreamy intermingling of forms should have been restful.

'Why do you have the sound turned down?'

'Don't.'

She squatted next to him, picked up the remote-control from the carpet, and depressed the volume button. The only sound was the faint static hiss of the speakers.

She scanned just one channel farther up on the dial, and the booming voice of an excited sportscaster and the cheering of a crowd at a football game exploded through the living room. She quickly decreased the volume.

When she scanned back to the previous channel, the Technicolor Lava lamp was gone. A Daffy Duck cartoon filled the screen instead and, judging by the frenetic pace of the action, was drawing toward a pyrotechnic conclusion.

'That was odd,' she said.

'I liked it,' Toby said.

249

She scanned farther down the dial, then farther up than before, but she could not find the strange display. She hit the OFF button, and the screen went dark.

'Well, anyway,' she said, 'time to grab breakfast, so we can get on with the day. Lots to do in town. Don't want to run out of time to buy those sleds.'

'Buy what?' the boy asked as he got to his feet.

'Didn't you hear me before?'

'I guess.'

'About snow?'

His small face brightened. 'It's gonna snow?'

'You must have enough wax built up in your ears to make the world's biggest candle,' she said, heading for the kitchen.

Following her, Toby said, 'When? When's it gonna snow, Mom? Huh? Today?'

'We could stick a wick in each of your ears, put a match to them, and have candlelight dinners for the rest of the decade.'

'How much snow?'

'Probably dead snails in there too.'

'Just flurries or a big storm?'

'Maybe a dead mouse or three.'

'*Mom?*' he said exasperatedly, entering the kitchen behind her.

She spun around, crouched in front of him, and held her hand above his knee. 'Up to here, maybe higher.'

'Really?'

'We'll go sledding.'

'Wow.'

'Build a snowman.'

'Snowball fight!' he challenged.

'Okay, me and Dad against you.'

'Not fair!' He ran to the window and pressed his face to the glass. 'The sky's blue.'

'Won't be in a little while. Guarantee,' she said, going to the

250

pantry. 'You want shredded wheat for breakfast or corn flakes?'

'Doughnuts and chocolate milk.'

'Fat chance.'

'Worth a try. Shredded wheat.'

'Good boy.'

'Whoa!' he said in surprise, taking a step back from the window. 'Mom, look at this.'

'What is it?'

'Look, quick, look at this bird. He just landed right smack in front of me.'

Heather joined him near the window and saw a crow perched on the other side of the glass. Its head was cocked, and it regarded them curiously with one eye.

Toby said, 'He just zoomed right at me, *whoooosh,* I thought he was gonna smash through the window. What's he doing?'

'Probably looking for worms or tender little bugs.'

'I don't look like any bug.'

'Maybe he saw those snails in your ears,' she said, returning to the pantry.

While Toby helped Heather set the table for breakfast, the crow remained at the window, watching.

'He must be stupid,' Toby said, 'if he thinks we have worms and bugs in here.'

'Maybe he's refined, civilized, heard me say "corn flakes".'

While they filled bowls with cereal the big crow stayed at the window, occasionally preening its feathers but mostly watching them with one coal-dark eye or the other.

Whistling, Jack came down the front stairs, along the hall, into the kitchen, and said, 'I'm so hungry I could eat a horse. Can we have eggs and horse for breakfast?'

'How about eggs and crow?' Toby asked, pointing to the visitor.

'He's a fat and sassy specimen, isn't he?' Jack said, moving to the window and crouching to get a close look at the bird.

'Mom, look! Dad's in a staring contest with a bird,' Toby said, amused.

Jack's face was no more than an inch from the window, and the bird fixed him with one inky eye. Heather took four slices of bread out of the bag, dropped them in the big toaster, adjusted the dial, depressed the plunger, and looked up to see that Jack and the crow were still eye to eye.

'I think Dad's gonna lose,' Toby said.

Jack snapped one finger against the window pane directly in front of the crow, but the bird didn't flinch.

'Bold little devil,' Jack said.

With a lightning-quick dart of its head, the crow pecked the glass in front of Jack's face so hard that the *tock* of bill against pane startled Jack into a backward step that, in his crouch, put him off balance. He fell on his butt on the kitchen floor. The bird leaped away from the window with a great flapping of wings and vanished into the sky.

Toby burst into laughter.

Jack crawled after him on hands and knees. 'Oh, you think that was funny, do you? I'll show you what's funny, I'll show you the infamous Chinese tickle torture.'

Heather was laughing too.

Toby scampered to the hall door, looked back, saw Jack coming, and ran to another room, giggling and shrieking with delight.

Jack scrambled to his feet. In a hunchbacked crouch, growling like a troll, he scuttled after his son.

'Do I have one little boy on my hands or two?' Heather called after Jack as he disappeared into the hall.

'Two!' he replied.

The toast popped up. She put the four crisp pieces on a plate, and slipped four more slices of bread into the toaster.

Much giggling and maniacal cackling was coming from the front of the house.

Heather went to the window. The *tock* of the bird's bill had been so loud that she more than half expected to see a crack in the glass. But the pane was intact. On the sill outside lay a single black feather, rocking gently in a breeze that could not quite pluck it out of its sheltered niche and whirl it away.

She put her face to the window and peered up at the sky. High in that blue vault, a single dark bird carved a tight circle, around and around. It was too far away for her to be able to tell if it was the same crow or another bird.

17

THEY STOPPED at Mountain High Sporting Goods and purchased two sleds (wide, flat runners; clear pine with polyurethane finish; a red lightning bolt down the center of each), as well as new insulated ski suits, boots, and gloves for all of them. Toby saw a big Frisbee specially painted to look like a yellow flying saucer, with portholes along the rim and a low red dome on top, and they bought that too. At the Union 76, they filled the fuel tank, then went on a marathon shopping expedition at the supermarket.

When they returned to Quartermass Ranch at one-fifteen, only the eastern third of the sky remained blue. Masses of gray clouds churned across the mountains, driven by a fierce high-altitude wind – though, at ground level, only an erratic breeze gently stirred the evergreens and shivered the brown grass. The temperature had fallen below freezing, and the accuracy of the weatherman's prediction was manifest in the cold, humid air.

Toby went immediately to his room, dressed in his new red-and-black ski suit, boots, and gloves. He returned to the kitchen with his Frisbee to announce he was going out to play and to wait for the snow to start falling.

Heather and Jack were still unpacking groceries and arranging supplies in the pantry. She said, 'Toby, honey, you haven't had lunch yet.'

'I'm not hungry. I'll just take a raisin cookie with me.'

She paused to pull up the hood on Toby's jacket and tie it under his chin. 'Well, all right, but don't stay out there too long at a stretch. When you get cold, come in and warm up a little, then go back out. We don't want your nose freezing and falling off.' She gave his nose a gentle tweak. He looked so cute. Like a gnome.

'Don't throw the Frisbee toward the house,' Jack warned him. 'Break a window, and we'll show no mercy. We'll call the police, have you committed to the Montana Prison for the Criminally Insane.'

As she gave Toby two raisin cookies, Heather said, 'And don't go into the woods.'

'All right.'

'Stay in the yard.'

'I will.'

'I mean it.' The woods worried her. This was different from her recent irrational spells of paranoia. There were good reasons to be cautious of the forest. Wild animals, for one thing. And city people, like them, could get disoriented and lost only a few hundred feet into the trees. 'The Montana Prison for the Criminally Insane has no TV, chocolate milk, or cookies.'

'Okay, okay. *Sheeeesh*, I'm not a baby.'

'No,' Jack said, as he fished cans out of a shopping bag. 'But, to a bear, you *are* a tasty-looking lunch.'

'There's bears in the woods?' Toby asked.

'Are there birds in the sky?' Jack asked. 'Fish in the sea?'

'So stay in the yard,' Heather reminded him. 'Where I can find you easy, where I can see you.'

As he opened the back door, Toby turned to his father and said, 'You better be careful too.'

'Me?'

'That bird might come back and knock you on your ass again.'

Jack pretended he was going to throw the can of beans that he was holding, and Toby ran from the house, giggling. The door banged shut behind him.

*

Later, after their purchases had been put away, Jack went into the study to examine Eduardo's book collection and select a novel to read, while Heather went upstairs to the guest bedrooms where she was setting up her array of computers. They had taken the spare bed apart and moved it to the cellar. The two six-foot folding tables, which had been among the goods delivered by the movers, now stood in place of the bed and formed an L-shaped work area. She'd unpacked her three computers, two printers, laser scanner, and associated equipment, but until now she'd had no chance to make connections and plug them in.

As of that moment, she really had no use for such a high-tech array of computing power. She had worked on software and program design virtually all of her adult life, however, and she didn't feel complete with her machines disconnected and boxed up, regardless of whether or not she had an immediate project that required them. She set to work, positioning the equipment, linking monitors to logic units, logic units to printers, one of the printers and logic units to the scanner, all the while happily humming old Elton John songs.

Eventually she and Jack would investigate business opportunities and decide what to do with the rest of their lives. By then the phone company would have installed another line, and the modem would be in operation. She could use data networks to research what population base and capitalization any given business required for success, as well as find answers to hundreds if not thousands of other questions that would influence their decisions and improve their chances for success in whatever enterprise they chose.

Rural Montana enjoyed as much access to knowledge as Los Angeles or Manhattan or Oxford University. The only things needed were a telephone line, a modem, and a couple of good database subscriptions.

At three o'clock, after she'd been working about an hour – the equipment connected, everything working – Heather got up from her chair and stretched. Flexing the muscles in her back, she went to the window to see if flurries had begun to fall ahead of schedule.

The November sky was low, a uniform shade of lead-gray, like an immense plastic panel behind which glowed arrays of dull fluorescent tubes. She fancied that she would have recognized it as a snow sky even if she hadn't heard the forecast. It looked as cold as ice.

In that bleak light, the higher woods appeared to be more gray than green. The backyard and, to the south, the brown fields seemed barren rather than merely dormant in anticipation of the spring. Although the landscape was nearly as monochromatic as a charcoal drawing, it was beautiful. A different beauty from that it offered under the warm caress of the sun. Stark, somber, broodingly majestic.

She saw a small spot of color to the south, on the cemetery knoll not far from the perimeter of the western forest. Bright red. It was Toby in his new ski suit. He was standing inside the foot-high fieldstone wall.

I should have told him to stay away from there, Heather thought with a twinge of apprehension.

Then she wondered at her uneasiness. Why should the cemetery seem any more dangerous to her than the yard immediately outside of its boundaries? She didn't believe in ghosts or haunted places.

The boy stood at the grave markers, utterly still. She watched him for a minute, a minute and a half, but he didn't move. For an eight-year-old, who usually had more energy than a nuclear plant, that was an extraordinary period of inactivity.

The gray sky settled lower while she watched.

The land darkened subtly.

Toby stood unmoving.

*

The arctic air didn't bother Jack – invigorated him, in fact – except that it penetrated especially deeply into the thigh bones and scar tissue of his left leg. He did not have to limp, however, as he ascended the hill to the private graveyard.

He passed between the four-foot-high stone posts that, gateless, marked the entrance to the burial ground. His breath puffed from his mouth in frosty plumes.

Toby was standing at the foot of the fourth grave in the line of four. His arms hung straight at his sides, his head was bent, and his eyes were fixed on the headstone. The Frisbee was on the ground beside him. He breathed so shallowly that he produced only a faint mustache of steam that repeatedly evaporated as each brief exhalation became a soft inhalation.

'What's up?' Jack asked.

The boy did not respond.

The nearest headstone, at which Toby stared, was engraved with the name THOMAS FERNANDEZ and the dates of birth and death. Jack didn't need the marker to remind him of the date of death; it was carved on his own memory far deeper than the numbers were cut into the granite before him.

Since they'd arrived Tuesday morning, after staying the night with Paul and Carolyn Youngblood, Jack had been too busy to inspect the private cemetery. Furthermore, he'd not been eager to stand in front of Tommy's grave, where memories of blood and loss and despair were certain to assail him.

To the left of Tommy's marker was a double stone. It bore the names of his parents – EDUARDO and MARGARITE.

Though Eduardo had been in the ground only a few months, Tommy for a year, and Margarite for three years, all of their graves looked freshly dug. The dirt was mounded unevenly and no grass grew on it, which seemed odd, because the fourth grave was flat and covered with silky brown grass. He could understand that grave-diggers might have disturbed the surface of Margarite's plot in order to bury Eduardo's coffin beside hers, but that didn't explain the condition of Tommy's site. Jack made a mental note to ask Paul Youngblood about it.

The last monument, at the head of the only grassy plot, belonged to Stanley Quartermass, patron of them all. An inscription in the weathered black stone surprised a chuckle out of Jack when he least expected one: *Here lies Stanley Quartermass/ dead before his time/ because he had to work/ with so damned many/ actors and writers.*

Toby had not moved.

'What're you up to?' Jack asked.

No answer.

He put one hand on Toby's shoulder. 'Son?'

Without shifting his gaze from the tombstone, the boy said, 'What're they doing down there?'

'Who? Where?'

'In the ground.'

'You mean Tommy and his folks, Mr Quartermass?'

'What're they doing down there?'

There was nothing odd about a child wanting to fully understand death. It was no less a mystery to the young than to the old. What seemed strange to Jack was the way the question had been phrased.

'Well,' he said, 'Tommy, his folks, Stanley Quartermass . . . they aren't really here.'

'Yes, they are.'

'No, only their bodies are here,' Jack said, gently massaging the boy's shoulder.

'Why?'

'Because they were finished with them.'

The boy was silent, brooding. Was he thinking about how close his own father had come to being planted under a similar stone? Maybe enough time had passed since the shooting for Toby to be able to confront feelings that he'd been repressing.

The mild breeze from out of the northwest stiffened slightly.

Jack's hands were cold. He put them in his jacket pockets and said, 'Their bodies weren't them, anyway, not the real them.'

The conversation took an even stranger turn: 'You mean, these weren't their original bodies? These were puppets?'

Frowning, Jack dropped to his knees beside the boy. 'Puppets? That's a peculiar thing to say.'

As if in a trance, the boy focused on Tommy's headstone. His gray-blue eyes stared unblinking.

'Toby, are you okay?'

Toby still didn't look at him but said, 'Surrogates?'

Jack blinked in surprise. 'Surrogates?'

'Were they?'

'That's a pretty big word. Where'd you hear that?'

Instead of answering him, Toby said, 'Why don't they need these bodies any more?'

Jack hesitated then shrugged. 'Well, son, you know why – they were finished with their work in this world.'

'This world?'

'They've gone on.'

'Where?'

'You've been to Sunday school. You know where.'

'No.'

'Sure you do.'

'No.'

'They've gone on to Heaven.'

'They went on?'

'Yes.'

'In what bodies?'

Jack removed his right hand from his jacket pocket and cupped his son's chin. He turned the boy's head away from the gravestone, so they were eye to eye. 'What's wrong, Toby?'

They were face to face, inches apart, yet Toby seemed to be looking into the distance, through Jack and at some far horizon.

'Toby?'

'In what bodies?'

Jack released the boy's chin, moved one hand back and forth in front of his face. Not a blink. His eyes didn't follow the movement of the hand.

'In what bodies?' Toby repeated impatiently.

Something was wrong with the boy. Sudden psychological ailment. With a catatonic aspect.

Toby said, 'In what bodies?'

Jack's heart began to pump hard and fast as he stared into his son's flat, unresponsive eyes, which were no longer windows on a soul but mirrors to keep out the world. If it was a psychological problem, there was no doubt about the *cause*. They'd been through a traumatic year, enough to drive a grown man – let alone a child – to a breakdown. But what was the trigger, why now, why here, why after all these many months during which the poor kid had seemed to cope so well?

'In what bodies?' Toby demanded sharply.

'Come on,' Jack said, taking the boy's gloved hand. 'Let's go back to the house.'

'In what bodies did they go on?'

'Toby, stop this.'

'Need to know. Tell me now. Tell me.'

Oh, dear God, don't let this happen.

Still on his knees, Jack said, 'Listen, come back to the house with me so we can—'

Toby wrenched his hand out of his father's grasp, leaving Jack with the empty glove. '*In what bodies?*'

The small face was without expression, as placid as still water, yet the words burst from the boy in a tone of ice-cold rage. Jack had the eerie feeling that he was conversing with a ventriloquist's dummy that could not match its wooden features to the tenor of its words.

'*In what bodies?*'

This wasn't a breakdown. A mental collapse didn't happen this suddenly, completely, without warning signs.

'*In what bodies?*'

This wasn't Toby. Not Toby at all.

Ridiculous. Of course it was Toby. Who else?

Someone talking *through* Toby.

Crazy thought, weird. *Through* Toby?

Nevertheless, kneeling there in the graveyard, gazing into his son's eyes, Jack no longer saw the blankness of a mirror, although he was aware of his own frightened face in twin reflections. He didn't see the innocence of a child, either, or any familiar quality. He perceived – or was imagining – another presence, something both less and more than human, a strangeness beyond comprehension, peering out at him from within Toby.

'*In what bodies?*'

Jack couldn't work up any saliva. Tongue stuck to the roof of his mouth. Couldn't swallow, either. He was colder than the wintry day could explain. Suddenly much colder. Beyond freezing.

He'd never felt anything like it before. A cynical part of him thought he was being ridiculous, hysterical, letting himself be swept away by primitive superstition – all because he could not face the thought of Toby having a psychotic episode and slipping into mental chaos. On the other hand, it was precisely the primitive nature of the perception that convinced him another presence shared the body of his son: he *felt* it on a primal level, deeper than he had ever felt anything before; it was a knowledge more certain than any that could be arrived at by intellect, profound and irrefutable animal instinct, as if he'd captured the scent of an enemy's pheromones; his skin was tingling with the vibrations of an inhuman aura.

His gut clenched with fear. Sweat broke out on his forehead, and the flesh crimped along the nape of his neck.

He wanted to spring to his feet, scoop Toby into his arms, run down the hill to the house, and remove him from the influence of the entity that held him in its thrall. Ghost, demon, ancient Indian spirit? No, ridiculous. But something, damn it. Something. He hesitated, partly because he was transfixed by what he thought he saw in the boy's eyes, partly because he feared that forcing a break of the connection between Toby and whatever was linked with him would somehow harm the boy, perhaps damage him mentally.

Which didn't make any sense, no sense at all. But then *none* of it made sense. A dreamlike quality characterized the moment and the place.

It was Toby's voice, yes, but not his usual speech patterns or inflections: '*In what bodies did they go on from here?*'

Jack decided to answer. Holding Toby's empty glove in his hand, he had the terrible feeling that he must play along or be left with a son as limp and hollow as the glove, a drained shell of a boy, form without content, those beloved eyes vacant forever.

And how insane was *that?* His mind spun. He seemed poised on the brink of an abyss, teetering out of balance. Maybe *he* was the one having the breakdown.

He said, 'Th-they didn't need bodies, Skipper. You know that. Nobody needs bodies in Heaven.'

'They are bodies,' the Toby-thing said cryptically. 'Their bodies are.'

'Not any more. They're spirits now.'

'Don't understand.'

'Sure you do. Souls. Their souls went to Heaven.'

'Bodies are.'

'Went to Heaven to be with God.'

'Bodies are.'

Toby stared through him. Deep in Toby's eyes, however, like a coiling thread of smoke, something moved. Jack sensed that something was regarding him intensely. 'Bodies are. Puppets are. What else?'

Jack didn't know how to respond.

The breeze coming across the flank of the sloped yard was as cold as if it had skimmed over a glacier on its way to them.

The Toby-thing returned to the first question that it had asked: 'What are they doing down there?'

Jack glanced at the graves, then into the boy's eyes, deciding to be straightforward. He wasn't actually talking to a little boy, so he didn't need to use euphemisms. Or he was crazy, imagining the whole conversation as well as the inhuman presence. Either way, what he said didn't matter. 'They're dead.'

'What is dead?'

'They are. These three people buried here.'

'What *is* dead?'

'Lifeless.'

'What is lifeless?'

'Without life.'

'What is life?'

'The opposite of death.'

'What is death?'

Desperately, Jack said, 'Empty, hollow, rotting.'

'Bodies are.'

'Not forever.'

'Bodies *are*.'

'Nothing lasts forever.'

'Everything lasts.'

'Nothing.'

'Everything becomes.'

'Becomes what?' Jack asked. He was now beyond giving answers himself, was full of his own questions.

'Everything becomes,' the Toby-thing repeated.

'Becomes what?'

'Me. Everything becomes me.'

Jack wondered what in the hell he was talking to and whether he was making more sense to it than it was making to him. He

264

began to doubt that he was even awake. Maybe he'd taken a nap. If he wasn't insane, perhaps he was asleep. Snoring in the armchair in the study, a book in his lap. Maybe Heather had never come to tell him Toby was in the cemetery, in which case all he had to do was wake up.

The breeze felt real. Not like a dream wind. Cold, piercing. And it had picked up enough speed to give it a voice. Whispering in the grass, soughing in the trees along the edge of the higher woods, keening softly, softly.

The Toby-thing said, 'Suspended.'

'What?'

'Different sleep.'

Jack glanced at the graves. 'No.'

'Waiting.'

'No.'

'Puppets waiting.'

'No. Dead.'

'Tell me their secret.'

'Dead.'

'The secret.'

'They're just dead.'

'*Tell me.*'

'There's nothing to tell.'

The boy's expression was still calm, but his face was flushed. The arteries were throbbing visibly in his temples as if his blood pressure had soared off the scale.

'*Tell me!*'

Jack was shaking uncontrollably, increasingly frightened by the cryptic nature of their exchanges, worried that he understood even less of the situation than he thought he did and that his ignorance might lead him to say the wrong thing and somehow put Toby into even greater danger than he already was.

'*Tell me!*'

265

Overwhelmed by fear and confusion and frustration, Jack grabbed Toby by the shoulders, stared into his strange eyes. 'Who are you?'

No answer.

'What's happened to my Toby?'

After a long silence: 'What's the matter, Dad?'

Jack's scalp prickled. Being called 'Dad' by this thing, this hateful intruder, was the worst affront yet.

'Dad?'

'Stop it.'

'Daddy, what's wrong?'

But he wasn't Toby. No way. His voice still didn't have its natural inflections, his face was slack, and his eyes were *wrong*.

'Dad, what're you doing?'

The thing in possession of Toby apparently hadn't realized that its masquerade had come undone. Until now it had thought that Jack believed he was speaking with his son. The parasite was struggling to improve its performance.

'Dad, what did I do? Are you mad at me? I didn't do anything, Dad, really I didn't.'

'What are you?' Jack demanded.

Tears slid from the boy's eyes. But the nebulous *something* was behind the tears, an arrogant puppet-master confident of its ability to deceive.

'Where's Toby? You sonofabitch, whatever the hell you are, give him back to me.'

Jack's hair fell across his eyes. Sweat glazed his face. To anyone coming upon them just then, his extreme fear would appear to be dementia. Maybe it was. Either he was talking to a malevolent spirit that had taken control of his son or he was insane. Which made more sense?

'Give him to me, I want him back!'

'Dad, you're scaring me,' the Toby-thing said, trying to tear loose of him.

266

'You're not my son.'

'Dad, *please!*'

'Stop it! Don't pretend with me, you're not fooling me, for Christ's sake!'

It wrenched free, turned, stumbled to Tommy's headstone, and leaned against the granite.

Toppled on to all fours by the force with which the boy broke away from him, Jack said fiercely, 'Let him go!'

The boy squealed, jumped as if surprised, and spun to face Jack. 'Dad! What're you doing here?' He sounded like Toby again. 'Jeez, you scared me! What're you sneaking in a cemetery for? Boy, that's not funny!' They weren't as close as they had been, but Jack thought the child's eyes no longer seemed strange; Toby appeared to see him again. 'Holy Jeez, on your hands and knees, sneaking in a *cemetery.*'

The boy was Toby again, all right. The thing that had controlled him was not a good enough actor to be this convincing.

Or maybe he had always been Toby. The unnerving possibility of madness and delusion confronted Jack again.

'Are you all right?' he asked, rising on to his knees once more, wiping his palms on his jeans.

'Almost pooped my pants,' Toby said, and giggled.

What a marvelous sound. That giggle. Sweet music.

Jack clasped his hands to his thighs, squeezing hard, trying to stop shaking. 'What're you . . .' His voice was quavery. He cleared his throat. 'What are you doing up here?'

The boy pointed to the Frisbee on the dead grass. 'Wind caught the flying saucer.'

Remaining on his knees, Jack said, 'Come here.'

Toby was clearly dubious. 'Why?'

'Come here, Skipper, just come here.'

'You going to bite my neck?'

'What?'

'You going to pretend to bite my neck or do something and scare me again, like sneaking up on me, something weird like that?'

Obviously, the boy didn't remember their conversation while he'd been . . . possessed. His awareness of Jack's arrival in the graveyard began when, startled, he'd spun away from the granite marker.

Holding his hands out, arms open, Jack said, 'No, I'm not going to do anything like that. Just come here.'

Skeptical and cautious, puzzled face framed by the red hood of the ski suit, Toby came to him.

Jack gripped the boy by the shoulders, looked into his eyes. Blue-gray. Clear. No smoky spiral under the color.

'What's wrong?' Toby asked, frowning.

'Nothing. It's okay.'

Compulsively, he pulled the boy close, hugged him.

'Dad?'

'You don't remember, do you?'

'Huh?'

'Good.'

'Your heart's really wild,' Toby said.

'That's all right, I'm okay, everything's okay.'

'*I'm* the one scared poopless. Boy, I sure owe you one!'

Jack let go of his son and struggled to his feet. The sweat on his face felt like a mask of ice. He combed his hair back with his fingers, wiped his face with both hands, and blotted his palms on his jeans. 'Let's go back to the house and get some hot chocolate.'

Picking up the Frisbee, Toby said, 'Can't we play a while first, you and me? A Frisbee's more fun with two.'

Frisbee tossing, hot chocolate. Normality hadn't merely returned to the day; it had crashed down like a ton weight. Jack doubted he could have convinced anyone that he and Toby had so recently been deep in the muddy river of the supernatural. His own fear and his perception of uncanny forces were fading so rapidly that already he could not quite recall the power of what he'd felt. Hard gray sky, every scrap of blue chased away beyond the eastern horizon, trees shivering in the frigid breeze, brown grass, velvet shadows, Frisbee games, hot chocolate: the whole world waited for the first spiraling flake of winter, and no aspect of the November day admitted the possibilities of ghosts, disembodied entities, possession, or any other-worldly phenomena whatsoever.

'Can we, Dad?' Toby asked, brandishing the Frisbee.

'All right, for a little while. But not here. Not in this . . .'

It would sound so stupid to say *not in this graveyard*. Might as well segue into one of those grotesque Stepin Fetchit routines from old movies, do a double take and roll his eyes and shag his arms at his sides and howl, *Feets don't fail me now*.

Instead he said, '. . . not so near the woods. Maybe . . . down there closer to the stables.'

Carrying the flying-saucer Frisbee, Toby sprinted between the gateless posts, out of the cemetery. 'Last one there's a monkey!'

Jack didn't chase after the boy.

Hunching his shoulders against the chill wind, thrusting his hands in his pockets, he stared at the four graves, again troubled that only Quartermass's plot was flat and grass-covered. Freakish thoughts flickered in his mind. Scenes from old Boris Karloff movies. Grave-robbers and ghouls. Desecration. Satanic rituals in cemeteries by moonlight. Even considering the experience he'd just had with Toby, his darkest thoughts seemed too fanciful to explain why only one grave of four appeared long undisturbed; however, he told himself that the explanation, when he learned it, would be perfectly logical and not in the least creepy.

Fragments of the conversation he'd had with Toby echoed in his memory, out of order:

What are they doing down there? What is dead? What is life?
Nothing lasts forever.
Everything lasts.

269

Nothing.

Everything becomes.

Becomes what?

Me. Everything becomes me.

Jack sensed that he had enough pieces to put together at least part of the puzzle. He just couldn't see how they interlocked. Or *wouldn't* see. Perhaps he refused to put them together because even the few pieces he possessed would reveal a nightmare face, something better not encountered. He wanted to know, or thought he did, but his subconscious overruled him.

As he raised his eyes from the mauled earth to the three stones, his attention was caught by a fluttering object on Tommy's marker. It was stuck in a narrow crack between the horizontal base and the vertical slab of granite: a black feather, three inches long, stirred by the breeze.

Jack tilted his head back and squinted uneasily into the wintry vault directly overhead. The heavens hung low. Gray and dead. Like ashes. A crematorium sky. However, nothing moved above except great masses of clouds.

Big storm coming.

He turned toward the sole break in the low stone wall, walked to the posts, and looked downhill toward the stable.

Toby had almost reached that long rectangular building. He skidded to a halt, glanced back at his laggardly father, and waved. He tossed the Frisbee straight into the air.

On edge, the disc knifed high, then curved toward the south and caught a current of wind. Like a spacecraft from another world, it whirled across the somber sky.

Much higher than the greatest altitude reached by the Frisbee, under the pendulous clouds, a lone bird circled above the boy, like a hawk maintaining surveillance of potential prey, though it was likely a crow rather than a hawk. Circling and circling. A puzzle piece in the shape of a black crow. Gliding on rising thermals. Silent as a stalker in a dream, patient and mysterious.

18

AFTER SENDING Jack to discover what Toby was doing among the gravestones, Heather returned to the spare bedroom where she had been working with her computers. She watched from the window as Jack climbed the hill to the cemetery. He stood with the boy for a minute, then knelt beside him. From a distance, everything seemed all right, no sign of trouble.

Evidently she'd been worried for no good reason. A lot of that going around lately.

She sat in her office chair, sighed at her excessive maternal concern, and turned her attention to the computers. For a while she searched the hard disc of each machine, ran tests, and made sure the programs were in place and that nothing had crashed during the move.

Later, she grew thirsty and before going to the kitchen to get a Pepsi, she stepped to the window to check on Jack and Toby. They were almost out of her line of view, near the stables, tossing the Frisbee back and forth.

Judging by the heavy sky and by how icy cold the window was when she touched it, snow would begin to fall soon. She was eager for it.

Maybe the change of weather would bring a change in her mood, as well, and help her finally shed the city jitters that plagued her. It ought to be hard to cling to the old paranoia-soaked expectations

271

of life in Los Angeles when they were living in a white wonderland, sparkling and pristine, like a sequined scene on a Christmas card.

In the kitchen, as she opened a can of Pepsi and poured it into a glass, she heard a heavy engine approaching. Thinking it might be Paul Youngblood paying an unexpected visit, she took the tablet from the top of the refrigerator and put it on the counter, so she would be less likely to forget to give it to him before he went home.

By the time she went down the hall, opened the door, and stepped on to the front porch, the vehicle pulled to a stop in front of the garage doors. It wasn't Paul's white Bronco, it was a similar metallic-blue wagon, as large as the Bronco, larger than their own Explorer, but of yet another model with which she wasn't familiar.

She wondered if anyone in those parts ever drove cars. But, of course, she had seen plenty of cars in town and at the supermarket. Even there, however, pickup trucks and four-wheel-drive truck-style wagons outnumbered automobiles.

She went down the steps and crossed the yard to the driveway to greet the visitor, wishing she'd paused to put on a jacket. The bitter air pierced even her comfortably thick flannel shirt.

The man who climbed out of the wagon was about thirty, with an unruly mop of brown hair, craggy features, and light-brown eyes kinder than his rugged looks. Closing the driver's door behind him, he smiled and said, 'Howdy. You must be Mrs McGarvey.'

'That's right,' she said, shaking the hand he offered.

'Travis Potter. Pleased to meet you. I'm the vet in Eagle's Roost. One of the vets. A man could go to the ends of the earth, there'd still be competition.'

A big golden retriever stood in the back of the wagon. Its bushy tail wagged nonstop, and it grinned at them through the side window.

Seeing the direction of Heather's gaze, Potter said, 'Beautiful, isn't he?'

'They're such gorgeous dogs. Is he a purebred?'

'Pure as they come.'

272

Jack and Toby rounded the corner of the house. White clouds of breath steamed from them because they had evidently run from the hillside west of the stable, where they'd been playing. Heather introduced them to the vet. Jack dropped the Frisbee and shook hands. But Toby was so enchanted by the sight of the dog that he forgot his manners and went directly to the wagon to stare delightedly through the window at the occupant of the cargo space.

Shivering, Heather said, 'Doctor Potter—'

'Travis, please.'

'Travis, can you come in for some coffee?'

'Yeah, come on in and visit a spell,' Jack said, as if he had been a country boy all his life. 'Stay to dinner if you can.'

'Sorry, can't,' Travis said. 'But thanks for the invitation. I'll take a raincheck, if you don't mind. Right now, I've got calls to make – a couple of sick horses that need tending to, a cow with an infected hoof. With this storm coming, I want to get home early as I can.' He checked his watch. 'Almost four o'clock already.'

'Ten-inch snowfall, we hear,' said Jack.

'You haven't heard the latest. First storm's built strength, and the second's no longer a day behind it, more like a couple hours. Maybe two feet accumulation before it's all done.'

Heather was glad they had gone shopping that morning and that their shelves were well stocked.

'Anyway,' Travis said, indicating the dog, 'this fella's the real reason I stopped by.' He joined Toby at the side of the wagon.

Jack put an arm around Heather to help her keep warm, and they stepped behind Toby.

Travis pressed two fingers against the window, and the dog licked the other side of the glass enthusiastically, whined, and wagged his tail more furiously than ever. 'He's a sweet-tempered fella. Aren't you, Falstaff. His name's Falstaff.'

'Really?' Heather said.

'Hardly seems fair, does it? But he's two years old and used to it now. I hear from Paul Youngblood, you're in the market for just such an animal as Falstaff here.'

Toby gasped. He gaped at Travis.

'Hold your mouth open that wide,' Travis warned him, 'and some critter is going to run in there and build a nest.' He smiled at Heather and Jack. 'Was this what you had in mind?'

'Just about exactly,' Jack said.

Heather said, 'Except, we thought a puppy . . .'

'With Falstaff, you get all the joy of a good dog and none of that puppy mess. He's two years old, mature, housebroken, well behaved. Won't spot the carpet or chew up the furniture. But he's still a young dog, lots of years ahead of him. Interested?'

Toby looked up worriedly, as if it was beyond conception that such an enormous great good thing as this could befall him without his parents objecting or the ground opening and swallowing him alive.

Heather glanced up at Jack, and he said, 'Why not?'

Looking at Travis, Heather said, 'Why not?'

'*Yes!*' Toby made it a one-word expression of explosive ecstasy.

They went to the back of the wagon, and Travis opened the tailgate.

Falstaff bounded out of the wagon to the ground and immediately began excitedly sniffing everyone's feet, turning in circles, one way and then the other, slapping their legs with his tail, licking their hands when they tried to pet him, a jubilation of fur and warm tongue and cold nose and heart-melting brown eyes. When he calmed down, he chose to sit in front of Toby, to whom he offered a raised paw.

'He can shake hands!' Toby exclaimed, and proceeded to take the paw and pump it.

'He knows a lot of tricks,' Travis said.

'Where'd he come from?' Jack asked.

'A couple in town, Leona and Harry Seaquist. They had goldens all their lives. Falstaff here was the latest.'

'He seems too nice to just be given up.'

Travis nodded. 'Sad case. A year ago, Leona got cancer, was gone in three months. Few weeks back, Harry suffered a stroke, lost the use of his left arm. Speech is slurred, and his memory isn't so good. Had to go to Denver to live with his son, but they didn't want the dog. Harry cried like a baby when he said goodbye to Falstaff. I promised him I'd find a good home for the pooch.'

Toby was on his knees, hugging the golden around the neck, and it was licking the side of his face. 'We'll give him the best home any dog ever had anywhere anytime ever, won't we, Mom, won't we, Dad?'

To Travis, Heather said, 'How sweet of Paul Youngblood to call you about us.'

'Well, he heard mention your boy wanted a dog. And this isn't the city, everyone living in a rat race. We have plenty of time around here to meddle in other people's business.' He had a broad, engaging smile.

The chilling breeze had grown stronger as they talked. Suddenly it gusted into a whistling wind, flattened the brown grass, whipped Heather's hair across her face, and drove needles of cold into her.

'Travis,' she said, shaking hands with him again, 'when *can* you come for dinner?'

'Well, maybe Sunday a week.'

'A week from Sunday it is,' she said. 'Six o'clock.' To Toby, she said, 'Come on, peanut, let's get inside.'

'I want to play with Falstaff.'

'You can get to know him in the house,' she insisted. 'It's too cold out here.'

'He's got fur,' Toby protested.

'It's *you* I'm worried about, dummkopf. You're going to get a frostbitten nose, and then it'll be as black as Falstaff's.'

Halfway to the house, padding along between Heather and Toby, the dog stopped and looked back at Travis Potter. The vet made a go-ahead wave with one hand, and that seemed sufficient permission for Falstaff. He accompanied them up the steps into the warm front hall.

*

Travis Potter had brought a fifty-pound bag of dry dog food with him. He hefted it out of the back of the Range Rover and put it on the ground against a rear tire. 'Figured you wouldn't have dog chow on hand just in case someone happened by with a golden retriever.' He explained what and how much to feed a dog Falstaff's size.

'What do we owe you?' Jack asked.

'Zip. He didn't cost me. Just doing a favor for poor Harry.'

'That's nice of you. Thanks. But for the dog food?'

'Don't worry about it. In years to come, Falstaff's going to need his regular shots, general looking after. When you bring him to me, I'll soak you plenty.' Grinning, he slammed the tailgate.

They went around to the side of the Rover farthest from the house, using it to shelter themselves from the worst of the biting wind.

Travis said, 'Understand Paul told you in private about Eduardo and his raccoons. Didn't want to alarm your wife.'

'She doesn't alarm easy.'

'You tell her then?'

'No. Not sure why, either. Except . . . we've all got a lot on our minds already, a year of trouble, a lot of change. Anyway, wasn't much Paul told me. Just that the coons were behaving oddly, out in broad daylight, running in circles, and then they just dropped dead.'

'I don't think that was all of it.' Travis hesitated. He leaned back at an angle against the side of the Rover and bent his knees, slouching a little to get his head down out of the keening wind. 'I think Eduardo was holding out on me. Those coons were doing something stranger than what he said.'

'Why would he hold out on you?'

'Hard to say. He was a sort of quirky old guy. Maybe . . . I don't know, maybe he saw something he felt funny talking about, something he figured I wouldn't believe. Had a lot of pride, that man. He wouldn't want to talk about anything that might get him laughed at.'

'Any guesses what that could be?'

'Nope.'

Jack's head was above the roof of the Rover, and the wind not only numbed his face but seemed to be scouring off his skin layer by layer. He leaned back against the vehicle, bent his knees, and slouched, mimicking the vet. They stared out across the descending land to the south as they talked. Jack said, 'You think, like Paul does, it was something Eduardo saw that caused his heart attack, related to the raccoons?'

'And made him load a shotgun, you mean. I don't know. Maybe. Wouldn't rule it out. More'n two weeks before he died, I talked to him on the phone. Interesting conversation. Called him to give him the test results on the coons, wasn't any known disease involved—'

'The brain swelling.'

'Right. But no apparent cause. He wanted to know, did I just take samples of brain tissue for the tests or do a full dissection.'

'Dissection of the brain?'

'Yeah. He asked, did I open their brains all the way up. He seemed to expect, if I did that, I'd find something besides swelling. But I didn't find anything. So then he asks me about their spines, if there was something attached to their spines.'

'Attached?'

'Odder still, huh? He asks if I examined the entire length of their spines to see if anything was attached. When I ask him what he means, he says it might've looked like a tumor.'

'"Looked like".'

The vet turned his head to the right, to look directly at Jack, but Jack stared ahead at the Montana panorama. 'You heard it the same

277

way I did. Funny way to word it, huh? Not a tumor. Might've looked like one but not a real tumor.' Travis gazed out at the fields again. 'I asked him if he was holding out on me, but he swore he wasn't. I told him to call me right away if he saw any animals behaving like those coons – squirrels, rabbits, whatever – but he never did. Less than three weeks later, he was dead.'

'You found him.'

'Couldn't get him to answer his phone. Came out here to check on him. There he was, lying in the open doorway, holding on to that shotgun for dear life.'

'He hadn't fired it.'

'No. It was just a heart attack got him.'

Under the influence of the wind, the long meadow grass rippled in brown waves. The fields resembled a rolling, dirty sea.

Jack debated whether to tell Travis about what had happened in the graveyard a short while ago. However, describing the experience was difficult. He could outline the bare events, recount the bizarre exchanges between himself and the Toby-thing. But he didn't have the words – maybe there were no words – to adequately describe what he had felt, and feelings were the core of it. He couldn't convey a fraction of the essential supernatural nature of the encounter.

To buy time, he said, 'Any theories?'

'I suspect maybe a toxic substance was involved. Yeah, I know, there aren't exactly piles of industrial sludge scattered all around these parts. But there are natural toxins, too, can cause dementia in wildlife, make animals act damn near as peculiar as people. How about you? See anything weird since you've been here?'

'In fact, yes.' Jack was relieved that the postures they had chosen, relative to each other, made it possible to avoid meeting the veterinarian's eyes without causing suspicion. He told Travis about the crow at the window that morning – and how, later, it had flown tight circles over him and Toby while they played with the Frisbee.

'Curious,' Travis said. 'It might be related, I guess. On the other

278

hand, there's nothing that bizarre about its behavior, not even pecking the glass. Crows can be damned bold. It still around here?'

They both pushed away from the Rover and stood scanning the sky. The crow was gone.

'In this wind,' Travis said, 'birds are sheltering.' He turned to Jack. 'Anything besides the crow?'

That business about toxic substances had convinced Jack to hold off telling Travis Potter anything about the graveyard. They were discussing two utterly different kinds of mystery: poison versus the supernatural; toxic substances as opposed to ghosts and demons and things that go bump in the night. The incident on the cemetery knoll was evidence of a strictly subjective nature, even more so than the behavior of the crow; it didn't provide any support to the contention that something unspeakably strange was going on at Quartermass Ranch. Jack had no proof it had happened. Toby clearly recalled none of it and could not corroborate his story. If Eduardo Fernandez had seen something peculiar and withheld it from Travis, Jack sympathized with the old man and understood. The veterinarian was predisposed to the idea that extraordinary agents were at work, because of the brain swelling he'd found in the autopsies of the raccoons, but he was not likely to take seriously any talk of spirits, possession, and eerie conversations conducted in a cemetery with an entity from the Beyond.

Anything besides the crow? Travis had asked.

Jack shook his head. 'That's all.'

'Well, maybe whatever brought those coons down, it's over with. We might never know. Nature's full of odd little tricks.'

To avoid the vet's eyes, Jack pulled back his jacket sleeve, glanced at his watch. 'I've kept you too long if you want to finish your rounds before the snow sets in.'

'Never had a hope of managing that,' Travis said. 'But I should make it back home before there're any drifts the Rover can't handle.'

They shook hands, and Jack said, 'Don't you forget, a week from tomorrow, dinner at six. Bring a guest if you've got a lady friend.'

Travis grinned. 'You look at this mug, it's hard to believe, but there's a young lady willing to be seen with me. Name's Janet.'

'Be pleased to meet her,' Jack said.

He dragged the fifty-pound bag of dog chow away from the Rover and stood by the driveway, watching the vet turn around and head out.

Looking in the rearview mirror, Travis Potter waved.

Jack waved after him and watched until the Rover had disappeared around the curve and over the low hill just before the county road.

The day was a deeper gray than it had been when the vet arrived. Iron instead of ashes. Dungeon gray. The ever-lowering sky and the black-green phalanxes of trees seemed as formidably restricting as walls of concrete and stone.

Bitterly cold wind, sweetened by the perfume of pines and the faint scent of ozone from high mountain passes, swept out of the northwest. The boughs of the evergreens strained a low mournful sound from that rushing river of air; the grassy meadows conspired with it to produce a whispery whistle; and the eaves of the house inspired it to make soft hooting sounds like the weak protests of dying owls lying with broken wings in uncaring fields of night.

The countryside was beautiful even in that pre-storm gloom, and perhaps it was as peaceful and serene as they had perceived it when they'd first driven north from Utah. At that moment, however, none of the usual travel-book adjectives sprang to mind as a singular and apt descriptive. Only one word suited now. *Lonely*. It was the loneliest place Jack McGarvey had ever seen, unpopulated to distant points, far from the solace of neighborhood and community.

He hefted the bag of dog chow on to his shoulder.

Big storm coming.

He went inside.

He locked the front door behind him.

He heard laughter in the kitchen and went back there to see what was happening. Falstaff was sitting on his hindquarters, forepaws raised in front of him, staring up yearningly at a piece of bologna that Toby was holding over his head.

'Dad, look, he knows how to beg,' Toby said.

The retriever licked his chops.

Toby dropped the meat.

The dog snatched it in mid-air, swallowed, and begged for more.

'Isn't he great?' Toby said.

'He's great,' Jack agreed.

'Toby's hungrier than the dog,' Heather said, getting a large pot out of a cabinet. 'He didn't have any lunch and didn't even eat the raisin cookies I gave him when he went outside. Early dinner okay?'

'Fine,' Jack said, dropping the bag of dog chow in a corner with the intention of finding a cupboard for it later.

'Spaghetti?'

'Perfect.'

'We have a loaf of crusty French bread. You make the salads?'

'Sure,' Jack said as Toby fed Falstaff another bite of bologna.

Filling the pot with water at the sink, Heather said, 'Travis Potter seems really nice.'

'Yeah, I like him. He'll be bringing a date to dinner next Sunday. Janet's her name.'

Heather smiled and seemed happier than any time since they had come to the ranch. 'Making friends.'

'I guess we are,' he said.

As he got celery, tomatoes, and a head of lettuce out of the refrigerator, he was relieved to note that neither of the kitchen windows faced the cemetery.

*

The prolonged and subdued twilight was in its final minutes when Toby rushed into the kitchen, the grinning dog at his heels, and cried breathlessly, 'Snow!'

Heather looked up from the pot of bubbling water and roiling spaghetti, turned to the window above the sink, and saw the first flakes spiraling through the gloaming. They were huge and fluffy. The wind was in abeyance for the moment, and the immense flakes descended in lazy spirals.

Toby hurried to the north window. The dog followed, slapped its forepaws on to the sill, stood beside him, and gazed out at the miracle.

Jack put aside the knife with which he was slicing tomatoes and went to the north window as well. He stood behind Toby, his hands on the boy's shoulders. 'Your first snow.'

'But not my last!' Toby enthused.

Heather stirred the sauce in the smaller pot to be sure it was not going to stick, and then she squeezed in with her family at the window. She put her right arm around Jack and, with her left hand, idly scratched the back of Falstaff's head.

For the first time in longer than she could remember, she felt at peace. With no more financial worries, having settled into their new home in less than a week, with Jack fully recovered, with the dangers of the city schools and streets no longer a threat to Toby, Heather was finally able to put the negativity of Los Angeles behind her. They had a dog. They were making new friends. She was confident that the peculiar anxiety attacks afflicting her since their arrival at Quartermass Ranch would trouble her no more.

She had lived with fear so long in the city that she had become an anxiety junkie. In rural Montana, she didn't have to worry about drive-by gang shootings, car-jackings, ATM robberies that frequently involved casual murder, drug dealers peddling crack cocaine on every corner, follow-home stickups – or child molesters who slipped off freeways, cruised residential neighborhoods, trolled for prey, and then disappeared with their catch into the anonymous urban sprawl. Consequently, her habitual need to be afraid of *something* had given rise to the unfocused dreads and phantom enemies that had marked her first few days in these more pacific regions.

That was over now. Chapter closed.

Heavy wet snowflakes descended in battalions, in armies, swiftly conquering the dark ground, an occasional outrider finding the glass, melting. The kitchen was comfortably warm, fragrant with the aromas of cooking pasta and tomato sauce. Nothing was quite so likely to induce feelings of contentment and prosperity as being in a well-heated and cozy room while the windows revealed a world in the frigid grip of winter.

'Beautiful,' she said, enchanted by the breaking storm.

'Wow,' Toby said. 'Snow. It's really, really snow.'

They were a family. Wife, husband, child, and dog. Together and safe.

Hereafter, she was going to think *only* McGarvey thoughts, never Beckerman thoughts. She was going to embrace a positive outlook and shun the negativism that was both her family legacy and a poisonous residue of life in the big city.

She felt free at last.

Life was good.

*

After dinner, Heather decided to relax with a hot bath, and Toby settled in the living room with Falstaff to watch a video of *Beethoven*.

Jack went directly to the study to review the guns available to them. In addition to the weapons they'd brought from Los Angeles – a collection Heather had substantially increased after the shootout at Arkadian's service station – a corner case was stocked with hunting rifles, a shotgun, a .22 pistol, a .45 Colt revolver, and ammunition.

He preferred to select three pieces from their own armory: a beautifully made Korth .38; a pistol-grip, pump-action Mossberg 12-gauge; and a Micro Uzi like the one Anson Oliver had used, although this particular weapon had been converted to full automatic status. The Uzi had been acquired on the black market. It was odd that a cop's wife should feel the need to purchase an illegal gun – odder still that it had been so easy for her to do so.

He closed the study door and stood at the desk, working quickly to ready the three firearms while he still had privacy. He didn't want to take such precautions with Heather's knowledge because he would have to explain why he felt the need for protection.

She was happier than she'd been in a long time, and he could see no point in spoiling her mood until – and unless – it became necessary. The incident in the graveyard had been frightening; however, although he'd felt threatened, no blow had actually been struck, no harm done. He'd been afraid more for Toby than for himself, but the boy was back, no worse for what had happened.

And what *had* happened? He didn't relish having to explain what he had sensed rather than seen: a presence spectral and enigmatic and no more solid than the wind. Hour by hour, the encounter seemed less like something he had actually experienced and more like a dream.

He loaded the .38 and put it to one side of the desk.

He could tell her about the raccoons, of course, although he himself had never seen them and although they had done no harm to anyone. He could tell her about the shotgun Eduardo Fernandez had been clutching fiercely when he'd died. But the old man hadn't been brought down by an enemy vulnerable to buckshot; a heart attack had felled him. A massive cardiac infarction was as scary as hell, yes, but it wasn't a killer that could be deterred with firearms.

He fully loaded the Mossberg, pumped a shell into the breach, and then inserted one additional shell in the magazine tube. A bonus round. Eduardo had prepared his own gun in the same fashion shortly before he died . . .

If he tried to explain all of this to Heather now, he'd succeed in alarming her – but to no purpose. Maybe there would be no trouble. He might never again come face to face with whatever presence he had been aware of in the cemetery. One such episode in a lifetime was more contact with the supernatural than most people ever experienced. Wait for developments. Hope there were none. But if there were, and if he obtained concrete proof of danger, *then* he would have to let her know that maybe, just maybe, their year of tumult was not yet at an end.

The Micro Uzi had two magazines welded at right angles, giving it a forty-round capacity. The heft of it was reassuring. More than two kilos of death waiting to be dispensed. He couldn't imagine any enemy – wild creature or man – that the Uzi couldn't handle.

He put the Korth in the top right-hand desk drawer, toward the back. He closed the drawer and left the study with the other two weapons.

Before slipping past the living room, Jack waited until he heard Toby laughing, then glanced around the corner of the archway. The boy was focused on the TV, Falstaff at his side. Jack hurried to the kitchen at the end of the hall, where he put the Uzi in the pantry, behind extra boxes of corn flakes, Cheerios, and shredded wheat that wouldn't be opened for at least a week.

Upstairs in the master bedroom, breezy music played behind the closed door to the adjoining bathroom. Soaking in the tub, Heather had turned the radio to a golden-oldies station. '*Dreamin*'' by Johnny Burnette was just winding down.

Jack pushed the Mossberg under the bed, far enough back so she wouldn't notice it when they made the bed in the morning but not so far back that he couldn't get hold of it in a hurry.

'*Poetry in Motion*'. Johnny Tillotson. Music from an innocent age. Jack hadn't even been born yet when that record had been made.

He sat on the edge of the bed, listening to the music, feeling mildly guilty about not sharing his fears with Heather. But he just didn't want to upset her needlessly. She'd been through so much. In some ways, his being wounded and hospitalized had been harder on her than on him, because she'd been required to bear alone the pressures of day-to-day existence while he'd recuperated. She needed a reprieve from tension.

285

Probably nothing to worry about anyway.

A few sick raccoons. A bold little crow. A strange experience in a cemetery – which was suitably creepy material for some television show like *Unsolved Mysteries* but which hadn't been as threatening to life and limb as any of a hundred things that could happen in the average police officer's workday.

Loading and secreting the guns would most likely prove to have been an overreaction.

Well, he'd done what a cop should do. Prepared himself to serve and protect.

On the radio in the bathroom, Bobby Vee was singing '*The Night Has a Thousand Eyes*'.

Beyond the bedroom windows, snow was falling harder than before. The flakes, previously fluffy and wet, were now small, more numerous, and dry. The wind had accelerated again. Sheer curtains of snow rippled and billowed across the black night.

*

After his mom warned him against allowing Falstaff to sleep on the bed, after goodnight kisses, after his dad told him to keep the dog on the floor, after the lights were turned out – except for the red nightlight – after his mom warned him again about Falstaff, after the hall door was pulled half shut, after enough time had passed to be sure neither his mom nor his dad was going to sneak back to check on the retriever, Toby sat up in his alcove bed, patted the mattress invitingly, and whispered, 'Here, Falstaff. Come on, fella.'

The dog was busily sniffing along the base of the door at the head of the back stairs. He whined softly, unhappily.

'Falstaff,' Toby said, louder than before. 'Here, boy, come here, hurry.'

Falstaff glanced at him, then put his snout to the door sill again, snuffling and whimpering at the same time.

286

'Come here, we'll play covered wagon or spaceship or anything you want,' Toby wheedled.

Suddenly getting a whiff of something that displeased him, the dog sneezed twice, shook his head so hard that his long ears flapped loudly, and backed away from the door.

'*Falstaff!*' Toby hissed.

Finally the dog padded to him through the red light – which was the same kind of light you'd find in the engine room of a starship, or around a campfire out on a lonely prairie where the wagon train had stopped for the night, or in a freaky temple in India where you and Indiana Jones were sneaking around and trying to avoid a bunch of weird guys who worshiped Kali, Goddess of Death. With a little encouragement, Falstaff jumped on to the bed.

'Good dog.' Toby hugged him. Then in hushed, conspiratorial tones: 'Okay, see, we're in a rebel starfighter on the edge of the Crab Nebula. I'm the captain and ace gunner. You're a super-super-intelligent alien from a planet that circles the Dog Star plus you're psychic, see, you can read the thoughts of the bad aliens in the other starfighters trying to blow us apart, which they don't know. *They don't know.* They're crabs with sort of hands instead of just claws, see, like this, crab hands, *scrack-scrick-scrack-scrick*, and they're mean, really really vicious. Like after their mother gives birth to eight or ten of them at once, they turn on her and *eat her alive*! You know? Crunch her up. *Feed* on her. Mean as shit, these guys. You know what I'm saying?'

Falstaff regarded him face to face throughout the briefing, and then licked him from chin to nose when he finished.

'All right, you know! Okay, let's see if we can ditch these crab geeks by going into hyperspace – jump across half the galaxy and leave 'em in the dust. So what's the first thing we got to do? Yeah, right, put up the cosmic-radiation shields so we don't wind up full of pin holes from traveling faster than all the subatomic particles we'll be passing through.'

He switched on the reading lamp above his headboard, reached to the draw-cord – 'Shields up!' – and pulled the privacy drapes all the way shut. Instantly the alcove bed became a cloistered capsule that could be any sort of vehicle, ancient or futuristic, traveling as slow as a sedan chair or faster than light through any part of the world or out of it.

'Lieutenant Falstaff, are we ready?' Toby asked.

Before the game could begin, the retriever bounded off the bed and between the bunk drapes, which fell shut again behind him.

Toby grabbed the draw-cord and pulled the drapes open. 'What's the matter with you?'

The dog was at the stairwell door, sniffing.

'You know, dogbreath, this could be viewed as mutiny.'

Falstaff glanced back at him, then continued to investigate whatever scent had fascinated him.

'We got crabulons trying to kill us, you want to go play dog.' Toby got out of bed and joined the retriever at the door. 'I know you don't have to pee. Dad took you out already, and you got to make yellow snow before I ever did.'

The dog whimpered again, made a disgusted sound, then backed away from the door and growled low in his throat.

'It's nothing, it's some steps, that's all.'

Falstaff's black lips skinned back from his teeth. He lowered his head as if he was ready for a gang of crabulons to come through that door right now, *scrack-scrick-scrack-scrick*, with their eye stalks wiggling two feet above their heads.

'Dumb dog. I'll show you.'

He twisted open the lock, turned the knob.

The dog whimpered and backed away.

Toby opened the door. The stairs were dark. He flipped on the light and stepped on to the landing.

Falstaff hesitated, looked toward the half-open hall door as if maybe he would bolt from the bedroom.

288

'You're the one was so interested,' Toby reminded him. 'Now come on, I'll show you, just stairs.'

As if he had been shamed into it, the dog joined Toby on the landing. His tail was held so low that the end of it curled around one of his hind legs.

Toby descended three steps, wincing as the first one squeaked and then the third. If Mom or Dad was in the kitchen below, he might get caught, and then they'd think he was sneaking out to grab up some snow – in his bare feet! – to bring it back to his room to watch it melt. Which wasn't a bad idea, actually. He wondered whether snow was interesting to eat. Three steps, two squeaks, and he stopped, looked back at the dog.

'Well?'

Reluctantly, Falstaff moved to his side.

Together they crept down the tight, enclosed spiral. Trying to make as little noise as possible. Well, one of them was trying, anyway, staying close to the wall where the treads weren't as likely to creak, but the other one had claws that ticked and scraped on the wood.

Toby whispered, 'Stairs. Steps. See? You can go down. You can go up. Big deal. What'd you think was behind the door, huh? Doggie Hell?'

Each step they descended brought one new step into view. The way the walls curved, you couldn't see far ahead, couldn't see the bottom, just a few steps with the paint worn thin, lots of shadows because of the dim bulbs, so maybe the lower landing was just two steps below or maybe it was a hundred, five hundred, or maybe you went down and down and around and around for ninety *thousand* steps, and when you reached the bottom you were at the center of the earth with dinosaurs and lost cities.

'In doggie Hell,' he told Falstaff, 'the devil's a cat. You know that? Big cat, really big, stands on his hind feet, has claws like razors . . .'

Down and around, slow step by slow step.

'. . . this big devil cat, he wears a cape made out of dog fur, necklace out of dog teeth . . .'

Down and around.

'. . . and when he plays marbles . . .'

Wood creaking underfoot.

'. . . he uses dogs' eyes! Yeah, that's right . . .'

Falstaff whimpered.

'. . . he's one mean cat, big mean cat, mean as shit.'

They reached the bottom. The vestibule. The two doors.

'Kitchen,' Toby whispered, indicating one door. He turned to the other. 'Back porch.'

He could probably twist open the deadbolt, slip on to the porch, scoop up a double handful of snow, even if he had to go as far as the yard to get it, but still make it back inside and all the way up to his room without his mom or dad ever knowing about it. Make a real snowball, his first. Take a taste of it. When it started to melt, he could just put it in a corner of his room and, in the morning, there'd be no evidence. Just water. Which, if anyone noticed it, he could blame on Falstaff.

Toby reached for the doorknob with his right hand, and for the dead-bolt turn with his left.

The retriever jumped up, planted both paws on the wall beside the door, and clamped his jaws around Toby's left wrist.

Toby stifled a squeal of surprise.

Falstaff held the wrist firmly, but he didn't bite down, didn't really hurt, just held on and rolled his eyes at Toby, as if what he would have said, if he could speak, was something like, *No, you can't open this door, it's off limits, forget it, no way.*

'What're you doing?' Toby whispered. 'Let go.'

Falstaff would not let go.

'You're drooling on me,' Toby said as a rivulet of thick saliva trickled down his wrist and under the sleeve of his pajama top.

The retriever worked his teeth slightly, still not hurting his master but making it clear that he *could* cause a little pain any time he wanted.

'What, is Mom *paying* you?'

Toby let go of the doorknob with his right hand.

The dog rolled his eyes, relaxed his jaws, but didn't entirely let go of the left wrist until Toby released the thumb-turn on the lock and lowered his hand to his side. Falstaff dropped away from the wall, on to all fours again.

Toby stared at the door, wondering if he would be able to move quickly enough to open it before the dog could leap up and seize his wrist again.

The retriever watched him closely.

Then he wondered why Falstaff didn't want him to go outside. Dogs could sense danger. Maybe a bear was prowling around outside, one of the bears that Dad said lived in the woods. A bear could gut you and bite your head off so quick you wouldn't have a chance to scream, crunch your skull up like hard candy, pick its teeth with your arm bone, and all they'd find in the morning was a bloody scrap of pajamas and maybe a toe the bear had overlooked.

He was scaring himself.

He checked the crack between the door and the jamb to be sure the deadbolt was actually in place. He could see the dull brass shine of it in there. Good. Safe.

Of course, Falstaff had been afraid of the door above, too, curious but afraid. He hadn't wanted to open it. Hadn't wanted to come down here, really. But nobody had been waiting for them on the steps. No bear, for sure.

Maybe this was just a dog who spooked easy.

'My dad's a hero,' Toby whispered.

Falstaff cocked his head.

'He's a hero cop. He's not afraid of nothin' and I'm not afraid of nothin' either.'

The dog stared at him as if to say, *Yeah? So what next?*

Toby looked again at the door in front of him. He could just open it a crack. Take a quick look. If a bear was on the porch, slam the door fast.

'If I wanted to go out there and *pet* a bear, I would.'

Falstaff waited.

'But it's late. I'm tired. If there's a bear out there, he'll just have to wait till tomorrow.'

Together, he and Falstaff climbed back to his room. Dirt was scattered on the stairs. He'd felt it under his bare feet on the way down; now he felt it going up. On the high landing, he stood on his right leg and brushed off the bottom of his left foot, stood on his left foot and brushed off his right. Crossed the threshold. Closed the door. Locked it. Switched off the stair light.

Falstaff was at the window, gazing out at the backyard, and Toby joined him.

The snow was coming down so hard there would probably be nine feet of it by morning, maybe sixteen. The porch roof below was white. The ground was totally white everywhere, as far as he could see, but he couldn't see all that far because the snow was *really* coming down. He couldn't even see the woods. The caretaker's house was swallowed by whipping white *clouds* of snow. Incredible.

The dog dropped to the floor and trotted away, but Toby watched the snow a while longer. When he began to get sleepy, he turned and saw that Falstaff was sitting in the bed, waiting for him.

Toby slipped under the blankets, keeping the retriever on top of them. Letting the dog *under* the blankets was going one step too far. Infallible eight-year-old-boy instinct told him as much. If Mom or Dad found them like that – boy head on one pillow, dog head on the other pillow, covers pulled up to their chins – there would be big trouble.

He reached for the draw-cord to shut the drapes, so he and Falstaff could go to sleep on a train, crossing Alaska in the dead of winter to get to the gold-rush country and stake a claim, after which they'd change Falstaff's name to White Fang. But as soon as the drapes began to close, the dog sprang to its feet on the mattress, ready to leap to the floor.

'Okay, all right, Jeez,' Toby said, and he pulled the drapes wide open.

The retriever settled beside him again, lying so he was facing the door at the head of the back stairs.

'Dumb dog,' Toby muttered from the edge of sleep. 'Bears don't have door keys . . .'

*

In the darkness, when Heather slid against him, smelling faintly of soap from her hot bath, Jack knew he'd have to disappoint her. He wanted her, needed her, God knew, but he remained obsessed with his experience in the cemetery. As the memory grew rapidly less vivid, as it became increasingly difficult to recall the precise nature and intensity of the emotions that had been a part of the encounter, he turned it over and over more desperately in his mind, examining it repeatedly from every angle, trying to squeeze sudden enlightenment from it before it became, like all memories, a dry and faded husk of the actual experience. The conversation with the thing that had spoken through Toby had been about death – cryptic, even inscrutable, but definitely about death. Nothing was as certain to dampen desire as brooding about death, graves, and the moldering bodies of old friends.

At least, that's what he thought when she touched him, kissed him, and murmured endearments. Instead, to his surprise, he found not only that he was ready but rampant, not merely capable but full of more vigor than he'd known since long before the shooting back in March. She was so giving yet demanding, alternately submissive and aggressive, shy yet all-knowing, as enthusiastic as a bride embarking on a new marriage, sweet and silken and alive, so wonderfully *alive*.

Later, as he lay on his side and she drifted asleep with her breasts pressed to his back, the two of them like a pair of spoons, he understood that making love with her had been a rejection of the frightening yet darkly alluring presence in the cemetery. A day of brooding about death had proved to be a perverse aphrodisiac.

He was facing the windows. The draperies were open. Ghosts of snow whirled past the glass, dancing white phantoms, spinning to the music of the fluting wind, waltzing spirits, pale and cold, waltzing and pale, cold and spinning, spinning . . .

*

. . . in cloying blackness, blindly feeling his way toward the Giver, toward an offer of peace and love, pleasure and joy, an end to all fear, ultimate freedom, his for the taking, if only he could find the way, the path, the truth. The door. Jack knew he only had to find the door, to open it, and a world of wonder and beauty would lie beyond. Then he understood that the door was within himself, not to be found by stumbling through eternal darkness. Such an exciting revelation. Within himself. Paradise, paradise. Joy eternal. Just open the door within himself and let it in, let it in, as simple as that, just let it in. He wanted to accept, surrender, because life was hard when it didn't have to be. But some stubborn part of him resisted, and he sensed the frustration of the Giver beyond the door, frustration and inhuman rage. He said, *I can't, no, can't, won't, no.* Abruptly the darkness acquired weight, compacting around him with the inevitability of stone forming around a fossil over millennia, a crushing and unrelenting pressure, and with that pressure came the Giver's furious assertion: *Everything becomes, everything becomes me, everything, everything becomes me, me, me.* Must submit . . . useless to resist . . . let it in . . . paradise, paradise, joy forever . . . let it in. Hammering on his soul. *Everything becomes me.* Jarring blows at the very structure of him, ramming, pounding, colossal blows shaking the deepest foundations of his existence: let it in, let it in, let it in, LET IT IN, LET IT IN, *LET IT IN, LET IT ININININININ—*

A brief internal sizzle and crack, like the hard quick sound of an electrical arc jumping a gap, jittered through his mind, and Jack woke. His eyes snapped open. At first he lay rigid and still, so terrified he could not move.

Bodies are.

Everything becomes me.

Puppets.

Surrogates.

Jack had never before awakened so abruptly or so completely in an instant. One second in a dream, the next wide awake and alert and furiously *thinking*.

Listening to his frantic heart, he knew that the dream hadn't actually been a dream, not in the usual sense of the word, but . . . an intrusion. Communication. Contact. An attempt to subvert and overpower his will while he slept.

Everything becomes me.

Those three words were not so cryptic now as they had seemed before, but were an arrogant assertion of superiority and a claim of dominance. They had been spoken both by the unseen Giver in the dream and by the hateful entity that communicated through Toby in the graveyard yesterday. In both instances, waking and sleeping, Jack had felt the presence of something inhuman, imperious, hostile and violent, something that would slaughter the innocent without remorse but preferred to subvert and dominate.

A greasy nausea made Jack gag. He felt cold and dirty inside. Corrupted by the Giver's attempt to seize control and nest within him, even though it had not been successful.

He knew as surely as he had ever known anything in his life that this enemy was real: not a ghost, not a demon, not just the paranoid-schizophrenic delusion of a troubled mind, but a creature of flesh and blood. No doubt infinitely strange flesh. And blood that might not be recognized as such by any physician yet born. But flesh and blood nonetheless.

He didn't know what the thing was, where it had come from, or out of what it had been born, just that it existed. And that it was somewhere on Quartermass Ranch.

Jack was lying on his side, but Heather was no longer pressed against him. She had turned over during the night.

Crystals of snow tick-tick-ticked against the window, like a finely calibrated astronomical clock counting off every hundredth of a second. The wind that harried the snow made a low whirring sound. Jack felt as if he was listening to the heretofore silent and secret cosmic machinery that drove the universe through its unending cycles.

Shakily, he pushed back the covers, sat up, stood.

Heather didn't wake.

Night still reigned, but a faint gray light in the east hinted at the pending coronation of a new day.

Striving to quell his nausea, Jack stood in just his underwear until his shivering was a greater concern than his queasiness. The bedroom was warm. The chill was internal. Nevertheless, he went to his closet, quietly slid the door open, slipped a pair of jeans from a hanger, pulled them on, then a shirt.

Awake, he could not sustain the explosive terror that had blown him out of the dream, but he was still shaky, fearful – and worried about Toby. He left the master bedroom, intending to check on his son.

Falstaff was in the shadowy upstairs hall, intently staring through the open door of the bedroom next to Toby's, where Heather had set up her computers. An odd, faint light fell through the doorway and glimmered on the dog's coat. He was statue-still and tense. His blocky head was held low and thrust forward. His tail wasn't wagging.

As Jack approached, the retriever looked at him and issued a muted, anxious whine.

The soft clicking of a computer keyboard came from the room. Rapid typing. Silence. Then another burst of typing.

In Heather's makeshift office, Toby was sitting in front of one of the computers. The glow from the oversize monitor, which faced away from Jack, was the only source of light in the former bedroom, far brighter than the reflection that reached the hallway; it bathed the boy in swiftly changing shades of blue and green and purple, a sudden splash of red, orange, then blue and green again.

At the window behind Toby, the night remained deep because the gray insistence of dawn could not yet be seen from that side of the house. Barrages of fine snowflakes tapped the glass and were briefly transformed into blue and green sequins by the monitor light.

Stepping across the threshold, Jack said, 'Toby?'

The boy didn't glance up from the screen. His small hands flew across the keyboard, eliciting a furious spate of muffled clicking. No other sound issued from the machine, none of the usual beeps or burbles.

Could Toby type? No. At least, not like this, not with such ease and speed.

The boy's eyes glimmered with distorted images of the display on the screen before him: violet, emerald, a flicker of red.

'Hey, kiddo, what're you doing?'

He didn't respond to the question.

Yellow, gold, yellow, orange, gold, yellow – the light shimmered not as if it radiated from a computer screen but as if it was the glittering reflection of summer sunlight bouncing off the rippled surface of a pond, spangling his face. Yellow, orange, umber, amber, yellow . . .

At the window, spinning snowflakes glimmered like gold dust, hot sparks, fireflies.

Jack crossed the room with trepidation, sensing that normality had not returned when he'd awakened from the nightmare. The dog padded behind him. Together they rounded one end of the L-shaped work area and stood at Toby's side.

A riot of constantly changing colors surged across the computer screen from left to right, melting into and through one another, now fading, now intensifying, now bright, now dark, curling, pulsing, an electronic kaleidoscope in which none of the ceaselessly transfigured patterns had straight edges.

It was a full-color monitor. Nevertheless, Jack had never seen anything like this before.

He put a hand on his son's shoulder.

Toby shuddered. He didn't look up or speak, but a subtle change in his attitude implied that he was no longer as spellbound by the display on the monitor as he had been when Jack first spoke to him from the doorway.

His fingers rattled the keys again.

'What're you doing?' Jack asked.

'Talking.'

19

MASSES OF yellow and pink, spiraling threads of green, rippling ribbons of purple and blue.

The shapes, patterns, and rhythms of change were mesmerizing when they combined in beautiful and graceful ways – but also when they were ugly and chaotic. Jack sensed movement in the room, but he had to make an effort to look up from the compelling protoplasmic images on the screen.

Heather stood in the doorway, wearing her quilted red robe, hair tousled. She didn't ask what was happening. As if she already knew. She wasn't looking directly at Jack or Toby but at the window behind them.

Jack turned and saw showers of snowflakes repeatedly changing color as the display on the monitor continued its rapid and fluid metamorphosis.

'Talking to whom?' he asked Toby.

After a hesitation, the boy said, 'No name.' His voice was not flat and soulless as it had been in the graveyard, but neither was it quite normal.

'Where is he?' Jack asked.

'Not he.'

'Where is she?'

'Not she.'

Frowning, Jack said. 'Then what?'

The boy said nothing, gazed unblinking at the screen.

'It?' Jack wondered.

'All right,' Toby said.

Approaching them, Heather looked strangely at Jack. 'It?'

To Toby, Jack said, 'What is it?'

'Whatever it wants to be.'

'Where is it?'

'Wherever it wants to be,' the boy said cryptically.

'What is it doing here?'

'Becoming.'

Heather stepped around the table, stood on the other side of Toby, and stared at the monitor. 'I've seen this before.'

Jack was relieved to know the bizarre display wasn't unique, therefore not necessarily related to the experience in the cemetery, but Heather's demeanor was such that his relief was extremely short-lived. 'Seen it when?'

'Yesterday morning, before we went into town. On the TV in the living room. Toby was watching it . . . sort of enraptured like this. Strange.' She shuddered and reached for the master switch. 'Shut it off.'

'No,' Jack said, reaching in front of Toby to stay her hand. 'Wait. Let's see.'

'Honey,' she said to Toby, 'what's going on here, what kind of game is this?'

'No game. I dreamed it, and in the dream I came in here, then I woke up and I *was* here, so we started talking.'

'Does this make any sense to you?' she asked Jack.

'Yes. Some.'

'What's going on, Jack?'

'Later.'

'Am I out of the loop on something? What is this all about?' When he didn't respond, she said, 'I don't like this.'

'Neither do I,' Jack said. 'But let's see where it leads, whether we can figure this out.'

'Figure *what* out?'

The boy's fingers pecked busily at the keys. Although no words appeared on the screen, it seemed as if new colors and fresh patterns appeared and progressed in a rhythm that matched his typing.

'Yesterday, on the TV . . . I asked Toby what it was,' Heather said. 'He didn't know. But he said . . . he liked it.'

Toby stopped typing.

The colors faded, then suddenly intensified and flowed in wholly new patterns and shades.

'No,' the boy said.

'No what?' Jack asked.

'Not talking to you. Talking to . . . it.' And to the screen, he said, 'No. Go away.'

Waves of sour green. Blossoms of blood red appeared at random points across the screen, turned black, flowered into red again, then wilted, streamed, a viscous pus yellow.

The endlessly mutagenic display dazed Jack when he watched it too long, and he could understand how it could completely capture the immature mind of an eight-year-old boy, hypnotize him.

As Toby began to hammer the keyboard once more, the colors on the screen faded – then abruptly brightened again, although in new shades and in yet more varied and fluid forms.

'It's a language,' Heather exclaimed softly.

For a moment Jack stared at her, uncomprehending.

She said, 'The colors, the patterns. A language.'

He checked the monitor. 'How can it be a language?'

'It is,' she insisted.

'There aren't any repetitive shapes, nothing that could be letters, words.'

'Talking,' Toby confirmed. He pounded the keyboard. As before,

301

the patterns and colors acquired a rhythm consistent with the pace at which he input his side of the conversation.

'A tremendously complicated and expressive language,' Heather said, 'beside which English or French or Chinese is primitive.'

Toby stopped typing, and the response from the other conversant was dark and churning, black and bile-green, clotted with red.

'No,' the boy said to the screen.

The colors became more dour, the rhythms more vehement.

'No,' Toby repeated.

Churning, seething, spiraling reds.

For a third time: 'No.'

Jack said, 'What're you saying "no" to?'

'To what it wants,' Toby replied.

'What does it want?'

'It wants me to let it in, just let it in.'

'Oh, Jesus,' Heather said, and reached for the OFF switch again.

Jack stopped her hand as he'd done before. Her fingers were pale and frigid. 'What's wrong?' he asked, though he was afraid he knew. The words 'let it in' had jolted him with an impact almost as great as one of Anson Oliver's bullets.

'Last night,' Heather said, staring in horror at the screen. 'In a dream.' Maybe his own hand turned cold. Or maybe she felt him tremble. She blinked. 'You've had it, too, the dream!'

'Just tonight. Woke me.'

'The door,' she said. 'It wants you to find a door in yourself, open the door and let it in. Jack, damn it, what's going on here, what the *hell's* going on?'

He wished he knew. Or maybe he didn't. He was more scared of this thing than of anyone he'd confronted as a cop. He had *killed* Anson Oliver, but he didn't know if he could touch this enemy, didn't know if it could even be found or seen.

'No,' Toby said to the screen.

Falstaff whined and retreated to a corner, stood there, tense and watchful.

'No. No.'

Jack crouched beside his son. 'Toby, right now you can hear it and me, both of us?'

'Yes.'

'You're not completely under its influence?'

'Only a little.'

'You're . . . in between somewhere?'

'Between,' the boy confirmed.

'Do you remember yesterday in the graveyard?'

'Yes.'

'You remember this thing . . . speaking through you?'

'Yes.'

'What?' Heather asked, surprised. 'What about the graveyard?'

On the screen: undulant black, bursting boils of yellow, seeping spots of kidney red.

'Jack,' Heather said, angrily, 'you said nothing was wrong when you went up to the cemetery. You said Toby was daydreaming – just standing up there daydreaming.'

To Toby, Jack said, 'But you didn't remember anything about the graveyard right after it happened.'

'No.'

'Remember what?' Heather demanded. 'What the hell was there to remember?'

'Toby,' Jack said, 'are you able to remember now because . . . because you're half under its spell again but only half . . . neither here nor there?'

'Between,' the boy acknowledged.

'Tell me about this "it" you're talking to,' Jack said.

'Jack, don't,' Heather said.

She looked haunted. He knew how she felt. But he said, 'We have to learn about it.'

'Why?'

'Maybe to survive.'

He didn't have to explain. She knew what he meant. She had endured some degree of contact in her sleep. The hostility of the thing. Its inhuman rage.

To Toby, he said, 'Tell me about it.'

'What do you want to know?'

On the screen: blues of every shade, spreading like Japanese fans but without the sharp folds, one blue over the other, through the other.

'Where does it come from, Toby?'

'Outside.'

'What do you mean?'

'Beyond.'

'Beyond what?'

'This world.'

'Is it . . . extraterrestrial?'

Heather said, 'Oh, my God.'

'Yes,' Toby said. 'No.'

'Which, Toby?'

'Not as simple as . . . ET. Yes. And no.'

'What is it doing here?'

'Becoming.'

'Becoming what?'

'Everything.'

Jack shook his head. 'I don't understand.'

'Neither do I,' the boy said, riveted to the display on the computer monitor.

Heather stood with her hands fisted against her breast.

Jack said, 'Toby, yesterday in the graveyard, you weren't just between, like now.'

'Gone.'

'Yes, you were gone all the way.'

'Gone.'

'I couldn't reach you.'

'Shit,' Heather said furiously, and Jack didn't look up at her because he knew she was glaring at him. 'What *happened* yesterday, Jack? Why didn't you *tell* me, for Christ's sake? Something like this, why didn't you *tell* me?'

Without meeting her eyes, he said, 'I will, I'll tell you, just let me finish this.'

'What *else* haven't you told me,' she demanded. 'What in God's name's happening, Jack?'

To Toby, he said, 'When you were gone yesterday, son, where were you?'

'Gone.'

'Gone where?'

'Under.'

'Under? Under what?'

'Under it.'

'Under . . .?'

'Controlled.'

'Under this thing? Under its mind?'

'Yeah. In a dark place.' Toby's voice quavered with fear at the memory. 'A dark place, cold, squeezed in a dark place, hurting.'

'Shut it off, shut it down!' Heather demanded.

Jack looked up at her. She was glaring, all right, red in the face, as furious as she was frightened.

Praying that she would be patient, he said, 'We can shut the computer off, but we can't keep this thing out that way. Think about it, Heather. It can get to us by a lot of routes – through dreams, through the TV. Apparently even while we're awake, somehow. Toby was *awake* yesterday when it got to him.'

'I let it in,' the boy said.

Jack hesitated to ask the question that was, perhaps, the most critical of all. 'Toby . . . listen . . . when it's in control . . . does it

305

have to be actually *in* you? Physically? A part of it inside of you somewhere?'

Something in the brain that would show up in a dissection. Or attached to the spine. The kind of thing for which Eduardo had wanted Travis Potter to look.

'No,' the boy said.

'No seed . . . no egg . . . no slug . . . nothing that it inserts.'

'No.'

That was good, very good, thank God and all the angels, that was very good. Because if something was implanted, how did you get it out of your child, how did you free him, how could you cut open his brain and tear it out?

Toby said, 'Only . . . thoughts. Nothing in you but thoughts.'

'You mean, like it uses telepathic control?'

'Yeah.'

How suddenly the impossible could seem inevitable. Telepathic control. Something from beyond, hostile and strange, able to control other species telepathically. Crazy, right out of a science-fiction movie, yet it felt real and true.

'And now it wants in again?' Heather asked Toby.

'Yes.'

'But you won't let it in?' she asked.

'No.'

Jack said, 'You can really keep it out?'

'Yes.'

They had hope. They weren't finished yet.

Jack said, 'Why did it leave you yesterday?'

'Pushed it.'

'You pushed it out?'

'Yeah. Pushed it. Hates me.'

'For pushing it out?'

'Yeah.' His voice sank to a whisper. 'But it's . . . it . . . it hates . . . hates everything.'

306

'Why?'

With a fury of scarlet and orange swirling across his face and flashing in his eyes, the boy still whispered: 'Because . . . that's what it is.'

'It's hate?'

'That's what it does.'

'But why?'

'That's what it is.'

'Why?' Jack repeated patiently.

'Because it knows.'

'Knows what?'

'Nothing matters.'

'It knows . . . that nothing matters?'

'Yes.'

'What does that mean?'

'Nothing means.'

Dizzied by the only half-coherent exchange, Jack said, 'I don't understand.'

In a still lower whisper: 'Everything can be understood, but nothing can be *understood*.'

'I *want* to understand it.'

'Everything can be understood, but nothing can be *understood*.'

Heather's hands were still fisted, but now she pressed them to her eyes, as if she couldn't bear to look at her son in this half-trance any longer.

'Nothing can be understood,' Toby murmured again.

Frustrated, Jack said, 'But it understands us.'

'No.'

'What doesn't it understand about us?'

'Lots of things. Mainly . . . we resist.'

'Resist?'

'We resist it.'

'And that's new to it?'

'Yeah. Never before.'

'Everything else lets it in,' Heather said.

Toby nodded. 'Except people.'

Chalk one up for human beings, Jack thought. Good old Homo sapiens, bullheaded to the last. We're just not happy-go-lucky enough to let the puppetmaster jerk us around any way it wants, too uptight, too damned stubborn to love being slaves.

'Oh,' Toby said quietly, more to himself than to them or to the entity controlling the computer. 'I see.'

'What do you see?' Jack asked.

'Interesting.'

'What's interesting?'

'The how.'

Jack looked at Heather, but she didn't seem to be tracking the enigmatic conversation any better than he was.

'It senses,' Toby said.

'Toby?'

'Let's not talk about this,' the boy said, glancing away from the screen for a moment to give Jack what seemed to be an imploring or warning look.

'Talk about what?'

'Forget it,' Toby said, gazing at the monitor again.

'Forget *what*?'

'I better be good. Here, listen, it wants to know.' Then, with a voice as muffled as a sigh in a handkerchief, forcing Jack to lean closer, Toby seemed to change the subject, 'What were they doing down there?'

Jack said, 'You mean in the graveyard?'

'Yeah.'

'You know.'

'But it doesn't. It wants to know.'

'It doesn't understand death?' Jack said.

'No.'

'How can that be?'

'Life is,' the boy said, clearly interpreting a viewpoint that belonged to the creature with which he was in contact. 'No meaning. No beginning. No end. Nothing matters. It *is*.'

'Surely this isn't the first world it's ever found where things die,' Heather said.

Toby began to tremble, and his voice rose but barely. 'They resist, too, the ones under the ground. It can use them, but it can't know them.'

It can use them, but it can't know them.

A few pieces of the puzzle suddenly fit together. Revealing only a tiny portion of the truth. A monstrous, intolerable portion of the truth.

Jack remained crouched beside the boy in stunned silence. At last he said weakly, 'Use them?'

'But it can't know them.'

'How does it use them?'

'Puppets.'

Heather gasped. 'The smell. Oh, dear God. The smell in the back staircase.'

Though Jack wasn't entirely sure what she was talking about, he knew that she'd realized what was out there on the Quartermass Ranch. Not just this thing from beyond, this thing that could send the same dream to both of them, this unknowable *alien* thing whose purpose was to become and to hate. *Other* things were out there.

Toby whispered: 'But it can't know them. Not even as much as it can know us. It can use them better. Better than it can use us. But it wants to know them. Become them. And they resist.'

Jack had heard enough. Far too much. Shaken, he rose from beside Toby. He flipped the master switch to OFF, and the screen blanked.

'It's going to come for us,' Toby said, and then he ascended slowly out of his half-trance.

Bitter storm wind shrieked at the window behind them, but even if it had been able to reach into the room, it couldn't have made Jack any colder than he already was.

Toby swiveled in the office chair to direct a puzzled look first at his mother, then at his father.

The dog came out of the corner.

Though no one was touching it, the master switch on the computer flicked from the OFF to the ON position.

Everyone twitched in surprise, including Falstaff.

The screen gushed with vile and squirming colors.

Heather stooped, grabbed the power cord, and tore it out of the wall socket.

The monitor went dark again, stayed dark.

'It won't stop,' Toby said, getting up from the chair.

Jack turned to the window and saw that dawn had come, dim and gray, revealing a landscape battered by a full-scale blizzard. In the past twelve hours, at least fourteen to sixteen inches of snow had fallen, drifting twice that deep where the wind chose to pile it. Either the first storm had stalled, instead of moving farther eastward, or the second had blown in even sooner than expected, overlapping the first.

'It won't stop,' Toby repeated solemnly. He wasn't talking about the snow.

Heather pulled him into her arms, lifted and held him as tightly and protectively as she would have held an infant.

Everything becomes me.

Jack didn't know all that might be meant by those words, what horrors they might encompass, but he knew Toby was right. The thing wouldn't stop until it had become them and they'd become part of it.

Condensation had frozen on the inside of the lower panes in the French window. Jack touched the glistening film with a fingertip, but he was so frigid with fear that the ice felt no colder than his own skin.

*

Beyond the kitchen windows, the white world was filled with cold motion, the relentless angular descent of wind-driven snow.

Restless, Heather moved continuously back and forth between the two windows, nervously anticipating the appearance of a monstrously corrupted intruder in that otherwise sterile landscape.

They were dressed in the new ski suits they'd bought yesterday morning, prepared to get out of the house quickly if they came under attack and found their position indefensible.

The loaded Mossberg 12-gauge lay on the table. Jack could drop the yellow tablet and snatch up the shotgun in the event something – don't even *think* about what it might be – launched an assault on the house. The Micro Uzi and Korth .38 were on the counter by the sink.

Toby sat at the table, sipping hot chocolate from a mug, and the dog was lying at his feet. The boy was no longer in a trance state, was entirely disconnected from the mysterious invader of dreams; yet he was uncharacteristically subdued.

Although Toby had been fine yesterday afternoon and evening, following the apparently far more extensive assault he had suffered in the graveyard, Heather worried about him. He had come away from that first experience with no conscious memory of it, but the trauma of total mental enslavement had to have left scars deep in the mind, the effects of which might become evident only over a period of weeks or months. And he *did* remember the second attempt at control, because this time the puppetmaster hadn't succeeded in either dominating him or repressing the memory of the telepathic invasion. The encounter she'd had with the creature in a dream the night before last had been frightening and so repulsive that she had been overcome with nausea. Toby's experiences with it, much more intimate than her own, must have been immeasurably more terrifying and affecting.

Moving restively from one window to the other, Heather stopped behind Toby's chair, put her hands on his thin shoulders, gave him a squeeze, smoothed his hair, kissed the top of his head. Nothing must happen to him. Unbearable to think of him being touched by that thing, whatever it was and whatever it might look like, or by one of its puppets. Intolerable. She would do anything to prevent that. Anything. She would die to prevent it.

Jack looked up from the tablet after quickly reading the first three or four pages. His face was as white as the snowscape. 'Why didn't you tell me about this when you found it?'

'Because of the way he'd hidden it in the freezer, I thought it must be personal, private, none of our business. Seemed like something only Paul Youngblood ought to see.'

'You should've showed it to me.'

'Hey, you didn't tell *me* about what happened in the cemetery,' she said, 'and that's a hell of a lot *bigger* secret.'

'I'm sorry.'

'You didn't share what Paul and Travis told you, either.'

'That was wrong. But . . . now you know everything.'

'*Now*, yes, finally.'

She had been furious that he'd withheld such things from her, but she hadn't been able to sustain her anger; and she could not rekindle it now. Because, of course, she was equally guilty. She'd not told him about the uneasiness she'd felt during the entire tour of the property Monday afternoon. The premonitions of violence and death. The unprecedented intensity of her nightmare. The certainty that something had been in the back stairwell when she'd gone into Toby's room the night before last.

In all the years they had been married, there had not been as many gaps in their communication with each other as since they'd come to Quartermass Ranch. They had wanted their new life not merely to work but to be perfect, and they had been unwilling to express doubts or reservations. For that failure to reach out to each other, though motivated by the best intentions, they might pay with their lives.

312

Indicating the tablet, she said, 'Is it anything?'

'It's everything, I think. The start of it. His account of what he saw.'

He spot-read to them about the waves of virtually palpable sound that had awakened Eduardo Fernandez in the night, about the spectral light in the woods.

'I thought it would've come from the sky, a ship,' she said. 'You expect . . . after all the movies, all the books, you expect them to come in massive ships.'

'When you're talking about extraterrestrials, alien means truly different, deeply *strange*,' Jack said. 'Eduardo makes that point on the first page. Deeply strange, beyond easy comprehension. Nothing we could imagine – including ships.'

'I'm scared about what might happen, what I might have to do,' Toby said.

A blast of wind skirled under the back porch roof, as shrill as an electronic shriek, as questing and insistent as a living creature.

Heather crouched at Toby's side. 'We'll be okay, honey. Now that we know something's out there, and a little bit about what it is, we'll handle it.' She wished she was half as confident as she sounded.

'But I shouldn't be scared.'

Looking up from the tablet, Jack said, 'Nothing shameful about being afraid, kiddo.'

'You're never afraid,' the boy said.

'Wrong. I'm scared half to death right now.'

That revelation amazed Toby. 'You are? But you're a hero.'

'Maybe I am, and maybe I'm not. But there's nothing unique about being a hero,' Jack said. 'Most people are heroes. Your mom's a hero, so are you.'

'Me?'

'Sure. For the way you handled this past year. Took a lot of courage to deal with everything.'

313

'I didn't feel brave.'

'Truly brave people never do.'

Heather said, 'Lots of people are heroes even if they never dodge bullets or chase bad guys.'

'People who go to work every day, make sacrifices to raise families, and get through life without hurting other people if they can help it – those are the *real* heroes,' Jack told him. 'Lots of them out there. And once in a while all of them are afraid.'

'Then it's okay I'm scared?' Toby said.

'More than okay,' Jack said. 'If you were never afraid of anything, then you'd either be very stupid or insane. Now, I know you can't be stupid because you're *my* son. Insanity, on the other hand . . . well, I can't be too sure about that, since it runs in your mom's family.'

'Then maybe I can do it,' Toby said.

'We'll get through this,' Jack assured him.

Heather met Jack's eyes and smiled as if to say, *You handled that so well, you ought to be Father of the Year*. He winked at her. God, she loved him.

'Then it's insane,' the boy said.

Frowning, Heather said, 'What?'

'The alien. Can't be stupid. It's smarter than we are, can do things we can't. So it must be insane. It's *never* afraid.'

Heather and Jack glanced at each other. No smiles this time.

'Never,' Toby repeated, both hands clasped tightly around the mug of hot chocolate.

Heather returned to the windows, first one, then the other.

Jack skimmed the tablet pages he hadn't yet read, found a passage about the doorway, and quoted from it aloud. Standing on edge, a giant coin of darkness. As thin as a sheet of paper. Big enough to drive a train through. A blackness of exceptional purity. Eduardo daring to put his hand in it. His sense that something was coming out of that fearful gloom.

314

Pushing the tablet aside, getting up from his chair, Jack said, 'That's enough for now. We can read the rest of it later. Eduardo's account supports our own experiences. That's what's important. They might've thought he was a crazy old geezer, or that we're flaky city people who've come down with a bad case of the heebie-jeebies in all this open space, but it isn't as easy to dismiss all of us.'

Heather said, 'So who're we going to call, the county sheriff?'

'Paul Youngblood, then Travis Potter. They already suspect something's wrong out here – though, God knows, neither of them could have a clue that it's anything *this* wrong. With a couple of locals on our side, there's a chance the sheriff's deputies might take us more seriously.'

Carrying the shotgun with him, Jack went to the wall phone. He plucked the handset off the cradle, listened, rattled the disconnect lever, punched a couple of numbers, and hung up. 'The line's dead.'

She had suspected as much even as he started toward the phone. After the incident with the computer, she had known that getting help wasn't going to be easy, although she hadn't wanted to think about the possibility that they were trapped.

'Maybe the storm brought down the lines,' Jack said.

'Aren't phone lines on the same poles as power lines?'

'Yeah, and we have power, so it wasn't the storm.' From the pegboard, he snatched the keys to the Explorer and to Eduardo's Cherokee. 'Okay, let's get the hell out of here. We'll drive over to Paul and Carolyn's, call Travis from there.'

Heather tucked the yellow tablet into the waistband of her pants, against her stomach, and zipped her ski jacket over it. She took the Micro Uzi and Korth .38 from the counter top, one in each hand.

As Toby scooted off his chair, Falstaff came out from under the table and padded directly to the connecting door between the kitchen and garage. The dog seemed to understand that they were getting out, and he heartily concurred with their decision.

Jack unlocked the door, opened it fast but warily, crossing the threshold with the shotgun held in front of him, as if he expected their enemy to be in the garage. He flipped the light switch, looked left and right, and said, 'Okay.'

Toby followed his father, with Falstaff at his side.

Heather left last, glancing back at the windows. Snow. Nothing but cold cascades of snow.

Even with the lights on, the garage was murky. It was as chilly as a walk-in refrigerator. The big sectional roll-up door rattled in the wind, but she didn't push the button to raise it; they would be safer if they activated it with the remote from inside the Explorer.

While Jack made sure that Toby got in the back seat and buckled his safety belt – and that the dog was in, as well – Heather hurried to the passenger side. She watched the floor as she moved, convinced something was under the Explorer and would seize her by the ankles.

She remembered the dimly and briefly glimpsed presence on the other side of the threshold when she had opened the door a crack in her dream Friday night. Glistening and dark. Writhing and quick. Its full shape had not been discernible, although she had perceived something large, with vaguely serpentine coils.

From memory she could clearly recall its cold hiss of triumph before she had slammed the door and exploded from the nightmare.

Nothing slithered from under either vehicle and grabbed at her, however, and she made it safely into the front passenger seat of the Explorer, where she put the heavy Uzi on the floor between her feet. She held on to the revolver.

'Maybe the snow's too deep,' she said as Jack leaned in the driver's door and handed her the 12-gauge. She braced the shotgun between her knees, butt against the floor, muzzle aimed at the ceiling. 'The storm's a lot worse than they predicted.'

Getting behind the wheel, slamming his door, he said, 'It'll be all right. We might push a little snow here and there with the bumper, but I don't think it's deep enough yet to be a big problem.'

'I wish we'd had that plow attached first thing.'

Jack jammed the key in the ignition, twisted the switch, but was rewarded only with silence, not even the grinding of the starter. He tried again. Nothing. He checked to be sure the Explorer wasn't in gear. Tried a third time without success.

Heather was no more surprised than she had been when the phone proved to be dead. Although Jack said nothing and was reluctant to meet her eyes, she knew he expected it, too, which was why he had also brought the keys to the Cherokee.

While Heather, Toby, and Falstaff got out of the Explorer, Jack slipped behind the wheel of the other vehicle. That engine wouldn't turn over, either.

He raised the hood on the Jeep, then the hood on the Explorer. He couldn't find any problems.

They went back into the house.

Heather locked the connecting door to the garage. She doubted that locks were of any use in keeping out the thing that now held dominion over Quartermass Ranch. For all they knew, it could walk through walls if it wished, but she engaged the deadbolt anyway.

Jack looked grim. 'Let's prepare for the worst.'

20

SHATTERS OF snow ticked and pinged against the windows in the ground-floor study.

Though the outer world was whitewashed and full of glare, little daylight filtered into the room. Lamps with parchment shades cast an amber glow.

Reviewing their own guns and those that Eduardo had inherited from Stanley Quartermass, Jack chose to load only one other weapon: a Colt .45 revolver.

'I'll carry the Mossberg and Colt,' he told Heather. 'You'll have the Micro Uzi and the thirty-eight. Use the revolver only as backup to the Uzi.'

'That's it?' she asked.

He regarded her bleakly. 'If we can't stop whatever's coming at us with this much firepower, a third gun isn't going to do either of us a damned bit of good.'

In one of the two drawers in the base of the gun cabinet, among other sporting paraphernalia, he found three game-hunting holsters that belted around the waist. One was crafted from nylon or rayon – some manmade fabric, anyway – and the other two were leather. Exposed to below-zero temperatures for an extended period, nylon would remain flexible long after the leather holster would stiffen; a handgun might snag or bind up slightly if the leather contracted around it. Because he intended to be outdoors while Heather remained inside, he gave her the most supple of the two leather rigs and kept the nylon for himself.

Their ski suits were replete with zippered pockets. They filled many of them with spare ammunition, though it might be optimistic to expect to have a chance to reload after the assault began.

That an assault would occur, Jack had no doubt. He didn't know what form it would take – an entirely physical attack or a combination of physical and mental blows. He didn't know whether the damn thing would come itself or through surrogates, neither when nor from what direction it would launch its onslaught, but he knew it *would* come. It was impatient with their resistance, eager to control and become them. Little imagination was required to see that it would next want to study them at much closer range, perhaps dissect them and examine their brains and nervous systems to learn the secret of their ability to resist.

He had no illusions that they would be killed or anesthetized before being subjected to that exploratory surgery.

*

Jack put his shotgun on the kitchen table again. From one of the cupboards he removed a round galvanized-tin can, unscrewed the lid, and extracted a box of wooden matches, which he put on the table.

While Heather stood watch at one window, Toby and Falstaff at the other, Jack went down to the basement. In the second of the two lower rooms, along the wall beside the silent generator, stood eight five-gallon cans of gasoline, a fuel supply they had laid in at Paul Youngblood's suggestion. He carried two cans upstairs and set them on the kitchen floor beside the table.

'If the guns can't stop it,' he said, 'if it gets inside, and you're backed into a corner, then the risk of fire might be worth taking.'

'Burn down the house?' Heather asked disbelievingly.

'It's only a house. It can be rebuilt. If you have no other choice, then to hell with the house. If bullets don't work—' He saw stark terror in her eyes. 'They will work, I'm sure of that, the guns will stop it, especially that Uzi. But if by some chance, some one-in-a-million chance, that *doesn't* stop it, fire will get it for sure. Or at least drive it back. Fire could be just what you need to give you time to distract the thing, hold it off, and get out before you're trapped.'

She stared at him dubiously. 'Jack, why do you keep saying "you" instead of "we"?'

He hesitated. She wasn't going to like this. He didn't like it much himself. There was no alternative. 'You'll stay here with Toby and the dog while I—'

'No way.'

'—while I try to get to the Youngbloods' ranch for help.'

'No, we shouldn't split up.'

'We don't have a choice, Heather.'

'It'll take us easier if we split up.'

'Probably won't make a difference.'

'I think it will.'

'This shotgun doesn't add much to that Uzi.' He gestured at the whiteout beyond the window: 'Anyway, we can't all make it through that weather.'

She stared morosely at the wall of blowing snow, unable to argue the point.

'I could make it,' Toby said, smart enough to know that he was the weak link. 'I really could.' The dog sensed the boy's anxiety and padded to his side, rubbed against him. 'Dad, please, just give me a chance.'

Two miles wasn't a great distance on a warm spring day, an easy walk, but they were faced with fierce cold against which even their ski suits were not perfect protection. Furthermore, the power of the wind would work against them in three ways: reducing the subjective air temperature at least ten degrees below what it was objectively, pounding them into exhaustion as they tried to make

320

progress against it, and obscuring their desired route with whirling clouds of snow that reduced visibility to near zero.

Jack figured he and Heather might have the strength and stamina required to walk two miles under those conditions, with snow up to their knees, higher in places, but he was sure Toby wouldn't get a quarter of the way, not even walking in the trail they broke for him. Before they'd gone far, they would have to take turns carrying him. Thereafter, they would quickly become debilitated and surely die in that white desolation.

'I don't want to stay here,' Toby said. 'I don't want to do what I might have to do if I stay here.'

'And I don't want to leave you here.' Jack squatted in front of him. 'I'm not abandoning you, Toby. You know I'd never do that, don't you?'

Toby nodded somberly.

'And you can depend on your mom. She's tough. She won't let anything happen to you.'

'I know,' Toby said, being a brave soldier.

'Good. Okay. Now I've got a couple of things to do yet, and then I'll go. I'll be back fast as I can – straight over to Ponderosa Pines, round up help, get back here with the cavalry. You've seen those old movies. The cavalry always gets there in the nick of time, doesn't it? You'll be okay. We'll all be okay.'

The boy searched his eyes.

He met his son's fear with a falsely reassuring smile and felt like the most deceitful bastard ever born. He was not as confident as he sounded. Not by half. And he *did* feel as if he was running out on them. What if he got help – but they were dead by the time he returned to Quartermass Ranch?

He might as well kill himself then. Wouldn't be a point in going on.

Truth was, it probably wouldn't work out that way, them dead and him alive. At best he had a fifty-fifty chance of making it all

the way to Ponderosa Pines. If the storm didn't bring him down
. . . something else might. He didn't know how closely they were
being observed, whether their adversary would be aware of his
departure. If it *did* see him go, it wouldn't let him get far.

Then Heather and Toby would be on their own.

Nothing else he could do. No other plan made sense. Zero options.
And time running out.

*

Hammer blows boomed through the house. Hard, hollow, fearful
sounds.

Jack used three-inch steel nails because they were the largest he
had been able to find in the garage tool cabinet. Standing in the
vestibule at the bottom of the back stairs, he drove those spikes at a
severe angle through the outside door and into the jamb. Two above
the knob, two below. The door was solid oak, and the long nails bit
through it only with relentless hammering.

The hinges were on the inside. Nothing on the back porch could
pry them loose.

Nevertheless, he decided to fix the door to the jamb on that flank,
as well, though only with two nails instead of four. He drove another
two through the upper part of the door and into the header, just
for good measure.

Any intruder that entered those back stairs could take two immediate routes once it crossed the outer threshold, instead of just one
as with the other doors. It could enter the kitchen and confront
Heather – or turn the other way and swiftly ascend to Toby's room.
Jack wanted to prevent anything from reaching the second floor
because, from there, it could slip into several rooms, avoiding a
frontal assault, forcing Heather to search for it until it had a chance
to attack her from behind.

After he'd driven the final nail home, he disengaged the dead-bolt

322

lock and tried to open the door. He couldn't budge it, no matter how hard he strained. No intruder could get through it quietly any more; it would have to be broken down, and Heather would hear it regardless of where she was.

He twisted the thumb-turn. The lock clacked into the striker plate again.

Secure.

*

While Jack nailed shut the other door at the back of the house, Toby helped Heather pile pots, pans, dishes, flatware, and drinking glasses in front of the door between the kitchen and the back porch. That carefully balanced tower would topple with a resounding crash if the door was pushed open even slowly, alerting them if they were elsewhere in the house.

Falstaff kept his distance from the rickety assemblage, as if he understood that he would be in big trouble if he was the one to knock it over.

'What about the cellar door?' Toby said.

'That's safe,' Heather assured him. 'There's no way into the cellar from outside.'

As Falstaff watched with interest, they constructed a similar security device in front of the door between the kitchen and the garage. Toby crowned it with a glassful of spoons atop an inverted metal bowl.

They carried bowls, dishes, pots, baking pans, and forks to the foyer. After Jack left, they would construct a third tower inside the front door.

Heather couldn't help feeling that the alarms were inadequate. Pathetic, actually.

However, they couldn't nail shut all of the first-floor doors because they might have to escape by one – in which case they could just shove the tottering housewares aside, slip the lock, and be gone. And they hadn't time to transform the house into a sealed fortress.

Besides, every fortress had the potential to become a prison.

*

Even if Jack had felt there was time enough to attempt to secure the house a little better, he might not have tried. Regardless of what measures were taken, the large number of windows made the place difficult to defend.

The best he could do was hurry from window to window upstairs – while Heather checked those on the ground floor – to make sure they were locked. A lot of them appeared to be painted shut and not easy to open in any case.

Pane after pane revealed a misery of snow and wind. He caught not a glimpse of anything unearthly.

In Heather's closet off the master bedroom, Jack sorted through her wool scarves. He selected one that was loosely knit.

He found his sunglasses in a dresser drawer. He wished he had ski goggles. Sunglasses would have to be good enough. He couldn't walk two miles to Ponderosa Pines with his eyes unprotected in that glare; he'd be risking snowblindness.

When he returned to the kitchen, where Heather was checking the locks on the last of the windows, he lifted the phone again, hoping for a dial tone. Folly, of course. A dead line.

'Got to go,' he said.

They might have hours or only precious minutes before their nemesis decided to come after them. He couldn't guess whether the thing would be swift or leisurely in its approach, because there was no way of understanding its thought processes or of knowing whether time had any meaning to it.

Alien. Eduardo had been right. Utterly alien. Mysterious. Infinitely strange.

324

Heather and Toby accompanied him to the front door. He held her briefly but tightly, fiercely. He kissed her only once. He said an equally quick goodbye to Toby.

He dared not linger, for he might decide at any second not to leave, after all. Ponderosa Pines was the only hope they had. *Not* going was tantamount to admitting they were doomed. Yet leaving his wife and son alone in that house was the hardest thing he had ever done, harder than seeing Tommy Fernandez and Luther Bryson cut down at his side, harder than facing Anson Oliver in front of that burning service station, harder by far than recovering from a spinal injury. He told himself that going required as much courage on his part as staying required of them, not because of the ordeal the storm would pose and not because something unspeakable might be waiting for him out there; but because, if they died and he lived, his grief and guilt and self-loathing would make life darker than death.

He wound the scarf around his face, from chin to just below his eyes. Although it went around twice, the weave was loose enough to allow him to breathe. He pulled up the hood and tied it under his chin to hold the scarf in place. He felt like a knight girding for battle.

Toby watched, nervously chewing his lower lip. Tears shimmered in his eyes, but he strove not to spill them. Being the little hero.

Jack put on his sunglasses, so the boy's tears would be less visible to him and, therefore, less corrosive of his will to leave.

He pulled on his gloves and picked up the Mossberg shotgun. The Colt .45 was holstered at his right hip.

The moment had come.

Heather appeared stricken.

He could hardly bear to look at her.

She opened the door. Wailing wind drove snow all the way across the porch and over the threshold.

Jack stepped out of the house and reluctantly turned away from everything he loved. He kicked through the powdery snow on the porch.

He heard her speak to him one last time – 'I love you' – the words distorted by the wind but the meaning unmistakable.

At the head of the porch steps he hesitated, turned to her, saw that she had taken one step out of the house, said, 'I love you, Heather,' then walked down and out into the storm, not sure if she had heard him, not knowing if he would ever speak to her again, ever hold her in his arms, ever see the love in her eyes or the smile that was, to him, worth more than a place in heaven and the salvation of his soul.

The snow in the front yard was knee-deep. He bulled through it.

He dared not look back again.

Leaving them, he knew, was essential. It was courageous. It was wise, prudent, their best hope of survival.

However, it didn't feel like any of those things. It felt like abandonment.

21

WIND HISSED at the windows as if it possessed consciousness and was keeping watch on them, thumped and rattled the kitchen door as if testing the lock, shrieked and snuffled along the sides of the house in search of a weakness in their defenses.

Reluctant to put the Uzi down in spite of its weight, Heather stood watch for a while at the north window of the kitchen, then at the west window above the sink. She cocked her head now and then to listen closely to those noises that seemed too purposeful to be just voices of the storm.

At the table, Toby was wearing earphones and playing with a Game Boy. His body language was different from that which he usually exhibited when involved in an electronic game – no twitching, leaning, rocking from side to side, or bouncing in his seat. He was playing only to fill the time.

Falstaff lay in the corner farthest from a window, the warmest spot in the room. Occasionally he lifted his noble head, sniffing the air or listening; but mostly he lay on his side, staring across the room at floor level, yawning.

Time passed slowly. Heather repeatedly checked the wall clock, certain that ten minutes had gone by, only to discover that just two minutes had elapsed since she'd last looked.

The two-mile walk to Ponderosa Pines would take maybe twenty-five minutes in fair weather. Jack might require an hour or even an hour and a half in the storm, allowing for the hard slogging through knee-deep snow, detours around the deeper drifts, and the incessant resistance of the gale-force wind. Once there, he should need half an hour to explain the situation and marshal a rescue team. Less than fifteen minutes would be required for the return trip even if they had to plow open some snowbound stretches of road and driveway. At most he ought to be back in two hours and fifteen minutes, maybe half an hour sooner than that.

The dog yawned.

Toby was so still he might have been asleep sitting up.

They had turned the thermostat down so they could wear their ski suits and be ready to desert the house without delay if necessary, yet the place was still warm. Her hands and face were cool, but sweat trickled along her spine and down her sides from her underarms. She unzipped her jacket, though it interfered with the hip holster when it hung loose.

When fifteen minutes had passed uneventfully, she began to think their unpredictable adversary would make no move against them. Either it didn't realize they were currently more vulnerable without Jack or it didn't care. From what Toby had said, it was the very definition of arrogance – *never* afraid – and might operate always according to its own rhythms, plans, and desires.

Her confidence was beginning to rise – when Toby spoke quietly and not to her. 'No, I don't think so.'

Heather stepped away from the window.

He murmured, 'Well . . . maybe.'

'Toby?' she said.

As if unaware of her, he stared at the Game Boy screen. His fingers weren't moving on the controls. No game was under way: shapes and bold colors swarmed across the miniature monitor, similar to those she had seen twice before.

'Why?' he asked.

She put a hand on his shoulder.

'Maybe,' he said to the swirling colors on the screen.

Always before, responding to this entity, he had said 'no'. The 'maybe' alarmed Heather.

'Could be, maybe,' he said.

She took the earphones off him, and he finally looked up at her. 'What're you doing, Toby?'

'Talking,' he said in a half-drugged voice.

'What were you saying "maybe" to?'

'To the Giver,' he explained.

She remembered that name from her dream, the hateful thing's attempt to portray itself as the source of great relief, peace, and pleasure. 'It's not a giver. That's a lie. It's a taker. You keep saying "no" to it.'

Toby stared up at her.

She was shaking. 'You understand me, honey?'

He nodded.

She was still not sure he was listening to her. 'You keep saying "no", nothing but "no".'

'All right.'

She threw the Game Boy in the waste can. After a hesitation, she took it out, placed it on the floor, and stomped it under her boot, once, twice. She rammed her heel down on it a third time, although the device was well crunched after two stomps, then once more for good measure, then again just for the hell of it, until she realized she was out of control, taking excess measures against the Game Boy because she couldn't get at the Giver, which was the thing she really wanted to stomp.

For a few seconds she stood there, breathing hard, staring at the plastic debris. She started to stoop to gather up the pieces, then decided to hell with it. She kicked the larger chunks against the wall.

Falstaff had become interested enough to get to his feet. When Heather returned to the window at the sink, the retriever regarded her curiously, then went to the trashed Game Boy and sniffed it as if trying to determine why it had elicited such fury from her.

Beyond the window, nothing had changed. A wind-driven avalanche of snow obscured the day almost as thoroughly as a fog rolling off the Pacific could obscure the streets of a California beach town.

She looked at Toby. 'You okay?'

'Yeah.'

'Don't let it in.'

'I don't want to.'

'Then don't. Be tough. You can do it.'

On the counter under the microwave, the radio powered up of its own accord, as if it incorporated an alarm clock set to provide five minutes of music prior to a wake-up buzzer. It was a big multiple-spectrum receiver the size of two giant-economy-size boxes of cereal, and it pulled in six bands, including domestic AM and FM; however, it was not a clock and could not be programmed to switch itself on at a pre-selected time. Yet the dial glowed with green light, and strange music issued from the speakers.

The chains of notes and overlapping rhythms were not music, actually, just the essence of music in the sense that a pile of lumber and screws amounted to the essence of a cabinet. She could identify a symphony of instruments – flutes, oboes, clarinets, horns of all kinds, violins, timpani, snare drums – but there was no melody, no identifiable cohesive structure, merely a *sense* of structure too subtle to quite hear, waves of sound that were sometimes pleasant and sometimes jarringly discordant, now loud, now soft, ebbing and flowing.

'Maybe,' Toby said.

Heather's attention had been on the radio. With surprise, she turned to her son.

Toby had gotten off his chair. He was standing by the table, staring across the room at the radio, swaying like a slender reed in

330

a breeze only he could feel. His eyes were glazed. 'Well . . . yeah, maybe . . . maybe . . .'

The unmelodious tapestry of sound coming from the radio was the aural equivalent of the ever-changing masses of color that she had seen swarming across the television, computer and Game Boy screens: a language that evidently spoke directly to the subconscious. She could feel the hypnotic pull of it herself, although it exerted only a small fraction of the influence on her that it did on Toby.

Toby was the vulnerable one. Children were always the easiest prey, natural victims in a cruel world.

'. . . I'd like that . . . nice . . . pretty,' the boy said dreamily, and then he sighed.

If he said 'yes', if he opened the inner door, he might not be able to evict the thing this time, as he had done before. He might be lost forever.

'No!' Heather said.

Seizing the radio cord, she tore the plug out of the wall socket hard enough to bend the prongs. Orange sparks spurted from the outlet, showered across the counter tile.

Though unplugged, the radio continued to produce the mesmerizing waves of sound.

She stared at it, aghast and uncomprehending.

Toby remained entranced, speaking to the unseen presence, as he might have spoken to an imaginary playmate. 'Can I? Hmmm? Can I . . . will you . . . will you?'

The damn thing was more relentless than the drug dealers in the city, who did their come-on shtick for kids at schoolyard fences, on street corners, in videogame parlors, outside movie theaters, at the malls, wherever they could find a venue, indefatigable, as hard to eradicate as body lice.

Batteries. Of course. The radio operated off either direct or alternating current.

'. . . maybe . . . maybe . . .'

331

She dropped the Uzi on the counter, grabbed the radio, popped open the plastic cover on the back, and tore out the two recharge-able batteries. She threw them into the sink, where they rattled like dice against the backboard of a craps table. The siren song from the radio had stopped before Toby had acquiesced, so Heather had won that roll. Toby's mental freedom had been on the line, but she had thrown a seven, won the bet. He was safe for the moment.

'Toby? Toby, look at me.'

He obeyed. He was no longer swaying, his eyes were clear, and he seemed to be back in touch with reality.

Falstaff barked, and Heather thought he was agitated by all of the noise, perhaps by the stark fear he sensed in her, but then she saw that his attention was on the window above the sink. He rapped out hard, vicious, warning barks meant to scare off an adversary.

She spun around in time to see something on the porch slip away to the left of the window. It was dark and tall. She glimpsed it out of the corner of her eye, but it was too quick for her to see what it was.

The doorknob rattled.

The radio had been a diversion.

As Heather snatched the Micro Uzi off the counter, the retriever charged past her and positioned himself in front of the pots and pans and dishes stacked against the back door. He barked ferociously at the brass knob, which turned back and forth, back and forth.

Heather grabbed Toby by the shoulder, pushed him toward the hall door. 'Into the hall but stay close behind me – quick!'

The matches were already in her jacket pocket. She snared the nearest of the five-gallon cans of gasoline by its handle. She could only take one because she wasn't about to put down the Uzi.

Falstaff was like a mad dog, snarling so savagely that spittle flew from his chops, hair standing up straight on the back of his neck, his tail flat across his butt, crouched and tense, as if he might spring at the door even before the thing outside could come through it.

The lock opened with a hard *clack*.

The intruder had a key. Or maybe it didn't need one. Heather remembered how the radio had snapped on by itself.

She backed on to the threshold between the kitchen and ground-floor hall.

Reflections of the overhead light trickled scintillantly along the brass doorknob as it turned.

She put the can of gasoline on the floor and held the Uzi with both hands. 'Falstaff, get away from there! *Falstaff!*'

As the door eased inward, the tower of housewares tottered.

The dog backed off as she continued to call to him.

The security assemblage teetered, tipped over, crashed. Pots, pans, and dishes bounced-slid-spun across the kitchen floor, forks and knives rang against one another like bells, and drinking glasses shattered.

The dog scrambled to Heather's side but kept barking fiercely, teeth bared, eyes wild.

She had a sure grip on the Uzi, the safeties off, her finger curled lightly on the trigger. What if it jammed? Forget that; it wouldn't jam. It had worked like a dream when she'd tried it out against a canyon wall in a remote area above Malibu several months ago: automatic gunfire echoing along the walls of that narrow defile, spent shell casings spewing into the air, scrub brush torn to pieces, the smell of hot brass and burned gunpowder, bullets banging out in a punishing stream, as smooth and easy as water from a hose. It wouldn't jam, not in a million years. *But, Jesus, what if it does?*

The door eased inward. A narrow crack. An inch. Then wider.

Something snaked through the gap a few inches above the knob. In that instant the nightmare was confirmed, the unreal made real, the impossible suddenly incarnate, for what intruded was a tentacle, mostly black but irregularly speckled with red, as shiny and smooth as wet silk, perhaps two inches in diameter at the thickest point that she could see, tapering as thin as an earthworm at the tip. It quested into the warm air of the kitchen, fluidly curling, flexing obscenely.

That was enough. She didn't need to see more, didn't want to see more, so she opened fire. *Chuda-chuda-chuda-chuda*. The briefest squeeze of the trigger spewed six or seven rounds, punching holes in the oak door, gouging and splintering the edge of it. The deafening explosions slammed back and forth from wall to wall of the kitchen, sharp echoes overlaying echoes.

The tentacle slipped away with the alacrity of a retracted whip.

She heard no cry, no unearthly scream. She didn't know if she had hurt the thing or not.

She wasn't going to go and look on the porch, no way, and she wasn't going to wait to see if it would storm into the room more aggressively the next time. Because she didn't know how fast the creature might be able to move, she needed to put more distance between herself and the back door.

She grabbed the can of gasoline at her side, Uzi in one hand, and backed out of the doorway, into the hall, almost tripping over the dog as he scrambled to retreat with her. She backed to the foot of the stairs, where Toby waited for her.

'Mom?' he said, voice tight with fear.

Peering along the hall and across the kitchen, she could see the back door because it was in a direct line with her. It remained ajar, but nothing was forcing entry yet. She knew the intruder must still be on the porch, gripping the outside knob, because otherwise the wind would have pushed the door all the way open.

Why was it waiting? Afraid of her? No. Toby had said it was never afraid.

Another thought rocked her: if it didn't understand the concept of death, that must mean it couldn't die, couldn't be killed. In which case guns were useless against it.

Still, it waited, hesitated. Maybe what Toby had learned about it was all a lie, and maybe it was as vulnerable as they were or more so, even fragile. Wishful thinking. It was all she had.

She was not quite to the midpoint of the hall. Two more steps would put her there, between the archways to the dining and living rooms. But she was far enough from the back door to have a chance of obliterating the creature if it erupted into the house with unnatural speed and power. She stopped, put the gasoline can on the floor beside the newel post, and clutched the Uzi in both hands again.

'Mom?'

'Sssshhhh.'

'What're we gonna do?' he pleaded.

'Sssshhhh. Let me think.'

Aspects of the intruder were obviously snakelike, although she couldn't know if that was the nature of only its appendages or of its entire body. Most snakes could move fast – or coil and spring substantial distances with deadly accuracy.

The back door remained ajar. Unmoving. Wisps of snow followed drafts through the narrow gap between the door and jamb, into the house, spinning and glittering across the tile floor.

Whether or not the thing on the back porch was fast, it was undeniably big. She'd sensed its considerable size when she'd had only the most fleeting glimpse of it slipping away from the window. Bigger than she was.

'Come on,' she muttered, her attention riveted on the back door. 'Come on, if you're never afraid, come on.'

Both she and Toby cried out in surprise when, in the living room, the television switched on, with the volume turned all the way up.

Frenetic, bouncy music. Cartoon music. A screech of brakes, a crash and clatter, with comic accompaniment on a flute. Then the voice of a frustrated Elmer Fudd booming through the house: 'OOOHHH, I *HATE* THAT WABBIT!'

Heather kept her attention on the back door, beyond the hall and kitchen, altogether about fifty feet away.

So loud each word vibrated the windows, Bugs Bunny said: 'EH, WHAT'S UP, DOC?' And then a sound of something bouncing: *BOING, BOING, BOING, BOING, BOING.*

'STOP THAT, STOP THAT, YOU CWAZY WABBIT!'

Falstaff ran into the living room, barking at the TV, and then scurried into the hall again, looking past Heather where he, too, knew the real enemy still waited.

The back door.

Snow sifting through the narrow opening.

In the living room, the television program fell silent in the middle of a long comical trombone glissando that, even under the circumstances, brought to mind a vivid image of Elmer Fudd sliding haplessly and inexorably toward one doom or another. Quiet. Just the keening wind outside.

One second. Two. Three.

Then the TV blared again, but not with Bugs and Elmer. It spewed forth the same weird waves of unmelodious music that had issued from the radio in the kitchen.

To Toby, she said sharply, 'Resist it!'

Back door. Snowflakes spiraling through the crack.

Come on, come on.

Keeping her eyes on the back door at the far side of the lighted kitchen, she said, 'Don't listen to it, honey, just tell it to go away, say no to it. No, no, no to it.'

The tuneless music, alternately irritating and soothing, pushed her with what seemed like real physical force when the volume rose, pulled on her when the volume ebbed, pushed and pulled, until she realized that she was swaying as Toby had swayed in the kitchen when under the spell of the radio.

In one of the quieter passages, she heard a murmur. Toby's voice. She couldn't catch the words.

She looked at him. He had that dazed expression. Transported. He was moving his lips. He might have been saying 'yes, yes', but she couldn't tell for sure.

Kitchen door. Still ajar two inches, no more, as it had been. Something still waiting out there on the porch.

She *knew* it.

The boy whispered to his unseen seducer, soft urgent words that might have been the first faltering steps of acquiescence or total surrender.

'Shit!' she said.

She backed up two steps, turned toward the living-room arch on her left, and opened fire on the television. A brief burst, six or eight rounds, tore into the TV. The picture tube exploded, thin white vapor or smoke from the ruined electronics spurted into the air, and the darkly beguiling siren song was hammered into silence by the clatter of the Uzi.

A strong, cold draft swept through the hallway, and Heather spun toward the rear of the house. The back door was no longer ajar. It stood wide open. She could see the snow-covered porch and, beyond the porch, the churning white day.

The Giver had first walked out of a dream. Now it had walked out of the storm, into the house. It was somewhere in the kitchen, to the left or right of the hall door, and she had missed the chance to cut it down as it entered.

If it was just the other side of the threshold between the hall and kitchen, it had closed to a maximum striking distance of about twenty-five feet. Getting dangerously close again.

Toby was standing on the first step of the staircase, clear-eyed once more but shivering and pale with terror. The dog was beside him, alert, sniffing the air.

Behind her, another pot-pan-bowl-flatware-dish alarm went off with a loud clanging of metal and shattering of glass. Toby screamed, Falstaff erupted into ferocious barking again, and Heather swung around, heart slamming so hard it shook her arms, made the gun jump up and down. The front door was arcing inward. A forest of long red-speckled black tentacles burst through the gap between door and jamb, glossy and writhing. So there were *two* of them, one at the front of the house, one at the back. The Uzi chattered.

Six rounds, maybe eight. The door shut. But a mysterious dark figure was hunched against it, a small part of it visible in the beveled-glass window in the top of the door.

Without pausing to see if she'd actually hit the sonofabitch or scored only the door and wall, she spun toward the kitchen yet again, punching three or four rounds through the empty hallway behind her even as she turned.

Nothing there.

She had been sure the first one would be striking at her back. Wrong. Maybe twenty rounds left in the Uzi's double magazine. Maybe only fifteen.

They couldn't stay in the hall. Not with one of the damned things in the kitchen, another on the front porch.

Why had she thought there'd be only one of them? Because in the dream there was only one? Because Toby had spoken of just a single seducer? Might be more than two. Hundreds.

The living room was on one side of her. Dining room on the other. Ultimately, either place seemed likely to become a trap.

In different rooms all over the ground floor, windows imploded simultaneously.

The clink-jangle-tink of cascading glass and the shrieking of the wind at every breach decided her. Up. She and Toby would go up. Easier to defend high ground.

She grabbed the can of gasoline.

The front door came open behind her again, banging against the scattered items with which they had built the alarm tower. She assumed something other than the wind had shoved it, but she didn't glance back. The Giver hissed. As in the dream.

She leaped for the stairs, gasoline sloshing in the can, and shouted at Toby, 'Go, go!'

The boy and the dog raced to the second floor ahead of her.

'Wait at the top!' she called as they scrambled upward and out of sight.

338

At the top of the first flight, Heather halted on the landing, looked back and down into the front hall, and saw a dead man walking. Eduardo Fernandez. She recognized him from the pictures they had found while sorting through his belongings. Dead and buried more than four months, he nevertheless moved in a shambling and stiff-jointed manner, kicking through the dishes and pans and flatware, heading for the foot of the stairs, accompanied by swirling flakes of snow like ashes from the fires of Hell.

There could be no self-awareness in the corpse, no slightest wisp of Ed Fernandez's consciousness remaining in it, for the old man's mind and soul had gone on to a better place before the Giver had requisitioned his body. The soiled cadaver was evidently being controlled with the same power that had switched on the radio and the TV at long distance, had opened the deadbolt locks without a key, and had caused the windows to implode. Call it telekinesis, mind over matter. Alien mind over earthly matter. In this case, it was decomposing organic matter in the rough shape of a human being.

At the bottom of the steps, the corpse stopped and gazed up at her. Its face was only slightly swollen, though darkly empurpled, mottled with yellow here and there, a crust of evil green under its clogged nostrils. One eye was missing. The other was covered with a yellow film; it bulged against a half-concealing lid that, though sewn shut by a mortician, had partially opened when the rotting threads had loosened.

Heather heard herself muttering rapidly, rhythmically. After a moment she realized she was feverishly reciting a long prayer she had learned as a child but had not repeated in eighteen or twenty years. Under other circumstances, if she had made a conscious effort to recall the words, she couldn't have come up with half of them, but now they flowed out of her as they had when she'd been a young girl kneeling in church.

The walking corpse was less than half the reason for her fear, however, and *far* less than half the reason for the acute disgust that knotted her stomach, made breathing difficult, and triggered her gag reflex. It was gruesome, but the discolored flesh was not yet dissolving from the bones. The dead man still reeked more of embalming fluid than of putrescence, a pungent odor that blew up the staircase on a cold draft and instantly reminded Heather of long-ago high-school biology classes and slippery specimen frogs fished from jars of formaldehyde for dissection.

What sickened and repelled her, most of all, was the Giver that rode the corpse as it might have ridden a beast of burden. Though the light in the hallway was bright enough to reveal the alien clearly, and though she might have wanted to see *less* of it rather than more, she was nevertheless unable to precisely define its physical form. The bulk of the thing appeared to hang along the dead man's back, secured by whiplike tentacles – some as thin as pencils, some as thick as her own forearm – firmly lashed around the mount's thighs, waist, chest, and neck. The Giver was mostly black, and such a deep black that it hurt her eyes to stare at it, though in places the inky sheen was relieved by blood-red speckles.

Without Toby to protect, she might not have been able to face this thing, for it was too strange, incomprehensible, just too damned much. The sight of it dizzied like a whiff of nitrous oxide, brought her to the edge of desperate giddy laughter, a humorless mirth that was perilously close to madness.

Not daring to take her eyes off the corpse or its hideous rider, for fear she would look up to find it one step below her, Heather slowly lowered the five-gallon can of gasoline to the floor of the landing.

Along the dead man's back, at the heart of the churning mass of tentacles, there might have been a central body akin to the sac of a squid, with glaring inhuman eyes and a twisted mouth – but, if it was there, she couldn't catch a glimpse of it. Instead, the thing seemed to be all ropy extremities, ceaselessly twitching, curling, coiling, and unraveling. Though oozing and gelatinous within its skin, the Giver occasionally bristled into spiky shapes that made her think of lobsters, crabs, crawfish – but in a blink, it was all sinuous motion once more.

In college, a friend of Heather's – Wendi Felzer – had developed liver cancer and had decided to augment her doctors' treatments with a course of self-healing through imaging therapy. Wendi had pictured her white blood cells as knights in shining armor with magic swords, her cancer as a dragon, and she had meditated two hours a day, until she could see, in her mind, all of those knights slaying the beast. The Giver was the archetype for every image of cancer ever conceived, the slithering essence of malignancy. In Wendi's case, the dragon had won. Not a good thing to remember now, not good at all.

It started to climb the steps toward her.

She raised the Uzi.

The most loathsome aspect of the Giver's entanglement with the corpse was the extent of its intimacy. The buttons had popped off the white burial shirt, which hung open, revealing that a few of the tentacles had pried open the thoracic incision made by the coroner during his autopsy; those red-speckled appendages vanished inside the cadaver, probing deep into unknown reaches of its cold tissues. The creature seemed to revel in its bonding with the dead flesh, an embrace that was as inexplicable as it was obscene.

Its very existence was offensive. That it could *be* seemed proof that the universe was a madhouse, full of worlds without meaning and bright galaxies without pattern or purpose.

It climbed two steps from the hall, toward the landing.

Three. Four.

Heather waited one more.

Five steps up, seven steps below her.

A bristling mass of tentacles appeared between the dead man's parted lips, like a host of black tongues spotted with blood.

341

Heather opened fire, held the trigger down too long, used up too much ammunition, ten or twelve rounds, even fourteen, although it was surprising – considering her state of mind – that she didn't empty both magazines. The 9mm slugs stitched a bloodless diagonal line across the dead man's chest, through body and entwining tentacles.

Parasite and dead host pitched backward to the hallway floor below, leaving two lengths of severed tentacles on the stairs, one about eighteen inches long, the other about two feet. Neither of those amputated limbs bled. Both continued to move, initially twisting and flailing the way the bodies of snakes writhe long after being separated from their heads.

Heather was transfixed by the grisly sight because, almost at once, the movement ceased to be the result of misfiring nerves and randomly spasming muscles; it began to appear *purposeful*. Each scrap of the primary organism seemed aware of the other, and they groped toward each other, the first curling down over the edge of a step while the second rose gracefully like a flute-charmed serpent to meet it. When they touched, a transformation occurred that was essentially black magic and beyond Heather's understanding even though she had a clear view of it. The two became as one, not simply entwining but melding, flowing together as if the soot-dark silken skin sheathing them was little more than surface tension that gave shape to the oozing protoplasm within. As soon as the two combined, the resulting mass sprouted eight smaller tentacles; with a shimmer like quick shadows playing across a puddle of water, the new organism bristled into a vaguely crablike – but still eyeless – form, though it was as soft and flexible as ever. Quivering, as if to maintain even a marginally more angular shape required monumental effort, it began to hitch down the steps toward the mothermass from which it had become separated.

Less than half a minute had passed from the moment when the two severed appendages had begun to seek each other.

Bodies are.

Those words were, according to Jack, part of what the Giver had said through Toby in the cemetery.

Bodies are.

A cryptic statement then. All too clear now. Bodies are – now and forever, flesh without end. Bodies are – expendable if necessary, fiercely adaptable, severable without loss of intellect or memory and therefore in infinite supply.

The bleakness of her sudden insight, the perception that they could not win regardless of how valiantly they struggled or how much courage they possessed, kicked her across the borderline of sanity for a moment, into madness no less total for its brevity. Instead of recoiling from the monstrously *alien* creature stilting determinedly down the steps to rejoin its mothermass, as any sane person would have done, she plunged after it, off the landing with a strangled scream that sounded like the thin and bitter grievance of a dying animal in a sawtooth trap, the Micro Uzi thrust in front of her.

Although she knew she was putting herself in terrible jeopardy, unconscionably abandoning Toby at the top of the stairs, Heather was unable to stop. She went down one, two, three, four, five steps in the time that the crablike thing descended two. They were four steps apart when the thing abruptly reversed directions without bothering to turn around, as if front and back and sideways were all the same to it. She stopped so fast she almost lost her balance, and the crab ascended toward her a lot quicker than it had descended.

Three steps between them.

Two.

She squeezed the trigger, emptied the Uzi's last rounds into the scuttling form, chopping it into four-five-six bloodless pieces that tumbled and flopped down a few steps, where they lay squirming. Squirming ceaselessly. Supple and snakelike again. Eagerly and silently questing toward one another.

Its silence was almost the worst thing about it. No screams of pain when it was shot. No shrieks of rage. Its patient and silent

343

recovery, its deliberate continuation of the assault, mocked her hopes of triumph.

At the foot of the stairs, the apparition had pulled itself erect. The Giver, still hideously bonded to the corpse, started up the steps again.

Heather's spell of madness shattered. She fled to the landing, grabbed the can of gasoline, and scrambled to the second floor, where Toby and Falstaff were waiting.

The retriever was shuddering. Whining rather than barking, he looked as if he'd sensed the same thing Heather had seen for herself: effective defense was impossible. This was an enemy that couldn't be brought down with teeth or claws any more than with guns.

Toby said, 'Do I have to do it? I don't want to.'

She didn't know what he meant, didn't have time to ask. 'We'll be okay, honey, we'll make it.'

From the first flight of steps, out of sight beyond the landing, came the sound of heavy footsteps ascending. A hiss. It was like the sibilant escape of steam from a pinhole in a pipe – but a cold sound.

She put the Uzi aside and fumbled with the cap on the spout of the gasoline can.

Fire might work. She had to believe it might. If the thing burned, nothing would be left to remake itself. Bodies are. But bodies, reduced to ashes, could not reclaim their form and function, regardless of how alien their flesh and metabolism. Damn it, fire *had* to work.

'It's never afraid,' Toby said in a voice that revealed the profound depths of his own fear.

'Get away from here, baby! Go! Go to the bedroom! Hurry!'

The boy ran, and the dog went with him.

*

At times Jack felt that he was a swimmer in a white sea under a white sky on a world every bit as strange as the planet from which

344

the intruder at Quartermass Ranch had traveled. Though he could feel the ground beneath his feet as he slogged the half mile to the county road, he never got a glimpse of it under the enduring white torrents cast down by the storm, and it seemed as unreal to him as the bottom of the Pacific might seem to a swimmer a thousand fathoms above it. The snow rounded all forms, and the landscape rolled like the swells of a mid-ocean passage, although in some places the wind had sculpted drifts into scalloped ridges like cresting waves frozen in the act of breaking on a beach. The woods, which could have offered contrast to the whiteness that flooded his vision, were mostly concealed by falling and blowing snow as obscuring as fog at sea.

Disorientation was an unremitting threat in that bleached land. He got off course twice while still on his own property, recognizing his error only because the flattened meadow grass underneath the snow provided a spongier surface than the hard-packed driveway.

Step by hard-fought step, Jack expected something to come out of the curtains of snow or rise from a drift in which it had been lying, the Giver itself or one of the surrogates that it had mined from the graveyard. He continually scanned left and right, ready to pump out every round in the shotgun to bring down anything that rushed him.

He was glad that he had worn sunglasses. Even with shades, he found the unrelieved brightness inhibiting. He strained to see *through* the wintry sameness to guard against attack and to make out familiar details of the terrain that would keep him on the right track.

He dared not think about Heather and Toby. When he did so, his paced slowed and he was nearly overcome by the temptation to go back to them and forget about Ponderosa Pines. For their sake and his own, he blocked them from his thoughts, concentrated solely on covering ground, and virtually became a hiking machine.

The baleful wind shrieked without surcease, blew snow in his face, and forced him to bow his head. It shoved him off his feet twice – on one occasion causing him to drop the shotgun in a drift, where he had to scramble frantically to find it – and became almost as real an adversary as any man against whom he'd ever been pitted. By the time he reached the end of the private lane and paused for breath between the tall stone posts and under the arched wooden sign that marked the entrance to Quartermass Ranch, he was cursing the wind as if it could hear him.

He wiped one gloved hand across the sunglasses to scrape off the snow that had stuck to the lenses. His eyes stung as they sometimes did when an ophthalmologist put drops in them to dilate the pupils prior to an examination. Without the shades, he might already have been snowblind.

He was sick of the taste and smell of wet wool, which flavored the air he drew through his mouth and scented every inhalation when he breathed through his nose. The vapor he exhaled had thoroughly saturated the fabric, and the condensation had frozen. With one hand he massaged the makeshift muffler, cracking the thin, brittle ice and crumbling the thicker layer of compacted snow; he sloughed it all away so he could breathe more easily than he'd been able to breathe for the past two or three hundred yards.

Though he found it difficult to believe that the Giver didn't know he had left the house, he had reached the edge of the ranch without being assaulted. A considerable trek remained ahead, but the greatest danger of attack would have been in the territory he had already covered without incident.

Maybe the puppetmaster was not as omniscient as it either pretended or seemed to be.

*

A distended and ominous shadow, as tortured as that of a fright figure in a funhouse, rose along the landing wall: the puppetmaster and its decomposing marionette laboring stiffly but doggedly toward

346

the top of the first flight of stairs. As the thing ascended, it no doubt absorbed the fragments of strange flesh that bullets had torn from it, but it didn't pause to do so.

Although the thing was not fast, it was too fast for Heather's taste, too fast by half. It seemed to be *racing* up the damned stairs.

In spite of her shaky hands, she finally unscrewed the stubborn cap on the spout of the fuel can. Held the container by its handle. Used her other hand to tip the bottom. A pale gush of gasoline arced out of the spout. She swung the can left and right, saturating the carpet along the width of the steps, letting the stream splash down the entire top flight.

On the first step below the landing, the Giver appeared in the wake of its shadow, a demented construct of filth and slithering sinuosities.

Heather hastily capped the gasoline can. She carried it a short distance along the hall, set it out of the way, and returned to the stairs.

The Giver had reached the landing. It turned to face the second flight.

Heather fumbled in a jacket pocket where she thought she had stowed the matches, found spare ammo for both the Uzi and the Korth, no matches. She tried another zipper, groped in the pocket, more cartridges, no matches, no matches.

On the landing, the dead man raised his head to stare at her, which meant the Giver was staring, too, with eyes she couldn't see.

Could it smell the gasoline? Did it understand that gasoline was flammable? It was intelligent. Vastly so, apparently. Did it grasp the potential for its own destruction?

A third pocket. More bullets. She was a walking ammo dump, for God's sake.

One of the cadaver's eyes was still obscured by a thin yellowish cataract, gazing between lids that were sewn half shut.

The air *reeked* of gasoline. Heather had difficulty drawing a clear breath; she was wheezing. The Giver didn't seem to mind, and the corpse wasn't breathing.

Too many pockets, Jesus, four on the outside of the jacket, three inside, pockets and more pockets, two on each leg of her pants, all of them zippered.

The other eye socket was empty, partially curtained by shredded lids and dangling strands of mortician's thread. Suddenly the tip of a tentacle extruded from inside the skull.

With an agitation of appendages, like the tendrils of a black sea anemone lashed by turbulent currents, the thing started up from the landing.

Matches.

A small cardboard box, wooden matches. Found them.

Two steps up from the landing, the Giver hissed softly.

Heather slid open the box, almost spilled the matches. They rattled against one another, against the cardboard.

The thing climbed another step.

*

When his mom told him to go to the bedroom, Toby didn't know if she meant her bedroom or his. He wanted to get as far as possible from the thing coming up the front stairs, so he went to his bedroom at the end of the hallway, though he stopped a couple of times and looked back at her and almost returned to her side.

He didn't want to leave her there alone. She was his *mom*. He hadn't seen all of the Giver, only the tangle of tentacles squirming around the edge of the front door, but he knew it was more than she could handle.

It was more than he could handle, too, so he had to forget about doing anything, didn't *dare* think about it. He knew what had to be done, but he was too scared to do it, which was all right, because even heroes were afraid, because only insane people were never

ever scared. And right now he knew he sure wasn't insane, not even a little bit, because he was scared bad, so bad he felt like he had to pee. This thing was like the Terminator and the Predator and the alien from *Alien* and the shark from *Jaws* and the velociraptors from *Jurassic Park* and a bunch of other monsters rolled into one – but *he* was just a kid. Maybe he was a hero, too, like his dad said, even if he didn't feel like a hero, which he didn't, not one bit; but if he *was* a hero, he couldn't do what he knew he should do.

He reached the end of the hall, where Falstaff stood trembling and whining.

'Come on, fella,' Toby said.

He pushed past the dog into his bedroom, where the lamps were already bright because he and Mom had turned on just about every lamp in the house before Dad left, though it was daylight outside.

'Get out of the hall, Falstaff. Mom wants us out of the hall. Come on!'

The first thing he noticed, when he turned away from the dog, was that the door to the back stairs stood open. It should have been locked. They were making a fortress here. Dad had nailed shut the lower door, but this one should also be locked. Toby ran to it, pushed it shut, engaged the deadbolt, and felt better.

At the doorway, Falstaff had still not entered the room. He had stopped whining.

He was growling.

*

Jack at the ranch entrance. Pausing only a moment to recover from the first and most arduous leg of the journey.

Instead of soft flakes, the snow was coming down in sharp-edged crystals, almost like grains of salt. The wind drove it hard enough to sting his exposed forehead.

A road crew had been by at least once, because a four-foot-high wall of plowed snow blocked the end of the driveway. He clambered over it, on to the two-lane.

*

Flame flared off the match head.

For an instant Heather expected the fumes to explode, but they weren't sufficiently concentrated to be combustible.

The parasite and its dead host climbed another step, apparently oblivious of the danger – or certain that there was none.

Heather stepped back, out of the flash zone, tossed the match.

Continuing to back up until she bumped into the hallway wall, watching the flame flutter in an arc toward the stairwell, she had a seizure of manic thoughts that elicited an almost compulsive bark of mad laughter, a single dark bray that came dangerously close to ending in a thick sob: *Burning down my own house, welcome to Montana, beautiful scenery and walking dead men and things from other worlds, and here we go, flame falling, may you burn in Hell, burning down my own house, wouldn't have to do that in Los Angeles, other people will do it for you there.*

WHOOSH!

The gasoline-soaked carpet exploded into flames that leaped all the way to the ceiling. The fire didn't spread through the stairwell; it was simply everywhere at once. Instantaneously the walls and railings were as fully involved as the treads and risers.

A stinging wave of heat hit Heather, forcing her to squint. She should at once have moved farther away from the blaze because the air was nearly hot enough to blister her skin, but she had to see what happened to the Giver.

The staircase was an inferno. No human being could have survived in it longer than a few seconds.

In that swarming incandescence, the dead man and the living

beast were a single dark mass, rising another step. And another. No screams or shrieks of pain accompanied its ascent, only the roar and crackle of the fierce fire, which was now lapping out of the stairwell and into the upstairs hallway.

*

As Toby locked the stairhead door and turned from it, and as Falstaff growled from the threshold of the other door, orange-red light flashed through the hall behind the dog. His growl spiraled into a yelp of surprise. Following the flash were flickering figures of light that danced on the walls out there: reflections of fire.

Toby knew that his mom had set the alien on fire – she was tough, she was smart – and a current of hope thrilled through him.

Then he noticed the second wrong thing about the bedroom. The drapes were closed over his recessed bed.

He had left them open, drawn back to both sides of the niche. He only closed them at night or when he was playing a game. He had opened them this morning, and he'd had no time for games since he'd gotten up.

The air had a bad smell. He hadn't noticed it right away because his heart was pounding and he was breathing through his mouth.

He moved toward the bed. One step, two.

The closer he drew to the sleeping alcove, the worse the smell became. It was like the odor on the back stairs the first day they'd seen the house, but a lot worse.

He stopped a few steps from the bed. He told himself he was a hero. It was okay for heroes to be afraid but, even when they were afraid, they had to *do* something.

At the open door, Falstaff was just about going crazy.

*

Blacktop was visible in a few small patches, revealed by the flaying wind, but most of the roadway was covered by two inches of fresh powder. Numerous drifts had formed against the snow walls thrown up by the plow.

Judging by the available signs, Jack figured the crew had made a circuit through this neighborhood about two hours ago, certainly no more recently than an hour and a half. They were overdue to make another pass.

He turned east and hurried toward the Youngblood spread, hopeful of encountering a highway-maintenance crew before he had gone far. Whether they were equipped with a big road grader or a salt-spreading truck with a plow on the front – or both – they would have microwave communications with their dispatcher. If he could persuade them that his story was not just the raving of a lunatic, he might be able to convince them to take him back to the house to get Heather and Toby out of there.

Might be able to persuade them? Hell, he had a shotgun. For sure, he'd convince them. They'd plow the half-mile driveway clean as a nun's conscience to the front door of Quartermass Ranch, smiles on their faces from start to finish, as jolly as Snow White's short protectors, singing, *Heigh-ho, heigh-ho, it's off to work we go* if that's what he wanted them to do.

*

Impossible as it seemed, the creature on the stairs appeared even more grotesque and frightful in the obscuring embrace of fire, with smoke seething from it, than it had been when she'd had a clear look at its every feature. Yet another step it rose. Silently, silently. Then another. It ascended out of the conflagration with all the panache of His Satanic Majesty on a day trip out of Hell.

The beast was burning, or at least the portion of it that was

Eduardo Fernandez's body was being consumed, and yet the demonic thing climbed one more step. Almost to the top now.

Heather couldn't delay any longer. The heat was unbearable. She'd already exposed her face too long and would probably wind up with a mild burn. The hungry fire ate across the hallway ceiling, licking at the plaster overhead, and her position was perilous.

Besides, the Giver was not going to collapse backward into the furnace below, as she had hoped. It would reach the second floor and open its arms to her, its many fiery arms, seeking to enfold and become her.

Heart thudding furiously, Heather hurried a few steps along the hall to the red can of gasoline. She snatched it up with one hand. It felt light. She must have used three of the five gallons.

She glanced back.

The stalker came out of the stairwell, into the hallway. Both the corpse and the Giver were ablaze, not merely a smouldering gnarl of charred organisms but a dazzling column of tempestuous flames, as if their entwined bodies had been constructed of dry tinder. Some of the longer tentacles coiled and lashed like whips, casting off streams and gobs of fire that spattered against the walls and floor, igniting carpet and wallpaper.

*

As Toby took one more step toward the curtained bed, Falstaff finally dashed into the room. The dog blocked his path and barked at him, warning him to back off.

Something moved on the bed behind the drapes, brushing against them, and each of the next few seconds was an hour to Toby, as if he had shifted into super slow-mo. The sleeping alcove was like the stage of a puppet theater just before the show began, but it wasn't Punch or Judy back there, wasn't Kukla or Ollie, wasn't any of the

Muppets, nothing you'd ever find on *Sesame Street*, and this wasn't going to be a funny program, no laughs in this weird performance. He wanted to close his eyes and wish it away. Maybe, if you just didn't *believe* in it, the thing wouldn't exist. It was stirring the drapes again, bulging against them, as if to say, *Hello there, little boy*. Maybe you had to *believe* in it just like you had to believe in Tinker Bell to keep her alive. So if you closed your eyes and thought good thoughts about an empty bed, about air that smelled of fresh-baked cookies, then the thing wouldn't be there any more, and neither would the stink. It wasn't a perfect plan, maybe it was even a *dumb* plan, but at least it was something to do. He had to have something to do or he was going to go nuts, yet he couldn't take one more step toward the bed, not even if the retriever hadn't been blocking his way, because he was just too scared. Numb. Dad hadn't said anything about heroes going numb. Or spitting up. Did heroes ever spit up? Because he felt as if he was going to spew. He couldn't run, either, because he'd have to turn his back to the bed. He wouldn't do that, couldn't do that. Which meant closing his eyes and wishing the thing away was the plan, the best and only plan – except he was *not* in a billion years going to close his eyes.

Falstaff remained between Toby and the alcove but turned to face whatever waited there. Not barking now. Not growling or whimpering. Just waiting, teeth bared, shuddering in fear but ready to fight.

A hand slipped between the drapes, reaching out from the alcove. It was mostly bone in a shredded glove of crinkled leathery skin, spotted with mould. For sure, this couldn't really be alive unless you believed in it, because it was more impossible than Tinker Bell, a hundred million times more impossible. A couple of fingernails were still attached to the decaying hand, but they had turned black, looked like the gleaming shells of fat beetles. If he couldn't close his eyes and wish the thing away, if he couldn't run, he at least had to scream for his mother, humiliating as that would be for a kid who was almost nine. But then *she* had the machine gun, after all, not him. A wrist became visible, a forearm with a little more meat on it, the ragged and stained sleeve of a blue blouse or dress. *Mom!* He shouted the word but heard it only in his head, because no sound would escape his lips. A red-speckled black bracelet was around the withered wrist. Shiny. New-looking. Then it moved and wasn't a bracelet but a greasy worm, no, a tentacle, wrapping the wrist and disappearing along the underside of the rotting arm, beneath the dirty blue sleeve. *Mom, help!*

*

Master bedroom. No Toby. Under the bed? In the closet, the bathroom? No, don't waste time looking. The boy might be hiding but not the dog. Must've gone to his own room.

Back into the hall. Waves of heat. Wildly leaping light and shadows. The crackle-sizzle-growl-hiss of fire.

Other hissing. The Giver looming. *Snap-snap-snap-snap*, the furious whipping of fiery tentacles.

Coughing on the thin but bitter smoke, heading toward the rear of the house, the can swinging in her left hand. Gasoline sloshing. Right hand empty. Shouldn't be empty.

Damn!

She stopped short of Toby's room, turned to peer back into the fire and smoke. She'd forgotten the Uzi on the floor near the head of the steps. The twin magazines were empty, but her zippered ski-suit pockets bulged with spare ammunition. Stupid.

Not that guns were of much use against the freakish thing. Bullets didn't harm it, only delayed it. But at least the Uzi had been *something*, a lot more firepower than the .38 at her hip.

She couldn't go back. Hard to breathe. Getting harder. The fire sucking up all the oxygen. And the burning, lashing apparition already stood between her and the Uzi.

Crazily, Heather had a mental flash of Alma Bryson loaded down with weaponry: pretty black lady, smart and kind, cop's widow, and one tough damned bitch, capable of handling anything. Gina Tendero, too, with her black-leather pantsuit and red-pepper mace and maybe an unlicensed handgun in her purse. If only they were here now, at her side. But they were down there in the City of Angels, waiting for the end of the world, ready for it, when all the time the end of the world was starting here in Montana.

Billowing smoke suddenly gushed out of the flames, wall to wall, floor to ceiling, dark and churning. The Giver vanished. In seconds Heather was going to be completely blinded.

Holding her breath, she stumbled along the wall toward Toby's room. She found his door and crossed the threshold, out of the worst of the smoke, just as he screamed.

22

WITH THE Mossberg 12-gauge gripped in both hands, Jack moved eastward at an easy trot, in the manner of an infantryman in a war zone. He hadn't expected the county road to be half as clear as it was, so he was able to make better time than planned.

He kept flexing his toes with each step. In spite of two pairs of heavy socks and insulated boots, his feet were cold and getting colder. He needed to keep full circulation in them.

The scar tissue and recently knitted bones in his left leg ached dully from exertion; however, the slight pain didn't hamper him. In fact, he was in better shape than he had realized.

Although the whiteout continued to limit visibility to less than a hundred feet, sometimes dramatically less, he was no longer at risk of becoming disoriented and lost. The walls of snow from the plow defined a well-marked path. The tall poles along one side of the road carried telephone and power lines, and served as another set of route markers.

He figured he had covered nearly half the distance to Ponderosa Pines, but his pace was flagging. He cursed himself, pushed harder, and picked up speed.

Because he was trotting with his shoulders hunched against the battering wind and his head tucked down to spare himself the sting of the hard-driven snow, looking only at the roadway immediately in front of him, he did not at first see the golden light but only the reflection of it in the fine, sheeting flakes. There was just a hint of yellow at first, then suddenly he might have been running through a storm of gold dust rather than a blizzard.

When he raised his head, he saw a bright glow ahead, intensely yellow at its core. It throbbed mysteriously in the cloaking veils of the storm, the source obscured, but he remembered the light in the trees of which Eduardo had written in the tablet. It had pulsed like this, an eerie radiance that heralded the opening of the doorway and the arrival of the traveler.

As he skidded to a halt and almost fell, the pulses of light grew rapidly brighter, and he wondered if he could hide in the drifts to one side of the road or the other. There were no throbbing bass sounds like those Eduardo had heard and felt, only the shrill keening of the wind. However, the uncanny light was everywhere, dazzling in the sunless day: Jack standing in ankle-deep gold dust, molten gold streaming through the air, the steel of the Mossberg glimmering as if about to be transmuted into bullion. He saw multiple sources now, not one light but several, pulsing out of sync, continuous yellow flashes overlaying one another. A sound above the wind. A low rumble. Building swiftly to a roar. A heavy engine. Through the whiteout, tearing apart the obscuring veils of snow, came an enormous machine. He found himself standing before an oncoming road grader adapted for snow removal, a brawny skeleton of steel with a small cab high in the center of it, pushing a curved steel blade taller than he was.

*

Entering the cleaner air of Toby's room, blinking away tears wrung from her by the caustic smoke, Heather saw two blurry figures, one small and one not. She desperately wiped at her eyes with her free hand, squinted, and understood why the boy was screaming.

Towering over Toby was a grotesquely decomposed corpse,

draped in fragments of a rotted blue garment, bearing another Giver, aswarm with agitated black appendages.

Falstaff sprang at the nightmare, but the writhing tentacles were quicker than they had been before, almost faster than the eye. They whipped out, snared the dog in mid-leap, and flicked him away as casually and efficiently as a cow's tail might deal with an annoying fly. Howling in terror, Falstaff flew across the room, slammed into the wall beside the window, and dropped to the floor with a squeal of pain.

The .38 Korth was in Heather's hand though she didn't remember having drawn it.

Before she could squeeze the trigger, the new Giver – or the new aspect of the only Giver, depending on whether there was one entity with many bodies or, instead, many individuals – snared Toby in three oily black tentacles. It lifted him off the floor and drew him toward the leering grin of the long-dead woman, as if it wanted him to plant a kiss on her.

With a cry of outrage, furious and terrified in equal measure, Heather rushed the thing, unable to shoot from even a few steps away because she might hit Toby. Threw herself against it. Felt one of its serpentine arms – cold even through her ski suit – curling around her waist. The stench of the corpse. *Jesus.* The internal organs were long gone, and extrusions of the alien were squirming within the body cavity. The head turned toward her, face to face, red-stippled black tendrils with spatulate tips flickering like multiple tongues in the open mouth, bristling from the bony nostrils, the eye sockets. Cold slithered all the way around her waist now. She jammed the .38 under the bony chin that was bearded with graveyard moss. She was going for the head as if the head still mattered, as if a brain still packed the cadaver's cranium; she could think of nothing else to do. Toby screaming, the Giver hissing, the gun booming, booming, booming, old bones shattering to dust, the grinning skull cracking off the knobby spine and lolling to one side, the gun booming again

– she lost count – then clicking, the maddening clicking of the hammer on empty chambers.

When the creature let go of her, Heather almost fell on her ass because she was already straining so hard to pull loose. She dropped the gun, and it bounced across the carpet.

The Giver collapsed in front of her, not because it was dead but because its puppet, damaged by gunfire, had broken apart in a couple of key places and now provided too little support to keep its soft, heavy master erect.

Toby was free too. For the moment.

He was white-faced, wide-eyed. He'd bitten his lip. It was bleeding. But otherwise he seemed all right.

Smoke was beginning to roil into the room, not much, but she knew how abruptly it could become blindingly dense.

'Go!' she said, shoving Toby toward the back stairs. 'Go, go, *go!*'

He scrambled across the floor on his hands and knees, and so did she, both of them reduced by terror and expediency to the locomotion of infancy. Got to the door. Pulled herself up against it. Toby at her side.

Behind them was a scene out of a madman's nightmare: the Giver sprawled on the floor, resembling nothing so much as an immensely complicated octopus, although stranger and more evil than anything that had ever lived in the seas of Earth, a tangle of wriggling ropy arms. Instead of trying to reach for her and Toby, it was struggling with the disconnected bones, attempting to pull the mouldering corpse together and lever itself erect on the damaged skeleton.

She wrenched the doorknob, yanked.

The stairhead door didn't open.

Locked.

On the shelf behind the alcove bed, Toby's clock-radio came on all by itself, and rap music hammered them at full volume for a second or two. Then that *other* music. Tuneless, strange, but hypnotic.

'No!' she told Toby as she struggled with the deadbolt turn. It was maddeningly stiff. 'No! Tell it no!' The lock hadn't been stiff before, damn it.

At the other door, the first Giver lurched out of the burning hall and through the smoke, into the room. It was still wrapped around and through what was left of Eduardo's charred corpse. Still afire. Its dark bulk was diminished. Fire *had* consumed part of it.

The thumb-turn twisted slowly, as if the lock mechanism was rusted. Slowly. Slowly. Then: *clack*.

But the bolt snapped into the jamb again before she could pull open the door.

Toby was murmuring something. Talking. But not to her.

'No!' she shouted. 'No, no! Tell it no!'

Grunting with the effort, Heather twisted the bolt open again and held tightly to the thumb-turn. But she felt the lock being re-engaged against her will, the shiny brass slipping inexorably between her thumb and forefinger. The Giver. This was the same power that could switch on the radio. Or animate a corpse. She tried to turn the knob with her other hand, before the bolt slammed into the striker plate again, but now the *knob* was frozen. She gave up.

Pushing Toby behind her, putting her back to the door, she faced the two creatures. Weaponless.

*

The road grader was painted yellow from end to end. Most of the massive steel frame was exposed, with only the powerful diesel engine and the operator's cab enclosed. This no-frills worker drone looked like a big exotic insect.

The grader slowed when the driver realized a man was standing in the middle of the road, but Jack figured the guy might speed up again at first sight of the shotgun. He was prepared to run alongside the machine and board it while it was on the move.

But the driver brought it to a full stop in spite of the gun. Jack ran around to the side where he could see a door on the cab about ten feet off the ground.

The grader sat high on five-foot-tall tires with rubber that looked heavier and tougher than tank tread, and the guy up there was not likely to open his door and come down for a chat. He would probably just roll down his window, keep some distance between them, have a shouted conversation above the shrieking wind – and, if he heard something he didn't like, he'd tramp the accelerator and haul ass out of there. In the event that the driver wouldn't listen to reason, or wanted to waste too much time with questions, Jack was ready to climb up to the door and do whatever he *had* to do to get control of the grader, short of killing someone.

To his surprise, the driver opened his door all the way, leaned out, and looked down. He was a chubby guy with a full beard and longish hair sprouting under a John Deere cap. He shouted over the combined roar of the engine and the storm, 'You got trouble?'

'My family needs help!'

'What kind of help?'

Jack wasn't even going to try to explain an extraterrestrial encounter in ten words or less. 'They could die, for God's sake!'

'Die? Where?'

'Quartermass Ranch!'

'You the new fella?'

'Yeah!'

'Climb on up!'

The guy hadn't even asked him why he was carrying a shotgun, as if everyone in Montana went nearly everywhere with a pistol-grip, pump-action 12-gauge. Hell, maybe everyone did.

Holding the shotgun in one hand, Jack hauled himself up to the cab, careful where he placed his feet, not foolish enough to try to leap up like a monkey. Dirty ice was crusted on parts of the frame. He slipped a couple of times but didn't fall.

When Jack arrived at the open door, the driver reached for the shotgun to stow it inside. He gave it to the guy, even though for a moment he worried that, relieved of the Mossberg, he would get a boot in the chest and be knocked back to the roadway.

The driver was a good Samaritan to the end. He stowed the gun and said, 'This isn't a limousine, only one seat, kinda cramped. You'll have to swing in here behind me.'

The niche between the driver's seat and the back wall of the cab was less than two feet deep and five feet wide. The ceiling was low. A couple of rectangular toolboxes were on the floor, and he had to share the space with them. While the driver leaned forward, Jack squirmed headfirst into that narrow storage area and pulled his legs in after himself, sort of half lying on his side and half sitting.

The driver shut the door. The rumble of the engine was still loud, and so was the whistling wind.

Jack's bent knees were behind the driver, and his body was in line with the gear shift and other controls to the right of the man. If he leaned forward only inches, he could speak directly into his rescuer's ear.

'You okay?' the driver asked.

'Yeah.'

They didn't have to shout inside the cab, but they did have to raise their voices.

'So tight in here,' the driver said, 'we may be strangers now, but by the time we get there, we'll be ready for marriage.' He put the grader in gear. 'Quartermass Ranch, all the way up at the main house?'

'That's right.'

The grader lurched then rolled smoothly forward. The plow made a cold scraping sound as it skimmed the blacktop. The vibrations passed through the frame of the grader, up through the floor, and deep into Jack's bones.

*

Weaponless. Her back to the stairhead door.

Fire was visible through the smoke at the hall doorway.

Snow at the windows. Cool snow. A way out. Safety. Crash through the window, no time to open it, straight through, on to the porch roof, roll to the lawn. Dangerous. Might work. Except they wouldn't make it that far without being dragged down.

The volcanic eruption of sound from the radio was deafening. Heather couldn't think.

The retriever shivered at her side, snarling and snapping at the demonic figures that threatened them, though he knew as well as she did that he couldn't save them.

When she'd seen the Giver snare the dog, pitch him away, and then grab Toby, Heather had found the .38 in her hand with no memory of having drawn it. At the same time, also without realizing it, she had dropped the can of gasoline; now it stood across the room, out of reach.

Gasoline might not have mattered, anyway. One of the creatures was already on fire, and that wasn't stopping it.

Bodies are.

Eduardo's burning corpse was reduced to charred bone, bubbling fat. All the clothes and hair had gone to ashes. And there was barely enough of the Giver left to hold the bones together, yet the macabre assemblage lurched toward her. Apparently, as long as any fragment of the alien body remained alive, its entire consciousness could be exerted through that last quivering scrap of flesh.

Madness. Chaos.

The Giver *was* chaos, the very embodiment of meaninglessness, hopelessness, malignancy, madness. Chaos in the flesh, demented and strange beyond understanding. Because *there was nothing to understand.* That was what she believed of it now. It had no explicable purpose but existence. It lived only to live. No aspirations. No meaning except to hate. Driven by a compulsion to Become and destroy, leaving chaos behind it.

A draft pulled more smoke into the room.

The dog hacked, and Heather heard Toby coughing behind her. 'Pull your jacket over your nose, breathe through your jacket!'

But why did it matter whether they died by fire – or in less clean ways? Maybe fire was preferable.

The other Giver, slithering on the bedroom floor among the ruins of the dead woman, suddenly shot a sinuous tentacle at Heather, snaring her ankle.

She screamed.

The Eduardo-thing tottered nearer, hissing.

Behind her, sheltered between her and the door, Toby shouted, 'Yes! All right, yes!'

Too late, she warned him: 'No!'

*

The driver of the grader was Harlan Moffit, and he lived in Eagle's Roost with his wife, Cindi – with an 'i' – and his daughters Luci and Nanci – each of those with an 'i', as well – and Cindi worked for the Livestock Cooperative, whatever that was. They were life-long residents of Montana and wouldn't live anywhere else. However, they'd had a lot of fun when they'd gone to Los Angeles on vacation a couple of years ago and had seen Disneyland, Universal Studios, and an old broken-down homeless guy being mugged by two teenagers on a corner while they were stopped at a traffic light. Visit, yes; live there, no. All of this he somehow imparted by the time they had reached the turnoff to Quartermass Ranch, as if he felt obliged to make Jack feel among friends and neighbors in his time of trouble, regardless of what that trouble might be.

They entered the private lane at a higher speed than Jack would have thought possible, considering the depth of the snow that had accumulated in the past sixteen hours.

Harlan raised the angled plow a few inches to allow the speed. 'We don't need to scoop off everything down to bare dirt and maybe risk jamming up on a big bump in the road.' The top three-quarters of the snow cover plumed to the side.

'How can you tell where the lane is?' Jack worried, because the rolling mantle of white blurred definitions.

'Been here before. Then there's instinct.'

'Instinct?'

'Plowman's instinct.'

'We won't get stuck?'

'These tires? This engine?' Harlan was proud of his machine, and it really was churning along, rumbling through the untouched snow as if carving its way through little more than air. 'Never get stuck, not with me driving. Take this baby through Hell if I had to, plow away the melting brimstone and thumb my nose at the devil himself. So, what's wrong up there with your family?'

'Trapped,' Jack said cryptically.

'In snow, you mean?'

'Yes.'

'Nothing steep enough around here for an avalanche.'

'Not an avalanche,' Jack confirmed.

They reached the hill and headed for the turn past the lower woods. The house should be in view any second.

'Trapped in the snow?' Harlan said, worrying at it. He didn't look away from his work, but he frowned as if he would have liked to meet Jack's eyes.

The house came into view. Almost hidden by sheeting snow but vaguely visible. Their new house. New life. New future. On fire.

*

Earlier, at the computer, when he'd been mentally linked to the Giver but not completely in its power, Toby had gotten to know it, feeling around in its mind, being nosy, letting its thoughts slide into him while he kept saying 'no' to it, and little by little he had learned about it. One of the things he learned was that it had never encountered any species that could get inside *its* mind the way it could force itself into the minds of other creatures, so it wasn't even aware of Toby in there, didn't feel him, thought it was all one-way communication. Hard to explain. That was the best he could do. Just sliding around in its mind, looking at things, terrible things, not a good place but dark and frightening. He hadn't thought of it as a brave thing to do, only what must be done, what Captain Kirk or Mr Spock or Luke Skywalker or any of those guys would have done in his place, or when meeting a new and hostile intelligent species out on the galactic rim. They'd have taken any advantage, added to their knowledge in any way they could.

So did he.

No big deal.

Now, when the noise coming out of the radio urged him to open the door – *just open the door and let it in, let it in, accept the pleasure and the peace, let it in* – he did as it wanted, though he didn't let it enter all the way, not half as far as *he* entered into *it*. As at the computer this morning, he was now between complete freedom and enslavement, walking the brink of a chasm, careful not to let his presence be known until he was ready to strike. While the Giver was rushing into his mind, confident of overwhelming it, Toby turned the tables. He imagined that his own mind was a colossal weight, a billion trillion tons, even heavier than that, more than the weight of all the planets in the solar system combined, and even a zillion times heavier than that, pressing down on the mind of the Giver, so much weight, crushing it, flattening it into a thin pancake and holding it there, so it could think fast and furiously but could not *act* on its thoughts.

*

The thing let go of Heather's ankle. All of its sinuous and agitated appendages retracted and curled into one another, and it went still, like a massive ball of glistening intestines, four feet in diameter.

The other one lost control of the burning corpse with which it was entwined. Parasite and dead host collapsed in a heap and were also motionless.

Heather stood in stunned disbelief, unable to understand what had happened.

Smoke churned into the room.

Toby had opened the deadbolt and the stairhead door. Tugging at her, he said, 'Quick, Mom.'

Beyond confusion, in a state of utter bafflement, she followed her son and the dog into the back stairwell and pulled the door shut, cutting off the smoke before it reached them.

Toby hurried down the stairs, the dog at his heels, and Heather plunged after him as he followed the curving wall out of sight.

'Honey, wait!'

'No time,' he called back to her.

'Toby!'

She was terrified about descending the stairs so recklessly, not knowing what might be ahead, assuming another of those things had to be somewhere near at hand. *Three* graves had been disturbed at the cemetery.

In the vestibule at the bottom, the door to the back porch was still nailed shut. The door in the kitchen was wide open, and Toby was waiting for her with the dog.

She would have thought her heart couldn't have beat any faster or slammed any harder than it did on the way down those stairs; but, when she saw Toby's face, her pulse quickened and each *lub-dub* was so forceful that it sent a throb of dull pain across her breast.

If he had been pale with fear, he was now a far whiter shade of pale. His face didn't look like that of a living boy so much as like a death mask of a face, rendered now in cold hard plaster as colorless as powdered lime. The whites of his eyes were gray, one pupil large and the other just a pinpoint, and his lips were bluish. He was in the grip of terror, but it wasn't terror alone that drove him. He seemed strange, haunted – and then she recognized the same fey quality that he'd exhibited when he'd been in front of the computer this morning, not in the grip of the Giver but not entirely free. *Between*, he had called it.

'We can get it,' he said.

Now that she recognized his condition, she could hear the same flatness in his voice that she had heard this morning when he'd been in the thrall of that storm of colors on the IBM monitor.

'Toby, what's wrong?'

'I've got it.'

'Got what?'

'*It.*'

'Got it where?'

'Under.'

Her heart was exploding. 'Under?'

'Under me.'

Then she remembered, blinked. Amazed.

'It's under *you*?'

He nodded. So pale.

'You're controlling it?'

'For now.'

'How can that be?' she wondered.

'No time. It wants loose. Very strong. Pushing hard.'

A glistening beadwork of sweat had appeared on his brow. He chewed his lower lip, drawing more blood.

Heather raised a hand to touch him, stop him, hesitated, not sure if touching him would shatter his control.

'We can get it,' he repeated.

*

369

Harlan damned near drove the grader into the house, halting the plow inches from the railing, casting a great crashing wave of snow on to the front porch.

He leaned forward in his seat to let Jack squeeze out of the storage area behind him. 'You go, take care of your people. I'll call the depot, get a fire company out here.'

Even as Jack went through the high door and dismounted from the grader, he heard Harlan Moffit on the cellular system, talking to his dispatcher.

He had never known fear like this before, not even when Anson Oliver had opened fire at Arkadian's service station, not even when he'd realized something was speaking through Toby in the graveyard yesterday, never a fear half this intense, with his stomach knotted so tightly it hurt, a surge of bitter bile in the back of his throat, no sound in the world but the pile-driving thunder of his own heart. Because this wasn't just his life on the line. More important lives were involved here. His wife, in whom his past and future resided, the keeper of all his hopes. His son, born of his own heart, whom he loved more than he loved himself, immeasurably more.

From outside, at least, the fire appeared to be confined to the second floor. He prayed that Heather and Toby weren't up there, that they were on the lower floor or out of the house altogether.

He vaulted the porch railing and kicked through the snow that had been thrown up against the front wall by the plow. The door was standing open in the wind. When he crossed the threshold, he found tiny drifts beginning to form among the pots and pans and dishes that were scattered along the front hall.

No gun. He had no gun. He'd left it in the grader. Didn't matter. If they were dead, so was he.

Fire totally engulfed the stairs from the first landing upward, and it was swiftly spreading down from tread to tread toward the hallway, flowing almost like a radiant liquid. He could see well because drafts were sucking nearly all the smoke up and out the roof: no flames in the study, none beyond the living-room or dining-room archways.

'Heather! Toby!'

No answer.

'*Heather!*' He pushed the study door all the way open and looked in there, just to be sure. '*Heather!*' From the archway he could see the entire living room. Nobody. The dining-room arch. '*Heather!*' Not in the dining room, either. He hurried back across the hall, into the kitchen. The back door was shut, though it had obviously been opened at some point because the tower of housewares had been knocked down. '*Heather!*'

'Jack!'

He spun around at the sound of her voice, unable to figure where it had come from. '*HEATHER!*'

'Down here, we need help!'

The cellar door was ajar. He pulled it open, looked down.

Heather was at the landing, a five-gallon can of gasoline in each hand. 'We need all of it, Jack.'

'What're you doing, the house is on fire! Get out of there.'

'We need the gasoline to do the job.'

'What're you talking about?'

'Toby's got it.'

'Got what?' he demanded, going down the steps to her.

'It. He's got *it*. Under him,' she said breathlessly.

'Under him?' he asked, taking the cans out of her hands.

'Like *he* was under *it* in the graveyard.'

Jack felt as if he'd been shot, not the same pain but the same impact as a bullet in the chest. 'He's a boy, a little boy, he's just a little *boy*, for Christ's sake!'

'He paralyzed it, the thing itself and all its surrogates. You should've seen! He says there isn't much time. The goddamned thing is strong, Jack, it's powerful. Toby can't keep it under him very long, and when it gets on top, it'll never let him go. It'll hurt him, Jack. It'll make him

371

pay for this. So we have to get it first. We don't have time to question him, second-guess him, we just do what he says.' She turned away from him, retreated down the lower steps. 'I'll get two more cans.'

'The house is on fire!' he protested.

'Upstairs. Not here yet.'

Madness.

'Where's Toby?' he called as she turned out of sight below.

'The back porch!'

'Hurry and get yourself out of there,' he shouted as he lugged ten gallons of gasoline up the basement stairs of a burning house, unable to repress mental images of the flaming rivers of gasoline in front of Arkadian's station.

He went on to the porch. No fire there yet. No reflections of second-story flames on the backyard snow, either. The blaze was still largely at the front of the house.

Toby was standing in his red ski suit at the head of the porch steps, his back to the door. Snow churned around him. The little point on the hood gave him the look of a gnome.

The dog was at Toby's side. He turned his burly head to look at Jack, wagged his tail once.

Jack put down the gasoline cans and hunkered beside his son. If his heart didn't turn over in his chest when he saw the boy's face, he *felt* as if it did.

Toby looked like death.

'Skipper?'

'Hi, Dad.'

His voice had little inflection. He seemed to be in a daze, as he had been in front of the computer this morning. He didn't look at Jack but stared uphill toward the caretaker's house, which was visible only when the dense shrouds of snow were drawn apart by the capricious wind.

'Are you between?' Jack asked, dismayed by the tremor in his voice.

'Yeah. Between.'

'Is that a good idea?'

'Yeah.'

'Aren't you afraid of it?'

'Yeah. That's okay.'

'What're you staring at?'

'Blue light.'

'I don't see any blue light.'

'When I was asleep.'

'You saw a blue light in your sleep?'

'In the caretaker's house.'

'Blue light in a dream?'

'Might have been more than a dream.'

'So that's where it is?'

'Yeah. Part of me too.'

'Part of you is in the caretaker's house?'

'Yeah. Holding it under.'

'We can actually burn it?'

'Maybe. But we've got to get all of it.'

Harlan Moffit clumped on to the back porch, carrying two cans of gasoline. 'Lady in there give me these, told me to bring 'em out here. She your wife?'

Jack rose to his feet. 'Yeah. Heather. Where is she?'

'Went down for two more,' Harlan said, 'like she doesn't know the house is on fire.'

In the backyard, there were reflections of fire on the snow now, probably from the main roof or from Toby's room. Even if the blaze hadn't yet spread all the way down the front stairs, the whole house would soon be engulfed when the roof fell into second-floor rooms and second-floor rooms fell into those below them.

Jack started toward the kitchen, but Harlan Moffit put down the fuel cans and grabbed him by the arm. 'What the hell's going on here?'

Jack tried to pull away from him. The chubby, bearded man was stronger than he looked.

'You tell me your family's in danger, going to die any minute, trapped somehow, but then we get here and what I see is your family *is* the danger, setting fire to their own house by the look of it.'

From the second floor came a great creaking and a shuddering crash as something caved in, wall or ceiling.

Jack shouted, 'Heather!'

He tore loose of Harlan and made it into the kitchen just as Heather climbed out of the basement with two more cans. He grabbed one of them from her, guided her toward the back door.

'Out of the house now,' he ordered.

'That's it,' she said. 'No more down there.'

Jack paused at the pegboard to get the keys to the caretaker's cottage, then followed Heather outside.

Toby had already started up the long hill, trudging through snow that was knee-high in some places, hardly up to his ankles in other places. It was nowhere as deep as out on the fields because the wind relentlessly swept the slope between the house and the higher woods, even scouring it to bare ground in a few spots.

Falstaff accompanied him, a brand new dog but as faithful as a lifelong companion. Odd. The finest qualities of character – rare in humankind and perhaps rarer still in what other intelligent species might share the universe – were common in canines. Sometimes, Jack wondered if the species created in God's image was, in fact, not one that walked erect but one that padded on all fours with a tail behind.

Picking up one of the cans on the porch to go with the one she already had, Heather hurried into the snow. 'Come on!'

'You going to burn down the house uphill now?' Harlan Moffit asked dryly, evidently having glimpsed that other structure through the snow.

'And we need your help.' Jack carried two of the remaining four cans to the steps, knowing Moffit must think they were all mad.

The bearded man was obviously intrigued but also spooked and wary. 'Are you people plumb crazy, or don't you know there's better ways of getting rid of termites?'

There was no way to explain the situation in a reasonable and methodical fashion, especially not when every second counted, so Jack went for it, took the plunge off the deep end, and said, 'Since you knew I was the new fella in these parts, maybe you also know I was a cop in L.A., not some flaky screenwriter with wild ideas, just a cop, a working stiff like you. Now, it's going to sound nuts, but we're in a fight here against something that isn't of this world, something that came here when Ed—'

'You mean *aliens*?' Harlan Moffit interrupted.

He could think of no euphemism that was any less absurd. 'Yeah. Aliens. They—'

'I'll be a fucking sonofabitch!' Harlan Moffit said, and smacked one meaty fist into the palm of his other hand. A torrent of words burst from him: 'I *knew* I'd get to see one sooner or later. Read about them all the time in the *Enquirer*. And books. Some are good aliens, some bad, and some you'll never figure out in a month of Sundays – just like people. These are real bad bastards, huh? Come whirling down in their ships, did they? Holy shit on a holy shingle! And *me* here for it!' He grabbed the last two cans of gasoline and charged off the porch, uphill through the bright reflections of flame that rippled like phantom flags across the snow. 'Come on, come on, let's waste these fuckers!'

Jack would have laughed if his son's sanity and life had not been balanced on a thin line, a thread, a filament. Even so, he almost sat down on the snow-packed porch steps, almost let the giggles and the guffaws come. Humor and death were kin, all right. Couldn't face the latter without the former. Any cop knew as much. And life was absurd, down to the deepest foundations of it, so there was always something funny in the middle of whatever hell was blowing up around you at the moment. Atlas wasn't carrying the world on his shoulders, no giant muscular hulk with a sense of responsibility; the world was balanced on a pyramid of clowns, and they were always tooting horns and wobbling and goosing each other. But even though it was absurd, though life could be disastrous and funny at the same time, people still died. Toby might still die. Heather. All of them. Luther Bryson had been making jokes, laughing, seconds before he took a swarm of bullets in the chest.

Jack hurried after Harlan Moffit.

The wind was cold.

The hill was slippery.

The day was hard and gray.

*

Climbing the sloped backyard, Toby pictured himself in a green boat on a cold black sea. Green because it was his favorite color. No land anywhere in sight. Just his little green boat and him in it. The sea was old, ancient, older than ancient, so old that it had come alive in a way, could think, could want things and need to have its way. The sea wanted to rise on all sides of the little green boat, swamp it, drag it down a thousand fathoms into the inky water, and Toby with it, ten thousand fathoms, twenty thousand, down and down to a place with no light but strange music. In his boat, Toby had bags of Calming Dust which he'd gotten from someone important, maybe from Indiana Jones, maybe from ET, maybe from Aladdin, probably from Aladdin who got it from the Genie. He kept scattering the Calming Dust on the sea as his little green boat puttered along, and though the dust seemed light and silvery in his hands, lighter than feathers, it became *hugely* heavy when it hit the water, but heavy in a funny way, in a way that didn't make it sink, magical Calming Dust that crushed the water flat, made the sea as smooth and ripple-free as a mirror. The ancient sea wanted to rise up, swamp the boat, but the Calming Dust weighed it down, more than iron, more than lead, weighed it down and kept it calm, defeated it. Deep in the darkest and coldest canyons below its surface, the sea raged, furious with Toby, wanting more than ever to kill him, drown him, bash his body to pieces against shoreline rocks, wear him away with its waters until he would be just sand. But it couldn't rise, couldn't rise, all was calm on the surface, peaceful and calm, calm.

*

Perhaps because Toby was concentrating so intensely on keeping the Giver under him, he lacked the strength to climb the entire hill, though the snow was not piled dauntingly high on that windswept ground. Jack put down the fuel cans two-thirds of the way to the higher woods, carried Toby to the stone house, gave Heather the keys, and returned for the ten gallons of gasoline.

By the time Jack reached the fieldstone house again, Heather had opened the door. The rooms inside were dark. He hadn't had time to discover the reason for the malfunctioning lights. Nevertheless, now he knew why Paul Youngblood couldn't get power to the house on Monday. The dweller within hadn't wanted them to enter.

The rooms were still dark because the windows were boarded over, and there was no time to pry off the plywood that shielded the glass. Fortunately Heather had remembered the lack of power and had come prepared. From two pockets of her ski suit, she produced a pair of flashlights instead of bullets.

It always seems to come down to this, Jack thought: going into a dark place. Basements, alleyways, abandoned houses, boiler rooms, crumbling warehouses. Even when a cop was chasing a perp on a bright day and the chase led only outdoors, in the final confrontation, when you came face to face with evil, it was always a dark place, as if the sun could not find that one small patch of ground where you and your potential murderer tested fate.

Toby walked into the house ahead of them, either unafraid of the gloom or eager to do the deed.

Heather and Jack each took a flashlight, and a can of gasoline, leaving two cans just outside the front door.

Harlan Moffit brought up the rear with two more cans. 'What're these buggers like, they all hairless and big-eyed like those geeks who kidnapped Whitley Strieber?'

In the unfurnished and unlighted living room, Toby was standing in front of a dark figure, and when their flashlight beams found what the boy had found before them, Harlan Moffit had his answer. Not hairless and big-eyed. Not the cute little guys from a Spielberg movie. A decomposing body stood with legs spread, swaying but in no danger of crumpling to the floor. A singularly repulsive creature was draped across the cadaver's back, bound to it by several greasy tentacles, *intruded* into its rotting body, as though it had been trying to become one with the dead flesh. It was quiescent but obviously alive: queer pulses were visible beneath its wet-silk skin, and the tips of some appendages quivered.

The dead man with which the alien had combined was Jack's old friend and partner, Tommy Fernandez.

*

Heather realized, too late, that Jack had never actually seen one of the walking dead with its puppetmaster in full saddle. That sight alone was sufficient to undermine a lot of his assumptions about the inherently benign – or at least neutral – character of the universe and the inevitability of justice. There was nothing benign or just about what had been done with Tommy Fernandez's remains – or about what the Giver would do to her, Jack, Toby, and the rest of humanity while they were still alive if it had the opportunity. The revelation had more sting because these were Tommy's remains in this condition of profound violation, rather than those of a stranger.

She turned her own flashlight away from Tommy and was relieved when Jack lowered his own quickly as well. It would not have been like him to dwell on such a horror. She liked to believe that, in spite of anything he might have to endure, he would always hold fast to the optimism and love of life that made him special.

'This thing has gotta die,' Harlan said coldly. He had lost his natural ebullience. He was no longer Richard Dreyfuss excitedly chasing his close encounter of the third kind. The most ominous apocryphal fantasies of evil aliens that the cheap tabloids and science fiction movies had to offer were not merely proved foolish by the grotesquerie that stood in the caretaker's house; they were proved naive, as well, because their portrayals of extraterrestrial malevolence were shabby funhouse spookery compared to the endlessly imaginative abominations and tortures that a dark, cold universe held in store. 'Gotta die right now.'

Toby walked away from Tommy Fernandez's body, into the shadows.

Heather followed him with her flashlight beam. 'Honey?'

'No time,' he said.

'Where are you going?'

They followed him to the back of the lightless house, through the kitchen, into what might have once been a small laundry room but now was a vault of dust and cobwebs. The desiccated carcass of a rat lay in one corner, its slender tail curled in a question mark.

Toby pointed to a blotchy yellow door that no doubt had once been white. 'In the cellar,' he said. 'It's in the cellar.'

Before going down to whatever awaited them, they put Falstaff in the kitchen and closed the laundry-room door to keep him there.

He didn't like that.

As Jack opened the yellow door on perfect blackness, the frantic scratching of the dog's claws filled the room behind them.

*

Following his dad down the sway-backed cellar stairs, Toby concentrated intensely on that little green boat in his mind, which was really well built, no leaks at all, unsinkable. Its decks were piled high with bags and bags of silvery Calming Dust, enough to keep the surface of the angry sea smooth and silent for a thousand years, no matter what it wanted, no matter how much it raged and stormed in its deepest canyons. He sailed on and on across the waveless ocean, scattering his magical powder, the sun above him, everything just the way he liked it, warm and safe. The ancient sea showed him its own pictures on its glossy black surface, images meant to scare him and make him forget to scatter the dust – his mother being eaten alive by rats; his father's head split down the middle and nothing inside it but cockroaches; his own body pierced by the tentacles of a Giver that was riding on his back – but he looked away from them quickly, turned his face to the blue sky instead, and wouldn't let his fear make a coward of him.

The cellar was one big room with a broken-down furnace, a rusted water heater – and the real Giver from which the other smaller Givers had detached. It filled the back half of the room, all the way to the ceiling, bigger than a couple of elephants.

It scared him.

That was okay.

But don't run. Don't run.

It was a lot like the smaller versions, tentacles everywhere, but with a hundred or more puckered mouths, no lips, just slits, and all of them working slowly in its current calm state. He knew what it was saying to him with those mouths. It wanted him. It wanted to rip him open, take out his guts, stuff itself into him.

Toby started shaking and tried very hard to make himself stop but couldn't.

Little green boat. Plenty of Calming Dust. Putter along and scatter, putter along and scatter.

As the beams of the flashlights moved over it, he could see gullets

380

the color of raw beef beyond those mouths. Clusters of red glands oozed clear syrupy stuff. Here and there the thing had spines as sharp as any on a cactus. There wasn't a top or bottom or front or back or head to it; just everything at once, everywhere at once, all mixed up. All over it, the working mouths were trying to tell him it wanted to push tentacles in his ears, mix *him* up too, stir his brains, become him, use him, because that's all he was, a thing to be used, that's all anything was, just meat, just meat to be used.

Little green boat.

Plenty of Calming Dust.

Putter along and scatter, putter along and scatter.

*

In the deep lair of the beast, with its monstrous hulk looming over him, Jack splashed gasoline across the paralyzed python-like append-ages, across other more repulsive and baroque features that he dared not stare at if he ever hoped to sleep again.

He trembled to think that the only thing caging the demon was a small boy and his vivid imagination.

Or maybe, when all was said and done, the imagination was the most powerful of all weapons. It was the imagination of the human race that had allowed it to dream of a life beyond cold caves and a possible future in the stars.

He looked at Toby. So wan in the backsplash of the flashlight beams. As if his small face was carved of pure white marble. He must be in emotional turmoil, half scared to death, yet he remained outwardly calm, detached. His placid expression and marble-white skin was reminiscent of the beatific countenances on the sacred figures portrayed in cathedral statuary, and he was, indeed, their only possible salvation.

A sudden flurry of activity from the Giver. A ripple of movement through the tentacles.

Heather gasped, and Harlan Moffit dropped his half-emptied can of gasoline.

Another ripple, stronger than the first. The hideous mouths opened wide as if to shriek. A thick, wet, repugnant *shifting*.

Jack turned to Toby.

Terror disturbed the boy's placid expression, like the shadow of a warplane passing over a summer meadow. But it flickered and was gone. His features relaxed.

The Giver grew still once more.

'Hurry,' Heather said.

*

Harlan insisted on being the last one out. He poured the trail of gasoline to which they would touch a match from the safety of the yard. Passing through the front room, he doused the corpse and its slavemaster.

He had never been so scared in his life. He was so loose in the bowels that he was amazed he hadn't ruined a good pair of corduroys. No reason why he had to be the last one out. He could have let the cop do it. But that thing down there . . .

He supposed he wanted to be the one to lay down the fuse because of Cindi and Luci and Nanci, because of all his neighbors in Eagle's Roost, too, because the sight of that thing had made him realize how much he loved them, more than he'd ever thought. Even people he'd never much liked before – Mrs Kerry at the diner, Bob Falkenberg at Hensen's Feed and Grain – he was eager to see again, because suddenly it seemed to him that he had a *world* in common with them and so much to talk about. Hell of a thing to have to experience, hell of a thing to have to *see*, to be reminded you're a human being and all it meant to be one.

*

His dad struck the match. The snow burned. A line of fire streaked back through the open door of the caretaker's house.

The black sea heaved and rolled.

Little green boat. Putter and scatter. Putter and scatter.

The explosion shattered the windows and even blew off some of the big squares of plyboard that had covered them. Flames crackled up the stone walls.

The sea was black and thick as mud, churning and rolling and full of hate, wanting to pull him down, calling him out of the boat, out of the boat and into the darkness below, and a part of him almost wanted to go, but he stayed in the little green boat, holding tight to the railing, holding on for dear life, scattering the Calming Dust with his free hand, weighing down the cold sea, holding on tight and doing what had to be done, just what had to be done.

*

Later, with sheriff's deputies taking statements from Heather and Harlan in patrol cars, with other deputies and firemen sifting for proof in the ruins of the main house, Jack stood with Toby in the stables, where the electric heaters still worked. For a while they just stared through the half-open door at the falling snow and took turns petting Falstaff when he rubbed against their legs.

Eventually Jack said, 'Is it over?'

'Maybe.'

'You don't know for sure?'

'Right near the end,' the boy said, 'when it was burning up, it made some of itself into little boring worms, bad things, and they tunneled into the cellar walls, trying to get away from the fire. But maybe they were all burned up anyway.'

'We can look for them. Or the right people can, the military people and the scientists who'll be here before long. We can try to find every last one of them.'

'Because it can grow again,' the boy said.

The snow was not falling as hard as it had been all through the night and morning. The wind was dying down as well.

'Are you going to be all right?' Jack asked.

'Yeah.'

'You sure?'

'Never the same,' Toby said solemnly. 'Never the same . . . but all right.'

That is, Jack thought, the way of life. The horror changes us, because we can never forget. Cursed with memory. It starts when we're old enough to know what death is and realize that sooner or later we'll lose everyone we love. We're never the same. But somehow we're all right. We go on.

*

Eleven days before Christmas, they topped the Hollywood Hills and drove down into Los Angeles. The day was sunny, the air unusually clear, and the palm trees majestic.

In the back of the Explorer, Falstaff moved from window to window, inspecting the city. He made small, snuffling sounds as if he approved of the place.

Heather was eager to see Gina Tendero, Alma Bryson, and so many other friends, old neighbors. She felt that she was coming home after years in another country, and her heart swelled.

Home was not a perfect place. But it was the only home they had, and they could hope to make it better.

That night, a full winter moon sailed the sky, and the ocean was spangled with silver.

384

LIGHTNING

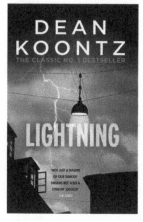

The first time the lightning strikes Laura Shane is born . . .

The second time it strikes the terror starts . . . though eight-year-old Laura is saved by a mysterious stranger from the perverted and deadly intentions of a drug-crazed robber. Throughout her childhood she is plagued by ever more terrifying troubles, and with increasing courage she finds the strength to prevail – even without the intervention of her strange guardian. But, despite her success as a novelist, and her happy family life, Laura cannot shake the certainty that powerful and malignant forces are controlling her destiny.

Then the lightning strikes once more and shatters her world. The adventure – and the terror – has only just begun . . .

headline

MIDNIGHT

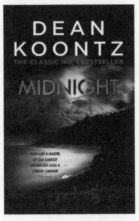

What is the dark secret that haunts Moonlight Cove?

A string of inexplicable deaths has occurred in this picturesque coastal town; sinister, shadowy figures stalk the streets in the dead of night and four people are drawn together by terrifying circumstance.

A young woman determined to find the truth behind her sister's suicide, an undercover federal agent, a child on the run from her parents and a wheelchair-bound veteran.

As darkness descends, these four must confront the chilling nightmare of Moonlight Cove.

headline

THE BAD PLACE

Frank Pollard awakens in an alley, knowing nothing but his name and that he is in danger. Over the next few days he develops a fear of sleep because when he wakes he finds blood on his hands and bizarre and terrifying objects in his pockets.

When a distraught and desperate Frank begs husband-and-wife detective team, Bobby and Julie Dakota, to get the bottom of his mysterious, amnesiac fugues, it seems a simple job. But they are drawn into ever-darkening realms where they encounter the nightmare, hate-filled figure stalking Frank. And their lives are threatened, as is that of Julie's gentle, Down's-syndrome brother, Thomas.

To Thomas, death is the 'bad place' from which there is no return. But as each of them ultimately learns, there are equally bad places in the world of the living, places so steeped in evil that, in contrast, death seems almost to be a relief . . .

headline

COLD FIRE

Schoolteacher Jim Ironheart flies on an impulse to Portland, Oregon. There he risks his life to save a child from being killed. Reporter Holly Thorne witnesses his heroism, and is impressed by his self-effacement when he declines to be interviewed.

Burnt out, cynical, and looking for a life beyond journalism, Holly finds her newshound's instincts rekindled when she discovers Jim has quietly performed twelve last-minute rescues in twelve far-flung places over the past four months. Realising she is on to the biggest story of her life, Holly traces Jim to California. He insists he is not a psychic; he simply believes God is working through him. Holly thinks his explanation is too easy, that there is no wonder in life, no great mystery.

She is dead wrong. For she and Jim are soon plunged into a dark sea of wonder, mystery – and stark terror. And, on the run for their lives, they will be forced to confront a savage and uncannily powerful adversary . . .

headline

HIDEAWAY

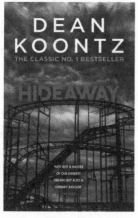

Although accident victim Hatch Harrison dies en route to the hospital, a brilliant physician miraculously resuscitates him. Given this second chance, Hatch and his wife Lindsey approach each day with a new appreciation of the beauty of life – until a series of mysterious and frightening events brings them face to face with the unknown. Although Hatch was given no glimpse of an afterlife during the period when his heart had stopped, he has reason to fear that he has brought a terrible presence back with him . . . from the land of the dead.

When people who have wronged the Harrisons begin to die violently, Hatch comes to doubt his own innocence – and must confront the possibility that this life is just a prelude to another, darker place.

headline